I0666576

This was a detour worth taking . . .

For as long as she can remember, Meilin Wu has had her life mapped out, and she's well down her chosen path—which had no warning signs about a tall, golden Brit who would bowl her over the night before her arranged marriage . . .

Drew Robinson has nearly finished his formal education and is ready to face the world when he meets Meilin, an exquisite beauty with Chinese ancestry. He doesn't mind she's ten years older, and the fact she knows Mandarin only makes her that much more a perfect fit for his upcoming adventures in China. He just has to get her to dump her fiancé and convince her that a trip in China will only enhance her established design business.

Easy for a guy who's known for seeing sunshine wherever he goes. Right?

Visit us at www.kensingtonbooks.com

Books by Shea McMaster

The Robinsons series
Her Foreign Affair
Her Unexpected Affair

Rachel Dahlrumple

Published by Kensington Publishing Corporation

Her Unexpected Affair

The Robinsons Series

Shea McMaster

LYRICAL PRESS
Kensington Publishing Corp.
www.kensingtonbooks.com

Lyrical Press books are published by
Kensington Publishing Corp. 119 West 40th Street New York, NY 10018

Copyright © 2016 by Shea McMaster

All rights reserved. No part of this book may be reproduced in any form or by any means without the prior written consent of the Publisher, excepting brief quotes used in reviews.

All Kensington titles, imprints, and distributed lines are available at special quantity discounts for bulk purchases for sales promotion, premiums, fund-raising, and educational or institutional use.

Special book excerpts or customized printings can also be created to fit specific needs. For details, write or phone the office of the Kensington Special Sales Manager:
Kensington Publishing Corp.
119 West 40th Street
New York, NY 10018
Attn. Special Sales Department. Phone: 1-800-221-2647.

Kensington and the K logo Reg. U.S. Pat. & TM Off.
Lyrical Press and the L logo are trademarks of Kensington Publishing Corp.

First Electronic Edition: June 2016
eISBN-13: 978-1-60183-820-9
eISBN-10: 1-60183-820-4

First Print Edition: June 2016
ISBN-13: 978-1-60183-822-3
ISBN-10: 1-60183-822-0

Printed in the United States of America

To the Mills College Women who helped shape this and many of my books, specifically:

Jennifer Weilbach, Beth Woolbright, Kerstin Mancini, Marybeth McLaughlin, Olivia Lovett, Martha McMaster Quimby, and Doris George (In Memoriam).

For you girls belong to Mills, and Mills belongs to you.

Acknowledgements

This book came together with the help of many, many people. In no particular order, I offer my gratitude to:

Martin Biro of Kensington for suggesting a trilogy when I'd considered Her Foreign Affair a stand-alone novel.

Editor Paige Christian for her humor, patience, wisdom, and encouragement.

Long time friend Jennifer Weilbach for her never-ending help with plotting and Alpha-reading – the one person who has read every single word since I started writing in 2004.

Marybeth McLaughlin for help with the few Chinese sentences I felt brave enough to use, insight into a Chinese immersion school experience, and for beta reading – it's been fun to reconnect after so many years and hear about your adventurous life.

Kerstin Mancini for once again providing her home and hospitality, both in life and in fiction.

Beth Woolbright for helping with research and providing companionship on my trip to California in the middle of writing this book.

Sister Helena for insight into great dramatic plot twists.

Author and close friend Lizbeth Selvig for taking time out of her busy schedule to provide an in-depth critique, which, as usual, was very spot on in so many ways.

Sprint-writing partner, Carmen Bydalek, who provided the wind beneath my wings. Without your support this book would have never been finished on time. You'll never know how many times your dedication to writing on Thursday afternoons and brainstorming pushed me forward when inspiration was low.

Most of all, to Husband Extraordinaire, 'Mr. McMaster' the love of my life for these thirty-some years. With this book, you bravely jumped into the role of critiquer and sounding board, providing excellent information and ideas. You also took on the role of househusband and lifted much of the burden of housekeeping, errand running, and mother herding from my shoulders. Life hasn't always been easy, but it's usually been interesting.

Author's Foreword

In part, the idea for this story came from the book Fifth Chinese Daughter. It seems this book has always been part of my life, or rather, the title has. I didn't actually read the book until starting this one.

Jade Snow Wong is a graduate of Mills College. At the time her book was first published, my mother was a student at Mills College. She has a signed copy of the first edition. I also graduated from Mills College, but more than forty years after Ms. Wong.

I was born the fifth child. My parents consulted with some Chinese-American friends who did some research and came back with the word Wu as the translation for Five or Fifth. So growing up, I was often called (Shea) Wu, fifth Chinese Daughter. A nickname that sometimes pops up today.

While it may have seemed odd to call a redheaded child Chinese Daughter, it generally brought some chuckles. However, although my roots are in no way Chinese, my family has ties to China/Asia. My mother spent six years during the 1930s living in the Philippines. Her father was an Army officer and when asked why he wanted a third tour of duty there replied, "It's the only place in the world I can live as a gentleman on my salary."

We also have, what I fear is badly damaged by now, film of my mother with her parents and brother in China somewhere around 1938. Those years, and later living near San Francisco, influenced my mother's taste greatly and we grew up with furnishings and art that reflected this. My house today has several elements of Asian design. We also enjoyed a period of time when Mother developed an interest in Chinese cooking.

I'm no expert in China or her history, but I do find myself drawn to elements of her society. It is my great hope that I have done justice with my limited knowledge in the portrayal of my heroine, Meilin Wu. If there are mistakes, the blame belongs to my own imagination and ignorance.

Prologue

Satisfaction filled his soul, much like how the now decimated feast being cleared from the table filled his body. Andrew Christian Robinson sat back in his seat at the long dining table, surveying the joyous debris. Christmas Eve tradition demanded that the Robinson family hold an extravagant dinner for not only extended family, but several of the local dignitaries, the Reverend of the family church, and a few family friends with nowhere else to go this night.

However, there was nothing traditional about this year's celebration. Glasses were raised and congratulations echoed to the heavy Tudor beams overhead. Once he knew Birdie watched from across the table, he glanced toward the ceiling and nodded. As if acknowledging one of the ghosts he'd told her resided in the house. Indeed, it was highly likely a few did haunt the old place. He'd just never seen one. Didn't stop him from trying to torment her.

Still, if there were ghosts in the rafters, Drew imagined one or two might approve, although some might not. Either way, his father was getting married. Not that any of the humans attending dinner thought that was horrible, but he was now committed to marrying an American he'd fallen in love with twenty-three years earlier. A love that had produced a girl, Drew's sister, Birdie, whom no one had known about until a month ago. The same one now giving him a skeptical eye from across the table.

Drew wasn't displeased at all. In fact, he was thrilled to have a sister and a new mother. One who was warm, loving, funny, and very mother-like. Perhaps he'd never be able to lay to rest the ghost of his own mother, good old Beatrice. However, Randi Jean Dailey Ferguson, soon to be Robinson, would at last take her rightful place at his father's side. Drew already loved her. Had from the moment she'd opened her home to him for Thanksgiving only weeks ago. An invite that'd grown to include his father who'd flown over to visit him at school for his first American holiday.

Seated at their father's left, his sister kept shooting glances upward. Only three months younger than he, she might have been his twin. It still amazed him that he hadn't recognized the Robinson golden hair, blue eyes, and sunny disposition in her. He'd met her as Birdie, a fun nickname, but her real name hadn't been clear until her mother, and their father, were forced to confess their prior relationship. The timing had been damn close as Drew had been trying to figure out how to steal a kiss.

A thought that still twisted his stomach.

Yeah, he'd been attracted to her as he'd never been attracted to another female. He hadn't understood the feeling, and he'd wanted to investigate it further. Had the story not been told, Drew's stomach clenched, well, some pretty devastating damage could have occurred. He was still attracted to Birdie, but as a sister, on a soul-deep level. He also felt damned protective of her. Some latent Neanderthal programming to be sure, but she was his sister. And he wasn't going to let a California meat-headed, beach bum jock use her like a party girl. Not on his watch.

Apparently giving up on ghost hunting for the moment, Birdie smiled at him and tipped her head at their parents sitting to her right, faces dangerously close. Drew lifted his champagne to her, and they shared a silent toast to their new relationship. Next to Birdie, Larry Attenborough, an old school chum of his father, bounced his gaze between Drew and Bird with hawk-sharp eyes.

"Now, really, did you have to keep this secret from me?" Larry asked.

"Too right we did," Drew answered. "If you'd known earlier, London would be reading about it right now. Instead they'll have to wait for Boxing Day to get the news."

Larry made a disgusted sound and dismissed Drew, turning his attention to Birdie. "Tell me about you. Courtney or Birdie? What's your real name?"

His sister managed to look down her adorable nose at the veteran gossip with an air of regal distain that amused Drew. That look could only be bred into a person, not taught. "My legal name is Courtney, but I've always been called Birdie. However, I'm changing that. You may call me Courtney."

"Named after your old man, eh?" Larry nodded at Court, who paid them no attention whatsoever.

"Yes," she answered simply. "Although my last name should have been Robinson all along, I'm keeping Ferguson to honor the man who raised me as his own."

"Right, right. The honorable man who married your mum, knowing she carried another man's child." Larry nodded thoughtfully. "Not sure I could be so noble. Looks as if he did a good job of it, though."

Drew silently agreed. Although Courtney—hell, how was he supposed to adjust to that name? The hell with it, he wouldn't change—had suffered at the news, she appeared to be coming to grips with it. She'd loved Wyatt Ferguson, the man she'd known as her father all her life, and had mourned his death for the last two years. Now she had to make the mental switch. Certainly she'd taken the news the hardest.

Drew glanced down the table to where his maternal grandparents sat with his paternal grandmother. No, Courtney wasn't the only one to take the news hard. His mother's parents weren't pleased at all, for different reasons, with the news of not only the newfound daughter but the marriage to the woman Court had loved all along instead of their beloved Beatrice.

There would be time to work it out. Drew was first in line to assume the leadership of the family companies from his father. Probably sooner than planned. The newlyweds would want time alone, and that would take his father away from the office.

Which made it imperative that Drew do well with his International Law degree. Followed by the ten week Chinese language immersion program. The path had been laid out four years earlier, geared toward giving him better negotiating skills with China. Court had never been comfortable working through interpreters, never completely sure the deals they'd worked so far had been fair.

With a knowledge of law, and an understanding of the language, Drew planned to spend a fair amount of the next several years in China, working that end of the business, making sure their employees in the Beijing office were loyal to the company.

Those were also worries for another time. Dinner was coming to an end, and it was time to mingle with the guests, including a handful of elderly aunts and uncles on short leave from their nursing homes. Somehow he didn't think his father and mother-to-be were keen on visiting the drawing room for long. Although Randi looked radiant with happiness, she and her father, RJ, had only arrived that afternoon after nearly twenty-four hours of travel from California. There were shadows under her eyes that said she needed several hours of sleep.

No time like the present, he decided. Drew stood and faced the table of well-fed attendees. "Let's take ourselves off to the drawing room for brandy, coffee, and some carols to warm up our throats for church, shall we?"

His father sent him a look of gratitude as he stood and helped Randi to her feet. "Excellent idea." He clasped Drew's arm and spoke quietly. "We'll come in for a bit, a chance to talk with the elders, and then we'll slip away. Randi is definitely on her last leg."

"No worries, old man. I've got this. Make your rounds, then take yourselves off. We won't start anything until noon tomorrow. The lads are old enough to enjoy a sleep-in." He nodded at his cousins, now young teenagers. "If you're not downstairs by noon, we'll sic Martin on you."

His father groaned and Randi elbowed him in the side. "We'll be downstairs, dressed, with bells on," she assured him. Warmth spread through Drew when she placed a hand on his arm. "Thank you."

"For what?"

"For being you." She smiled up at him, and the glow in Drew spread and deepened.

The feeling was bittersweet because his own mother had never said something as nice to him. She'd been there to correct his manners, critique his schoolwork, shame him into straightening his clothes, and would only send a short nod to indicate approval. Never had she smiled at him for just being. He swallowed around the sudden lump in his throat and leaned down to kiss Randi on the cheek. "I'm pretty happy to have you around, myself."

Chapter 1

"I don't know, Jack...." Drew grimaced as he rubbed the back of his neck. Normally he was all for going out and blowing off the steam of studying. Only this wasn't just ordinary studying. He'd survived the grilling, passed the grueling exams, and earned his degree. Soon to be supplemented with a ten week crash course in Mandarin Chinese. Five weeks at Stanford, five weeks at Peking University in Beijing. Not like he would be leaving Stanford in the immediate future. Graduation ceremonies in a week—his parents were arriving from London tonight for it and a recreation of their spring break wedding for the California friends—and then the following Monday he dove right back into studying. Absolutely no rest for the wicked or exhausted.

Yeah, he really could use a night out. But he was so damn drained he barely knew his name. All he wanted to do was sleep for the next week, waking only to cross the stage and accept his Master of the Science of Law degree.

"Come on, Drew. You're the party animal. Besides, I have a place in mind where the women are beautiful and you can get a head start on your Chinese course." Jack spread his hands as if pleading his final argument. One guaranteed to win the hearts of jurors.

"Chinese women specifically?" He frowned. "Why does that matter? Do they speak Mandarin?"

Jack nodded so much his over-long straight, black hair flopped in his eyes. "Look, you're headed to Beijing in, what? Six weeks, right? These ladies are the closest you'll get to the real deal here. The high caste, the cream of the society. The ones with true traditional values, including speaking Mandarin at home, while also embracing the modern times. A hundred fifty years ago these women would have come straight out of the Imperial Court."

While his interest was piqued at the possibility of finding people to practice Mandarin with, Drew wasn't sure he was up to high society. A burger and beer, or three, down at The Oasis Beer Garden sounded more his speed tonight, but it was still second choice to a six pack in the apartment while zoning out to whatever movie was on TV. Something violent, but other than that, he didn't particularly care. Possibly the O, where other students were sure to be blowing off the steam of exams, would provide enough of a party atmosphere. Lord knew he'd barely survived the last week when he'd probably had a total of four hours sleep combined. Most of that acquired in thirty minute blocks.

Drew ran a hand through his hair, ending at the back of his neck. "Sounds pretty interesting, but awfully tame. I'm close enough to falling asleep on my feet as it is."

"Nah. These girls love the music loud, the drinks frothy, and the lights bright. No sleeping there, unless you're truly dead."

One last ditch effort. "Look, my folks fly in tonight. I need to get out to the house in San Ramon and help with arrangements for next week. Graduation Saturday morning, then their second wedding and my grad party immediately after. Sort of a two-fer. Then the following Monday it's back here bright and early to check in for the next five weeks. I'm sure tomorrow night or a night during the week will work as well."

Jack slid him a sly look. "I'll teach you some more phrases guaranteed to get the attention of a lovely Mandarin princess."

Just what he needed. Right. Drew sighed. "Who would be interested in a bloke from England...why?"

"Because you're nothing like the men they're used to. Men like me." He gestured at himself. "Men who are American to the bone. Many barely civilized and trying to hide it under Armani. You, you're civilization personified. Polite, classy, refined, mildly humorous, in a tasteful way. You're like Prince William to them. Tall, blond, killer accent which should make your Chinese accent adorable to them, and you're not hidebound by Chinese tradition. Only English tradition."

"Amusing, Jack." Sure, Drew had been raised with formal manners, but was he really anymore civilized than the next man? Not sure he liked that description, he rested his head on the back of the sofa in the apartment he'd started sharing with his sister in January. If only she were home at the moment, she'd distract Jack and Drew could escape the pressure to go out. And the self-introspection Jack seemed determined to force on him.

"Birdie should be back in a minute. Why don't you take her to dinner?"

Jack's dark eyes flew open in surprise. "Really? Now you give me permission to ask her out?"

Yeah, so he wasn't thrilled about Jack, or any of the other guys he'd met in California, asking out his sister. If that wasn't a sign of his desperate need for sleep, he didn't know what was.

"She had a tough quarter too and still has her exams next week. Treat her like an English princess and I'll grant you this one favor."

Jack sat back on the other end of the sofa and frowned. "Seriously?"

The fact Jack questioned the offer showed he was tempted. Seriously tempted. Then Jack threw out his next idea. "Why not just bring her with us? She can help vet any woman you meet."

A groan started at the base of his stomach and crawled up his throat. That's all he needed. Chaperone his sister while having Jack hunt down a woman for him. Nope. Not happening.

"Look, I'll contribute a hundred bucks to a nice dinner. Something low key. Just leave me alone tonight. I have a date with a six-pack and my suitcase. If I know my folks, they'll swing by here when they leave the airport before heading home." Come to think of it, he wasn't sure how happy they'd be if Birdie were out with the Chinese American version of Slick Eddie. Jack Ling was just a touch too smooth, too practiced, too oily. A nice enough guy, really, and not seriously a jerk, but just one of those guys who always seemed to be working something to his advantage. Sort of like the furniture salesman on TV. The one who looked like Carrot-top and had a crazy deal every week. Only more subtle.

Jack stared at him through narrowed eyes. The wheels grinding in his head searching for the angle could almost be heard from the other end of the couch.

God. What was he thinking? He'd spent all spring warning his friends off his sister. And now he'd throw her to the most opportunistic of the bunch? Birdie was still adjusting to their new family dynamics and had plenty of her own friends to hang out with.

"Nah, never mind, mate." Drew tipped his beer bottle to his lips. "I can't do that to her."

Jack drew back in mock affront. "What? What's wrong with me? I'm a nice guy. I know the classiest places to party. Nice, clean fun with drinks, dinner, and dancing. Besides, it's your entrée into the local Chinese-American society I'm talking about, man. These are connections you'll need."

"I know, I know. Just not tonight, Jack. I'm whipped. Usually I'd be the first guy to put on his dancing shoes to go meet lovely ladies, but I doubt I'd be good company." That was the truth. He wanted to be sharp when meeting the high brow of society, if that truly was who Jack meant to introduce him to.

An hour later, with Birdie in the back of Jack's spit-shined hybrid SUV, the three were headed into the City. San Francisco's Chinatown to be exact. Or a place on the outskirts of it. They'd had a quick dinner of deli sandwiches while showering and dressing for a night on the town, much to Drew's disgust. Further proof of how tired he was. Normally he didn't let himself be persuaded against his gut feelings, but Jack had insisted and Bird had flown through the door in time to catch closing arguments and added her pressure as well. At least she and Jack kept up the conversation all the way up the peninsula while the energy shot he'd guzzled worked into his system. It was nearly enough to make a grown man cry.

While Jack piloted the vehicle and Birdie bombarded him with questions about their destination, Drew pulled out his cell phone and sent a text to both his father and shining new stepmother. Their plane was due to land in an hour, and he didn't want them to make the stop by the apartment to find it empty. At the same time, he set the phone to vibrate. He probably wouldn't be able to hear it wherever they ended up, but hopefully he'd feel it when a return text came through.

"So what's this about another wedding?" Jack tossed the question back at Birdie. "Thought your parents were already married? Isn't that why you two flew back to London over spring break?"

"This one is for the friends here who couldn't be there," Birdie explained. "Mom's lawyer says he wants proof before he starts rewriting the will. I think he just wants a party and a chance to get to know Dad a little more."

"This is all so confusing." Although Drew had given Jack the brief overview, the man thrived on details. Something that had served him well in many a mock court. "So back in the late 80s, your father"—Jack glanced in his direction—"met her mother, had an affair that resulted in Birdie. But your mother—at the time your father's ex—was already pregnant with you, unbeknownst to anyone. Right?"

"Right." Drew gave the one word answer, knowing there was no avoiding the topic.

"And when she found out she was pregnant with Birdie—"

"My name is Courtney. It's far more appropriate for the business world."

"Right, forgive me—Courtney. Your mother didn't stay to fight for her man?"

"No, she didn't." Courtney leaned forward more, her head now between the two front seats so she'd hear Drew better. "She'd overheard the announcement that my father was marrying my mother because of her pregnancy with me. She didn't want to make our father choose between children. Randi didn't know anything about my mother's circumstances and figured she'd have a better chance of making a go of it as a single mother. Which, while entirely noble of her, may not have been in everyone's best interest."

"So you and Bird—excuse me, *Courtney*—are half brother and sister, separated in age by only a few months."

"Three months." The clarification came from the back seat. "Which doesn't mean he's any wiser or smarter than I am." A sharp-nailed finger poked Drew's shoulder in emphasis. An argument they'd had many times since learning of their blood-tie.

"You're younger, smaller, and far more sheltered than I ever was, Bird. That makes me your big brother with all the rights and responsibilities therefore attached."

"Oh brother. I'm so glad I missed all that misogyny while growing up. I'm an independent woman, *And*rew."

"Then explain why we're sharing an apartment, sister dear."

"Because Dad is paying for it—"

"So I can keep an eye on you."

"So *I* can keep an eye on *you*."

Drew snorted and Jack grinned. "Right."

"Ah, sibling love." Jack sighed dramatically, hand over his heart. "Nothing like it in the world. You two are such amateurs. I should take you both home for Sunday dinner at the Ling household sometime soon. There's where you'll get a real lesson in how siblings act."

"Oh?" Birdie leaned forward. "How many do you have?"

Jack glanced at her in the rearview mirror. "I'm the eldest of eight. Three sisters, four brothers. All overachievers. You two don't know a thing about sibling competition."

"We're learning," Drew muttered. He loved his sister. Absolutely. No question. But she was far from the sweet, shy, biddable creature he'd first imagined her to be. Back before he knew he had a sister. Back when he'd been almost stalking her across campus trying to find out who she was, trying to find a way to meet her that didn't seem creepy.

Like that had worked. After learning her name, her schedule, even a little about her from some of the guys he'd met while playing a pickup game or two of rugby, who were also attracted to her, he'd finally seen his chance one morning at a campus coffee shop. She'd tripped over his size twelve foot and nearly broken her arm. So smooth. But it had worked. They'd met the next several mornings for coffee in the same spot before she'd invited him to her home for Thanksgiving as a stray. A foreign student without family connections for one of the biggest American holidays of the year.

Only to find out she was his unknown half-sister not even his father had known about and never expected to find when looking for the elusive love of his life from twenty years earlier. Surprise, surprise. Although Drew never let on, it still choked him up. His new stepmother, Randi, was all he could have hoped for in a mother. Not only did she make his father ecstatically happy, she'd brought a light of love and warmth into his world unlike any he'd ever known. In some ways it made him feel twelve again. Not just the stereotypical California friendly sort of warmth, but genuine love radiated from her entire being. Something sorely missing from his life up to then.

Where Randi had been open, loving, and accepting from the get-go, Birdie had a tougher time accepting the secrets of her past. Sometimes it still took her aback, leading to snark instead of easy going cheer. The girl just didn't fall in with the program of him being her protector. She didn't appreciate him vetting her dates and trying to steer her away from some of the more obnoxious suitors clamoring for her attention. Didn't she realize that he knew those guys? What they thought when they looked at her? What they wanted from her? It had been bad enough watching her those first weeks with those sharks disguised as law students, MBAs, and jocks circling her at the beginning of fall semester. But once they'd realized she was connected to him, connected to the Robinson international money, it had added a level of frenzy to the chumming around her. Not only did they see a beautiful, lithe blonde with a cheerful smile, they also saw connections to be made. The very idea of networking with someone as renowned as Courtland Robinson, the head of Lynford International Importers based in London, had opened up the sky of future possibilities for those in the International Law program. They were not only horny buggers, they were conniving networkers.

However, he never let Birdie's lack of appreciation for his help deter him from his accepted role of big brother. With calm and logic, he stayed the course and gently herded her along the path he thought best. If she broke from the herding, he merely sidestepped her and eased her back to the trail. Usually without her realizing his aim. Of course, her own graduate work mostly made his job easy. Like him, she didn't have much time for dating or carousing. She'd shifted from the plain old MBA program to International Business. In fact, she'd stay on in their apartment over the summer and take summer classes to move her along that much faster toward her goal of getting to London as their father's executive assistant. Hell, she'd probably end up in the CEO position when the old man was ready to retire. Drew grinned at the thought. Although he was also up for the position, there was one other in the wings. The nephew of a family friend. With three of them vying for the top spot, the future promised to be mighty interesting.

However, for tonight, all he had to do was survive a few hours of drinking and dancing with some Chinese beauties. He'd keep an eye on old Jack Ling and his ambitions to move in on Birdie, and perchance he'd meet someone for himself.

Chapter 2

Meilin Wu placed her order for a Napa Valley red wine and looked around the Golden Phoenix Club while her friends shouted their orders to the waitress. As usual, the place was hopping for a Friday night. Many of the faces were young, barely legal as far as she could tell. Probably new graduates celebrating their freedom from college. She'd been there ten years earlier and recognized the relief on the faces around her. The scent of wild celebration permeated the air. The music was faster, louder, the roving lights a tad brighter tonight. The dancers moved wildly, out of control, or as much out of control as the tightly restrained Asian upbringing allowed them to be. Mostly Chinese, there were a few other mixes in the crowd. White, black, and other Asians.

"Meilin!" One of her friends shouted over the music. "Let's dance!"

She rolled her eyes and made a shooing motion to the table of friends. "Go! I'll watch the table!" she shouted back.

Like a colorful flock of birds, they rose as one, grabbed each other's hands, and ran for the crowded dance floor. Half of them were married women out for a night of girls-only partying, their husbands at home with the toddlers and infants. They were far more excited about tonight than she was.

Unofficially, this was her last night as a single woman. The very thought was depressing. Instead of holding out for true love, as nearly the last single daughter of her parents' social circle, she'd finally caved to the pressure to marry. Tonight was her last night to be free from the five thousand years of tradition that had suffocated her most of her life.

Tomorrow night, at a classy hotel, wearing something closer to traditional and more modest than her current very short, peek-a-boo, red lace dress, with a carefully selected guest list of the San Francisco elite of the Chinese-American population and a few others tossed in—mostly her father's esteemed business associates—she'd officially sign the contract and accept the proposal of a man who'd been groomed his whole life to take over his family's dynasty. Shan Lin, as the Americans would call him. Lin Shan if one were being traditional. A man ten years her senior, he was ready to take a wife. She was the one chosen by their two families.

At least Shan didn't seem to object to her career, although it had been made clear to her she was expected to produce the all-important heir and a spare, or three, to cement the family future. At thirty-three she was very nearly at the end of her time to be fruitful, in the words of her mother. The time to have babies was now. They'd find a way to indulge her career as an interior designer along the way. Or not.

Never mind she had an active client list with people waiting up to a year for her to be free to decorate their homes, offices, and condos with the very best in Asian décor mixed with her own eclectic touch of European antiquity and Modernist utility. The crème of the crop sought her out, looking for that mix of dignity and style. People who appreciated the truly fine antiques from three continents and multiple countries mixed with tasteful modern treasures. No one disputed her talent for finding just the right balance of color, style, and sophistication to fit every client.

How that would work with a nursery full of the next generation, she had no clue. Especially since she had little experience with rug rats. Somehow the mother gene had never made a connection with her biological clock. No alarms ringing there.

Shan Lin was everything a modern woman should want in a husband. He was relatively tall, handsome, solid in build but kept in shape with mixed martial arts, could cement a deal in the boardroom that made all parties feel as if they'd come out on top, knew how to dance at formal occasions, and even made time to spend weekends out on the bay on the impressive sailboat he moored at the St. Francis Yacht Club. He could talk politics with the men without offending anyone, hold court with the ladies and make each one feel as if only she held his attention. He could even charm those under ten.

It didn't hurt he'd even had the good taste to hire her to decorate his condo. It had been a big job, including public rooms and private. He'd left many details to her, accepting her suggestions with few demands. In fact, he'd been as close to a perfect client as she'd ever had. Large budget, interested in the best without being ostentatious, and didn't get in her way too much. Especially since he'd been away on business during the bulk of the work. They'd met in his condo twice. Once when she showed him her design boards and again when the work was done. In between they'd communicated by e-mail, and she'd kept him up to date with digital photos. She could easily argue she knew his housekeeper and secretary better than she knew him.

On paper he was the perfect man.

In reality, he left her yawning.

Her mother and many of her friends thought she was crazy.

Hell, even she thought she was crazy at times. Certainly missing some streak of romance that would allow her to see him for the perfect specimen he was.

Although, she had to ask herself, if he was so perfect, why had he remained unmarried up to the ripe old age of forty-three? What made her so special that suddenly he had stars in his eyes only for her? They'd never even had a date. She didn't count the dinner with both sets of their parents the previous month when she'd learned of their desire to facilitate a marriage between her and Shan. An idea that had left her blinking in surprise. Hadn't seen that one coming, but on reflection, she'd decided, why not?

Even before he'd hired her, they'd crossed paths at social events, both of them networking their way across the room and occasionally sitting at the same table through endless rubber chicken dinners making small talk. She knew who he was, his reputation in the community, what charities he contributed to. He'd always been polite and not too forward, although she'd caught a certain appreciation in his eyes when she caught him looking at her. Once his regard from across the room had made her blush. But she'd turned and seen a very beautiful socialite behind her and decided his gaze had not been for her at all.

Meilin's parents had known his parents long before either of them had been born. The family friendship, or business relationship to be honest, probably went back to the days when their great-grandparents and grandparents had immigrated from China. Back then the families had stuck together, building Chinatown from the ground up, building their business interests from extremely humble beginnings to the very top of the social ladder.

Their families weren't unique in that legacy. Hundreds of families had done the same. And although she'd asked her mother what had suddenly made her stand out from so many other eligible women as the only one for him, she'd never received a satisfying answer.

Tomorrow she'd ask her mother again and possibly the question would be answered at the engagement bash for three hundred of their closest friends. Could it be during their first dance together she'd feel a spark of attraction?

The waitress arrived with the half dozen drinks, and Meilin handed over her credit card. "Run us a tab, will you, Junlei? And get the next round set up, please."

"Sure thing. Who's the celebration for tonight?"

"That would be me. Getting engaged tomorrow."

"Lucky girl!"

Meilin shrugged. "I guess. My parents think so."

Junlei set down the last drink. "Arranged, eh?" Sympathy filled her face. She patted Meilin on the shoulder. "Good luck to you," she said and whirled away toward the next table.

Good thing Shan was rich. As part of the engagement, he'd be taking on her bills. He could afford this party and not even notice. However, with him covering her living expenses, she could pay for this one on her own.

Meilin picked up her drink and downed a healthy sip. Thank God she'd put aside enough cash for a cab home. She intended to crawl out of this place at closing time and not a moment before. After this, it would be one party after another so everyone in Chinatown could toast the soon-be-wed couple. She faced three months of invitations, thank-you notes, and wedding planning. Her mother already had the California Ballroom at the St. Francis Hotel booked, as well as the nave at Grace Cathedral. Both large enough to accommodate the four hundred estimated wedding guests. A number large enough to make her head hurt.

Movement from the doorway caught her eye and she turned her head to see Jack Ling enter and stop to survey the room. Second cousin so many times removed they were hardly related, he'd been a pest to her most of his life. She'd spent more family gatherings tasked with keeping track of the brat than she could count until she'd escaped to college.

Ready to dismiss him, she paused to note the blond couple with him. The tall man towered over Jack by a good five inches, not that Jack was tall, but this guy had to be six-one at least. The blue oxford shirt and pressed khakis spoke of a man used to dressing with care, or at least in expensive clothing. The revolving colored lights bounced off his golden blond hair, making it look artistically colored. He surveyed the room, but had his hand on the back of the girl beside him. A girl who could have been his twin, although she was shorter than him; In heels she was about even with Jack. Both of them extremely attractive. The girl also dressed with style, but with more glitz, ready for a night of dancing much like Meilin's friends. And they both looked as young as Jack. Too bad. The blond man looked interesting. Sort of like Alex Pettyfer but with a better haircut. Next to Jack, who vibrated like a raw nerve as usual, the blond oozed calm reserve, giving the impression of being a high-born Brit. The girl was pure Californian with her long sun-streaked hair, wholesome, smiling face, tank mini-dress in neon blue, sparkly heels, and swinging earrings. Interesting.

However, Meilin tore her gaze from the group and turned to face the dance floor once more, not interesting enough. Jack's friends were always too young for her and tonight was all about being with her girls. A pre-bridal shower party. A pre-engagement blow-out. Let Jack and his friends find their own table, preferably far, far away from hers.

When the couple at the table next to hers got up to leave, she had a sinking feeling. It was confirmed when a hand landed on her shoulder.

"Cousin! Didn't expect to see you here."

Meilin sighed and carefully set down her drink before looking up at Jack. "Jack Ling. Fancy seeing you here. Finals over already?"

"Graduation is a week from tomorrow, which I'm sure you know. Hope you buy me an appropriate gift. Come, Meilin, let me introduce you to some friends of mine." His hand on her shoulder urged her to turn on her stool until she faced the young couple. "I've been teaching Drew here some phrases in Chinese."

Internally, her muscles tightened. Jack had done this before, taught a white friend a ghastly phrase while saying it was nothing more than a greeting.

"Meilin, may I present to you, Drew Robinson and Courtney Ferguson. Brother and sister raised far apart. Long story but very entertaining."

She extended her hand to the girl first. "Pleased to meet you, Courtney."

"Likewise," the girl replied with a wide-open friendly smile and gentle handshake. Warm and exactly appropriate, she didn't cling a moment longer than necessary.

Next, Meilin extended her hand to the man called Drew. "Drew, pleased to make your acquaintance. Do you both know my cousin from the university?"

Drew's large hand enclosed hers, and the flash of heat that surrounded her hand before zipping up her arm stole her breath. Enough so her eyes blinked wide open. In response, his blue eyes dilated in a flash, and his hand flexed a little, almost as if he wanted to pull her closer. Not that she'd mind, she was surprised to realize. The feeling left her disconcerted and breathless. She tugged her hand from his grip.

"Meilin. Did I say that correctly?"

"Yes, yes you did. You both may call me Mei, if you like." Flustered, she folded her hands in her lap, her gaze politely on his when she wanted to look anywhere but at his too handsome face. That was a lie. She wanted nothing more than to gaze upon his beautiful, perfect features now that she had a clear view, up close and personal. Blue eyes, golden hair, strong chin, chiseled jaw, perfectly shaped lips, hard body. This man was the total package.

His large hand rose and rubbed his perfectly sculpted chin. "Let me see if I have this right... *Wo hen gaoxìng dài qiánbao.*"

Holding back the smile and chuckle so desperate to break free, she replied, "I am sure, but the contents of my purse will remain where they are. You should slap Jack for playing such a trick on you."

The flush burning Drew's cheeks as he dropped his hand was almost disguised by the low lights and the flashing dance spotlights. Almost. The wicked twinkle in Jack's eyes was merely enhanced while Courtney lifted a hand to muffle her giggles.

"*Xièxie*, at least I'm pretty sure that means 'thank you.' I just may have to cause Jack some harm," Drew said easily. "I meant to say I was honored to meet you. Guess that's not even close, and I probably should forget the rest of the phrases he's been teaching me."

"No doubt." Meilin allowed her smile to break free. "Don't trust a word that trickster says. Especially when it comes to Chinese lessons, either language or culture. However, you did get 'thank you' right."

Jack held up his hands. "No harm intended, just a little fun for me."

The dark glance Drew directed at her cousin promised some sort of retribution. The twinkle in his blue eyes reduced the severity. He had a sense of humor. That endeared him to her more than she expected. Jack had a sense of humor, but as far as she knew, Shan did not. Much like her own father and brother seemed to be missing funny bones.

"Looks like we found a table," Drew said.

"Yes, yes," Jack agreed. "Let's pull it closer. Have you been abandoned by your giggling friends?"

Resigned and a little thrilled at the prospect of them sharing, she pushed Yuahua's chair away. "Not abandoned. Someone had to hold down the table."

Once the table was situated, Meilin couldn't help but notice Drew sitting next to her, an act that further caught her gaze. The man was that beautiful. At the end of the table Jack sidled up to Courtney. Meilin hoped the girl could see Jack for the restless boy he was. Then again, if Drew knew Jack, he'd probably already warned her Jack was often described as a player.

Jack waved for the waitress, then leaned over the table. "What are you doing here?"

"Girls' night out." At Jack's slow nod, she knew he'd figured it out. "How do you all know each other?" She redirected the conversation before it revealed too many details. She did not want to discuss her pending engagement.

"Drew's in the law program and we shared a room last fall. He and Courtney share an apartment now. She just started her MBA program while we just finished our law degrees."

"Congratulations," she said to Drew. "Are you two twins?"

All three of them laughed, but Drew answered. "Same father, different mothers, born a few months apart. Long story."

Meilin raised a brow. "As Jack mentioned, it sounds like an interesting tale."

Drew shrugged his wide shoulders, shoulders that moved with the grace of honed muscle beneath the fine cotton of his shirt. "A broken engagement, a relationship with an exchange student, marriage to the ex-fiancée brought on by pregnancy, departure of the exchange student who kept her pregnancy quiet… We all connected quite by accident last fall. Now her widowed mother is married to our widowed father and we're one big happy family." He turned just enough to grin at his sister. "Always wanted a sibling. Just had to wait a couple decades to meet her."

Meilin almost envied the cheeky grin the younger woman aimed at her brother. "Just trying to keep you on your toes."

Drew snorted and leaned toward Meilin to mutter, "That she does. And her mother too. Her mission is to drive our father bonkers and he loves it."

A stab of jealousy knifed Meilin in the heart. Other people found grand passion, and here she was about to commit the rest of her days to a union with a man who failed to inspire the rush of heat she'd experienced by just shaking Drew's hand. Insane. She didn't know these people well enough to envy them so fiercely. And yet, that emotion was a thousand times stronger than any emotion she'd ever felt for Shan.

It confused her.

And when confused, she turned to small talk.

"I detect more than a little pluminess in your accent, sir, but none in your sister's. I'm guessing you were raised in England? Father and mother both British?"

"Good ear, not that it's hard to decipher. I did the whole boarding school with proper elocution thing while Courtney was raised here in California as wild and free as a bird."

"How very interesting. Are you to the manor born?" She did her best to say it in a British accent. Not that she'd had much practice, but who didn't love a good BBC program from time to time?

Drew laughed. "No fancy titles in our branch, but we do have the biggest house in the district. My father likes to pretend he's a lord of some sort at Christmas."

The notion wasn't foreign to Meilin.

Junlei arrived with the second round of drinks for her table and turned to Jack's party to take their orders.

Her own father, directly descended from minor nobility turned laborer in California, liked to do the same. The reminders of how the family had started high born, fell to the lowest depths of society, then rose to the upper ranks were drummed into them all, chapter and verse at each large gathering. Come to think of it, at almost any gathering, large or small. The ancestors were well revered.

"Tell me about yourself," Drew said. "Jack has told us nothing about you."

Before she could open her mouth to politely turn the conversation again, Jack leaned across the table in order to be heard. "She's an interior designer. One of the best in the city. Possibly in all California if not the west coast. Big time bigwig woman."

Frowning at Jack did no good. She always let her work do her bragging for her, never did she need to toot her own horn. The wave of girls, fluttering like butterflies, returned to their table, relieving her from answering.

"Jack, what a surprise."

"Hey, cousin."

"Jack, you mangy dog, what are you doing here? Spying on Meilin's last night out? We should kick you out of here."

"Not while he has friends here." Sunchu, one of her few remaining single friends, leaned over from the far side of the table to extend her hand to Drew. "And who might you be, tall, golden, and handsome?"

Drew stood and exchanged handshakes all around as the entire group of five women settled at the table. Sure, they included Courtney, but Drew had ninety-nine percent of their attention. And why not? Exactly as Sunchu had said, he *was* tall, golden, and very handsome. Not only did he have a perfect tan, but he smelled good too. Not one whiff of heavily scented aftershave teased Meilin's nose. He was as fresh as a forest. Clean water and towering pines came to mind. Maybe a hint of citrus, possibly lime, but his scent was light and refreshing. She'd have to find out what he used.

What in the hell was she doing sniffing him up like that? No, she would not ask him what scent he wore. Especially because his proximity made her pulse thrum wildly in her veins. His thigh brushed against hers and she swallowed a gasp, as the contact acted like a raindrop landing on a smooth lake, sending ripples of goosebumps down her leg and up her body.

It took only a second to drain her first drink, set it down, and reach for the second. This was all she needed. A short, intense attraction to a foreigner on the eve of her engagement. Sort of like a very short-term foreign exchange. Surprised at her comparison to a semester abroad, she laughed to herself.

Not happening. Not now, not ever.

And then he had to ask, "Would you like to dance?"

Chapter 3

Hand extended to her, Drew stood close enough she could feel the heat from his body.

It took strength pulled from her center of calm to nod coolly and accept his offer. With the support of his gentle grip, she slid from the seat and followed him, dodging the crowded tables to the packed dance floor. Wasn't it just her luck the DJ chose to slow things down with the next song?

The fact Drew had been raised a gentleman was evident in the way he held her in a classic dance pose, one hand lightly resting on her waist, the other holding her right hand not too close to his body. A few inches separated them. Discreet. Respectful. However, both contact points tingled with awareness such that she wanted to press her body against his. The care with which he guided her to the rhythm of the slow tune indicated many hours of dance lessons. Better than most of the men she'd danced with. Following his lead was easy and comfortable. Rather it would have been easy and comfortable if not for the high voltage energy zinging back and forth between them. Not at all what she'd expected. Better than she'd ever dreamed a dance partner could be.

There, in the middle of the floor, she could better see the blue of his eyes. The blue pulled her in, much like a cool mountain lake on a hot day.

Ha! The ancestors and deities were having fun with her by throwing this prime specimen of man at her at this moment. He moved with athletic grace, his body talking to hers, the flexing of strong muscles moving under her hand, seducing more than the twinkle in his eyes. Eyes that held a faint shadow that looked suspiciously like exhaustion.

"So, you just completed your degree?" Anything to distract her from the surprising warmth purling around her limbs.

"International law. Everything was checked off this afternoon. I'm allowed to graduate with my class. Next stop is a ten week Chinese school.

Guess I'll have to unlearn everything Jack tried to teach me, won't I?" A small smile played around the corners of his mouth.

"Not everything, I'm sure. Mostly you'll have to work on your tones and inflections."

He nodded. "I've learned that much. I don't have the best ear, so that will be tough. Not all I've learned has come from Jack. I had a bit of exposure at school, although now I'm suspicious my roommate at Eton may have also been playing tricks on me."

Meilin laughed lightly. "I'm sure you'll do fine. So you're entering this program where?"

"Stanford."

"I know the program. Have even substituted on occasion. Why learn Chinese?"

"The family business. My father would like to be more confident in the interpretations when we do business in China. I'll spend a few years over there learning my way around, expanding our contacts, gaining new contracts. Any chance you'll show up at the school this summer?"

Meilin ignored his last question. Undoubtedly, Arnie, better known to the students as Professor An Cheng Chung, would call on her to sub at some point. Or help with tutoring. "And the business is?"

"Import. With an eye toward the higher end. Beyond tea and trinkets. I'm pretty sure my mother wants some authentic antiques in our catalogue."

At her raised brow, he clarified himself. "My stepmother, Randi. But already she's accepted me as if she'd given birth to me and I've adopted her back."

"Indeed. I'm not sure many women would so readily accept a grown man as their son."

"Is that a polite way of asking my age?" An elegant brow, slightly darker than his golden hair, rose enticingly.

Feigning disinterest, she shrugged one shoulder. "Making conversation. I'm not experienced with stepmothers and the like."

"Well, for clarification, I'm twenty-three. I know better than to ask your age, but I would place you close to twenty-five."

Meilin laughed. "Nice try, but no, I won't confess. A woman who will tell her age will tell everything. And I never tell everything."

The grin on his face widened. "That's fine by me. I like a woman full of mystery. Makes the getting to know her much more interesting."

"You're young to have completed a law degree. Although it happens, Jack's two years older than you and he's considered young for a JD. I'm surprised."

"I grew up spending school holidays working in the offices, and I skipped a few levels at school." He shrugged as if it were nothing unusual. "My experiences and scores got me into the program a few years ahead of my peers. All the better to be here at this point in time."

His grin created a longing to get to know him better deep inside, twisting her stomach at the words she had to speak. "I must disappoint us both, I confess; tomorrow I become engaged to a man who has been a close friend of the family for many years."

"Sounds…arranged." A slight wrinkle formed between his perfect eyes.

"Many marriages around the world are arranged for many reasons. Doesn't mean it's a bad thing. My parents are quite happy with the arrangements made by my grandparents."

"I wasn't criticizing. My own parents were expected to marry from the time they were toddlers. Sadly, for them, it wasn't quite the harmonious pairing many such arrangements bring about."

"I'm sorry to hear that." She really was. Most often it was the children who suffered when discord between the parents erupted. How had it affected him?

In an attempt to deflect the conversation from herself, she asked, "So, Mandarin school for you, then a place in the family business? This is what you want?"

"Absolutely. Many generations have paved the way to expanding the business globally. But I'm sure you don't want to hear those details. I'm more interested in you. Interior design?"

Sure, it was immodest to speak of her successes, but few people in her family were kind enough to pretend interest. "I keep busy. If your mother is interested in some fine antique pieces, she is welcome to come by my shop when she's in the area. I'm guessing your parents are based in England?"

"Until last December, Randi lived just across the Bay. That's where my sister was born and raised. In a nice, upper middle class suburban neighborhood. Randi's father does business with the vineyards up and down the entire west coast and until recently she worked for him. She and my father are flying in tonight not only for graduation, but to repeat their vows for the friends who live here."

"That's very sweet." Just the idea of saying vows with Shan once was enough. Repeating them? Not likely. Unless it was several years down the road and they were truly in love.

Although she'd already committed to the path, the faint vision she'd had of taking vows and living with Shan wavered like a fine mist on a foggy morning.

Enough, she told herself. Tonight was about a final fling celebrating freedom. It wasn't the time to change the path she'd chosen. The future wasn't yet here and she didn't want it to intrude on her fun. Besides, Drew wouldn't be around for long. Here tonight, gone in six weeks or so.

* * * *

Drew watched the emotions playing in Meilin's eyes. If only the light were better so he could see their true color. Something told him her eyes were a rare shade of green.

Pragmatically it was an indication of his frazzled self, but something about holding this woman ever so lightly in his arms brought a sense of calm, despite the way his blood raced through his body. Even when the music picked up speed again he had no desire to let her go. Nor did she seem to notice the energy once more pulsing from the speakers loud enough to block conversation. Palm to palm, one arm about her waist, they didn't need words. Their eyes, their bodies, communicated quite well without the distraction of talking.

In heels, the top of Meilin's head reached his chin, making her tall enough to be comfortable in his arms. Her frame was slight and delicate, her features classically Chinese, her skin pale and smooth, much like pearls. He liked the way her straight, thick, black hair fell to her shoulders like a rich, silk curtain. The soft cloud of scent surrounding her was light, yet rich and exotic. The way she held herself brought to mind the images of ladies of the Chinese court he'd seen in the books in his father's library in Sussex. He'd had plenty of time to sit and gaze at examples of beautiful women painted by the masters of many centuries and many countries depicted in those art books. At odds with her modern, short, lacy, sleeveless dress, he could easily imagine her draped in thick silk robes, her hair arranged to support an elaborate headdress of gold, framing her finely boned features. Better yet, the image of Meilin reclined on a bed of silk sheets, one small finger crooked, inviting him to join her, now there was a fantasy he'd like to bring to life.

"Okay, you two!" A firm hand landed on his shoulder, startling him out of the trance he'd fallen into. Meilin flinched in his arms and pulled away, an enticing flush coloring her cheeks.

"Jack," she scolded. "That was rude."

Unrepentant, his friend laughed. "You two are looking far too serious out here! We're here to party, not gaze deeply into the eyes of strangers."

Jack's hand fell on his cousin's shoulder, not at all subtle about putting distance between the two of them. "Did I tell you Meilin is getting engaged tomorrow night? She's taken, man. Let me introduce you to some very nice single ladies. All from good families."

Scowling at this time wouldn't be polite, so Drew forced a genial smile onto his face. One he'd learned at a very early age. The one that diffused tense situations better than anything else he'd ever tried. Part of that stiff upper lip business his mother had drilled into him. Well, his father, too, but not as adamantly as his mother.

Jack drew forward another woman. "This is Yuahua, another, far more distant, cousin of mine. She's a career girl like Meilin, but four years younger, much closer to me in age."

Yuahua flushed, and gave Drew a shy smile before glaring at Jack. "Our Jack, he's too rude by far. But I am pleased to meet you, Drew from England. I adore your accent."

"Thank you. I'm rather enamored with the California accents around me." From his peripheral vision, he caught Meilin being pulled into a circle of her friends who danced to the fast beat. "Dance with me?" he asked the woman Jack practically pushed into his arms.

"Love to!" She grabbed his hand and pulled him deeper into the mass of writhing, hopping bodies.

He danced the entire set with one woman after another, all from Meilin's group of six, not a one of them touching his senses as Meilin did. Three were married, judging by the rings weighing down their fingers. Not one of them a shy flower. Not one of them as enticing as Meilin.

Meilin. Soon to be engaged. The very thought disturbed his peace of mind. He wanted to growl in a way he'd never experienced before. No matter who he danced with, some internal string had attached itself to her and each second he knew precisely where she was. It didn't take much effort to dance near the group of ladies around Meilin, all of them laughing, showing off their moves, dancing with the random men who gravitated to their group. Despite the ball of lead weighing him down, he laughed enough to find himself having fun.

Once or twice he looked around to find Birdie.

And found her dancing, closely, with Jack.

Now that didn't sit right with him. Truthfully he just didn't like any guy being so close to her. A totally irrational, but logical, big brother reaction he tried to shrug off. Hell, Jack didn't fit in with Birdie's plan and that fact guaranteed she'd keep the flirtation light. As she told Drew frequently, she was a big girl and could watch out for herself.

Meilin claimed his attention with her sensual moves. The night became a blur around him as his focus grew tighter on her face. Her joy at dancing and laughing with him and her friends, the way her gaze flirted with him, the expressions on her face, all the little details drew him to her.

He forgot she was all but engaged. He forgot they were surrounded. Nothing else held his attention longer than a half second. She was beauty and grace personified.

Eventually the dance floor began to clear, and the DJ played slower tunes. Meilin came into his arms easily enough and the distance between them closed until they swayed, their bodies synchronized, heartbeats aligned. When the last call went out, as natural as breathing he touched his lips to hers and discovered the true origin of lightning. Forget Mr. Franklin and his kite string. Forget Los Alamos and their mega bombs. Her kiss leveled his heart with a jolt of pure fire, igniting his body in ways he'd never experienced before.

By her gasp of surprise, he deduced she felt it too. The trembling of her slight frame shook him to his core where he trembled as well. Just touching his mouth to hers wasn't enough for him. Parting his lips, the tip of his tongue found hers. Need burned deep, although he fought to keep the kiss gentle when he wanted to ravage and conquer. Meilin melted against him, both her hands sliding up his chest to circle around his neck. The world dropped away, and blind instinct strained at the leash he'd put on it. Just one night…

"Enough of that!" Jack startled them from the moment. "Meilin, you're practically a married woman. Don't take advantage of the young lad that way. You're killing him."

Heat rushed to Drew's cheeks and he wanted nothing more than to plant his hand over Jack's face and push.

Blushing as well, Meilin stood before him, hands brushing away imaginary wrinkles from her flawless red dress. A light sheen of perspiration coated her pearlescent skin, glowing with smooth perfection under the swirling lights. A shaking hand pushed her hair from her face. "Jack, you're a pig."

"No, I'll be dead if word of that little scene gets back to your parents."

One of her friends stepped up and smacked Jack upside the head. "Leave her alone. It's her last night as a single woman. Let her have a little fun."

Rubbing his head, Jack turned on the woman. "You condone this?"

She shrugged. "It's no big deal. It's some dancing and a kiss."

Drew resisted the temptation to clear his throat, although he rubbed a hand over his chest, right in the center where a funny little pinch formed.

Was it just a harmless flirtation on her part? It sure felt like more. A hell of a lot more. Had the kiss not been interrupted, he had the feeling he might have seen the future. He tried looking to confirm it, but Meilin kept her eyes lowered and directed anywhere but him.

"Let it go, Jack. I'm a big girl and it was just some fun. As Suhua said, tonight is just a last chance to party like a single woman instead of a corporate wife. Things will get much duller from here on out. Endless events and such."

Drew forced his patented, calming smile to his lips. "Exactly, Jack. Everyone here was just blowing off a little steam tonight. No need to make a case out of it." He slapped a hand on Jack's shoulder. Possibly landing a little harder than intended. Easy enough to blame on the alcohol.

Jack's gaze sharpened as he searched Drew's face for any indication of a lie. Jack could spin with the best litigation lawyers, but Drew had confidence in his perfected poker face. The tension drained from Jack's shoulders. "Yeah, okay, but no more of that stuff. Shan and my uncle would both have my beautiful golden hide up on their walls if they learn about it." He shot a glare at Meilin's friends now gathered around them.

One woman held up her hands and nearly lost her balance. Clearly she'd freely imbibed. "No one here will say a thing. We all know exactly what's she feeling and facing. Meilin doesn't play much, and after tonight I doubt she'll ever get a chance to play like this again. Give her a break. Shan doesn't own her yet."

Drew was beginning to hate the name of this Shan guy.

But there wasn't a damn thing he could do about it. He had no time for a serious romance. Not even time for a light one. Not with a woman already established, as Meilin was from what he'd been able to get her to talk about.

"Meilin!" The call came from the bar. "Your cab is out front."

"Thanks, Bastion." She waved back. "That's it, ladies, time to head home."

Drew held out his arm. "Let me walk you out. We're leaving as well."

Meilin nodded and Drew hung back with her. He helped the women gather their purses and wraps if they had them, and made sure the tabs were settled. He and Jack tossed down handfuls of bills. Meilin signed a slip while her friends tossed smaller bills on the table. The waitress was well compensated in tips as far as he could gauge. At last they had little excuse but to follow their friends to the street. Jack, he noted, ushered Courtney with a hand on her lower back and an eye over his shoulder to make sure Drew and Meilin followed.

"Is there a way I—or rather my mother—can reach you?" he asked.

Meilin paused just outside the club door. A mixture of exhaust, common street filth, and a hint of salt in the misty air teased his nostrils. He wanted to smell nothing but her, the rich scent clinging to her hair and skin.

Letting his hand drift to her lower back, he once again experienced the jolt of electric awareness.

"Um, sure." She dug into her small purse. "I'm pretty sure I have a card in here somewhere…" A smile curved her lips upward as she pulled the small rectangle of cardstock from her purse. "Here it is. My cell phone is also on there, so if, um, she misses me at the office, she can try there. What's her name again?"

"Randi Robinson. Formerly Ferguson."

"Oh, I think I know her. Absolutely do"—Meilin's breath hitched—"have *her* give me a call at any time." Drew suspected Meilin had just given him permission to call her, rather than his mother. Did he dare hope?

The card slipped between his fingers as hers brushed his for a moment. "I'll do that." He looked as deeply as the dark night allowed and saw an answering heat flare in her eyes. "You get home safely."

"Thanks. I will."

"Meilin!" her friends called from the packed cab. "Meter's running, let's go!"

She waved at her giggling friends. "I must go. I've enjoyed meeting you, Drew Robinson. Best of luck straightening out your Chinese."

And if she'd really given him permission to call, he wanted to be sure. "May I call you if I need help studying?"

For a very long moment, she gazed into his eyes. "That might not be a good idea," she finally said quietly, the roar of Jack's SUV pulling up behind the cab almost covering her voice. The hand she held out was delicate, just like her. "Although it's possible your professor may call me for teaching assistance. We may yet meet again in the few weeks before the class moves to Peking University. Give my best to your sister. She's lucky to have you."

While his heart pounded at the thought of seeing her again, even if only for tutoring, Meilin turned and ducked into the front seat of the cab. The rest of her friends were piled two deep, one sitting on the laps of the others in the back. The driver pulled away with a screech of his tires to the squeals of his passengers. Meilin's wave was tiny and it left Drew's soul feeling empty as he watched her cab disappear around a corner. The sight of her face turned to the window, her green eyes looking back at him before being whisked down the street.

He had to let her go. One did not find true love at a bar the night before her engagement party.

The blast from Jack's horn broke him from his reverie and his feet dragged and stumbled against the ancient cement sidewalk as he made his way to the vehicle.

Drew had never considered himself a romantic, but something had shifted in his world tonight. Inside he knew he'd finally learned the secret to the poems written by men over the centuries. The aching loss of the possibility of a glorious future. Some of the sparkle went out of Drew's generally golden life. Meilin was one of a kind. Exotic and extraordinary. Lord, he must be more exhausted than he'd thought. It felt as if he'd never find another like her if he lived a hundred lives.

Climbing into Jack's SUV, he shook his head. Exhaustion, plus alcohol, dizzying lights, and deafening music, all combined to metaphorically dump him on his arse. A rare moment of fancy, that. Surely he'd manufactured the whole drama in his own head. Besides, in six weeks he was leaving for China. Where would he have time to fit in a seduction? Suddenly what had felt like an endless amount of time seemed far, far too short.

Chapter 4

"Turn up the music, Jack," Birdie called from the back seat.

"Enough, Bird," Drew complained. "I've got a splitting headache coming on."

"You're getting old, brother dear." The tease made him smile. But for a few measly months, they were the same age.

"Not old, just exhausted."

"Yeah, yeah. You poor baby. All tuckered out and no rest in sight. Have you heard from the parents?" She started digging into her purse. "Guess we wouldn't have heard our phones in there."

"No, I didn't check for messages." But he pulled his phone from his pocket.

"Guess that means you had a good time tonight." Jack's smile was back to being a little sly. "Didn't think I'd ever see you hitting on a woman ten years your senior."

Ten years? "Didn't seem like she was." Gaze on his phone, he swiped the screen and saw there were a few messages waiting.

"They're home!" Birdie chirped. "What time do we see them tomorrow?"

"Not too early." Drew groaned, reading his own messages. The two of them had received the same texts.

"In graduate school and still letting your parents know what you're up to every night? I'm impressed. My mother hasn't followed my antics since I finished high school." Jack turned on the wipers to clear the drops of mist forming on the windscreen.

"Won't your parents be at graduation?" Drew asked absently as he typed a reply. "They should be at the house about now," he commented over his shoulder. "Probably as wiped out as we are and jetlagged."

"Not too bad," Birdie replied. "They spent last night in New York. It's easier flying west. This way they gain several hours instead of losing them."

"Bet they're already falling into bed." The ding of a message arriving belied his prediction.

"Nope, they're too wired to sleep, Mom says. Headed for the hot tub." A snort left Drew's nose. Not something he wanted to think about. He'd caught them *au naturel* in the backyard spa once, not that they'd seen him. They'd been far too busy to notice Drew escaping the house for a late night soak. While he was thrilled for them—nice to know that in twenty years he could look forward to an active love life—it wasn't something he'd wanted to see. A glimpse had been enough, and he'd quietly retreated back into the house and left them to it.

Still, he'd never seen affection of any kind between his father and his mother, good old Bea. So, yeah, while parent sex squicked him out, he was happy for them. They'd each had very different lives the twenty two years they'd been apart. He and his father had never known about Birdie. Not a whisper. The frozen, formal life they'd lived with Beatrice was a far cry from the warm, loving, emotional women they'd met by accident. Well, his father, a widower of six years, had been actively searching for Randi, a girl he'd known as Jean Dailey. The shock had shaken things up considerably. But the attraction between the two had been undeniable.

"They'd like us there by noon." Birdie confirmed the text on his phone.

"Manageable. Barely." The drive from Stanford to San Ramon would take an hour at least. Weekend traffic on any of the bridges crossing the San Francisco Bay could be as heavy as the week day commute. Depended on what was happening where. A baseball game, a marathon, or some festival could account for weekend backups. Throw in never ending road repair by CalTrans and it could slow things down even more. "We'll leave as close to eleven as possible, if not a few minutes before."

Absence of late night traffic had them home within twenty minutes. A minute later they waved good-bye to Jack and let themselves into their apartment, doing their best to not disturb the neighbors.

"So you're hooked on an older woman?" Birdie's smile was silly as she swayed while kicking off her heels.

"And you were dancing with men shorter than you with those shoes on. What's your point?"

"Going to call her?"

Feigning nonchalance, he shrugged. "She's getting engaged tomorrow. Some big deal party. Not likely we could get anything going."

"Ah, that sucks." The look of sadness on her face was genuine. Birdie couldn't hide an emotion to save her life. He regularly walked away with her money after playing poker. Or Monopoly. Or any other game they wagered on. Sometimes he let her win, but recently time for games had been few and far between. With a little luck they could schedule some poker nights over the summer to break up the intense study ahead of him. Depended on how heavy her summer class load turned out to be.

"Well, it was a fun night."

The sappy smile on her face and deep sigh gave him cause for alarm. "Yeah, it was fun. I never knew there were so many hot guys out there."

"Didn't you mostly dance with Jack?" Again, he kept his face neutral. Friendly. Just like the Golden Retriever dogs his father compared him to. That was him, just easy going, happy to be where he was, thrilled to have anyone to talk to, but happy to lie about in the sun when the opportunity arose. All true, and part of his carefully constructed outward persona. Worked perfect for the lawyer gig. Also made life a lot easier by letting him step back from the drama that could break out at a moment's notice.

"Mostly, but there were five or six other guys I danced with. They also bought me drinks."

That fact was evident in the way she staggered from the foyer to the kitchen for a glass of water. Damn, she was shit-faced and he hadn't even noticed.

"Come on, Bird, off to bed with you. I'll bring you a big glass of water and some aspirin." He grabbed her upper arm and redirected her towards her bedroom.

"I'm fine. Lay off." Although she protested, she didn't fight him as he steered her into her room.

"I'll let you undress yourself."

"Damn right you will," she grumbled on her way face down onto the bed.

Drew sighed. She was out cold. He threw a blanket over her. At some point she'd wake up and get herself situated. In the meantime, he filled a large covered cup with a straw with cold water and set it on the nightstand with a couple tablets. Sure she could breathe, he left her room and shut the door. Lightweight.

A text pinged through and he checked his phone. It was Randi. *Birdie okay? She didn't answer.*

Drew tapped in a response. *Passed out. We went dancing in the City. She's wrung out from end of the quarter. Still has finals next week.*

A moment later Randi replied. *You are too. Thanks for keeping an eye on her. Sweet dreams. CBR sends his love to you both.*

A grin curled his lips. *Backatcha, Mum.*

Only a few seconds passed before she responded with a heart. Damn, if that didn't fill him with warmth.

Drew tossed his phone down on the bed and undressed in the dark of his room. If he dreamed of one certain Asian beauty, his sleep would certainly be sweet. Tortured, but sweet. Briefly he entertained the thought of calling her in the morning and seeing if he could talk her out of the engagement. Right. Some fantasy that was. She'd been out for a final fling with her friends. The next time might not happen until another one was getting married, and then she'd be far less open to flirtation. Much less a kiss.

Ah, that kiss. It would haunt him for years to come.

* * * *

Meilin paid the cab driver, the last one to be dropped off. The girls had all shoved money into her hand to cover their share. The man had a pretty good tip for making sure each one of them made it safely to their homes. The husbands who'd been waiting up had met each wife at the door and called out good night with a wave.

Would Shan be so amused and tolerant on the very rare nights she'd go out with the girls? Granted they might do it once a year, but would his social standing be flexible enough to allow her a night of fun even then? Or would she be limited to stuffy formal affairs mixed with family holiday gatherings? Would she and her friends have to limit themselves to Bunco or Mahjong parties?

She managed to enter her building and make her way up three flights of stairs to her apartment off the west end of California Avenue. An older building in the Richmond District, not far south of the Presidio, it was redolent of cooking from the older tenants and years of dust that no longer easily vacuumed out of the carpet. Her parents weren't impressed with the building, but it was cozy, convenient to transportation, the rent was reasonable, and she loved the neighbors.

She didn't have much time to spare for them, but from time to time she helped carry groceries up the stairs, or sat down to tea with octogenarians who'd been young children during the Great Depression. One had lived in the Philippines with her parents during the worst of the Depression and loved to go through Meilin's catalogues and design books, talking about the beautiful Chinese furniture and *objets d'art*. Meilin had tried to take her down to Gump's during the Christmas season, but, Edna had sighed, it just wasn't the same once they'd moved from the original location. And while Neiman Marcus and Saks were beautiful, they just didn't have the same sophistication as the old City of Paris and I. Magnin. Edna still had her wedding dress purchased at the latter in the early fifties and had many times shown Meilin the pictures of her wedding to a handsome young Coast Guard officer. Now faced with what she was sure would be a huge, showy, society wedding, Meilin found herself a tad envious of the simple ceremony pictured in Edna's album. Few guests in a cozy venue, the young men handsome in their uniforms, the two bridesmaids looking fresh in their dresses fluffed out with crinolines.

Inside her apartment, she flicked the three door locks and turned on only a table lamp in the small living room. She'd lived here six years now and didn't really relish the idea of moving into Shan's sleek, modern, high rise condo. On the other hand, his condo building did have an elevator. A couple months after she'd redone the design, he'd hosted a cocktail party there for a small group of his parents' friends and colleagues. He hadn't specifically invited her, at least not to show off her work, but she'd attended at her mother's insistence. Had Mom been matchmaking all those months ago? Probably.

That was most likely when the negotiations had begun.

Funny she should see it now, but hadn't noticed then. Hadn't wanted to notice.

In the bathroom she slowly removed her clothes before dropping the dress into the dry cleaning hamper. Shan's condo didn't have a bathroom with hand-laid hexagonal tiles that covered the floor and climbed the lower half of the walls, or a claw-footed cast iron tub. Instead of renovating, she'd merely decorated his private bath, a room about the size of her living room, with glass and chrome everywhere. It had already been outfitted with a tub big enough for four, and marble lined the floor and walls. She'd added huge fluffy towels to hang on the towel heater, painted the walls gold and black, and added a few accessories. That part of the job had been very easy. Not much different than other installations she'd sold to other clients. And not once had she been thinking it would be hers someday.

She shouldn't be complaining. Instead, she should be thinking of all the connections that would open up to her. There wasn't much she'd have to do to Shan's condo, but there were things she could still do to put her personal stamp on the spaces. Things that would bring in more new clients for her. The extra business would keep her busy enough not to worry about her lack of independence.

Shan had his business, she had hers. Unless he insisted she become a society wife and leave her work behind. Then things would get sticky. If he were willing to put off children a couple years, enough so that she could bring in other designers to handle most of the work, she could retreat to a hands-off, directorial position, keeping a hand in the jobs but not handling the small details. She could combine motherhood with work then.

The big question for her came down to needing to know how traditional he felt about life in general. Relationship roles. Maybe her mother would have some deeper insight. Something she hadn't really taken the time to worry about. Now with the engagement imminent, she was forced to think things through. Had she buried her head in the sand on purpose?

Having her parents arrange the marriage had seemed like a short cut since she hadn't made time to cultivate a romantic relationship. Was it more of a cop-out?

Lord, she was so tired. She didn't have the energy to contemplate it tonight.

Wiping the cream cleanser and the makeup from her face, she briefly contemplated a bath. Or a faster shower. Tomorrow—or rather today— was tightly booked with a trip to a spa to prepare for the party. She had to look her best, which put sleep at the top of her priorities. So. No bath, no shower. Cold water from the tap filled her plastic cup and she drank it down. Cool and refreshing. Now she just had to face her lonely bed and try to put the memory of one certain, young Englishman and his kiss from her mind.

Yeah, like that could work.

Chapter 5

"Why are we driving across the Bay today?" Birdie groaned from the passenger seat as they crossed the Bay Bridge. "I just have to go back tomorrow."

"It's the plan. We have to help get ready for the party next weekend." He'd packed his suitcase for the coming week and started setting aside what he needed to move into the dorm with the other immersion students.

Only staying overnight before going back for her finals, Birdie would have preferred to stay in their apartment and sleep. Seemed she still suffered from her hangover despite his efforts to help minimize it.

"Why do you have to move out?"

"It's part of the learning experience. I need to be near the other Mandarin students so as to stay in the language as much as possible." But he could get away from time to time. Depended on how stagnating the company might be.

"Not that I'll mind having our apartment to myself. At least then I can do what I want, have friends over or hang out in my pajamas all day without you nagging me."

Drew laughed to himself. Sure, living alone left one a lot of personal freedom but for all her bluster he knew they both liked having the other around. Raised without siblings all their lives, having one now, sharing an apartment, made up for the loneliness back then. Sort of. It went a long way toward helping him feel more and more comfortable in California. It was a lifestyle he'd quickly grown to like.

"You'll miss me, brat."

"Not when you're being an overprotective, bossy, know-it-all Neanderthal," she mumbled. "And don't call me brat."

"Don't act like one."

Birdie sighed as she leaned against the window of the sedan they shared. Because parking was at a premium almost everywhere they went, the two of them had decided to share the vehicle rather than each have their own. Not that Drew had ever enjoyed the luxury when he'd been at school in London, another place where parking came at a cost. For getting around and across the Stanford campus they each had a bicycle.

Still, the sedan was a bit old-fashioned. They could upgrade to something sportier. However, the car had belonged to the man who'd raised Birdie as his own and she wasn't ready to let go, so no one pushed. Much. Well, he didn't push much. The parents left it alone entirely.

"Okay, so tonight we spend with the parents, then I hike it back to campus in the morning, and suffer through my finals. On Thursday I return home."

"Right. We have a day to finalize all the party plans, and then we all go back to Palo Alto for my graduation Saturday."

"After which we turn right around, back to San Ramon, have a quick renewal of vows, then on with the graduation party and wedding reception. All at the house. How the hell do they think we're going to fit a hundred people there?"

He had to agree with his sister. The house Birdie had been raised in was a decent size, but not that big. Forty, perhaps fifty people max. Then again, not everyone who'd been invited would show. Randi was probably counting on that. And most of them would be neighbors such as the lawyer who lived across the street on the straight stretch leading into the circle of the cul-de-sac they lived on.

"I'm sure all the details have been planned for. Mum is good at this stuff, and Martin surely has it in hand." Lord forbid they hold an event without the butler to oversee everything. John Martin, his father's domestic right hand man, would be a mess of nerves and precise control. If he didn't fall over his own feet at the sight of Birdie.

A glance sideways showed Birdie smiling for the first time all day. It brightened up her face, and he could see her fighting her way out from under the effects of last night's binge.

"I like hearing you call her mum."

"I like having her as my mum. Love that you allow me to share her."

"She adores you too."

"I make a pretty awesome son. Any woman would be happy to have me as hers." He ducked to the side before Birdie's fist could connect with any sort of strength against his shoulder. "No violence now."

She laughed and something tense unwound inside him. His sunny sister was back. "So what was that with you and Jack last night?"

"What was with you and Meilin last night? That's her name, right?" Birdie rubbed her temples as if her head still hurt.

"Yes, Meilin."

"Pretty name even if it sounds a little Pokémon-ish. Meilinchu."

Drew winced. "Don't ever say that. Don't ever let it be a possibility she might overhear it. Besides, Pokémon is Japanese, not Chinese."

"She's too pretty, too classy to be a Pokémon. What's she do, again? Didn't Jack say something about it?"

Drew merged into traffic headed for the Caldecott tunnel, then glanced at her. "Is your memory so bad? Or were you too busy checking out the talent?"

"It was loud. I didn't catch even half of what anyone said."

"She's an interior designer. I'd like to look up her business and see what she does. Mum might know more about her."

"Probably. Mom has an interest in all things Bay Area, and with her tea set collection, she's very interested in Asian items."

True, Randi had an extensive, impressive, collection of tea pots and tea services from around the world. Nearly every country who revered tea was represented in some way. Dad teased her about it often. And since the family business had begun as tea importation nearly two centuries before, it all tied together.

"Why take this route?" Birdie asked. "The other way is faster."

"This is prettier."

"Did you invite Jack to the party?"

Surprised by the swift topic change, he took a moment to switch gears. "I did, but like us, he has a family who wants to celebrate their way. I'm sure we'll bump into him sometime over the summer. He'll be working from some relative's law office in the lower peninsula area. I'm sure he'll want to torture me with more bad Chinese phrases."

"What did you actually say to her last night? The look on her face was pretty funny."

"I'm not sure. Something to do with wanting something in her purse instead of a polite hello."

Birdie laughed again. Her good humor was definitely coming back.

"Bet she loved that. What other phrases did Jack teach you?"

"I have no idea, and I'm not about to try them on anyone until I know for sure. So what was with you snuggling up to him last night? Especially in that dress that fit like a rubber band."

Birdie shrugged. "I'd had a few to drink, and I was just having fun. Don't worry, I won't fall for him. I know what he is, and he doesn't fit in my plan."

"Ah, the plan. Still set on the London office?"

"Absolutely. I have one more full year to go, even if I start my thesis work this summer. Have to add some international business courses. Then Dad won't be able to put me off any longer."

Drew snorted. "Who knew I'd have to compete with you for the ultimate job when he's ready to retire."

"Which won't be soon, will it? I mean, he could at almost any time, now that he has Mom back in his life. Of course, they want more time off, but there's such a thing as retiring too early, isn't there?" A small pinch creased between her eyes. "I know I'm not prepared to step up now. Neither are you."

"No, we both have some years to put in first. I've got at least two, maybe three years to spend in the Far East office. Besides, if we fail, there's always Oswald to step in. But again, not for some time to come. Even if Dad does retire early, he'll wait at least ten years. Maybe fifteen. Long way to go."

Other than a snort at the mention of Larry Attenborough's nephew, a rising exec in the Lynford London office, Birdie ignored the implication there was a third in line for the top job. "You looking forward to China? I can't believe you'll be there in only six or seven weeks."

He had been. Yeah, he still was. But meeting Meilin last night had cast a shadow on his long-term plan. He hadn't expected to get slapped upside the head with such a strong attraction. Then again, it probably had just been the moment. Maybe if he saw her another time the pull wouldn't be there. And then there was that whole engagement thing for her. Even if he did fall hard, timing was off in a bad way. The woman already had her career established, and he was just starting down that path.

"Yeah, of course I am. Been planning it for years. I've been studying the economy, the culture, the traditions."

"Is that why you spent so much time dancing with Meilin? Is she your ideal Chinese princess?"

Drew forced himself to laugh. "I'm pretty sure she doesn't have time for me. Never mind there's ten years between us, ya know? And she's getting engaged tonight. So no, I don't see her figuring in my future plans." Which was a bloody shame, even if there was time for an all-out wooing.

"Yeah, I can see where that would be a problem. But it didn't seem to bother her so much last night. The age difference or the fiancé in the wings."

"Last night was not real life. It was a moment out of time. Not enough to make big changes in carefully laid out plans."

"But you're thinking about those changes, aren't you?"

Birdie was a shrewd one for sure. If anything, her insight painfully reminded him of her Robinson genetics. Although Randi had said more than once Birdie's brains came from her father's side of the family, Drew knew her mother's side had their fair share. Birdie had been raised by people who worked within their own family business. RJ Dailey had a successful business selling vintner's supplies to many of the vineyards up and down the west coast. Her mother did the accounting for the business and the man who'd raised Birdie had run the sales department. She'd been around for much of it and already had a head trained for business. Transferring those smarts to Lynford would be a snap for her. Which is where her attention should focus, not on his supposed love life.

"When have I had time?" They'd made it through the tunnel and to the other side of the golden brown hills. Dark green oak trees broke up the expanse of dried grasses as they headed for the next freeway junction that would run them past Walnut Creek and south to San Ramon.

"True. But you know they'll see something in your face if you let those thoughts occupy you tonight."

Very true. Randi was a little too observant. At least his dad would be more focused on her than him, but she'd eventually clue him in. There were times when being on his own was a good thing. Tonight would have been a good time to be very much alone with his thoughts.

* * * *

"What's up with you?" From the chair beside her, the elegant and still beautiful woman who had given birth to her shattered the nap Meilin had been trying to take.

Meilin kept her eyes closed as the technician massaged her legs. The pedicure was the last step before getting her hair done for the evening. If she didn't open her eyes, maybe her mother would think she'd fallen asleep and hadn't heard the question.

"Meilin, I know when you're faking sleep."

Mentally she heaved a big sigh. Mother was like that. Far too observant.

The peaceful moment gone like mist burned away by the sun, Meilin opened her eyes and glanced at her mother. "Nothing's up with me. I'm just trying to get into my zone, find my Zen, for tonight."

Perched like a queen in the large, vibrating pedicure chair, her mother waved her hand. As if that wave could dispel all of Meilin's concerns. "You like Shan well enough. This is not a horrible thing happening tonight."

"Shan's okay." Well, he was. From their limited working relationship months ago, she hadn't seen anything to indicate otherwise. If he'd been anything other than okay, there would have been whispers long ago. One had to trust the community grapevine.

"In time he'll be more than okay to you. He's a good man. Successful. Polished. Kind. He'll be good to you." As mentally sharp as her mother was, Meilin knew there was a kernel of truth there. Everyone who knew Lin Shan said he was a good man.

"I know. But as much as I want to know why he picked me, I also want to know if he will be exciting. Will he be comforting? Or too focused on business to notice anything more than how perfect a hostess I am?" Like anyone would believe that of her. She rarely had a hand in any sort of party planning, unless it was to decorate for a wedding or corporate event, and her assistant usually handled those details. Did Shan's housekeeper or secretary currently handle those details for him, just as they'd handled many of the details of his condo remodel?

Her mother softly scoffed. "Of course he'll be most attentive. He knows how to cherish a wife."

"He's never had a wife, so how can you know that? Will I ever be more to him than another accessory in his perfect life? Will he tolerate my imperfections?" Not that she'd tried to hide them, but she did have some. She grew impatient from time to time. Liked to leave her shoes by the front door of her apartment. Didn't always make her bed and sometimes ate ice cream for dinner. When she actually ate at home. She also loved to spend Saturdays in her pajamas with her nose in a book or watching a drippy, sappy movie on Netflix. When she had a Saturday at home. Something that happened only about twice a year.

"All beauty has some imperfection, you know this. You plan for it in your designs. He knows this as well."

Surely dear old Mom was making some of this up as she went along. Or did she know about the cuckoo clock her latest clients insisted on including? "How do you know he knows this? Do you know him personally?"

"I know what his parents have told us, and they know him better than anyone. Same with you. We have not misrepresented you during the marriage negotiations."

Oh goodie. She could just imagine. "What have you told him?" Hopefully not about her sloppy Saturdays. Just one more thing that would probably disappear forever now.

"About what? We told him you were raised to respect your heritage. You honor your ancestors and respect the old ways. But he can also see you're a modern woman. As he is a modern man. As we all have to be to thrive in this world. We've chosen this life away from China. We've adapted. As have all who emigrated when our ancestors did. We adapted without forgetting our roots."

Roots that extended across the wide Pacific Ocean and deep into the soil of China. A land that had changed so much from the one her great-grandparents had left so long ago. So changed that those old days were more a dream than history. Her two years in China had shown her many alterations from the stories told down the generations.

"But being a modern woman doesn't mean you've turned your back on our ways. You know what he expects of you. A sophisticated woman on his arm, a hostess for his home, a lover in his bed, a companion and helpmate, and children to continue the legacy."

"Ah, children. Now there's a concept." Not one she'd ever spent any time contemplating. Children belonged to her brother, cousins, and friends. She was the favorite Auntie who happily returned them to their parents when they needed feeding, changing, or a nap.

"Believe it or not, children will bring joy to your life. Most days."

The laugh at her mother's sly expression escaped before Meilin could stop it. "I'm sure. Some days more than others."

"Today should be one of those days, and yet, I find my heart uneasy. You agreed to this, Meilin. And while you haven't been exactly over the moon, you seemed happy enough about it. It's time to take on the next role. Time to do your share to honor the sacrifice your ancestors made by leaving China."

"My honored brother already has three children. The family legacy is secure." Her sarcasm rolled right over her mother's head. "Why I have to add to it, I'm not quite sure, but you've always told me someday this would come to pass." She raised a hand to her temple and rubbed. Traces of her night out lingered, and she could use a good long nap. "So I've agreed to do my duty. I'll be the best wife I can be and hope he is forgiving when I fall short."

"You won't fall short. And if you do, there will be times he does as well. He'll miss a dinner, or school event, or even forget a birthday or anniversary. It won't be because he wants to, but rather business will demand it. A business that is there to keep you and your children dry, warm, and safe. To give you a life of security and dignity. To provide your children with the best advantages to make sure their futures are solid. It's what good parents do."

Yes, her own father had missed events on occasion. Not often enough she'd ever truly felt abandoned, but it had happened. Mom had always been there. "As you've done for me. I get it. It's my turn to do the giving and not the taking."

"So what has changed? Today you seem more reluctant than ever. Stop thinking about what you're giving up and start thinking of what you'll gain."

"I'm trying, Mother. I'm trying. But last night…"

She didn't have to look to know her mother shot a sharp glare her direction. "What about last night? I knew that girls' night out with your friends was a bad idea. Did Jade tell you horror stories of childbirth?"

"What?" Meilin's eyes popped open. "Of course not! She's the first one to talk about marital bliss and how adorable her children are."

"Then what happened?"

"I… I don't know. I got home and I started looking at my apartment. Started thinking about my neighbors. How no one will be around to have tea with Edna and have her page through the latest design catalogues. She has very good taste."

"For a poor white woman," her mother grumbled. "What does she know of Asian art and furniture?"

"Quite a lot, actually. She's given me some great ideas. I won't have time for her once I'm married. Maybe once in a blue moon I'll be able to visit her. Take her to Union Square at Christmas. But it won't be the same. You know it won't."

"That old woman means more to you than your own grandmother."

"Not true, but my own grandmother doesn't recognize me anymore."

"She does. She just can't say it, but deep down, she does."

This time the sigh was heavy and audible. "So you say. I adore my grandmother. I miss her terribly. But she's being well cared for. Edna is all alone. Her son lives across the Bay and only makes it over to see her about every six months. She says they talk at least once a week, but he has grandchildren of his own now."

"Again, not your problem. I'd think you'd be happy to leave that old apartment behind. That building needs a top to bottom renovation."

"I love that building. It has character. It has warmth and charm. All of which is lacking in Shan's high rise condo."

"I'm sure he'll be looking for a house very soon. Children should not be raised in such a place. They need room to run."

A home that will be every much as formal and pristine as his condo, she felt sure. Huge and cold.

"But even if Shan doesn't look into buying a house in the near future, Meilin, you could make it a family home without sacrificing style. But this can't be the whole issue. A house is just a place to live. What's important is the relationship."

"I don't love him, Mother."

At this, she scoffed and waved her hand again. "Love will follow."

"I'm not attracted to him, not the way a woman should be attracted to the man she marries."

"Why are you bringing this up now? It didn't seem to matter last week. Besides, that will change. Love grows and passion follows. Even then, passion may very well cool, but love will remain. Have your children and when passion in the bedroom changes, put your passion into your children."

"And my work."

"Your work." Her mother practically snorted. "Your work will fit in or it won't, and there are many designers out there ready to fill your shoes. No one can replace you in your marriage or with your children. A career just fills time until you take the next step Destiny has provided."

A burst of anger, barely leashed, filled Meilin's chest with fire. "How dare you discount my career? It's kept me from sponging off you for the last twelve years. I'm good at what I do; I'm sought after, my reputation impeccable. My career has brought no shame to our family."

"Easy, daughter, easy. Your career has brought you much respect, and the family by association. But it also brings questions. Why are you not married? It brings doubts. Is there something wrong with you that you aren't married? Shan's suit has ended those questions. It has brought you a new level of approval."

The anger simmered. Was she a dog to do as she was told, to seek a pat on the head for following her master's plan instead of her own? Getting out on her own had been hard, but she'd stuck to it, worked up the ranks to achieve success on her own terms. Of course she still had to work within the basic rules of her field, but she knew when to bend the rules, when to toe the line. And she'd paved a way for other young Asian designers. Women who fought not only gender bias, but racial prejudices as well. Although the landscape had changed over the decades, there were still pockets of people who couldn't forget the division of Asian from white, white from black, or anyone else. People who paid her commissions but still believed themselves to be her betters, all because of their white skin.

"I don't need society's approval, Mother."

"Stop growling at me. Of course you need society's approval. Without it you'd have no business. We're all scraping for approval from somebody, be it husbands, children, parents, colleagues, or clients. It's how the world works. Step too far out of line and the backlash is considerable. Depending on the line." The shrug she offered was fatalistic and reminded Meilin of her grandmother.

Swallowing a pang, she had to acknowledge her mother's point. "True."

"But none of this explains what happened last night to change your mind about this next step in your life."

No. She was right about that. Meeting Drew had changed everything. The attraction she felt couldn't have been all on her side. The way he'd held her, gazed at her, kissed her... It all spoke of a man who felt every bit of the electricity zipping between them. Something she'd never once felt in the presence of Shan or any other man. And it was the one thing she could never tell her mother.

Luckily, the technician finished by easing the disposable foam flip-flops onto Meilin's feet as the hair stylist came for her. For now, she escaped, but not without the feel of her mother's eyes glaring into her back.

Chapter 6

The house in San Ramon welcomed Drew and Birdie home. With summer's heat settling in, the warm, dry air held the scent of sweet flowers and the refreshing scent of the tall redwoods forming a barrier on the uphill side of the lot. Charcoal also coasted on the slight breeze and Drew's mouth watered. Would dinner be a barbeque on the back deck overlooking the pool? Good thing he kept a pair of swim togs in the room Randi had changed from craft room to his own space. There was also a chaise lounge out back with his name on it. Something he meant to take advantage of as often as possible until he left for China.

The greetings from both parents were effusive. Randi glowed with love and happiness; his father couldn't stop grinning. The tension between Drew's shoulders ramped down a notch or two. Coming here today had been the right decision.

Randi's soft hand stopped on his cheek, forcing him to look down at her concerned face. "You look tired. Were exams tough?"

"They're over; that's the best thing about them." Drew bent enough to wrap his arms around her waist and lift her up for a tight hug. She smelled of Chanel and barbeque sauce and something else elusive and comforting. Like a mother should smell.

At her squeak, he set her down again. "I'm starved. What's for dinner?"

"Your arse if you don't unhand my wife." Drew looked to his father and caught the laugh that belied the rebuke.

"She's my mother now. I get to hug her whenever I want, or beg for kisses whenever my boo-boos need to be kissed all better."

"Get your own girlfriend," his father said easily and pulled Randi back against his chest. "This one's mine."

"Men." Randi huffed, then laughed. "The chicken is nearly ready to go on the grill. Dump your packs, and then you and Birdie can set the table out back."

"Mum, you're a mind reader." Drew contented himself with a small whoop and a kiss on her cheek.

"No, I just know you. You're a man of simple wants. Only the best, but simple. Barbeque and sunshine. Toss in a beer or two. You, I have figured out." She shooed him away.

Did he mind that she considered him simple? Nah, not really. After all, she was mostly right. And she had anticipated his hunger for chicken on the grill. Well, any kind of meat on the grill, really. Ribs, steak, crab legs, chicken, didn't matter much. Football and barbeque were two of Drew's favorite things in America. Sunshine and swimming pools figured high on the list as well. Girls in bikinis didn't hurt, either. Girls in general never hurt.

As he undressed and glanced at the clock, he wondered what time Meilin's engagement party started. Remembering her looking back at him from the window of her cab, he couldn't help but wonder… Would she go through with it? She hadn't been wearing a ring yet. Would she accept it tonight? Or some other engagement gift? Thinking about what might be happening at any moment over in the City gave him only frustration. Not a damn thing he could do about it. Had he met her a couple of months ago… Would it have made a difference? Chances were their paths probably would never cross again. In a city the size of San Francisco, their meeting had been purely a fluke, despite Jack's family ties to her. Jack had little time for family as far as Drew knew. They'd shared a room Autumn quarter at Stanford. In between classes and small parties with the other law students, Jack had spent most of his time hitting the books just as Drew had.

And while Drew had moved into the two bedroom apartment with his sister, Jack had still been around more than anyone else. As friendly as Jack was, Drew suspected his overly polished, slightly smarmy personality kept many people away as it appeared Jack had few, if any, close friends. A cover to hide a soft heart? Sentiment and Jack didn't seem to be compatible words, but hey, what guys let their deepest feelings hang out on their sleeves? When it came to relatives other than his siblings, Drew had no clue what Jack thought. Meilin was evidence that suggested he had an extended family in the area. How often did they meet? Would Meilin and her future husband attend local family events?

What a wanker. What right did he have to get wound up about a woman he'd met at a night club? He pulled up the baggy swim togs and tossed his clothes to the corner to be sorted later. Right now all his brain could handle was a short swim, a long soak in the outdoor spa, and a big dinner. Not necessarily in that order. Food first. Drink and swim second.

Randi had a pile of plates and silverware on the island when he entered the kitchen with a pool towel slung around his neck. "Birdie's taken out the placemats and napkins. Can you get this bunch?"

"Sure. Where's the old man?"

Randi's laughing eyes looked up at him from where she tossed a green salad in a large bowl. "He's manning the grill."

"I hope there's a backup plan when he burns the chicken."

"He's learning. He's been practicing."

"In London?" That didn't seem likely.

"When we go to the Sussex house on the weekends. He had a charcoal grill installed and Cook's been having a fine time watching him learn to cook something more than toast and eggs. He's getting better."

"How many chickens were sacrificed to the fire?" Sure, the guys who lived all around them here knew the fine art of cooking over open flames, but it wasn't something done across the pond. Not by men who could hire cooks, butlers, and maids.

"Not many. Fewer than I expected, actually. I've never fully mastered the outside grill."

"Sure, and you have a fine indoor one."

"Completely different animals, I assure you."

Birdie bounced into the kitchen wearing a one-piece suit with a sarong tied around her hips. "What else? Drinks are on the table."

Randi handed her the salad bowl. "I'll bring the dressings. Drew has the plates and silver. All we need is the corn from the fridge and the bread from the oven."

"Fab. I'm starving," Drew said as his stomach growled.

"You're always starving." Both women spoke at the same time.

Drew grabbed up his assignment and left them to their giggles in the kitchen. He pretended to be annoyed, but really, he loved the teasing. This was what it meant to be a family. Something he'd vaguely missed, but hadn't realized how much until he'd been gifted with these two women. This life he could easily learn to love. Perhaps he should let Birdie take over the London office and he could be a California beach bum.

* * * *

Meilin stood beside Shan in a small anteroom to the side of the ballroom booked for their engagement party. He was dressed impeccably in a tux with black tie, his thick dark hair perfectly groomed, shoulders straight, looking every bit the handsome tycoon. On the outside he appeared cool and comfortable. Who knew what he felt on the inside. His face gave nothing away, nor did he fidget.

Allowing herself a small nervous swallow, she tried to emulate his stance. The elegant, traditionally styled red silk dress fit her better than any formal gown she'd ever worn in her life. If the appraising perusal Shan had given her a moment before meant anything, she'd cleaned up quite well. A hint of a smile hovered around his lips and a slight warmth filled his eyes, making her think he'd noticed enough to be pleased, but his mind wasn't entirely on her. Was he nervous too?

From beyond the door into the ballroom, the sounds of conversation and string music filtered in. Occasionally a laugh lifted above the murmurs, but nothing loud and crass. So unlike the loud dancing music of the night before. No conversations shouted to be heard over the music. No magical LED lightshows to help build the frenzy of those lost in the music.

She wanted to sigh. She held it back. No doubt it would make Shan frown, and they couldn't have that.

"Before we go in," Shan said, turning to fully face her.

"Yes?"

He reached into his breast pocket and pulled out a long narrow dark leather case. "A gift." He simply handed it to her.

Knowing there would be an engagement ring ceremoniously given in front of the guests, she raised a questioning brow.

"Open it. I hope you like it." Not a drop of nerves appeared in his expression.

Meilin lifted the hinged lid and both brows rose at the sight of the diamond bracelet inside. Pairs of diamonds were separated by waves of pavé set diamonds. The man had exquisite taste. Or his mother did. "It's beautiful."

Shan cleared his throat. "I thought to get something larger...showier, but... Well, this seems more fitting for your beauty. More delicate." He reached around the lid and lifted the bracelet. "May I?"

"Yes. Please." She lifted her left wrist and let him work to secure the fine catch.

He fumbled a little. "I can see this will take a little practice to master." The smile he gave her actually bordered on shy. A layer of ice fell away from her heart. Maybe he did have some feeling for her. "There. I think it's secure. I hope so." At least he wasn't practiced at fastening expensive bracelets on the wrists of women. Did that mean he didn't give expensive gifts or that he'd never been with a woman worthy of such a gift?

"I wouldn't want to lose it. Thank you." With her head dipped, she looked up at him through her lashes. Although she wore heels, he still had a few inches on her. Not so tall he towered over her, but enough to make her feel feminine. Not that he made her feel as delicate as Drew had. Damn, this was not the time to think of the youngster from England. To cover her thoughts of another man, she leaned forward meaning to kiss his cheek. But Shan moved, and their lips touched. Softly. A mere whisper. A brush of air that sent exactly zero tingles of electricity through her body.

She pulled back. Shan stepped closer until his chest brushed her breasts. One hand touched her waist, then settled there. His other hand rose to cup her cheek. "That was nice, but I'd prefer you kiss me like this."

His lips settled more firmly on hers, not enough to crush or bruise, but enough she noticed how surprisingly soft they were. Shan's eyelids lowered as he nibbled on her lips. Automatically she responded in kind, hoping, dreaming, he'd draw some heat from her. A hint of passion that would confirm her decision to take this step. With him.

At the moment the heat should have kicked in, the door from the ballroom opened.

"Oh ho! Looks like they can't be trusted alone just yet!" Jack rudely interrupted, his voice loud enough to project back into the larger room.

Shan moved back just far enough to put space between their lips, but not their bodies. "Bad timing," he muttered. For a long moment, he held her close, and to her shock, she discovered why. The kiss had aroused Shan to the point he took time to adjust his dinner jacket to hide it.

"Time to greet your guests, you two lovebirds!" Jack called out loud enough for the entire ballroom to hear.

"I'm going to kill you, Jack," Meilin said in her sweetest voice.

"No, you won't. You love me, dearest cousin." Jack's smirk took in her flushed face and the way Shan positioned himself slightly behind her, his arm across her back, his hand possessively resting on her hip.

"Let's go," Shan said, and she had no choice but to do as he said. They followed Jack into the ballroom and faced the crowd that burst into applause punctuated by whistles from a select group of younger attendees despite the frowns from their parents. At the dais stood her parents and Shan's. Both sets looked extremely pleased.

If only the doubts hadn't invaded her mind since last night.

Guess it was time to put her acting experience to work. Never mind she'd been ten when she'd been chosen to be Mary in the Christmas pageant at church. She had more in common with the lamb being led to slaughter than she did the Mother of Christ.

Like a modest Chinese bride, she stood on the dais at Shan's side, his arm an anchor and a small comfort while their fathers made short speeches. Then Shan made one, and all she had to say was she accepted his offer for her hand. Once she'd voiced her agreement, he slid a large diamond set in platinum on her left hand, a ring that sparkled nearly as much as the platinum and diamond bracelet on her wrist.

She held her serene smile as cameras flashed, and managed more of a smile when Jack called out for a repeat of the kiss he'd interrupted. "So everyone can see!"

Holding her smile, she also sent him a glare that only increased his grin of mischief. She didn't have to fake feeling shy about kissing in front of three hundred of their closest friends and business associates.

This kiss was pretty much the same as the last, although a little longer. Shan held her closer, his lips teased a little more, but held back the tongue. Thankfully. All in all, it was a modest kiss, quite unlike Drew's kiss the night before.

At the thought of Drew, she abruptly pulled back just enough to break the connection. Amusement twinkled in Shan's eyes. His chest lightly rubbed against her nipples, and she was mortified to realize they'd stiffened into small hard points. The lazy look in Shan's eyes told her he assumed the kiss had affected her as it had affected him. Although he seemed pleased, she'd held her passion back. At least in public. The smile on his face promised her he looked forward to later when he might get her alone.

Good God. He thought he'd turned her on. Embarrassment heated her cheeks, and she turned her face away from the crowd. A move that pleased their audience as Shan hugged her closer to him.

"I'm very happy," he said quietly, his warm breath brushing the shell of her ear. "I promise to do everything in my power to make you the happiest woman alive."

A shudder worked down her spine, and he hugged her closer.

"It's all official except for the actual wedding. Come home with me tonight."

Surprised at his request, Meilin turned to look at him. A very slight flush warmed his cheeks as his eyes dilated.

"I—I'm not sure I'm ready for that step."

Shan lifted a curled finger to stroke her cheek. "That's fair. I can wait. For now, let's enjoy our party."

To the applause and cheers of their guests, he led her off the dais to the dance floor. The small orchestra started up a tune perfect for a long slow-dance. Doing her best, she relaxed in his arms and followed his lead with little effort.

Well, he had that going for him. Shan was a good partner. Not exciting or thrilling, but solid and steady. No flash, just style.

"Have I mentioned how beautiful you are?" Shan said halfway through the dance.

"Have I mentioned how dashing you are tonight?" she responded with a cheeky smile.

"No, I don't believe you have until now. Thank you."

"And a very fine dance partner," she added.

"It bodes well for other areas of our future together." The smile he gave her left no doubt in her mind exactly where he expected them to dance well together.

It wasn't something she wanted to think about just yet.

From there the party picked up juice. Meilin lost count of how many people she danced with. Many of them elders. Uncles, they called themselves. Even Jack managed to cut in once.

"Have much of a hangover this morning?" he asked cheerfully.

Thank God he was too close a cousin and an original character. She shuddered to think she might have ended up with him, or someone like him, for a husband. In contrast, Shan looked very acceptable. "No, not really. Water and a pre-emptive aspirin work wonders. You? Did you manage to get home without a DUI?"

"No worries. I didn't drink much. Had to keep an eye out on our blond siblings. They really are too adorable together, although Drew is a mite over protective when it comes to his sister. Next Saturday I'm invited to a party at their mother's house across the Bay. Since the family is having a party for me, I doubt I'll make it."

"Is there a reason for this story?" She didn't have to fake the yawn she tried to hide behind her hand. "They were fun to dance with."

"Looked like you and Drew had more fun than just dancing usually entails."

"He's a nice kid. About ten, twelve years too young. Besides, as you know, I'm engaged now. That's what this"—she waved a hand indicating the crowd of well-dressed people around them—"is all about. It's an engagement party."

"So it is." Jack laughed and spun her around. "For my favorite cousin. But I will tell you something I've noticed between last night and now."

"What?" She heaved a sigh.

"You don't look nearly as happy tonight as you did last night."

"Last night was about letting loose, having fun. Tonight is a more serious event."

"Ah, but you should smile more. And not that little smile of mystery good little Chinese girls are taught from birth. You should have a big, bright American smile on your pretty face."

Meilin laughed. "Jack, you never cease to amaze me for your ability to poke, prod, and generally cause mischief. Leave well enough alone and pretend your mother raised you to behave properly in polite company."

"My mother gave up a long time ago. Some people just can't be tamed. I once thought you were one of my kind."

"Never, Jack. I studied my lessons like a dutiful daughter."

Jack snorted. "Lie to yourself if you must but don't lie to me. You taught me most of what I know about mischief."

"You're delusional."

"You're brainwashed." He smiled cheerfully enough, but there was a knife between the layers of sweet cake.

"So, will you begin work soon with your shiny new degree framed and tacked to the wall?"

"Ah, change the subject. Very well. No, I go back into the library and begin studying for the bar exam. After I take a week at Lake Tahoe to play and relax. Then I begin working at Uncle Za's firm until I pass the exam. After that, we'll see if they have an associate position for me. I intend to make my mark in the field of law. Some of it may take me to China, much like Drew expects his career to."

"China?"

"First he'll go learn some proper Mandarin—"

"—and not the silly phrases you taught him."

Conceding the point, he gave her a brief nod. "—and once the Beijing portion of his class is done, he's set to go right into the Beijing offices of his father's company. Lynford International Importers. If I find corporate law boring, I could make myself useful to him over there."

"Such lofty plans." And not long before Drew was out of the picture completely. That would make it easier for her to focus on her upcoming life with Shan.

"One must plan for the future. Or so my father has been telling me for years." His bright eyes crinkled with laughter.

"Admirable."

"But I'm not here to talk business."

"Because this is my engagement party. You know, you should be singing the praises of Shan like a canary from a golden cage instead of talking about your friend."

"Caged is not my style."

"Funny how I knew that." This crazy kid, the cousin who'd given her the most trouble when babysitting, had grown into a handsome young man. If only he'd stop the games and let people see how sweet he could be.

"May I cut in? Haven't danced with my fiancée much this evening."

Jack gave her a quick smile, then turned it on Shan. "You'll have to dance with this lovely woman for the rest of your life. What's the hurry now?"

Shan smiled only for Meilin. "Why waste more time? An offer was made, accepted, everyone is happy; it's time to move forward." He smoothly inserted himself between her and Jack and pulled her into his arms. Closer than he had with their first dance.

"Excuse us, will you, Jack?" Shan didn't wait for an answer, but expertly guided Meilin to the middle of the dance floor.

"That was mildly rude." She lightened her tone to make it sound teasing.

"Jack's persistent; I'll say that for him."

"He is. And deep down, he's really a decent guy."

"Never said he wasn't." Shan easily led her in a spin, pulling her closer until they were molded together from chest to thigh. Close enough she could appreciate how firm he was. Not rock hard, but well muscled. "About next Saturday…"

"Next Saturday?" Jack's graduation and party. She hadn't yet spoken to Shan about it but assumed he'd accompany her. Built-in date and all that, now.

Shan's steady gaze held hers. "Did you get my message? I don't recall a response."

Meilin shook her head. "I don't know what you're talking about. I didn't get a message."

"I guess that explains the lack of response. I need to double check the numbers I have for you. No matter now. I've been invited to a party. A combined wedding reception and graduation thing. The groom is someone I knew when I was in London for my undergrad exchange. The graduate is his son. I'll pick you up about four."

"Saturday is Jack's graduation. I'm obligated to attend the family function."

"Ah. So am I. I'll pick you up at twelve-thirty. We'll celebrate Jack's graduation, then head across the Bay to the other. It will have to count as our first date as I had unexpected business pop up and I have to fly to

LA tomorrow afternoon. I expect to be back no later than Friday. Maybe sooner. But definitely home for Saturday."

"Oh." She blinked at him, doing her best to process the invitation presented as a command. "I suppose that will work." She'd been hoping to spend the last part of Saturday at home with a movie.

"We won't stay late. I've only seen this guy once in the twenty some odd years since school. He was kind to a misplaced foreigner. I'd like to pay my respects."

"Well, when you put it like that..." There went her early night. At least she had time to reschedule and have a sloppy Sunday instead. Unless Shan came up with something else.

Shan smiled. "I also want to show him my happiness. Drink a toast to each other's good fortune. It seems auspicious for a happy beginning to our life together."

"Now there's the smooth operator I've heard about." She grinned at him to soften the intended rebuke.

"No more talk about pasts, darling. It's all about the future and how we're going to make it blissful."

Doing her best to appear on board with that idea, she let him cup her skull and pull her head to his shoulder. His lips softly touched her temple and for one moment she let herself believe there was a chance everything would work out fine. No, she didn't love him, nor did his touch set her blood on fire, but she didn't feel cold. The warmth was there, although slight, but it was enough that maybe, just maybe it could build to something comforting and lasting.

"All right, I'll be ready by twelve-thirty."

Chapter 7

After what seemed like hours in the intense sun, Drew was relieved to be ensconced in the back seat of his parents' air conditioned car. The fancy new dark green Jaguar XJ-R had a cooling option in the seats, not just in front, but the back as well. The car was so new it still had the temporary plate and the scent of new leather. He'd already removed the graduation robes and tugged his tie loose. Next up, the renewal of wedding vows for his parents and then the combined reception and graduation party for a hundred of their closest California friends and a few from London. Most of whom would be Randi's neighbors and her father's business associates. Birdie had called in her friends to grow the ranks of people their age and once the formalities were covered, they'd turn the bash into a pool party. Something he highly approved of.

In the front seat, Randi was on her phone first with Martin, their butler who'd flown over from London—because, really, they couldn't have a party without Martin in charge—then her friend from across the street, Kelly Tucker. The first time he'd met Kelly she'd been the one to comment on Birdie's resemblance to him and his father. Kelly had since apologized a dozen times over for her big mouth. Her husband, Brad Tucker, known to family and friends as simply Tuck, had covered her mouth more than once. Seemed like a regular thing for them. In truth, they were more an extension of the family despite Tuck being Randi's lawyer.

Because of the Tucker brood, there'd be younger kids at the party, so things couldn't get too terribly out of hand. Probably no throwing girls in the pool or nonsense like that. Too bad.

"Okay." Randi swiped the screen of her phone. "That's done. Kelly is supervising Martin who is supervising the caterers so everything should be in place by the time we get there."

"Excellent." His father glanced at his wife and grinned. "So the guests begin arriving at one, at one-thirty we bare our souls to them, and by two we'll be deep in toasts."

Randi laughed and swatted his arm. "You can't wait to gush out your vows again and you know it."

"True, but I'm not sure why you're making me do it in front of an audience. I'd rather keep it private."

Knowing where this was headed, Drew cleared his throat while Birdie squealed and covered her ears.

Randi laughed and swatted his arm again. "Behave. We'll warp the children."

"Too late, they're already warped."

"Bleach!" Birdie called out. "I need eye and ear bleach!"

Drew chuckled as the parents laughed. It felt good being like this. He hoped it never got old.

Randi glanced over her shoulder, and Drew caught the roll of her eyes. Didn't stop her from resting her hand on his dad's thigh. It could be Birdie had the right idea about the bleach. Especially when his dad rested his hand over Randi's and squeezed.

Their happiness thrilled him. No denying that, but he wasn't used to seeing the easy way they expressed affection. His mother wouldn't have allowed it even if his father had been so inclined to touch her publically. As she'd once explained, public displays were beneath them. The jewels she wore, all gifts from his father, were plenty to indicate the strength of their marriage. However, he saw it another way. The cold diamonds had merely reflected the ice building thicker and thicker each year between and around them.

His father didn't give Randi diamonds, unless they were secondary to the other stones. Emeralds and sapphires suited her far better. Australian fire opals. Stones set in gold rather than platinum to reflect the warmth of her spirit.

Rubies. Not for Randi, but for Meilin. Red would suit her exquisitely. As the banter in the car continued, he imagined her in a red dress of thick Chinese silk, heavily embroidered with dragons and delicate birds. Black hair flowing straight, shining and heavy as the silk of her dress would provide the right backdrop for a cascade of rubies and diamonds hanging from her small earlobes like tongues of dragon fire. Not the kind that consumed and burned, but the kind that licked and teased, stroked and excited. Red lips parted, long nails covered in red lacquer... Oh yeah. He had dreams. Big dreams that had kept him up most of the night.

"Drew!" A small fist connected with his bicep, shattering his daydream.

"What?" He shot her an irritated glance. "Why'd you do that?"

"Your phone dinged. You might want to check your messages."

Annoyed, he reached into his breast pocket for the phone.

"It's from Jack," he muttered.

"Doesn't he have his own family soiree?"

Reading the message, he grimaced. "He did. It seems a distant, but ancient and venerable, uncle collapsed under the heat. They're postponing the big celebration until tomorrow, so after lunch with his immediate family, he's coming over to join our party."

"Sorry for the reason," Randi said, reaching for her phone. "But glad he chose to join us. I'll have the caterer add his name to the graduation cake."

"He won't expect you to go to that amount of trouble," Drew said.

"No trouble. Not for me. And I'm sure the caterer has had far worse wrenches thrown in her plans. This is just two words."

After she hung up, nodding in satisfaction, Drew leaned forward and rested a hand on her shoulder. "Thank you. I'm sure he'll be thrilled."

Randi patted his hand. "No trouble to make a guest feel welcomed, especially when it's his day to celebrate too. The more the merrier."

Now if only he'd found a way to invite Meilin to the party. Yeah right. She was probably all tied up in her fiancé and wedding plans. Probably had spent the night with him. He'd seen Jack's parents and siblings in the crowd at the graduation ceremony, but there'd been no sign of Meilin. In all likelihood she wasn't a close enough cousin to be invited for the actual ceremony. Would she have been at the family party scheduled for this afternoon? The one now postponed? Like he should be worrying about it. After a mental eye roll, he set it aside and concentrated on his own immediate future as they pulled into the garage at the house.

* * * *

As Shan handed Meilin into the passenger seat of his dark gray Aston Martin, he told her they had a change of plans.

She'd already received word that Jack's party was on hold.

"If we hurry, and traffic isn't bad, we can make the renewal of vows part of the afternoon."

As he walked to his side of the car she wondered, how many couples, on any given Saturday, would be making or renewing vows?

Shan settled himself, checked for a break in traffic, then pulled onto the street.

"Exactly where are we headed?" She settled her purse at her feet and watched out the window as the apartment buildings and small stores passed by.

"San Ramon." A small niggle slipped down her spine. "I met Courtland Robinson when I did a year at the London School of Economics. Nice guy, maybe a little too nice. I met his fiancée a couple times. She was a bit of a bitch. Haven't really kept up with him directly, but my mother follows some of the London tabloids, and from time to time she'll notice a piece where he's mentioned. Attendance at this society gala or that fundraiser. When his wife died it made the news, and he became something of a playboy according to the papers. Not that he ever made the front page like the royals and movie stars."

"I'm surprised, Shan. Following the gossip rags," she gently teased.

He laughed. "Not me. My mother. She was spellbound with the stories I wrote in my letters home, and the one time they came to visit she met Court. Loved him, so she's kept up. Every now and again his company makes the trades, *Wall Street Journal* and such. I was surprised when he looked me up this last spring, to tell you the truth."

"Contacts are good," she murmured, still fighting the premonition tapping on her shoulder.

"That they are. His new wife is something of a tea service collector, I believe. That should give the two of you something to talk about."

"No doubt."

"Anyhow, since we're going earlier than planned, we won't have to stay as late." Shan grinned at her before checking over his shoulder and changing lanes, easing onto the Bay Bridge with the flow of traffic. "I thought we could watch the sunset while we have dinner at the Claremont."

"Sounds lovely, but I don't want to be out too late. I have a very busy week coming up. I generally take Sunday to do prep work and visit with my neighbor."

"Today gives us a chance to talk about our expectations for the future. You know you won't have to work after we're married. In fact, you could start winding down now if you like. Things will only get busier the closer the wedding comes."

Meilin opened her mouth to speak, but nothing came out. Not that she should be surprised in any way; she'd expected pretty much this very discussion.

"You don't have to answer right now, but Meilin, I want you to think it over. As my wife, there will be plenty to keep you busy. Especially after the children come. You won't have to spread yourself thin."

"I understand what you're saying, but, Shan, I've worked hard to build my reputation. I have employees and contractors who depend on me. I have clients who value me. I like what I do. You should know that from the work I did for you only a few months ago. Before you ask me to quit my business, you should know I am booked with upcoming projects for the next eighteen months."

"I know, I know. I understand, I really do," he soothed. "You're very good at what you do. This is merely opening the topic."

"Negotiations."

He chuckled. "If you like. Negotiation is a way of life in business."

And in marriage as well, apparently. She didn't say it out loud, but the sentiment was there.

"What do you expect from marriage, Meilin? I'm sure my wants are clear, but I don't know your thoughts."

"Do my thoughts matter?" After brunch last Sunday, spent with both sets of parents making wedding plans, she'd gotten the impression her voice didn't count for much. Both mothers had their expectations and what the bride and groom wanted mattered little. And now Shan had brought up the topic of leaving her design business behind.

"Of course they do. They always will. I can't make you happy if I don't know what makes you happy. I like to know my path. I study business details from the largest gain to the minutest detail. The pros, the cons. Who will benefit, who will be hurt, how to minimize the damage, because in every business deal there is a casualty of some kind. Maybe it is dead wood that needs to go, or it's a single mother who desperately needs her job and benefits. An older manager taking care of his parents."

As he spoke, he handled the car like an extension of his body. It seemed to respond to his thoughts, moving with the Saturday afternoon traffic heading east on the lower deck of the bridge.

Out on the sparkling water of the bay, boats with white sails flew across the light chop. Instead of going to a party, she almost wished they were out on the bay with the rest of the sailors. Not that she knew how to sail, but she could learn and would enjoy the breeze, the salt water, the freedom of flying across the water.

Shan didn't seem to notice her mind had wandered as he continued talking. "How can I make the necessary changes without destroying their lives, the income they depend on? I can't save every job, every person who desperately needs theirs, but sometimes I can put them in an equal, or better, position. In some cases there is no way to protect them, but I can make job placement or technical school available to send them down a new path. It's not always a popular idea with my stockholders, but in the long run it buys us goodwill. That's something no amount of money can ever guarantee."

"But you want me to give up my business to be your wife." The very thought was still difficult to take in. Wasn't her mother just the other day saying she could keep her job? And he claimed to value employees. What about her employees? Did he truly consider her work insignificant? Now that she thought about it, he hadn't gushed in pleasure over her work in his condo. Did he not recognize the work she'd put into blending his taste with convenience? What did he think she did with the design form she'd had him fill out?

His next question brought her back to the subject of being a wife. His wife. "Isn't that what you were raised to do? Didn't your mother give up her work to be a wife and mother? Mine did."

Meilin laughed. It didn't contain any mirth. "Yeah, because that is how all good Chinese girls are raised. To be wives and mothers. Not independent business women."

"Not mutually exclusive. Many a good Chinese woman has raised children and run the family business, many hoping their own daughters would never have to do the same. My great-grandmother did it because she had no other choice. You have choices, Meilin. You don't have to work yourself into an early grave like my great-grandmother did. She lived just long enough to see her daughter marry a successful businessman. If you want to work"—he shrugged as if it didn't matter—"then keep your business. But our marriage will compete for your time. I have business functions my wife is expected to attend. And before the children come along, I'd very much like to travel. We can see China, Australia, Europe, and Scandinavia all in the next year. A prolonged honeymoon if you will."

"All those places sound exciting and provide many opportunities for my business as well." They were all places she longed to visit on shopping trips. She just hadn't planned on taking months off to make them.

"Very true. While I'm in meetings, you can tour the shops and factories for your treasures."

She chose to ignore the hint of condescension in his tone. "Okay, it's possible I'll have to delegate more. Hire a designer to pick up my slack." If she had another designer on board, she could reduce the wait time for her services.

"Very wise."

"You're being very reasonable." It took effort, but she kept the sarcasm from her tone. Did he not think she'd fight to keep her business? Wouldn't he?

"I'm doing my best to see your side of this. I'm fairly set in my ways. Marriage is a big change for both of us. I've left it rather late, as my parents keep telling me." His lips tilted in a wry smile.

"Which leads us to the topic of children, I suppose." No, she really didn't want to go there, but it was the logical next step.

"A natural consequence of marriage, if all goes well. Why do we work if not to make a better life for our future family?"

"Neither of us had difficult childhoods. Mine was about as perfect as one could be." Although she had to admit, her mother didn't work outside the home. Rather she'd participated in charities, volunteered at school and the food pantry. But she'd usually been nearby, especially when Meilin didn't want her around.

"To be fair, so was mine. Good schools, supportive family, even if they did make it clear what path I was to follow. Not all was rosy, of course."

"Is that why you've put off marriage so long?"

He shot her a sideways glance and navigated the junction of one freeway to the next. "When I joined the family business, all was not well. My father did the best he could, but the economy and technology were changing and business had to change with it. The last twenty years have involved long hours, hundreds of thousands of miles of travel, more e-mails and phone conferences than I can ever hope to count, and as little sleep as I ever got in college. Things have turned around now and business has grown. I can make time for the important things in life."

Shan reached for her hand and she let him take it. He rested her hand on his knee, his over hers, keeping his options for grabbing the steering wheel open if needed. His thumb stroked the ring he'd placed on her hand a week ago. The two carat diamond was hefty without being garish. Elegant. A classic solitaire set in platinum.

"I hope you're not disappointed with the plain setting."

"It's classy without being ostentatious. I'm not a high maintenance woman."

Shan smiled. "I'm a man who likes simple things."

She gave him a look of disbelief. The Aston Martin, the Breitling watch on his wrist, the suit and shoes custom made in Hong Kong were not the simple possessions of a simple man.

"Sure you do."

Shan picked up on her slightly sarcastic tone with a brief smile. "Quality has everything to do with simplicity. The higher the quality, the easier life is." His hand tightened over hers. "Which is why when I see you working too hard, I'll step in. Your first job is our marriage. My business will fund our life together. If your business draws too much of your energy, I will put my foot down. However, until we have children you should be able to handle your new duties easily enough."

Meilin swallowed deeply. "I see." A hint of ice shimmered in the air, not that Shan seemed to notice.

"I've been over your financials. You do all right, but you're not raking in a large profit. Barely enough to cover your expenses and make your payroll. The apartment you live in is barely acceptable. It's small and middle class, sliding downward in value every year. The building needs many improvements, and with the seniors populating it, the owner is hampered. He can't charge enough rent to keep up the maintenance, much less take on renovations."

Meilin stiffened and tried to withdraw her hand, but he tightened his grip. Not painfully so, but enough she couldn't pull away without violently protesting. "You've been investigating me?" she asked, the disbelief quite clear in her voice, her heart jolting in an unpleasant way before the rushing of blood partially dimmed her hearing.

"It's how business works. I always know who I'm brokering a deal with."

Employing great self control, she forced her breathing to remain calm. Serene. Her mind raced, seeking to process his words. True, their marriage was arranged. They hadn't even dated. This counted as their first official date. But still. Didn't leave much room for the heart to have a say.

Surprised to find her voice calm, she said, "Marriage shouldn't be all about business, Shan. Is your heart engaged at all?"

He squeezed her hand. "Is yours? There hasn't been time, so I expect not. I hope today will change that. I like you. You're a beautiful woman with a kind heart. Over the past few years I've watched how you interact with family. I've watched you as your client. Some of my clients are the same as yours. Everyone has kind things to say about you, your character, the integrity with which you run your business. You're known for your good works with the Museum of Modern Art, as well as the Make A Wish Foundation. All things I've personally observed. These are good qualities in a wife."

"What about good qualities for a husband? What do you see as your best features to bring to marriage?" This ought to be good.

"I'm considerate. I have an excellent income, an expansive portfolio, so I'm a top notch provider. The household budget will be generous, and I'll leave you to sort out the household issues as you wish. I ask for clean laundry in the closet, a tidy, tranquil home, dinner on the table when we're not eating out. The children will require much more of your management than I will."

Obviously he'd thought things over far more than she had. "And you have a housekeeper and assistant at work to do these things for you now."

"Mrs. Chan, as you know, comes in everyday and sees to the laundry, gets the dry cleaning sent out, the groceries purchased, and dinner is usually made and in the oven or fridge waiting for me when I get home. My secretary, Julie Wong, you also know, keeps her apprised of my schedule."

She got along well with both women. "Will Mrs. Chan stay on after our marriage?"

"Yes, but it will be up to you to coordinate with her, which will take some of the burden off Julie. She will keep you notified of social events I'm obligated to attend for business. It will be up to you to handle our personal social scheduling, so you'll need to talk with her often."

"I should send her a gift then. Something to make her continue to think kindly of me."

Shan grinned and squeezed her hand again. "Great idea. She loves chocolate and trips to the spa. In fact, I will be grateful to turn such gifts of gratitude over to your care. I never know what to give her when the occasion calls for recognition of a job well done."

Not that she had much experience. Her own assistant received much verbal praise, but few gifts outside of holidays or her birthday. And those gifts tended to be small items, a jade figurine, a crystal vase, a small bunch of flowers. Nothing ostentatious. As for client gifts, her assistant usually handled those.

"By the end of the coming week I'll have a credit card for you for just such expenses. Business gifts as appropriate, family gifts such as Jack's graduation. Something for both of our parents to show our appreciation. Gifts for the wedding party."

"All right." At least he didn't expect her to pay out of her pocket, as thin as he knew it to be.

"You may also use the card for your current household expenses."

Tempted to mutter, "Big of you," she stuck to a simple thank you. At least she was seeing some of the arrogance she'd expected. The question was, could she live with it and his plans to change her?

Chapter 8

Drew looked out the front door to check for any last minute arrivals. He straightened the pale pink silk tie that matched his sister's bridesmaid dress. At least the linen suit that matched his father's was cooler than the wool tails they'd worn at the first wedding. The jacket and tie would disappear the moment the wedding photographer was done. Or when Randi said he could dump them.

He took one last look around, although he didn't expect anyone else. Jack had texted about his own plans falling through, but he wasn't expected to arrive for another hour at least because he was having lunch with his parents first.

A dark gray Aston Martin pulled into the court and circled around to stop in front of the pair of valets hired for the afternoon. Many of the neighbors had offered their driveways for overflow parking, as they'd walk to the party, but all those spots were taken, and there were only a few left at the curb. Soon, the valets would be parking cars around the corner and down the street, then dashing back to take care of the next arrivals. He didn't envy them or their job today. While rain would be the worst possible scenario, the intense sun combined with lack of breeze was probably the next worst.

He held up a hand for Martin, his father's butler, who fussed at RJ standing nearby waiting for the moment to escort Randi from the house, past the pool, and onto the lawn where chairs held the guests. More would arrive starting in an hour for the next part of the party. "One more arrival and then we should be good," he told the men.

Martin merely huffed and hustled over to mutter something to the DJ standing just outside the rear door ready to change the music for the procession. Birdie stood beside the chair where their grandmother waited for Drew to escort her to her seat.

Looking back to the street, he watched as the valet closest to the curb opened the passenger door and a female leg emerged. A slender, delicate leg in demure pumps, unlike some of the platforms he'd seen mincing across the grass out back.

Curious, he stood taller in the shadows of the doorway. The woman who stood from the car took his breath away when she faced the house. Meilin. Here. Arriving in a James Bond style car. The man from the driver's seat was obviously Asian, dressed in a light colored linen suit. He glanced around the neighborhood as he came around the car to offer his arm to the woman Drew hadn't been able to get out of his mind for the last week. And a day.

Meilin looked elegant in a sleeveless dress of golden lace that hugged her slim curves from neck to knee. The sun glanced off a spot on her hand. A huge diamond. That was new. As she took the arm of her date, the refraction of light was like a laser straight to his heart. This man must be the fiancé. Slightly older, a little stocky. They looked like a paired set. Which, in fact, they were. Both of them with pearl pale skin, black hair, and the features that indicated their Asian roots.

They came up the walk together, and the moment Meilin's gaze found his, her step faltered a little, causing her date to look at her with concern. She smiled and kept coming.

Drew cleared his throat. "Welcome. You're just in time. We have two seats left on the groom's side." He held out his hand to the man first. "Drew Robinson."

"Shan Lin and my fiancée, Meilin Wu."

"Mr. Lin. Please, come and be seated. As it is, we're running a couple minutes late, and the father of the bride is getting anxious." He turned to grin at RJ as he teased the older man.

"Lin," RJ greeted the couple as they traversed the foyer. "Didn't know you'd be here. Want to chat with you later about a new vineyard putting out some fine reds, but you'd better let the boy direct you to your seats. The wedding director is about to have kittens."

"Hush you." Randi spoke from the side hall leading to the master bedroom. Martin glared from his position near the back door. "The ceremony begins when I'm ready and not a moment before." Randi turned to smile at the new arrivals. "Meilin! I'm so pleased to see you here. And this must be Shan." She extended a hand and Lin bowed over it to press his lips to her knuckles. "Court has told me a little about you. What a small world we live in."

Lin rose from slobbering over Randi's hand. "So pleased to receive an invite. We were excited to be able to make it for the vows portion when a family event fell through at the last moment. An uncle was sent off to the hospital with heat stroke after the graduation this morning."

Okay, so the man didn't actually slobber, but Drew didn't like seeing the man so close to Meilin, or his mother.

Randi placed a hand over her heart. "Oh! That was your family? We saw the ambulance but didn't know the cause. I hope he's not too ill."

Meilin smiled. "Oh, he'll be fine. He does this at least once a summer. The sun is too bright for him. Congratulations, Randi. I didn't realize this was your event."

Randi blushed. "I'm still giddy with the rush of love. It's a long story and I'll tell you over cake and champagne. For now...Drew?" She turned to him. "Be a doll, seat them, then escort your grandmother to her seat, and get up by your father. We'll have this ceremony and then I'll introduce you properly."

"Of course, Mum." He bent down and kissed her cheek. "You're beautiful. See you at the altar."

He extended his arm for Meilin and spoke to her escort. "If you'll follow me?"

It was the strangest thing pretending he didn't know her. As she'd given no indication of their acquaintance, he followed her lead and pretended ignorance. But he couldn't ignore the tingle of awareness that came with the linking of her arm through his.

He saw them to their seats in the last row of the groom's side of the aisle, barely covered by the shade of the open tent overhead, reluctantly releasing Meilin to sidle over to her chair and make room for Lin. The bride's side was so full it had overflowed to the right. It didn't really matter, he supposed. As long as there were butts in the seats, to put it in Birdie's words.

He returned to the house and tucked his grandmother's hand around his arm. The imperious old woman stuck her nose in the air without comment and took her time walking up the aisle to her seat. At last, taking his place beside his father, he noted the old man was as fidgety as he'd been at the original ceremony over spring break. "What's got you worried now?" he asked his father as the music switched to the prelude before the bridal march.

"Not a thing. Just getting hot out here, despite the tent. Thinking about grabbing my bride and jumping into the pool."

Drew looked down to hide his grin as Birdie, wearing a pale pink dress, sauntered up the silk runner that covered the grass to form the aisle. Bet the bride and groom jumping into the cool water would go over well. Randi might laugh over it, but Bird would probably lay a few eggs in distress.

Once Birdie reached the end of the runner, the music switched to Randi's chosen processional. The guests rose and turned to watch her approach on her father's arm. The scene was every bit as moving as it had been only a few months ago in the village church.

"She's more beautiful now than she's ever been." His father actually sighed after making the quiet comment.

Drew glanced at his father then concentrated on Randi slowly walking in time to the music, wearing a short ivory linen sheath and ballet style flats. She looked young with the sun glinting off her hair picking out strands of gold from the red. Lifted off her neck, her hair was adorned with only a large creamy magnolia flower instead of the short veil she'd worn before. She held a giant, pink blossom as a simple bouquet. "You picked a winner. Never seen you so happy as you've been since Christmas."

"I've had a few days that pretty much equal this one. The next time I'm this happy will be the day you wed. Choose well."

"Since you've already taken the best woman ever born for a Robinson man to marry, I'm not eager to be looking for one of my own. Randi broke the mold."

His father snorted. "She's a tad old for you."

Drew's gaze slipped from Randi to Meilin, who watched the procession with a soft smile. "I don't mind older women. When she's the right one, she's the right one. Age doesn't matter a whit."

There was no time for an answer as Randi and her father completed the short walk, and the ceremony began when Tuck cleared his throat. As the officiate, he led them through their custom written vows, much differently worded, but making the same promises as the standard wedding service. The vows were spoken with great feeling, and more than a few people wiped their eyes as Randi and Court squeezed each other's hands tightly. Even Tuck seemed to forget he was a lawyer conducting a ceremony and had to use his handkerchief before they were done.

Finally, he had the final word. "Let no man put asunder what the Kingdom of England and the State of California have granted as a legal state of wedlock. I assure you, the legal mess would be horrendous to separate them, but as in love as these two are, and have always been, it's not an issue." Chuckles replaced the sniffs of sentiment. "Courtland Robinson, you may now kiss your bride."

Cheers erupted as Drew's father bent his bride over his arm and laid one on her. Birdie met Drew's gaze and they both rolled their eyes, even as they grinned. Double sealed, they were a family now for all time.

* * * *

Meilin dug into her purse for a tissue. Shan's left hand appeared in her blurred line of sight holding a square of folded linen while his right arm circled her shoulders.

"Thank you," she murmured and gently patted under her eyes with his handkerchief.

He bent his head to kiss her cheek. "Do you always cry at weddings? What about funerals?"

"Not always," she sniffed. "The vows were so beautiful, and beautifully spoken. Those two are very much in love and not afraid to show it." Much like she wanted for her own wedding, she realized. How had she ever thought she could have a business arrangement for a marriage?

"I'll be sure to tuck an extra hanky or two in my pockets for our wedding." The softly spoken words stirred a stray lock of hair that had escaped her careful style.

Was it possible their wedding could be as emotionally joyful as this one? Unable to help herself, she looked up into Shan's gaze. He smiled back at her, seemingly sincere enough, but she wasn't sure she saw love. Of course, it was far too soon, they didn't know each other well enough for it to be love. Still, she wondered if it could happen for them. The spark she'd felt only a week ago with a much younger man was lacking with Shan. Was it because they'd known of each other most of their lives, their circles touching, crossing, although they'd personally never circled close enough to touch more than a casual handshake? They were familiar rather than intimate. Was it Drew's difference, his youth, his foreign origins that sparked with her?

Unbidden, her gaze strayed toward the much taller man who stood out like a sunbeam. The touch of his gaze as they'd approached the house had been as mesmerizing as the first finger of dawn rising above the horizon. Even now, the blue of his eyes reached over the heads of the guests, seeking her out, locking on her for one scorching moment. Breathless, she made herself look away.

"Warm?" Shan asked, his arm slipping around her waist.

"Yes. I'm ready for something cold to drink." It was a good excuse.

"Hey everyone!" the young woman in pink she recognized as Courtney, yelled out. "Since the next part of this party is the graduation celebration, Mom's going to toss her bouquet now, so all single ladies please gather in the aisle while the men move the chairs aside."

"You should join them," Shan said. He pressed his lips to her temple. "Although we're engaged. It appears the only single ladies are very young indeed."

Most of them appeared to be teenagers. Some of them with shades of red hair much like the woman standing next to the officiate.

"No, no. As you said last night, the contract is basically signed. I'm officially off the market."

"I don't mind if you do. Chances are one of the young ones will make a leap and snatch it from the air."

Randi waved at her from the top of the aisle. "You too, Meilin! You're not married yet!"

And so she found herself standing at the back of a grouping of girls from ten to twenty-five. No one was more surprised than she when the gorgeous pink peony landed in her hands.

Shan's arms came around her from behind. "It's beautiful with your dress. Would you like to carry peonies at our wedding?"

Stunned by her capture, overwhelmed with congratulations and friendly pouts from the teenagers, she only murmured, "They'll be out of season then."

"Not an issue."

Of course not. She guessed that what Shan wanted, he generally got. Did that include her? Item—Bride. Bride—Meilin Wu. Check and check. Apparently.

Next they called for the single men. "That means you," she told him.

"I'm too old for such shenanigans."

"Not true." She nodded to Randi's father being escorted into the group waiting for the garter toss. From the front, the groom, a very handsome older version of Drew, pointed at Shan, then turned his hand over, crooking a finger in a "come here" gesture.

The laugh from Shan was stilted, but he left her side and moved to the back of the group. The groom lifted the bride onto a chair, made sure she was stable, then slid his hand up under her skirt. They stared into each other's eyes, small private smiles on their lips. The very air around them shimmered with love.

"No feeling her up in front of the kids!" someone from the crowd called out. "Grab the garter, man!"

The garter in question slowly descended until the article made of pink silk and frothy white lace loosened. Carefully it was pulled off over her foot, then the groom placed his hands on her waist and lifted her down, her body sliding the length of his. Meilin's chest ached with the beauty of their love. What they must have suffered to embrace their feelings so joyously. Not a feeling she'd ever felt for herself in regards to a man unless he was a hero in one of the novels she loved to read at night. How different their new marriage seemed to the one she'd just discussed with Shan. Had they considered all the angles, the repercussions to lives and careers the same way?

"Hands up, gentlemen!" Randi called out. "I want to see everyone's hands in the air!" Once she approved, her husband shot it like a rubber band into the grouping of men. It seemed the garter was headed for Shan, then a long arm reached out and snatched it from the air.

Drew.

"That's twice!" Courtney called out, laughing. "You're doubly in trouble from the matchmakers."

Shan returned to Meilin's side never noticing her gaze was locked with Drew's. "See, the Fates, or whomever are in charge of such things, already know I'm blessed with the next beautiful bride."

Tearing her gaze from the tall, young Englishman, she smiled faintly at Shan's hubris.

Now if only they'd serve the champagne.

Chapter 9

Drew endured the pounding that served as pats on the back. It was a silly custom, but if one believed it, then he was supposed to marry the woman who caught the bouquet. In this case, Meilin.

The thought of marrying Meilin left him short of breath.

Scared the hell out of him as well. Lord, he wasn't ready for marriage, not to anyone. He was leaving California soon and had at least three to four years of concentrated work ahead of him to secure his place in the family business. By then he'd be ready to think about his personal future. The time to date and get to know Meilin would be long past. She might very well have a couple kids by then.

How many months until her wedding? She'd probably told him while dancing. If she had, he couldn't remember a damn thing about it.

Jack would know. Or Randi would ask. That was the key, watch for when his new mother got Meilin aside, then find a way to be near enough to eavesdrop. He wasn't above eavesdropping. It was how a guy found out things. Like when his father had presented his mother with divorce papers and demanded custody of Drew. The very argument that had sent his mother rushing from the house in a rainstorm where she'd wrecked her car on slick roads. No divorce. No custody fight. From that dark day it had been just him and his dad until they'd found Randi and Birdie. Talk about Fate taking a hand in things. Now if only Fate would take an interest in his desire to get closer to Meilin.

He felt a sense of hopelessness that the opportunity would never appear. The man with her certainly displayed possessiveness, keeping a hand on her waist or hip. Drawing her close to kiss her temple. Drew had a brief fantasy of Lin reaching for her breast and Meilin decking the knobhead. Pretty much what he wanted to do, given an opportunity.

Drew did notice Meilin didn't return the signs of affection a woman might have for her fiancé. She didn't turn into his arms or nuzzle close.

Erect and proud, she held her spine straight, a polite smile on her perfect Cupid's bow mouth. A mouth he knew tasted of exotic honey. Like her dress, her skin shimmered in the sun, reminding him of the way she'd swayed and shimmied on the dance floor, laughing at the antics of her friends. Supple as a willow in a breeze. Not like an unbending flag pole, so polite and calm.

Drew let Martin and the photographer bully him into his place for pictures. First with his parents and sister. Then just his dad. Then with Randi. Then with Birdie. Then with the grandparents from both sides. The only time he felt his smile was genuine was when they made him pose with Meilin, him displaying the garter on his arm, her holding the flower she'd caught. Especially when he'd tipped her backward into a dip to the shrieks of laughter around them. It took great restraint not to kiss her, although he allowed himself a few seconds to stare into her startled eyes. Just long enough to see the jade green warm and a flush wash her cheeks. It took even more strength to let her go and watch her return to her glowering fiancé.

At last the photos were done and he could see relief on the faces of the guests hovering in the shade of the trees and the umbrellas set in the tables now scattered about the yard as the catering staff set up. A small dance floor was being laid on the ground under the open sided tent. Drinks were being handed out and food trays set on serving tables. Cases and cases of bottled water filled tubs of ice, all within easy reach of the guests. Buckets of ice held bottles of beer, wine, and soda supervised by a bartender. How he wanted a couple of those. He stared at Oswald, the third candidate in line for the top spot at Lynford, definitely envying the cold one in the man's hand.

While the photographer consulted with Martin, Randi patted Drew's arm. "Nice finish there. I think you embarrassed her and annoyed him."

Unrepentant, he merely grinned at Randi's mild chastisement. She huffed out her exasperation with him. "Oh you. Get out of that jacket and tie. Go mingle. Get Oswald to relax a little. Your friends should start showing up soon."

"At last." He heaved an exaggerated sigh and tugged on the tie. Although getting Oswald to relax wasn't so easy. Birdie liked to say the man had been born with a stick up his arse. She wasn't far off. Not a bad guy, just formal. Stiff. Drew had no problem with the man, but Birdie, now there was a different story. As he watched, she eyed the man in question before blowing out a huff and purposely turning her back on him.

Randi rolled on with her instructions, clearly not seeing the small display. "The little ones will want to be in the pool soon, but hold off a bit before assuming your preferred uniform." The smile she gave him was lopsided. She knew him so well. He'd already laid out his most obnoxious pair of swim trunks. Ones that would make Birdie scream that she was being blinded.

He bent down and kissed Randi's cheek. "Don't get burned, Mum." She already had new freckles dusting her nose.

"I won't. There's an umbrella with my name on it right over there." She pointed to the table closest to the pool. "I can play lifeguard and queen of the party all from the same location."

"Like you'll sit still that long."

"Oh, I will. Once this party switches to graduation celebration I'm no longer the official hostess. In fact, I think the entire party is now in Martin and Birdie's hands."

"Courtney," he reminded her.

"She's been Birdie since the first time she realized she could make noises. She chirped then; she chirps now. I can't think of her as Courtney to save my life."

Drew laughed and gave her a one-armed hug. "I'll leave that battle to you."

Randi's response was a very dry, "Thanks."

In a few minutes he was down to his shirt with the sleeves rolled up and held an icy beer in his hand as he took a position next to the still buttoned up Oswald. Or Ozzie as Birdie liked to taunt him. The nickname went over like a lead balloon. The first long pull of his beer went down like rain in the desert.

The last table was set, its umbrella unfurled, and guests flocked to the shade provided, plates loaded with cold appetizers. Food. What an excellent idea. "Come on, old man." He gave Oswald a light elbow to the ribs. "Get there before it's gone. They're not so polite over here about buffet tables."

That got a tight smile out of the stiff man. "Looks tasty."

Was it Drew's imagination or had Oswald just sneaked at look at Birdie? Hm. Hadn't seen that one coming.

At the table with salads on ice, he met up with Shan Lin and all thoughts about Oswald lusting after his sister disappeared. Lin lusting after Meilin was a problem in Drew's mind. No matter how irrational.

"I understand you've known my father for years." He opened the small talk. He was known for being friendly, so friendly conversation was called for.

"Yes," the man responded with cold politeness. "I spent a year of my undergrad in London. Your father was kind and helped me find my way around." His gaze dropped to the garter now snug around Drew's upper arm.

Doing his best not to grin, Drew nodded in response to the spoken words. Sounded exactly like Dad.

"We've stayed in contact a little over the years, but it wasn't until he started coming to California last year that we really talked in depth. I'm happy to see he's found good fortune in his new wife."

"Very good fortune. She's wonderful, and we're lucky to have her and Birdie."

"A second chance for both. It's easy to see how they care for each other. For her, a second good marriage is an exceptional fate. I'm sure she's most deserving."

Drew couldn't read the man's emotions. However, he seemed sincere. "I understand fortune in love is with you as well. Newly engaged?" He plopped a spoonful of potato salad on his plate.

"Yes. An exceptional young woman I've known many years."

* * * *

What in the world could Shan and Drew be talking about? From the shade of an umbrella over Randi's table, Meilin forced herself to look away and turn her attention to the bride.

Not that she knew Randi well. They'd met a few times at various functions and had somewhat bonded over discussions of décor and wine. Enough that she could see herself meeting Randi for lunch one day should they ever bump into one another on the street.

"I don't think I've ever seen you looking so happy," Meilin said.

"I've never been this happy. Well, except for a few short months when I was in London many years ago." The older woman glowed as her eyes sought out her husband near the bar.

"Ah London. Seems Shan also met your husband in London."

"Court said something about it briefly when he gave me Shan Lin's name to add to the invitation list. I wasn't really paying attention. Must have been before I made it there. Court was finishing his masters while I did a semester of my undergraduate there."

"I'd love to spend more than a few days in and around London."

Randi's sparkling green eyes turned to her. "We'd love to have you come down to the house in Sussex. It truly is a beautiful place. The gardens were just coming into full bloom when we left, but we'll be back long before they peak. Just a couple of weeks here and then back we go. Later in the summer, when Drew finishes the portion of the program over there, we'll go to Beijing for a few weeks. From the immersion program he's due to go straight to work in the offices there."

"I'd heard he was set to begin studying Mandarin soon."

"Yes. He starts Monday. I'm waiting to meet this friend of his. Jack. Apparently the boy is something of a prankster."

Meilin smiled. "He is at that. Drew quickly wised up to Jack's attempts to teach him some very funny phrases in Mandarin."

"You've met Drew?"

"A week ago Friday night. The girls took me out as a last fling before becoming engaged. Jack brought Drew and his sister along. Drew was very charming about the whole thing."

"Drew is very charming about everything." Randi smiled with a mother's fondness. "Smart as a whip, laid back as a Golden Retriever. Don't let that lazy smile fool you one bit. He's a sponge and soaks in everything. There's a reason he's the lawyer of the family." She nodded toward Drew and Shan, both still loading their plates. "Wonder what they're talking about…"

Just what Meilin had been wondering.

The moment to wonder passed as Jack came through the back door of the house onto the patio.

"Jack!" Randi's daughter called out and sauntered to his side. "You made it in time for the party, but you missed the vows."

"Sorry, sweet thing. Had to do lunch with the parents. They send their best wishes for great fortune and happiness upon the house of Robinson." Jack made a short bow and the girl laughed.

"Your daughter is beautiful," Meilin said.

"Thank you. Court is her biological father." A slight flush washed Randi's cheeks. "She's so much like him and Drew it's uncanny. I think most people knew she wasn't Wyatt's daughter, but few said anything to my face about it."

"She's lovely, and yes, I can see a resemblance to the men, but I see you in her as well."

Randi grinned. "Possibly, but what you see is probably from nurture rather than nature. The Robinson genetics run true in that one. And I suppose that is the infamous Jack."

Meilin laughed. "The rascal is a distant second or third cousin. I was put in charge of him many times when he was much younger. Let me make the introductions."

They stood and made their way to where Courtney escorted Jack past the various food tables headed for the bar.

"Jack, a moment," Meilin said, reaching out to touch his arm. Like the other men, he'd shed his jacket and rolled up his sleeves.

"Meilin Wu! My dearest cousin." He took her hand and bent to kiss her cheek. "I'm most surprised and pleased to see you here. And who is this lovely woman who could only be a secret sister to you?"

The three women snorted at his flowery speech and ridiculous flattery.

"Randi, may I present to you my incorrigible cousin, Jack Ling. Jack, this is Mrs. Randi Robinson, my esteemed friend, the mother of Courtney, stepmother to Drew, wife of Courtland Robinson, who is a friend of Shan Lin."

Jack took the hand Randi extended to him and bent over it to place a reverent kiss on her knuckles. "A very important person whom I am most pleased to meet. I've long heard your praises sung by your children and have been anxious to pay my respects."

"A very pretty oration." An amused smirk lifted one side of Randi's mouth. "I've heard a lot about you as well, Jack. Welcome and make yourself at home. Within reason."

Meilin laughed and Jack lifted a hand to his heart, amusement dancing in his eyes. "I see my reputation precedes me. I promise to be on my best behavior."

"A scoundrel for sure," Randi replied. "I believe I last saw Drew over by the drinks."

They turned and saw Drew and Shan standing off to the side, both men with stiff shoulders and false smiles. It was so unlike Shan, and apparently Drew, judging by the gasps from Randi and her daughter, that Meilin had the urge to run up and stand between them. Fortunately Drew's father seemed to have the same thought and stepped in from a closer position, relieving whatever tension had formed.

From beside her, Randi muttered, "What on earth?"

Indeed. What had the two men found to discuss to create such tension between them when they barely knew each other? As both men looked her way, her stomach sank. Had she been the topic of discussion?

Jack spoke up. "Might I escort you ladies through the buffet line and to a shaded seat? I see my friends are neglecting their jobs."

"Oh, yes, Jack." Courtney jumped right in. "Mom's been up for hours getting this all ready..." Her voice faded as she took his arm and steered him toward the loaded food tables.

Once more Meilin followed the line of Randi's gaze. It was fixed on Drew and Shan near the bar.

"I think I need a drink," Randi said.

Meilin could only agree. "I'll join you."

Chapter 10

Great. Just great. Drew the cool, the calm, the rational, was now a thing of the past as he knew it. He'd nearly been tempted into throwing his plate of sticky salads in the face of a man old enough to be his father. An esteemed business man who'd known his father longer than he'd been alive.

And he might nearly have gone through with his violent intent had his father not stepped in and diffused the situation. Tension still knotted his shoulders, unusual enough, but for the first time since his first month at Eton he really, really wanted to raise his fists and punch the smug expression off another man's face. Over time he'd learned to diffuse most situations with a calm word and a confident smile.

Instead he'd been forced to back down, return to acting gracious.

A brawl at his father's second wedding, his own graduation celebration, would have ruined more than one person's day. The very thought of the look on Randi's face was enough to dial his anger back one more notch. Not for the world would he ruin this day for his family. At least not on purpose.

His father nudged his shoulder in the direction of the tables. "Your hands are full. Let me gather some drinks for the ladies and let's go find a spot to sit a spell. I believe Randi has picked the table closest to the pool."

Drew expected to see her sitting there, but instead, Randi, Meilin, and Courtney stood in a knot with Jack, who'd just arrived. He'd been too focused on the rat bastard gloating over Meilin to notice his friend's arrival. More would be coming soon. Definitely not the time to start a brawl. Damn. It would have been satisfying, possibly even fun.

"Sure, Dad. I'll lead the way, then come back and assist."

"Just go. I'll get one of the staff to bring around a tray of champagne."

They met the small group headed their way as they stepped off the deck onto the patio.

"Drew! Shan, my man." Jack greeted them both with his usual enthusiasm, mischief sparking in his dark eyes. "I see you two have met."

"We're headed for that table." Drew nodded in the direction of the pool. "Get a drink, a plate, come join us. Mum, Dad's bringing over champagne." He used his shoulder to nudge her toward the table.

"Oh that sounds wonderful. Let me take something…" She reached for the beer bottle in his hand.

Drew lifted it out of her reach. "Nope. I've got it. And enough food here to get you ladies started."

Birdie jumped in. "I'll grab some more food and forks."

"Good thinking."

In maneuvering people into chairs, he made sure the ladies had the best shade and took a spot on one side of Meilin, but couldn't prevent Lin from sitting on her other side.

"I'll just sit for a moment," Randi said. "I have people to greet, and I need to oversee things."

"No, you sit, Mom." Birdie bounced up. "I'll see to hostess duties. Just save one chair for folks to come see you. I think Kelly is about to burst at the seams."

"I'm not so old yet," Randi muttered. "And you're making me feel like an ancient hag."

"No, you're gorgeous. But you are looking a tad overheated and need some water at the very least before you get up and start mingling."

Drew shared a grin with his sister over Randi's head. The woman promised to sit, but they both knew it might last five minutes before she was up and circulating. So far the guests invited for the vows only numbered about thirty, but when the friends invited for the receptions started rolling in, the list would easily double.

Kelly, a close friend from across the street, as small as Randi but twice as harried by her five kids, plopped a dripping bottle of water in front of Randi. "I hope you don't mind, but the kids couldn't wait a moment longer. Tuck's taken them across the street to put on their suits and shorts. I think he used that as an excuse to do the same."

"I don't mind a bit. That's why I'm seated closest to the water. I won't mind a few splashes."

Kelly laughed, then reached a hand across the table to Meilin. "I'm the nosy neighbor from across the street, Kelly Tucker. If you see red headed devil children running amuck, they're mine."

Drew stood to make the introductions. "Kelly, Meilin Wu and her fiancé, Shan Lin. The other character is my classmate, Jack Ling. I believe you've met Oswald?"

Meilin was gracious as she returned the handshake. "So pleased to meet you. I believe Randi has mentioned you a time or two."

"You've probably also met my in-laws. They have a house in Pacific Heights they're threatening to turn over to us in the next year or two. Louise and Brad Tucker Senior."

Also standing, Shan nodded. "Indeed. I've done business with your father-in-law's firm a time or two. I've heard tales of his grandchildren."

"Small world we live in, is it not?" Kelly grinned and sat. "And those stories of the kids you've heard? They're worse than he's lead you to believe."

Drew sat once more and pushed his plate to the center of the table. For a while Kelly dominated the conversation with stories of her five children, every once in a while a trace of her Boston accent slipping in.

Meilin asked the story of how she'd met her husband, and the story entertained them while Tuck settled beside his wife, now dressed more casually in cargo shorts and a loose linen shirt. Drew could hardly wait to do the same.

"Of course they now adore the quicksand I walk on." Kelly laughed. "But it took a few years and a couple children to bring them around."

From the corner of his eye, Drew watched Meilin. She sat straight with her hands in her lap, gently stroking the petals of the flower she'd caught, not making any show of affection toward Shan. What thoughts passed through her head? For a moment he allowed himself to wonder what her family would think of him. Not only was he English, but stand-out blond compared to their black hair. And younger than her thirty-three years, far younger than her fiancé, who Drew guessed was pushing forty-five. If only he were starting his position with the company in San Francisco and not Beijing. Very likely this whole thing was in his head. Meilin was engaged and not interested in him.

He'd about convinced himself when she leaned forward to pluck a deviled egg off a plate and her arm brushed his.

The shock of awareness that shot up his arm and straight to his heart was difficult to conceal. Especially since Meilin jerked slightly. She felt it too.

Gaze carefully averted, she sank back into her chair as if nothing had happened.

Randi distracted everyone at the table when she pushed back her seat. "New arrivals. Time to mingle and socialize a bit. Keep the wine flowing, and Drew, you have lifeguard duty." The warning came in the nick of time as the three youngest Tuckers spilled from the house, headed for the pool. "Oswald, you as well. Don't let them drown."

Kelly must have also caught the look of surprise on Oswald's face. "And there goes the peace," she joked and turned her chair halfway from the table so she could watch too.

Chapter 11

The afternoon was at once a delight and torture for Meilin. She mingled and met many of the Robinson's neighbors, was introduced to a few more of Jack's friends, and generally enjoyed the conversations around her. The kids in the pool weren't as rowdy as she'd feared, and their antics drew smiles from the guests. More than a few of the adults tucked up skirts or rolled up pant legs to dangle their feet into the cool, blue water. Smoke from the grill drifted in a fragrant cloud and laughter punctuated the air. She and Shan stayed long enough to see the wedding and graduation cakes cut, and take in a few small dramas.

For starters, she'd love to hear the story about the stoic, silent Oswald and Drew's vivacious sister. The two did their best to ignore each other, but when one ventured into the other's space, sparks flew hot enough to ignite the dry grasses beyond the fence. The very heat of their exchanged glances only highlighted how much Shan didn't set her own heart on fire, despite the way he always seemed to have a hand on her all afternoon. Still, it was amusing to watch the other two. Especially when Courtney talked the DJ into playing "Crazy Train." Oswald clearly wasn't amused to be taunted with Ozzy Osbourne's first hit single, which only made Birdie and Drew laugh, while Randi and Court shook their heads, biting back big grins. The butler showed his sympathy by patting Oswald on the shoulder as he passed by on some mission or another to keep the catering staff on their toes.

It pleased her to see Jack's honest surprise at the addition of his name to the graduation cake. For once he suffered a moment of being speechless, accompanied by an even rarer flush of pleasure on his cheeks. A rare event indeed.

There came a time when she danced a few songs, once with Shan where he pulled her far too close, making her feel self-conscious, followed by a fast paced hip-hop with Jack, even a passable swing with the laughing groom, and finally a ballad with Drew. The last stirred an unfamiliar longing inside, especially since he was dressed in a swim suit, baring his incredible, sun-kissed torso.

They didn't speak much and it was all she could do not to run her fingers over his leanly muscled chest or stare into the extraordinary blue of his eyes. Eyes that questioned. Although he kept enough distance between them to be proper, she still caught Shan's frown at the closeness demanded by the dreamy quality of the song. A pleasant haze of champagne bubbled in her veins, and she never wanted the dance to end. At least until Drew finally spoke.

"Why him?"

"Excuse me?" The question pulled her from her pleasant, floaty haze.

Drew blew out a breath and muttered, "Nothing. Not my business."

No, not his business, but a tiny part of her wanted it to be his business. It was a useless wish, much like the useless spark that flared between her and Drew. The ring from Shan weighed as heavy as a cement block on her finger. Oh to go back a few months and to have met Drew sooner. How her fate might have changed. Or not. The fact remained, he was so young. Too young. A mere infant in the business world. Just beginning to find his way beyond the hallowed halls of academia.

Reluctantly parting from Drew when the song changed, Meilin hid her surprise when Shan appeared at her shoulder. She noticed the possessive look on his face when he wrapped his arm around her, firmly gripping her hip intimately. For some reason it embarrassed her and her face burned, making it hard to look at Drew.

"It's time for us to say good-bye."

"Of course." She extended her hand to Drew and once more experienced the odd flow of energy between them, much like a jolting electrical charge. Her heart pounded as she did her best to remain cool and detached, her gaze on their hands and not his face. "Congratulations on your graduation. I wish you much good fortune on your road into the future."

The burning blue of his gaze said far more than his words. "I hope our paths cross again. Thank you for enjoying this day with…us."

It took a force of will, but she managed to reply without gushing. "My pleasure."

Losing the warmth of his hand was like losing a part of her soul, but she smiled as if it didn't matter.

Saying good-bye to the newlyweds involved personal space-invading hugs for both she and Shan. Not something she normally allowed, but these people had been so kind, so welcoming, she felt as close as family after a few hours. She made a mental note to add them to the guest list for her wedding. Her mother would possibly fuss, but on this she wouldn't budge. The Robinsons were good people, friends now, not just business contacts.

Once in the car, she adjusted the air vents to direct cool air on her face. Shan smoothly pulled away from the valet stand and heaved what sounded like a sigh of relief.

"Glad that's done."

"It was a lovely party. One I suspect will carry on late into the night." Were it not for the tension between Drew and Shan, she would have liked to stay. Both men in the same vicinity felt far too much like storing fireworks next to a bonfire.

"Most likely. But with the people pouring in, I'm sure they'll appreciate the space we occupied."

"Probably true." Biting her lip, she considered her next words carefully. "I'm adding them to the guest list."

Shan nodded. "Yes, I approve. There's a connection there I'd like to strengthen. And keep an eye on what they're doing in Beijing."

"Is their business in competition with yours?"

"Not so much, but it's good to keep in touch when someone seeks to increase their presence in our backyard, so to speak."

As if he and he alone did business in Beijing. "I wasn't aware your businesses overlapped."

"A little. Not enough to get territorial over. I'd like to see it stay that way."

"Of course."

"I'm not quite ready for dinner, feel like taking a drive through the hills?"

While intimate enough enclosed in the car, driving kept him, and his hands busy enough she could relax for a few. "That sounds like fun."

"Or we could check in at the hotel and have room service…" He sent a questioning look her direction.

Yeah, she should have seen that coming. "I'm not ready for that step, Shan. Yes, I've known you for years, but only on a very superficial level. I'm not prepared for intimacy of the sort you're hinting at."

"Can't blame a guy for trying." He reached for her hand. "It would be nice to confirm our compatibility in that area. The physical touch goes far in making a man ready to commit his whole life to one woman."

"There will be time enough for that."

Shan lifted her hand and flipped it over so he could kiss her palm. "A lifetime."

A small shudder worked its way through Meilin, and she fought the urge to pull her hand back. After dancing so closely with Drew, it was too soon to be so intimate with another man. And didn't that just confuse her more.

Shan turned off the freeway at Lafayette. "What do you think about sailing tomorrow? The weather is supposed to hold."

So much for her peaceful Sunday plans. Besides, she really would like to try sailing. "I'd like that."

Chapter 12

After watching Meilin leave with her smug fiancé, Drew found himself not much in the party mood. Didn't mean he didn't put on a good act. After an hour of giving the younger Tucker kids a chance to attempt to drown him, he pulled himself from the pool and threw himself onto a chaise in the sun. A few of Birdie's girlfriends from the neighborhood were eyeing him much like he eyed the lemon artichoke dip Randi had found somewhere. Oswald pulled up a chair, sat down beside him, and handed over an icy cold beer.

"Thanks," Drew said. Oswald wasn't much of a talker, but the man was solid. A nephew of Larry's, Oswald and Drew had sort of grown up together, although Oswald had four years on him. He'd been one of the older boys at Eton who'd stepped in before the younger ones got beat upon. Too much. Something Drew appreciated to this very day.

"Quite the interesting crowd your parents have gathered."

Understatement if he'd ever heard one. "It's California. You have to be baking. Lose the coat and tie, man. If you want a swim, I have spare trunks."

Oswald gave him a questioning look.

"Swim trunks. Suit. Board shorts. Whatever. I can dig you up a pair, and then the girls can stare at your abs too."

Oswald snorted. "Thanks, but no." Gaze searching the surrounding patio and deck, he sipped from a low crystal glass.

Probably some of the old man's expensive Talisker aged whisky. The really good stuff. Neat. Not even a single ice cube to cool it down a tad. Drew nearly rolled his eyes. The bloke was buttoned up tight. Always had been. But interestingly, the guy's search stopped when his gaze landed on Birdie, now barefoot and wearing a sundress with the strings of bikini top showing around her neck.

"Since you were at the wedding in March, why this one too?" Drew asked his friend.

"Court wants to have some sort of meeting with you, Courtney, and me tomorrow." Oswald's eyes never left Birdie as far as Drew could tell.

"Any idea what that's about?"

"I thought you might know."

Drew shrugged. "He's made a point of not talking business this past week. Too wrapped up in Mum's plans for today."

"Guess we'll find out tomorrow."

After a long draught of beer, Drew glanced sideways at Oswald. "What's with you and Bird? Can't keep your eyes off her today."

If Drew had startled him, it was hard to tell. Possibly it was the slight twitch of his mouth that gave him away.

"Nothing going on there, mate. Courtney hates my guts, or haven't you noticed the way her nose turns up every time she gets near me?"

Drew snorted and brushed some water drops from his chest. "Women. Can't live with 'em, can't shoot 'em."

Oswald raised a brow. "What's that mean anyway?"

"They're impossible creatures."

"Yeah, about that, want to tell me why you were mooning over one Asian beauty with a huge rock on her finger this afternoon?"

"Nice topic change," Drew muttered.

Oswald grinned briefly before taking another sip of his drink. "Who is she?"

Drew groaned and tossed his head back. "I met her a week ago at a club. Clicked immediately, only to find out the next night was her engagement party. The old guy with her today was the lucky suitor."

"Bad timing, since you're leaving here pretty much for good in a few weeks. What are you going to do about it?"

"Nothing. What can I do? As you said, I'm about to head into ten weeks of intensive language school. I'll be lucky to get away one night a week, and then only as far as my apartment across the street from campus. Won't find me out grinding at the clubs. Probably wouldn't find her there, either. I got the impression the night out was a one-off situation. A last fling at freedom for her." Above him the sky was beginning to darken just a little as the sun headed toward the hills to the west. Not that he expected sunset to slow the party down much.

"What did you say to yank his chain earlier? Looked like you two were about to break out in fisticuffs."

Drew laughed. "Bloody wanker had the nerve to tell me to back off today. Seems he didn't appreciate the dip thing." Personally. he'd loved it as much for holding Meilin in his arms as he had for tweaking the other guy's temper.

"Not like you to cause such a ruckus."

"Every man has his moments."

"Apparently," Oswald said dryly.

Slowly the elders were vacating the field while the twenty somethings poured out the back door. His grandmother Robinson and grandfather Dailey had already retreated to a hotel down the hill. Oswald had been offered a ride, one he'd refused. The very young were also departing as Tuck and Kelly instructed their eldest, a lad somewhere around seventeen, to escort the younger kids across the street and to supervise bed time. He already had the youngest, a red headed hellion about seven years old, falling asleep in his arms.

Jack pulled up a chair on the other side of Drew, a pair of fresh beers in his hand. Drew sucked down the last of the one Oswald had brought him and set aside the empty.

"Your sister is looking very fine tonight, Drew. Did I hear she was staying on campus this summer?"

Glaring at Jack, Drew swiped one of the beers from his hand. Jack barely noticed, his gaze tight on Birdie as she threw back her head and laughed at something one of the neighbors said. One of the middle-aged, male neighbors who was certainly enjoying the view provided by the tight top of Birdie's dress. Damned horny bastard. He made to sit up, but Oswald's hand on his shoulder stopped him.

"I'll take care of it."

Both Drew and Jack raised their brows at the declaration.

"But she hates you," Drew said.

"All the better. I'll engage the git in conversation, and she'll stomp off somewhere else. Gets her away from him that much faster." Glass in hand, Oswald stood, straightened his coat, and headed around the pool.

"Damn." Jack whispered the word, then softly whistled. "And I thought I had it bad for her. Who is that guy?"

"Oswald? He's been with the company for about six years. Backed up my dad some when we were going through the hassle after my mom's death. His uncle is an old school chum of my dad's. Pretty much grew up with him."

"Oswald. What a name. Does he ever shorten it?" Jack's lips twitched as Birdie predictably stormed off at the other man's approach. The old lecher drooling over her didn't look happy at the interruption.

"Never. Although Birdie started doing it when we were back there in March. She seems to take particular delight in tormenting him."

A huge sigh came from Jack. "Damn again. So the attraction goes both ways. Guess that kills my chances."

Drew laughed. "Unless you were planning on looking for a position in London, you never had a chance. Birdie's firmly set on the home office. Besides me, Oswald is her competition for the top spot when Dad decides to retire."

"A candidate who isn't related? Is that allowed?"

"We're very pragmatic that way. Must have a clear line of succession in place. Until Birdie popped up and indicated an interest, it was just me and Oswald. And although I have a slight nepotism edge, Oswald has more experience. Total toss-up. And hopefully a decision that won't need to be made for another twenty years unless the old man decides to retire early."

"And old Ozzie is besotted with your sister," Jack mused.

"Hmm, have to think about that. Not sure you've got that one right."

"For someone who is generally people smart, this seems to be a blind spot for you, my friend. Must be the family connection. Too close." Jack nodded to himself as if he were the greatest sage in all the world. "Trust me on this. Those two will tangle a lot more once Birdie's in the London office. Might want to suggest sending Oswald off to another office, say India or Spain, for a few years. Otherwise your old man will spend more time playing referee than CEO."

Drew glanced from where Oswald kept the neighbor in conversation to where Birdie hovered near the patio door with one of her girlfriends, her gaze firmly attached to Oswald's arse. Fascinating. Jack just might have a point. Didn't help him with Meilin, but since he had little he could do there, perhaps he should keep an eye on this situation.

Chapter 13

Sunday dawned bright, as promised by the weatherman, and Meilin found herself eager to be out on the water. Her only experiences had involved the ferry to Sausalito, a trip to Alcatraz, and a college casino night on a chartered boat. This time she might get to hold the steering wheel, rudder, or whatever they called it.

Shan arrived dressed in white jeans, deck shoes, and a blue T-shirt. All he needed was a captain's hat.

"I have a picnic basket Mrs. Chan prepared," he said, before stopping to look her up and down. "You look very cute."

Without her permission, a blush warmed her cheeks. She'd put on a pair of white capris that went with her blue and white striped boat-neck shirt, white Keds on her feet. Tied to her tote with essentials such as sunglasses, sunscreen, and bottled water, she had a nautical themed scarf to wrap around her hair. So maybe she'd gone slightly overboard, but "cute"? Hardly.

"Have a windbreaker and sweater in that bag?" He snagged a finger on the edge and peeked in.

"I have everything," she said and laughed at herself. "Probably too much."

"Let me carry it for you."

She surrendered the bag, locked her apartment, and followed him down the stairs to his car. It took twenty minutes to reach the marina and another ten to get through the crowds of people out enjoying a beautiful summer day. A smudge of dissipating fog clung to the Golden Gate over the mouth of the bay.

"Picture perfect," Shan said.

"So it seems." Meilin nodded toward the multitudes of amateur and professional photographers lining the path and lawns where kite flyers demonstrated their skill with huge kites in all shapes, then followed him onto the dock.

Shan stepped on board his sailboat with the picnic basket, then held a hand for her and her tote.

"What kind of boat is this?" She settled her bag on a built-in bench at the stern. The cockpit, she supposed.

"A thirty-seven foot Hunter 376. She's about twenty years old, but in great shape."

"Looks nearly new."

Shan grinned at her praise. "I grew up learning to sail her on weekends with my dad. He sometimes still takes her out, but mostly he's passed her on to me. She's a legacy worth great care."

"How did she get the name Zhen Tao? It's very pretty. Precious Peach?"

"Or Precious Long Life. My father and mother named her. I like it, so I chose not to re-christen her."

The sails, the electronics… It all looked so complicated she wasn't sure how she could help him. "Show me what to do."

Shan opened the hatch to the cabin below. "The boat is rigged so I can sail her solo. Why don't you stow the lunch in the galley and I'll get us out of the marina?"

"All right."

Stowing the picnic was easy, so she slathered on another layer of sunscreen and had a look around. Two staterooms. The one at the back even had a full bathroom, albeit cramped, including a shower. Handy if one needed to rinse off. When she felt the boat begin to move she tied the scarf around her head and went back up to the cockpit.

Up top she found Shan at the helm confidently guiding the boat out of the marina, mirrored sunglasses covering his eyes.

"Take a seat. We'll be on the bay in a few moments."

She was more than happy to sit at the stern, behind him and to the left a bit. The cry of seagulls blended with the shouts of greeting from other boaters. This close to shore the smell of boat fuel blended with fish. She hoped beyond the air would be fresher with the tang of salt.

Once on the open water, Meilin watched half in fear and half in amazement as Shan raised the sail and the boat picked up speed, all while avoiding collisions with the many other boats already out on the water.

Shan looked over his shoulder and caught the look on her face. Smiling, he reached back with his hand. "Come. It's not so scary from here."

Hoping he was right, she took his hand and found herself standing between him and the helm, his arms around her, his hands over hers on the wheel.

"This should help you feel more in control." He spoke close to her ear, and she wasn't sure if it was the breath from him or the salted breeze blowing past her ear that made her shiver. Shan took it as an opportunity to press closer to her back.

He was right about one thing, she wasn't nearly as frightened of the water and their course once she had a much clearer view of the water ahead.

"We'll head for the lee side of Angel Island. We can drop anchor there for our picnic."

Meilin nodded. The wind in her face, the sun sparkling off the water, and the warmth of Shan against her back all combined for a unique experience. At once exhilarated and a little nervous, she clung to the wheel and lifted her face to the sun.

He didn't quite take advantage, but his hands did slide to her waist, and his head dipped to her neck. "You're in total control now."

Her pulse jumped. Anticipation? Excitement? A touch of fear? She could barely breathe, much less interpret her body's reaction and if it related to steering the boat or Shan being so close.

She shrugged, hoping to dislodge him, and chuckled a little to cover her mixed up reactions. "Don't do that to me, Shan. I don't want to wreck your beautiful boat."

He laughed softly beside her ear. "I'm keeping an eye out. You won't wreck us."

Although he assured her they weren't traveling with great speed, it seemed to her they were flying. She learned to duck when the boom came around as they tacked back and forth, Shan behind her explaining why they made each turn.

Each time Meilin lost her footing, Shan was there to catch her.

"Are you playing or do you really have no sea legs?" he teased, righting her once again.

Meilin laughed, slightly embarrassed. "I have no balance on moving surfaces. I don't have the girly gene that makes me feign falling into men's arms."

Shan hugged her closer from behind. "I don't mind. We'll have to come out here more often."

"I'm afraid I'm hopeless. I was the girl who fell over during ballet class."

"I never would have known by the way you walk and dance. But no worries. We're almost where we want to be, and then we'll sit and enjoy lunch."

Shan's hands over hers on the helm, the boat rounded the island and slipped into calmer waters with three other sail boats spread out, seemingly with the same idea as they. With a button, Shan lowered the mainsail, and with another dropped an anchor, bringing their boat to a gentle stop.

"There. Now we can sit down and enjoy the sun and breeze." Shan turned her in his arms and brushed a stray strand of hair back under her scarf. "Getting a little sun on your nose." He stroked a finger over her cheek.

Meilin stared into his dark eyes and wondered. He genuinely seemed to be fond of her. "Hey, how about we grab that lunch and eat up here?"

Shan grinned. "You get the food; I'll put up the Bimini for some shade."

In the cabin she repacked the basket with the items she'd put in the fridge. Cheeses, cold cuts, pre-cut fruit, and sliced vegetables for sandwiches. She also found a bottle of chardonnay and plastic wine cups.

Shan poked his head through the hatch from above. "Need help?" He extended a hand down. "Hand me the basket."

She lifted it from the bottom, he swung it up and out of the way, then reached back to lend her a hand, since one held plates and utensils.

Lunch was pleasant sitting side by side as Shan told her stories of sailing trips past. One included helping a friend sail a boat from San Francisco down the coast to Marina Del Rey.

"We were young, stupid, and full of ourselves. Thankfully we had a couple retired Coast Guard guys on board. They talked some sense into us when we were absolutely convinced the compass was lying to us." He tossed back his second glass of wine.

"I don't know much about sailing equipment, but how can a compass lie?" Meilin tilted her head, trying to figure it out.

"Exactly." Shan winked at her. "A compass will never lie. But on the night watch with fog all around, it's easy to get confused."

They sat in companionable silence for a while, the boat rocking gently on the water. Meilin watched the seagulls flying, kids playing on the beach, and a man in a small boat with an outboard seemed to search for something in the water.

Shan sighed and stood. "I'll take the stuff down. Be back in a few minutes."

"All right." It was quite nice just sitting, feeling a little drowsy after a good lunch. A glass and a half of wine didn't hurt, either. Wonder if Shan would consider staying here a couple hours so she could lie down and have a little nap. With her busy schedule, lazy afternoons were very rare. The sun, the salty breeze, and the gentle rocking of the boat all were working to send her off to the land of Nod. Below, she could track Shan's movement in the cabin. In contrast to the quiet sounds, a gentle bumping sound came from the starboard side of the water line.

Curious, she stirred herself to stand and lean over the railing, thinking she'd see a piece of driftwood. What she didn't expect to see was a large glass float wrapped with hemp rope. A Japanese fishing float that looked quite old and very out of place. How the heck had it gotten out here?

She gingerly walked the side of the boat until she stood over the float. It had to be a good eight inches in diameter. Something someone would use in a nautical setting as decoration. As far as she knew, no one actually used them for fishing in these waters.

Hoping to reach it, she kneeled in the narrow space between the cabin roof and the railing. No, she'd have to lie down on her stomach.

Stretched on the white fiberglass surface, she eased her top half over the side, one hand on the railing above her head. The float was just barely out of her reach, but if the waves cooperated...and raised the float just a little... She was almost there... She let go of the top rail and grasped the railing pole down where it was attached to the deck.

Another inch and she'd have it, she was sure.

So focused on the float, she didn't hear Shan come topside.

"Meilin! What are you doing?" he yelled, startling her enough she slipped right over the side and into the icy water.

Chapter 14

Meilin came up spluttering and spitting out seawater, but she had a hand on the float. That was no small triumph in her mind.

"Meilin!" Shan shouted from the boat above her. "What in the world…? Can you swim?"

Coughing too much to speak, she nodded. Didn't help that the water was so cold her limbs were stiffening up.

A life ring landed in the water beside her. "Grab that," Shan ordered. "I'll pull you around to the swim step."

Without letting go of the precious glass float, she wrapped an arm around the solid form of the flotation ring. Salt water stung her eyes even as her coughing eased up. Chattering teeth took over.

In a matter of seconds that felt like long minutes, Shan stood on the swim deck, lifting her from the water to the narrow ledge.

"Is that what you went in for?" He tried to take the float from her, but she clutched it to her stomach. "Some old fishing float?"

"This isn't just some old piece of junk, Shan. Look at the color, the size, this is a very rare piece of memorabilia." She shook with cold and excitement. "I've seen these things go for well over five hundred dollars at auction."

At his skeptical look, she nodded. "I swear. This is a valuable treasure. And I have just the place for it in an upcoming job." She held it so he could see for himself. "This is a sweet piece of luck."

Shan shook his head, but with his hands on her shoulders, he gently pushed her up the step into the cockpit of the boat.

She heard the clunk of the life ring hitting the deck, then the thump of the seat folding back into place over the step to the swim platform.

"Here, sit on the railing seat and drip over the side while I find you a towel and a blanket."

The sun was already warming her. "Just a towel please. I'll be dry in no time."

Shan looked at her, her prize still clutched to her stomach, and shook his head. "Be right back."

Perched on a teak seat built into the stainless steel railing, she held her treasure to the sun. It was in perfect shape. Still shivering from the cold water, she gazed at its beauty, completely enraptured.

Shan returned with a large beach towel and wrapped it around her shoulders. "Will you let me hold it while you dry off? I found some sweats and a spare T-shirt you can change into below, and turned on the water heater so you can have a shower."

She took her eyes from the float long enough to look at him and see the concern on his face. "Yes, I suppose I should rinse off and change... But do you realize what a find this is? I wonder where it came from?"

"Ahoy!"

She and Shan looked to the side where a man approached in a small inflatable with an outboard. He killed the engine and let the dinghy coast their direction, until it lightly bumped against the sailboat.

"Hey, saw your lady go overboard. She okay?"

The man was probably in his fifties, dressed in clothes similar to Shan's. He wore a ball cap and sunglasses he removed. Shan tossed him a line which he caught one handed and used it to float near the boat.

"Yeah, she saw something in the water and fell in getting it."

"By any chance is it a glass float? Deep blue, about eight inches? Looks antique?"

Meilin's heart squeezed hard. "Yes. How did you know?"

Chagrin crossed the stranger's face. "I've been searching all day. My wife threw it overboard last night during an argument." A scowl at the memory of the argument crossed his face, but he erased it by pulling one hand over his forehead and down to his chin with a huge sigh. "My grandfather brought it back from Japan after the war. From my earliest memory it's always been the centerpiece of his collection on the sailboat."

Meilin glanced at Shan to see a deep frown on his face. "Shan?"

"Look," Shan said. "Finders keepers. She just went into the drink for this thing. She's an interior designer who has a place for it to go, a client who will want it."

"Hey," the man protested as Meilin put her hand on Shan's arm.

"It's okay. I'd be pretty upset if someone tossed something precious of mine overboard. I'd be grateful if a stranger recovered it and gave it back."

Shan's darkened gaze turned on her. "But you could have died going after it. Do you know how cold the water is? What if I hadn't seen you go over? What if you'd drowned?"

"It's okay, Shan. I can swim, and I was close to the boat. You would have heard me shout out, or I could have gotten myself to the stern and pulled myself out." A great shiver shuddered through her.

Shan grabbed her shoulders and started rubbing the towel up and down her arms.

"Meilin..."

"Really, Shan." She spoke over him. "It's all right. Giving it back is the right thing to do."

His lips thinned and his brows drew down in a fierce frown. Meilin gazed back at him, her eyes wide open, and she hoped, compelling.

"Look," the man in the dinghy said, "I'll pay you a recovery fee. What do you say? Fifty dollars cover it?"

Meilin glanced over and saw him pulling his wallet. "No, no. I don't need money for it."

"At least let me pay enough to replace your clothes. Sixty?"

Shan released a huge sigh of disgust. "Put your wallet way." He took the ball from Meilin's shaking hands and leaned over the rail enough to hand the float over with care. Meilin had the feeling he wanted to throw it in the water just as the angry wife had. "Take it and go."

The man clutched the glass ball in his lap and looked at Meilin. "I'm sorry you got dunked going after it, but I'm grateful you rescued it. You're a designer?"

Meilin nodded.

"Give me your name. My wife wants to redo the bedroom. If you recognized the value of this, I bet you know your stuff."

"Shan, I have some cards in my bag."

"I don't believe this," he muttered, but headed into the cabin below, coming back a few seconds later with her tote.

Fingers still damp and shaking, she found the cards and pulled out two, with three more spilling into the bottom of the bag. "Here." She handed them to Shan and indicated he should hand them over. Scowling something fierce, he did.

The man read one card, nodded, and stuck the pair of cards into his shirt pocket. "Thank you. From the bottom of my heart. I mean that."

"All right, all right," Shan said, and tugged on his line until the man released it. "We get it. Go. Enjoy."

He gave Shan a wary look, nodded at Meilin, then tugged on the starter of his outboard, and headed toward the west end of the island, the float secure on his lap.

Meilin stared after him. It was the right thing to do, but to have held that bit of history in her hands, even for a few minutes, left behind a longing. She'd have to check eBay later to confirm her guess, but she'd bet that float could easily go for several hundred dollars.

"Meilin?"

Shan's sharp tone broke her away from her musings.

"You need to get in a hot shower. Don't want you getting hypothermia." Strong hands lifted her by the waist and she set her frozen feet on the warm deck. "If you need help, just say the word."

That caught her attention fully and she snapped her gaze to his face. Traces of his tension remained, but he also wore a crooked grin. Yeah, he'd probably like to turn this into fun in the shower, but with what she recalled from her inspection of the head, there wasn't room for two in there.

"I think I can manage." A deep shiver shook her body. "You're right. I need to warm up."

"I'll make some tea while you shower."

"That would be great." She gave him a weak smile, followed him to the hatch where he went down first, then helped her down the steep steps.

Twenty minutes later she emerged from the tiny bathroom dressed in sweat pants she'd had to roll up at the waist and cinch tight. The T-shirt he'd also left for her was several sizes too big. He'd brought her tote down and she dug in it for her sweater. As a fashion statement, well, she missed completely, but it absorbed the little bit of water that dripped from her towel dried hair.

Shan held two steaming mugs. "Let's go topside. It's warm in the sun. We'll get your core temp back to normal soon."

She nodded and followed him up to the cockpit where he'd placed a folded blanket on the bench seat. With the mug of hot tea in her hands, she curled up on the blanket and stared out at the water. Damn, she'd hated to let that little treasure go.

"What possessed you to go after that alone?" Shan asked. At the tense tone in his voice she turned her head to look at him.

"I heard it bump against the boat and went to see what it was. When I saw it was something that didn't belong in the water here, I got curious. I honestly thought I could reach it."

Shan shoved a hand through his short hair. "It was a stupid thing to do."

Meilin stiffened. "Excuse me? Did you just call me stupid?" The icy water had nothing on the frostiness of her tone.

Shan's eyes bore into her. "I didn't say you were stupid. I said it was a stupid thing to do. There were so many other ways we could have fished it out."

"I didn't want it to get away."

"Don't do that again. Next time you think you see something worth salvaging, let me know. I'll get it for you."

"I'm not always so clumsy. I could have gotten myself out, and I nearly had it in my hand when you startled me. If you hadn't shouted at me, I'm sure I would have pulled it in without falling overboard."

Shan blew out a breath she took as frustration, but he held his tongue and stared into the distance for a long moment. "I won't take the blame for this. We're just lucky you didn't get in real trouble. Next time, if there is one, use your head. And don't contradict me in public."

It was oh so tempting to apologize to smooth things over. But was what she'd done really so wrong? "I won't apologize for giving that man back his possession. I hated to give it up, but it was the right thing to do."

"Rights of salvage made it yours. You found it; you should have kept it."

"And I would have felt small, mean, and guilty as if I'd stolen it. It meant much more to him than it did to me."

Shan dumped the remains of his tea into the water. "I tried to back you up and you turned on me today." He stood and glared down at her. "I tried to be your champion and you effectively chopped my dick off. Don't do that again."

Meilin also dumped the contents of her mug over the side of the boat. "Is that what you're mad about? I dented your male pride? Is it so fragile you can't set it aside to do the right thing?"

Shan's scowl deepened more as he clenched his fists at his side. "This is about you respecting me as the man in your life. You're my lady. I stuck up for you, and you kicked me aside in favor of some poor jerk who lost a fight with his wife. We will not fight, Meilin. Each ship can only have one captain, and in our relationship I'm the captain."

"I see, and what was that speech yesterday about my opinions mattering?"

"I say what I mean, Meilin. Your opinion matters, but someone has to be in charge of the final decision. Most of the time the matter will most likely go your way. In return I ask you to show respect at all times, particularly in public. If I say or do something you don't like, we will discuss it later. In private. This is what we're doing right now. Discussing our difference of opinion in private."

She wanted nothing more than to fume, but if she ever wanted to go home again, it was up to her to diffuse the situation. "Fine. But if I see something that needs to be discussed immediately, I will pull you aside then and there to discuss it. I couldn't let that man go away without his rightful property, which is why it may have seemed I disrespected you in front of him. However, you did not do me the courtesy of discussing it on the side, either. In this case, I rule we both have things to learn about how to communicate with each other."

For a long, long moment, Shan stared at her in silence before abruptly nodding. "I agree. We'll both work to be more in tune with each other in future situations that may be similar."

"That's all I can ask for. Now, please, I think I've had all the sun and sea I can stand for today."

"Again, I agree. Let's get you home so you can rest from your swim."

As Shan turned away to set the return trip in motion, Meilin curled up in the corner of the bench seating at the stern. They didn't speak another word until Shan pulled into his slip in the marina.

Mostly she chose to forget Shan's demeaning words. Instead, she wondered what Drew was up to. Was he spending the day with his family or was he already back on campus preparing for his course? Maybe she'd have to touch base with her cousin and get a feel for this year's class.

As he left her at her apartment door, Shan tried to break the ice by taking her in his arms for a soft, gentle kiss.

"Remember, dinner Wednesday night. The clients we're meeting with are very important, so please dress appropriately."

"Of course, Shan. I always do."

He gave her an odd look, then bent and lightly kissed her cheek. "I'll pick you up at six-thirty."

* * * *

Drew answered the front door late Sunday afternoon. Eyes hidden behind dark shades, Oswald stood on the step.

"Come in, man." Drew stepped back and invited the other man in. "You're family and don't need to knock."

"I'll always knock, just as I expect you to knock when coming to my flat." Oswald pulled off his sunglasses and carefully set them on the receiving table in the foyer.

Drew slapped a hand down on Oswald's oxford cloth covered shoulder. "Only if you keep the door locked."

"Which I always do. London is nothing more than a great seething cauldron of thieves."

Drew laughed. "Especially those dressed in suits from Seville Row with handmade custom shoes."

Rare for Oswald, a wide grin split his face for a moment. "We're the very worst, mate."

Birdie, dressed in shorts and a tight tank top, popped out from the back hallway. "What's so funny? Drew, did you actually make Ozzie laugh?" With a hand to her breast, she gasped dramatically. "It can smile! Who knew?"

Like the morning fog under relentless sunlight, Oswald's smile faded in an instant. "Courtney."

Birdie threw up her hands. "The only person in the world to call me by my real name and it has to be Lurch's brother." Turning on her heel, she headed through the formal living space toward the backyard. "Mom said dinner is nearly ready." She stopped at the glass slider door and looked over her shoulder, pinning Oswald with her blue eyes. "You're late." Turning again, she threw open the door and swished out to the patio.

"Dinner?" Oswald said, his eyes firmly directed at Birdie's backside.

Once again he was slapped in the face of Oswald being hot for Birdie. Drew wasn't sure how he felt about that. It was…weird. He hadn't wanted to think too much about it the day before when he'd caught Oswald eyeing Bird, but now… As Jack had said, he'd have to think about it more. "Yeah. Dad's burning more meat. Hamburgers this time, I think."

"Any idea what this meeting is about?"

Both men followed in Birdie's wake.

"Not a bloody idea. Old man hasn't even hinted. Just said we all needed to be here for dinner." Drew shrugged and let Oswald clear the door first before following and sliding the screen shut.

They sauntered over to the table where Randi waited as his dad set down a platter of cheeseburgers that didn't look burned. The man was improving at cooking over open flame. Bottles of wine and beer were already in place, as were a multitude of condiments and what looked like potato and macaroni salad left over from the party the day before.

"Looks great," Oswald said as he took a chair opposite from Birdie.

"Help yourself, everyone," Randi said and passed a basket of buns to Drew.

Dinner was filled with small talk, a rehashing of the previous day, and vague plans for a trip to Napa Valley and other wine regions. Drew held up his part, but mostly let it flow over and around him. Tonight he'd go back to the Palo Alto apartment with his sister and tomorrow begin his immersion program. The little experience he'd had at the mercy of

Jack made him a bit nervous. And the fact that Meilin sometimes taught there, and knew the instructor, had him wondering if he'd see her there. According to the course paperwork, he'd have damn little time for seeking her out. Although, he did have her phone number…

"What do you think, Drew?"

He looked at his father. "Excuse me, sir. I missed the discussion."

His dad chuckled. "We were wondering if you might be able to get away for a day next weekend and join us."

"Not really sure. The class outline looks quite ambitious. I might get a free night every now and again, but I gather Sundays will be pretty much as intense as the rest of the week. It's been designated homework day. A chance to catch up on anything we don't pick up during the week."

"Ah." His dad picked up a glass of deep red wine. "I guess we'll just have to play it by ear."

A glance at the table showed Drew they'd pretty much decimated the food. An inelegant belch confirmed it. "Pardon me. Good meal, Mum." The grin he gave her was as cheeky as he could make it.

Randi had an expression of half resignation, half affection on her face. "If that belch was any indication, then I guess so. Want to wait a bit on dessert?"

Oswald let out a small groan beside him while Birdie was more dramatic about hers. "I'm set, Mrs. Robinson. Great meal."

Drew held back his laugh when Birdie wrinkled her nose at Oswald. Although she didn't say it out loud, Drew knew exactly what she was thinking—brown-noser. Since he knew far more about Oswald than she did, he kept his comments to himself. Come to think of it, he was pretty sure he didn't know the whole of Oswald's background. Just that he was a good bloke to have around.

"Oswald," Randi said in a low voice. Almost a growl. "What's it going to take to get you to call me by my name? A man your age calling me Mrs. Robinson… Well, it just doesn't feel right."

Oswald set one of his rare grins free. "Since you're the wife of my boss, a man I call Mr. Robinson in the office, I guess there's not much you can do to change my mind."

Across the table, Birdie's mouth dropped open. Evidently she'd never seen Oswald's full megawatt smile. And judging by Randi's slight flush, neither had she.

"Oh bloody hell," Drew's dad muttered. "Stow it, Attenborough. That killer grin of yours has put more women than I can count in a state of vapors. I like you better when you're scowling."

At that Drew laughed, long, loud, and held his stomach. It was true. Oswald rarely smiled, mostly because when he did he found a line of women a city block long drooling after him. It was attention the very private man hated. Come to think of it, part of the reason Oswald was good at self defense was that very smile had earned him unwanted attention at school too.

Drew made an effort to catch his breath while Randi and Birdie stood to begin clearing the table, both women a little flustered, both stealing little glimpses of Oswald, who'd lost the smile.

Dad merely shook his head and stood to help with the clearing. But he had one last word for Oswald. "Better do as she says and call her Randi. Otherwise the words Mrs. Robinson coming out of your pretty face will put bad ideas in her head."

Oswald choked out a barely audible, and wholly horrified, "Yes, sir."

Drew took pity on his friend as his dad walked away. "We'd better grab the rest, then go pin the old man down as to this super secret meeting. Wonder if we'll need our decoder rings."

"Probably one of us will need body armor if Courtney doesn't like what she hears."

"Oh? You have an idea of what's coming?"

"Not a bloody clue, but something tells me I won't like it."

In the kitchen they set everything on the island. Randi handed them each a damp rag. "Please wipe everything down."

"Yes, ma'am." Drew gave her a cheeky grin, then danced out of the way of her swat.

When they came back, the food was put away and Randi was putting the last of the dishes into the dishwasher. "Anyone want coffee?" she asked.

"If you're making some, I'll have a cup," Drew said. "But if no one else is having any, don't bother."

"Now shoo. Into the family room, everyone. I'll be along in a minute."

Dad was already in the sturdy rocking chair, Birdie curled up in her corner at the far end of the long, curved sofa. Almost feeling like a kid called into the Headmaster's office, Drew settled himself a cushion width from his sister. Oswald sat beyond the curve, as far from Birdie as he could get. Was the man truly afraid of Bird? A question to ponder another time as Randi wandered in, rubbing lotion into her hands. Dad waved her over and pulled her down on his lap.

"I suppose you're all wondering why we called you here," Dad started.

"You could say that." Drew folded his arms across his chest. Otherwise he'd be tempted to tweak Birdie's toes and then the serious mood would be upset. Dad wouldn't appreciate it.

"Well, Randi and I have been talking, and now all the weddings are over, we want to make some plans."

"What sort of plans?" Birdie asked. Drew could certainly appreciate the suspicion in her tone.

"Well, I was about Drew's age when his grandfathers started seriously grooming me to run the company. Now he's headed off to China for at least a couple years. Maybe longer depending on how things go there. We've talked about this extensively. We need him there to personally oversee things and make sure all is according to the company interests. I'm not entirely sure our staff over there is one hundred percent loyal to us. Not even sure they're fifty percent."

Drew nodded. The plan they'd begun implementing soon after his mother's death. Acceleration through school, breaks spent in the London office working in various departments from the ground up. In fact, he'd started in the mail room. Much like he expected Birdie would, although she had her mind set on starting in the executive offices. She had a lot to learn. The last few years while he'd completed the courses required for the Stanford International Law program, he'd spent plenty of time in the legal offices and had passed the British Bar. One more session of school and he'd be more than ready to enter the company fully.

"With that in mind, it's time for me to make a tour of all our foreign offices and spend time with the staffs there, ensuring things remain on track."

"But what about the London office?" Birdie asked, a deep frown drawing her delicate brows together.

Drew cast a glance at Oswald and saw his lips flatten into a straight line. The man was fighting to keep a blank face, but for what reason. Did that mean...?

"Oswald's had several years working his way up the ladder in London. He's done some traveling to liaise with the satellite offices, but I've spent far too much time in London and far too little in the field, so to speak."

"You're turning London over to Ozzie?" Birdie asked in disbelief.

"At this time he's the most qualified," Dad confirmed. "Although the board of directors has indicated in the short term, Randi could probably run the company if I got run over by a bus."

"But-but..." Birdie spluttered.

"Randi?" Drew tossed in his own question. Certainly she had a business background from an accounting view, but to run the company?

"Sure," Dad said and nodded at Drew. "In fact, it was your grandfather Catchpole who suggested it."

Drew's mouth dropped open. "You're off your trolley. How'd that come about?"

Randi sat up and preened as she said, "He loves my turkey dinner with all the fixings."

"What?" Drew and Birdie spoke at the same time, then shared a look of disbelief.

Randi shrugged with a grin on her face. "Your dad wants a full turkey dinner for Thanksgiving, so your grandmother insisted we do a trial run so I could teach Cook how to do it right. Of course it's a big meal, so she invited the vicar and the Catchpoles to help eat it. While they still don't approve of me, we have a tentative truce." She and Dad shared a grin.

"And in his mind that qualifies you to run the company?" This wasn't making any sense to Drew. Bea's parents hated Randi and Birdie.

"Conversation at dinner included a review of Randi's resume. A grudging respect has been slowly growing," Dad said. "We'll take what we can get. However, the fact remains, Oswald is currently the most qualified to fill in, in the case of disaster," Dad said firmly. "Next year, Birdie, you'll join the London office as I've promised."

"But I'm to train as your assistant," Birdie said with barely a quiver in her voice.

"And you will," he assured her. "You'll learn your way up the corporate structure first, exactly the way Drew and Oswald have."

Birdie's mouth dropped open. "You're going to start me in the mail room?"

"Only fair, Bird," Drew jumped in. "Although I'm guessing your climb will be a little faster than mine. I spent an entire summer in the mail room."

Dad nodded. "The plan is a month, two at the most in each department on the way up the structure. You need to know people throughout the entire organization. No better way to do it than to jump into each department with a cheerful, helpful attitude. Spread a little honey, listen, learn everything you can from the people who will eventually be under you."

Birdie's mouth snapped shut. Well, Drew thought, she hadn't expected that. Better to tell her now rather than on her first day in the office with her shiny new degree. She'd have a year to get used to the idea.

"Oswald?" Dad asked the third person concerned in the room. "Ready to start assuming more duties?"

The stern man nodded silently, his expression blank as a slate.

"Excellent. Randi and I will return to London in another week or two, and then we'll start transitioning you into the temporary lead position. We'll see how that goes; then about the time Drew returns from China and Birdie is running the executive suites, he'll take a turn, allowing Oswald to travel the field and implement the changes I'll recommend. Or if Drew is happy out in the field, then you'll have your turn at the helm, Birdie. By then I'm sure you'll have the London offices eating out of your hand." Dad sent her a grin, but she only answered with barely a grimace.

"Sure thing, Dad."

Drew could see it wasn't the response his parents had hoped for, but contrary to Oswald's prediction, at least she wasn't throwing things.

And if the board was unbending enough to consider Randi a candidate to step in should Dad not be able to carry on, then maybe there was a way to convince Meilin to join him in China. Could they create a position that would dovetail with her design business?

A tad early to consider that thought, but it did bring up interesting questions.

He slid his gaze from Birdie to Oswald and back again. The two were currently engaged in a silent battle of some sort. Now that could make life more interesting in the offices.

Chapter 15

From the moment she stepped into the office Monday morning, Meilin knew, just knew, the week wasn't going to go her way.

"Mercury is in retrograde," her assistant Susan said, handing over a stack of messages.

"I never understood that," Meilin murmured as she sorted through the slips. Contractor delays, delivery issues, and clients with fickle taste all filled the dozen notes.

True hell started the moment she had to call Shan on Wednesday afternoon to tell him she couldn't make dinner that night.

"I explained how important tonight is, Meilin." His voice was tight, like he was trying not to yell, or not be overheard.

"And I can't plan for my contractor's son breaking his arm. Things happen, Shan, and with the furniture delivery tomorrow, I can't get another painter on such short notice. Unless you want to reschedule your dinner and come help me?" His scoffing noise came through loud and clear. "That's what I'll be doing tonight until the job is done. It's called stepping up and being a responsible business owner."

"A business you no longer need."

"Well, at least you finally came out and said it instead of dancing around the issue with placating words." She bit out the words as sharply as he had.

On the other end of the phone he let out a sigh. When he spoke again his voice was much softer. "Meilin, I want to work this out. It's just, well, timing sucks."

She softened her tone as well. "I get that. But when the school called and said his son had a compound fracture, what else could Paul do? He couldn't let the kid sit there scared and in pain. It's what parents do. They take care of their kids, and sometimes that means dropping the work mid-job. He'll make it up to me down the road, but right now I have a deadline that can't wait, and that's not his problem. It's mine."

A hint of impatience returned to Shan's voice. "And I have a problem in that I promised a very important client he'd meet my fiancée tonight. It's certainly more important than whether some walls get painted or not."

Meilin's back stiffened once more. "I can't help you tonight. I must meet my commitments or my reputation is worth nothing. Please extend my deepest apologies and explain my situation. Clearly, if they're any kind of business person, they'll understand my need to take care of my client. You should understand that."

"I understand it when meetings determine whether fresh food is delivered or medicines arrive on time. Surely those events are a higher priority on a global scale."

"Yes, they are. But my business, while small, is still important. Without my clients, craftsmen have fewer jobs to pay for the fresh food you ship to feed their families. Without my employees, yours would suffer. It's how the entire world comes together in the scheme of things."

Shan all but growled his frustration into the phone. "Fine. But don't do this to me again. I'll try to reschedule dinner for tomorrow night. And remember we're going away this weekend."

"I remember," she said, withholding the impatience from her tone. "Now, unless I want to spend the entire night here smelling paint fumes, I need to get to work."

Shan sighed, as if releasing his anger to the universe. When he spoke, his tone was much calmer. Nicer. "I'll call you if I get the dinner rescheduled. Do you need me to come by and escort you home? Whatever the hour, Meilin, I want to see you safely to your door."

With a smirk, she noticed he didn't offer to help with the painting. "Thanks, Shan, but I've got it. Going home late is pretty much routine and I feel perfectly safe when I do."

"Then please call me when you get home. For my peace of mind."

"Fine. Now, really, I've got to get moving on this paint job."

The huge sigh of relief she expelled a minute later released much of the tension, but not all. Shan was not happy. Well, that made two of them. So much for his talk of respecting her desire to continue working and running her own business. She grabbed her go-bag and headed for the bathroom to change.

* * * *

Things didn't improve when her cousin Arnie called and begged for her help.

"Meilin, my favorite cousin," he started.

"Get to the point, Arnie. I have four gallons of paint that need applying tonight." Dressed to paint, in jeans and an old T-shirt with a bandana covering her hair, she hardly looked elegant standing in the middle of her client's tarp draped living room.

"I need you this weekend at the school."

Meilin groaned. "You mean the immersion school at Stanford?"

"Yes. You know I'm teaching this summer's Mandarin session. You also know how critical the first week is for really dropping the students into the experience. I have to be gone Friday night through late Sunday. My father is having surgery on Friday and Mother needs me there first thing Saturday to bring him home. Monday she has a health aide coming in to assist, but the aide can't start before then. That leaves me. I have to fly to Seattle and won't make it back until very, very late Sunday night. I'll be there Monday morning, but I need you for the weekend. I don't trust Jack to teach them properly."

"With good cause." She sighed and looked up at the ceiling that had already been painted to look like a twilight sky. Arnie only called on Jack when there was absolutely no one else in the Bay Area who could fill in for a few hours. Meilin had to agree. She'd rather call her mother to teach than Jack. She'd filled in for Arnie before and worked with tutoring elementary kids from time to time. But Mother didn't like teaching adults and Meilin found it challenging. Teaching wasn't the problem. As Shan had said earlier, timing sucked.

Of course, Jack was no solution at all. Not with his tendency to cause mischief by teaching students the wrong phrases. Exhibit A, Drew week before last.

That Friday out with her friends seemed so far away as to be a barely remembered dream, but it had only been a matter of days since Jack had gotten a taste of teasing Drew. And wasn't Drew a student in the program? She could only imagine what damage Jack could do to his friend all in the name of fun. Learning Mandarin was difficult enough for adults well-versed in English.

"I assume the lesson plan is ready? I don't have to do any prep?" Because the thought of Drew in the class made her heart leap, she'd probably spend more time thinking about him than worrying about the other students. Could she really do this knowing he'd be there, watching her with those gorgeous blue eyes? Then again, seeing him in a class situation could very well drive home the fact how very young he was for her. Maybe this was just the chance she needed to make her brain understand Drew was a temporary infatuation.

"Not a bit. I'll go over it again and add as much detail as I can. All you have to do is follow it, correct pronunciations, answer questions, the usual. There are only five students and they're having the usual first week issues, although they're pretty smart and definitely enthusiastic."

"Yes, it helps when they want to be there. I'll have to explain it to Shan, of course, and he's already frustrated I had to cancel on him tonight. One more cancelation will be the icing on the cake."

"I'll make it up to both of you."

"No, you have a true emergency. What's going on with your father?"

Five minutes later, she had the details and Arnie's promise to e-mail her directions and the lesson plan. All she had to do was call Shan and cancel their weekend plans too. After their previous conversation, she'd changed her mind about looking forward to going away over the weekend. Relieved to have an excuse, she still didn't relish the thought of the discussion to come.

By Saturday morning, Meilin was ready to step outside her life and play substitute teacher for a weekend. Shan's icy displeasure had been hard to face. However, she'd finished the last job on time and on budget. Her client was over the moon and planning a party next week to show it off to her friends. Meilin and her plus one were invited. Shan's secretary had it on his calendar, and he was somewhat mollified. Once he saw what she'd accomplished, how she put her love of beauty into every job, she hoped he'd be so impressed he'd forgive her the transgressions of this week and weekend. The very thought she was seeking his forgiveness bugged her.

The day was already heating up when she parked her car and gathered her briefcase with Arnie's notes. Now all she had to do was find the classroom and face Drew in the most intimate setting yet. No loud music or swaying bodies to make conversation difficult. No fiancés, parents, neighbors, friends, or siblings there to run interference. Just Drew and four other students and lots of conversation in Chinese. Easy peasy.

In low sandals, a soft cotton skirt, and loose T-shirt, she wasn't fashionable, but she was comfortable. She'd only brushed on a light coat of mascara to emphasize her fine eyelashes, and a dash of lip gloss to protect from the sun and heat. Sunglasses shaded her eyes as she found the building and entered the cool hall.

The smell of floor wax, books, and their unique dust filled her head, reminding her of her years at school. The nostalgia took her by surprise as she found herself wishing she were back in school, eager to rush into the future and prove herself a savvy, independent woman who didn't need a man to complete her world. She'd proved herself a hundred times over.

What was wrong with her life that she'd agreed to marry anyone at all? Shan in particular? Maybe she was being fanciful for the first time in her life. Maybe he was being too practical and logical with his captain of the boat analogy. Maybe she was over reacting to something that would probably work out sensibly.

Her sandals slapped on the polished floors and she heard murmurs of conversation coming from the classrooms. The number was easy to find. The door was unlocked and she let herself into an empty room.

A few small tables were pushed together to make one larger table with a handful of chairs around it. The board at the front of the room was a white board, and Arnie had already outlined the lesson for the day in colorful markers. One less chore for her to take care of. At least he made it easy for his substitutes to step in.

She set her overnight bag in a corner and began emptying her briefcase of the printouts she'd prepared. A few minutes later the door opened and Drew stepped in.

Time stopped.

No, she hadn't imagined this man's good looks and presence. Beside his father last weekend, he'd stood out in a good way. Now he filled the classroom with a charisma that stole her breath. Didn't hurt that he wore cargo shorts and a tight T-shirt reminding her of his rock solid abs.

Drew's gaze locked on hers and he pulled in a deep breath. "Meilin."

The way he said her name was like a caress of his hand down her spine.

"Hi, Drew." She cleared her throat and forced herself to stand straight. "I'm subbing this weekend."

Clearly trying his best, he said in Mandarin, "*Wo hen gaoxìng jiàndào ni.*" *I am pleased to see you here.* Not bad. He was learning.

Speaking slowly, she replied, "*Wo hen gaoxìng cheng wei nide laoshi.*" *The pleasure is mine to be your teacher.*

He nodded and stepped farther into the room. Outside, footsteps of many people filled the halls. Once more he seemed to gather his words, but knowing he was just beginning, she knew he didn't have many. "May we speak later?" With his hand, he gestured between the two of them, indicating a wish to speak privately.

"*Shìde.*" She said the word in Mandarin and emphasized it with a nod.

"*Xièxie.*" Well, he knew that pretty well. She flashed a shy smile at him to indicate praise, and he huffed a small sigh as the door behind him opened.

The students ranged in age from late teens to late twenties, with Drew in the middle. She had each student say their name and age.

With a week under their belts, the class fell into the pattern set up by Arnie. Grammar and vocabulary in the morning. Then lunch where they sat together and practiced their words for the food and what they'd learned that morning. It also gave her time to learn a little about the students. They were just as curious about her and her qualifications to teach. They seemed satisfied when she told them about growing up bilingual and then the two years she'd spent with relatives in China not far from Beijing.

The afternoon was spent learning the characters to go with the words. Almost an art class, which she enjoyed, although Drew wasn't the best student when it came to drawing the symbols.

Dinner was the same as lunch, their group sitting together, only she let them speak in English. There had to be some break to help connect the two languages in their minds. Drew sat as close as he could without being obvious, and told the story of trying out a phrase or two at the nightclub. It kept the other students laughing until they told their own tales of silly mistranslations, not only in Chinese, but other languages as well. Each student was an accomplished traveler and as always, there was room for funny mishaps while in another country.

Drew in particular was very well traveled. He had stories from Italy, France, India, and Turkey. Even a run-in with a flock of Scottish sheep in the Highlands. He had a healthy sense of self-deprecation, which she found refreshing. And yet, he was easily the chosen leader of the group. A result of an unconscious, natural affinity for leadership.

"Are you staying over tonight?" Drew asked her quietly as they cleared their trays.

"I am. I'm here to help the students in this class with studying."

"Can we slip away during the movie tonight? I'd love to spend some time just talking. I could also stand to stretch my legs a bit. All this sitting is tough."

She weighed the pros and cons in her mind, then slowly nodded. It wasn't the right thing to do, movie night was meant to bring the entire school together, despite their different language focuses. But she, too, wanted to talk more, learn more about this fascinating man.

* * * *

Drew could barely breathe after Meilin agreed to walk with him. As much as he wanted to escape the suffocating air of the dorm, he wanted much more to talk alone with her. Something that hadn't yet happened since meeting her. This time it would be just the two of them. No loud music, no hovering cousins or fiancé, no sisters, parents, or classmates.

Just the two of them under the summer night sky, breathing in the scent of trees and flowers that perfumed the air.

As the movie started in the common room, they quietly made their exit and headed for the paths of the vast campus.

"I've always loved this place," Meilin said, breaking their silence.

"Did you go to school here?"

"No, but I have friends, and yes, cousins, who did. I went to college in the City."

"Tell me more about how you came to teach Chinese."

"Although I grew up speaking it at home, after college, as you know, I spent time in China. That's where I really refined the language and spent time combing markets for decorating ideas. I gained a good sense of history and the different styles of the dynasties. The time there served me well in business. Some of my clients long for the old country, whatever that means to them personally, and my skill with both language and design impressed them to no end. People without an ounce of taste can now pretend to be knowledgeable of their past and make it more illustrious than it truly is."

"Ah, even the Chinese have pretenders?" Drew chuckled. "Much like the courtesans who rose in society by attracting devilishly clever patrons who furnished them with the means to at least look as if they were close to the higher ranks of society."

"Exactly. For example, my family, along with Jack's and Shan's, came to the American shores as common laborers and servants during the gold rush and railroad years. They got lucky, found a few nuggets, made wise investments in property and professions, and turned it all into their own mini-dynasties here in San Francisco. Outsiders are under the impression we all came from the Imperial Court, or the class of noblemen."

"Not so different from the Lynfords and Robinsons who made some lucky investments in trade and built their name on imports not only from China, but India and Spain."

"Are your interests not solid in China?"

Drew glanced down at her pacing beside him. Like him, she had her hands folded behind her back. A sorry attempt to keep from touching, but it was all he had at the moment. "They're solid, but doing business in China, almost any country, is like standing on shifting sand. Some years we're solid, others we're looking to gain stronger ground as what we stood on has begun to crumble."

"I imagine that can be true for many economies."

"It is. But with quality dropping off, Lynford wants a stronger presence to oversee that the highest quality is maintained in the goods we sell. Hence, the heir apparent needs to spend some time there, learning the ins and outs of how to deal with our Chinese sources. Some of them are more slippery than eels."

Meilin laughed. "True. I can say that about some of my own family."

Drew flicked a glance her direction as she looked up at him. Together they smiled and said in unison, "Jack."

Without forethought, Drew let his hands swing free. As natural as breathing, Meilin did the same and their hands brushed. On the next swing, Drew opened his hand to hers, and without a hitch, her hand slipped into his as they strolled under the shadows of the tall palm trees lining their way.

The rush of warmth was enough for him to close his eyes for a moment just to savor her touch. Palm to palm, the heat slid up his arm like soft fire running through his veins. The air smelled sweeter, the barely there breeze fell soft as a blanket against his cheek, and the beating of his heart matched the cadence of hers as felt by his thumb against her wrist. For a moment, something wild and wonderful hovered just out of understanding. Something he'd never contemplated. It seemed his brain was about to fry, so he found a way to simplify the thought and decided this was heaven on earth. And if he was right, would there be retribution for daring to seek it out?

"So." He drew in a deep breath to push away the shadows of doubts and mixed up emotions he didn't want to acknowledge. "Tell me about you. Raised in San Francisco? Lived in China a couple years. Sometime teacher of Mandarin, full time interior designer, soon to be bride."

"There's not much to tell. I was a good girl. Did my homework and chores, ate my food without complaint, kept my room tidy, looked after my grandmother when I got home from school, and generally did my best to not make waves. Waves are frowned upon."

Drew thought of his paternal grandmother and her idea of not making waves. Until it came to the subject of Birdie, good old gran was the picture of English gentry. Impeccably dressed and groomed, her manners were perfect. Unless Birdie was in the room. Then the two tended to go at it like pugilists, only without fists. Ladylike, but no holds barred in their verbal warfare. Everything was up for criticizing. Birdie's posture, diction, clothing, eating habits, how she spoke on the phone or wrote a thank-you letter. Having endured much of the same, but from his mother, Drew had a lot of sympathy for his sister. But that didn't mean it wasn't for her own good, even if she managed to give back as much as she got in terms of making the old woman do her physical therapy.

"I can't believe you were good all the time."

A sly smile graced her lips. "I'm not telling. There's no proof."

Laughing out loud felt good. "I bet Jack would tell."

"Maybe, maybe not. If he knows what's good for him, he won't. Besides, aren't you going to be too busy with this studying to gossip about me with my cousin?"

"There is that." He pulled his free hand down his face. "I feel as if I'm learning nothing. This is so hard." Mandarin might as well be Klingon for all he understood.

A teasing grin crossed her face. "One fifth of the world speaks Chinese. It's possible to learn it."

"I think you're spreading propaganda. Aren't there a thousand dialects? I've nearly quit at least three times this week."

"The first week is the most difficult. It will come I assure you."

"I'll hold you to that. Will you fill in often?" He hoped so. She was much prettier than Professor Chung.

"You'll have many teachers. Professor Chung brings in experts for history as well as current events and etiquette. I may pop in from time to time, but not often. This was more of a fluke."

A sense of panic drove his heartbeat up a few beats per second. "Tell me you'll be back. If only to tutor me a night or two each week. If I have that hope, I can face anything."

Meilin squeezed his hand. "I'll think about it. It will depend on my time…"

"Which you don't have much of." Drew groaned. "I get it. I understand, really."

With a shake of her head, she spoke slowly. "No, I don't think you do."

"It's that fiancé of yours, isn't it?" Jealousy ran through him like a river of lava. The feeling was so astonishing it nearly knocked him over. Not a feeling he knew well unless it related to kids with loving mothers. Generally, people envied him, not the other way around.

Meilin shrugged. Her face was shadowed, but the light from street lamps touched her hair like a glaze, shifting with the silken strands. "He's part of it, but not all. I do have a business. Two nights ago I was on a ladder until one AM, finishing an interior paint job."

"Don't you hire those jobs out?"

"Usually, but my contractor had a family emergency. The painting had to be finished that night because the furnishings were delivered the next day.

I wasn't about to let a little pride get in my way, so I picked up the rollers and went to work. And missed an important client dinner with Shan."

Now that didn't break Drew's heart. "And this weekend? Did you have plans?"

"I did. But Arnie, I mean Professor Chung, called and I owe him a few favors, so here I am." She shrugged.

"Any thought about me being in the class?" No, he shouldn't have asked, but damn if he could keep his mouth shut.

Meilin ducked her head. "Perhaps one or two. His only other choice was Jack, but he's taken off for Nevada and I don't trust him to teach you the right words."

"I thank you." Hand over his heart, he gave her a shortened bow. Difficult to do while walking. In the distance, he spied a bench under the shadows of a tree. They were a bit off the main paths and it looked private. "Hey, let's go sit there." He pointed and she nodded.

As she sat, she groaned and released his hand. "I shouldn't be here with you."

The giant stone on her finger reflected the ambient light, reminding him she was engaged.

Swallowing his pride, he asked, "So tell me about him, this man you're going to marry."

Big round eyes looked up at him. "Why would I do that?"

"You're newly engaged. Isn't it something you want to talk about?"

"Surprisingly, no, I don't want to talk about it."

"Now that's interesting. I'd think it would be the only thing you wanted to talk about."

Meilin turned her head to look away from him. "I don't want to. It's an arranged marriage, not a love match. Very practical. He needs a wife; I have a duty to produce offspring. He's not ugly or poor. I'm okay in the looks department, and I know how to stage and host a party or business event. We both get something from the marriage. He gets a hostess, and mother for his children; I get financial stability and beautiful babies. I'll take my place in the family structure and supply the next set of building blocks. It's a chance to be part of something bigger than just me."

The speech sounded rehearsed. "For the record, you're better than okay looking. You're bloody gorgeous." He held her startled gaze for a long moment. "And that arrangement sounds rather cold to me," he muttered. "Not unlike my father's first marriage."

Her gaze softened. "Was your childhood unhappy?"

"No, not terribly, but it wasn't filled with a lot of maternal warmth, either."

"But your father seems to be a warm, loving sort of man."

Drew laughed. "Until Randi came along he would have bitten your head off for saying that. He was a manly man doing manly things in a manly manner."

"What does that even mean?" Meilin wrinkled her nose and crossed her eyes. It was incredibly adorable, and he wanted to kiss her nose.

"He was the quintessential English gentleman. He went shooting, taught me to play polo—although neither of us are especially good at it—fishing on the pond, things like that. Whenever we were out of sight of Bea—that's my birth mum—he'd let me run and yell like a hooligan. When she was around, we had to do the stiff upper lip thing. I wasn't allowed to get dirty, run, or make a mess."

"Mixed messages."

"Undoubtedly, but that was childhood for many of my friends. Especially those chosen for me by my mother and her friends in the upper crust."

Meilin bumped his shoulder. "Poor little rich boy." A sparkle of mischief lit up her eyes.

"Ha! It wasn't the same for you?"

"To some extent, maybe, but I was taught to honor our humble roots, the ancestors who suffered and worked to build a new life for future generations. There are photos of our great-grandfathers working the gold fields, the railroad, their first carts selling vegetables. Later the carts became grocery stores and restaurants. They worked until their fingers bled and their backs bent to make things better for their children and grandchildren. Then their children worked to improve and build upon those sacrifices so now we can say we helped build Chinatown, and brought our people into the mainstream."

A breeze wafted down the path and lifted a fringe of Meilin's hair. Drew forgot about the stories of the past and found himself reaching to brush the wayward strands from her face. The back of his finger touched soft skin and a rush of lust swept over him from head to toe.

Meilin's gaze softened more as she looked back at him, her breath hitched in her throat. The longing in her eyes matched what filled his heart.

He wanted nothing more than to lean down and kiss her. Her hand shifted on her lap and a shaft of light from a street lamp caught by the stone in her ring stabbed him in the eye. Damn. He didn't poach. Had never wanted to before.

He blew out a frustrated breath. Then opened his mouth and the words came tumbling out of their own free will. "Do you feel it too?" he whispered. "Do you feel what I'm feeling? The overriding urge to pull you into my arms and kiss you until we both burn to ash?"

Meilin swallowed, and he saw the pulse beating in the delicate hollow of her throat. "We can't..."

"But you want to, don't you? I want to." More than he wanted air at the moment.

Her lips flattened and stress drove her voice up a few notes. "That has no bearing. I made a promise. Signed a contract." The anguish in her eyes clawed at him, fueled a desperation unlike any he'd ever felt before.

"You're not married yet." His own heart hammered in his chest.

"I will be. In three months."

So soon? Damn. "Does he take your breath away like you take mine?"

Meilin's eyes grew sad, and she slowly shook her head. "That doesn't make it right. There's so much more to consider."

It would have been better to stand up and walk away than ask the question burning inside. "Do you love him?"

Her hair swayed as she shook her head. "No. I don't know him well enough to love him."

A thread of tension loosened in his chest. "But you know me. I know you."

Meilin broke their eye contact and tried to laugh. Wasn't much of one, more of a sob really, or so it sounded to him. "I don't know you; you don't know me. We've met, what, only three times now? There hasn't been time to know each other."

"Your heart knows. You don't love him, but it's possible there could be more, right here. There's something here, right between us."

Meilin stood and paced a few steps away, distancing herself from him. "No. Don't imagine what can't be."

"Why can't it be?"

"If I'd met you months ago, maybe we'd have time to work this out. But it's too late. I'm committed. You're committed here and then you're off to Beijing in a matter of weeks and for how many years? You're just starting your life, Drew. I've worked hard to establish myself, my reputation, my business. My mother tells me my biological clock is winding down. If I'm to have children and raise them before I'm using a walker, I need to do this now. I can't wait more than a couple years."

Was that all? In truth, what she said had merit, but it was just a detail. Details could be worked out. "Who says you have to?"

She spun on her heel and drilled her hot gaze into his eyes. "You don't understand. I'm ten years older than you! I'll be wrinkled and gray haired when you hit your prime in business and in life. If I wait any longer to get married and start a family as duty proclaims, I'll have trouble keeping up with my children. I'll be in a retirement home about the time they're having babies. I'll be well into my fifties by the time they reach college. My mother tells me she'll be too old to care for young grandchildren in another five years." She waved a hand. "As it is, my father is too old to get down on the ground and play with the young children of my brother and cousins. The look on his face is heart breaking when he wants to play horse with them."

"This is about our age differences? I don't care about your age. It doesn't mean a thing to me."

Facing him head on, she stood straight, hands clenched at her sides. "Because you're still young enough to spring out of bed and go-go-go until long after the sun goes down. Come ten o'clock at night I'm ready to close my eyes and drop dead to the world."

"You weren't asleep at ten o'clock the night we met."

Shoulders slumping, she sighed. "And the next day was excruciating. I had a hangover and bad attitude until nearly four o'clock, and it drove my mother crazy because I was supposed to be excited about the engagement party."

"Had you been excited, your attitude would have been better from the moment you woke. Have you considered you were dreading the party and what it meant?"

"Of course I have," she snapped. "But that's not what I agreed to. I agreed to be the loyal wife of a good man who looks after his employees and his community. I agreed to stand by his side and take part in those good works, many of which I'm already involved in. Like you were raised to have a hand in your family business, I was raised to have a hand in my community as a good wife."

Hands splayed, palms up, he adopted what he thought was a calm, reasonable, demeanor. "You can be a good wife anywhere you land."

"This is where my life is now." One finger pointed at the ground with a stabbing motion. "What are you saying? You want me to uproot and follow you to Beijing?" Disbelief filled her eyes as she threw up her hands.

Drew ran frustrated hands through his short hair. "Would that be so bad? I want to spend time with you. Here. Now. I don't want to worry about your fiancé. I wish he didn't exist so you and I would have time to spend getting to know one another. Find out if what we feel now can grow into something more. Is it just a surface thing? I don't think so, but with your engagement, we don't even have a chance to explore and find out." Maybe if he squeezed his head hard enough he'd find a solution. A way to put her engagement into neutral. Delay the wedding. Permanently.

"Look." He hated her deflated posture, the sad finality in her voice. "It's an impossible situation. I like you, Drew. I do. But I'm committed and I don't see any way out of it." With slumped shoulders she stood before him, sadness weighing her down.

Instinct to comfort pushed him to his feet. Before she could step back from him, he gently wrapped his hands around her slender arms. "Okay. That escalated fast. Far faster than I ever intended. More than anything, I want to be your friend. Can we be friends?" He bent his knees to stoop low enough to meet her gaze. "Please?"

Meilin hesitated a beat, then nodded. "Friends."

Chapter 16

Drew wanted to be the kind of friends who hugged and kissed. While endearing enough to make her smile even as she shook her head, Meilin knew it was destined to cause her grief.

Knowing it and living with it were two different beasts. After a sweet kiss good night, they'd parted outside the building, Drew insisting she go inside first so he'd know she was safe. Five minutes later she'd heard his footsteps in the hall outside her room in the dormitory. Sleep came slowly and filled with dreams of taking Drew around China, seeing Beijing, the countryside, walking the Great Wall. All while laughing, hugging, and kissing.

Upon waking, she felt as if she'd hardly slept a wink, so when she went to breakfast and found him bright and cheerful as a daisy at the table, laughing, teasing, and joking with anyone nearby, she wanted to smack him. The female students, and a few of the teachers, took note of his handsome face and flirted with him. He reminded her of a mischievous toddler. Much like Jack had been as a young child. It amazed her that she'd never actually taken time to wonder why the two were friends.

In class, his energy filled the room. The students worked harder at their vocabulary, even made some progress with pronunciation. Arnie would be pleased when he returned in the morning.

In the middle of a lesson he interrupted. "Teacher-san."

"Put down your hand, Mr. Robinson. Have you been reading *Sho-Gun*? In case you've forgotten, *san* is a Japanese term and we're here to learn Chinese." It just about killed her to keep a straight face. Severe was too much to ask for.

"Many pardons. I was wondering if courtship rituals will be a part of our cultural lessons."

"I don't know. Take it up with your regular teacher when he returns tomorrow. I assume the subject will be touched upon to some extent. It is almost a sure thing you may be invited to a social event while in Beijing, particularly if you stay more than a year or two."

Unfortunately, that set off a whole storm of questions, especially from the women.

"How are courtships conducted?"

"What is the general feeling about mixed race marriages in China?"

"Is it true men outnumber women by nearly twenty to one? I've heard polyandry—one wife, many husbands—marriages are becoming popular due to the shortage of women. Is this true?"

The questions kept coming for a solid fifteen minutes until Meilin held up her hands. "Enough. This is not part of our lesson plan, and it is entirely possible some of these questions will be answered in units down the road. May we please return to our scheduled lesson?"

It was impossible to miss the twinkle in Drew's eyes. The sneaky rat. If she set him up with Junlei, Ping, or Yauhua, would that distract him? Then again, it might take all three of her friends to keep him busy enough to stop him from planning more mischief with her. As it was, Arnie would be back tomorrow. She just had to make it through today. Less than eight hours and she'd be driving back to her apartment, getting ready for the week ahead—a week so busy she wasn't sure where she'd fit in dinner with Shan, much less see her parents, grandmother, or buy a new dress for the Schultz's house warming party to show off the newly decorated apartment.

Because the afternoon lesson included history, the question of romance came up again. This time she wrote five different characters on the white board. "Your homework is to find the definition to match these. I expect you all to turn in a paper with one sentence per word. I'll let your teacher know to expect it."

Drew was the first to laugh while groaning. "Will you get to read them?"

Hiding a smile, she shrugged. "It's possible. If you're creative enough to impress your teacher, I'm sure he'll pass the results along."

Ah, definitely challenged. The twinkle in Drew's eyes made it hard to keep her smile hidden, but in her heart, she laughed. They wanted romance; they'd find at least three of the characters could easily be adapted to something along those lines.

* * * *

"What's with the assignment you gave them?" On Tuesday Arnie called to touch base as Meilin was straightening her desk. It had been a long day, and she wasn't headed home yet. "I suddenly have a classroom of lovesick ducks."

Leaning back in her chair, Meilin laughed. "They kept asking me about romance and courtship rituals. It seems you have a class of lovelorn romantics."

"I don't even want to know how all that got started," he grumbled. "Each time you teach, at least one student falls in love. How come I never get that?"

"Ah, cousin, you don't throw off those vibes. You're a happily married man and if some pretty young thing tries to flirt with you, it goes completely over your head."

"I'm not that old or ugly." No, but he was a little nerdy. Although she'd never tell him so.

"No, you aren't. But you're obviously off the market, and I'm sure you lay down enough homework to keep them too busy to think of seduction." After picking up a pen, she doodled on her desk blotter calendar. She'd already circled the number in the square of the night she'd met Drew. Now little hearts started showing up.

From the phone, Arnie's harrumph made her laugh.

"Still, I thank you for covering the weekend. They've asked if you'll be back."

Looking at the dates coming up, she made tentative circles around the following Tuesday, and a fainter circle around the Thursday after. She knew better than to give him a firm date now. "I may be able to fill in for you a few evenings with tutoring."

"If you like. I'm committed for the summer, so it's not like my wife expects me home for dinner every night."

"I'd say commuting to Seattle isn't easy from here. How is your father?"

"He'll live. Tina and the kids are there to help my mother, plus she's hired that health aide. It seems the health aide is the kicker. My father hates him and is determined to get well fast. Much like the bitter tea my mother makes him drink."

"Good incentive to get well."

"So, you're willing to help with tutoring in the evenings?" At the hopeful note in Arnie's voice she quietly cringed.

"When I can. Not looking good this week." Tomorrow night was the unveiling party at the Schultz's apartment and she still had to buy a dress. Shan had agreed to go with her but made her swear she wouldn't skip dinner on Thursday night. Tonight was her only chance to shop, and Ping was meeting her at Saks in an hour.

"I'll take what you can give. Thursday?"

"No. I'm sworn to have dinner with Shan."

"Ah, the poor neglected fiancé. Sorry to mess up your plans last weekend."

"We're making up for it this weekend." When she'd rather be at the school. Odd.

"I'll have to call Shan and offer my apologies. Maybe he won't be so mad at you then."

"He's not mad." Exactly. Well, yes, he was, but Arnie didn't need to know that. "Just disappointed. He's trying to court me and my schedule gets in the way. Funny, I always expected his schedule to be the issue."

Arnie laughed. "Then he doesn't know you well. I'll call him anyway. Maybe he'll be more open to you tutoring. I'm astounded at what you accomplished in two days. The improvement in the basics is amazing. They're really trying."

"I'm sure that's just a matter of getting past the first week."

"I'm not so sure of that. Can I talk you into Friday night? It will give you a chance to see the results of your assignment. You and Shan aren't leaving for wine country until Saturday, are you?"

"Let me get through the next few nights. I'll let you know Friday morning."

Arnie sighed. "Fine. As I said, I'll take what I can get. Have to run now. Lunch is over and it's time for some history and culture."

"Have fun." She laughed as she hung up.

Chapter 17

On a deep breath, Meilin took Shan's offered hand and stepped from his car. A valet hired for the night drove the car away, and holding hands, they strolled into the lobby of the building. The guard at the desk nodded as they walked by. He knew her well from the weeks of work she'd done for the Shultz's.

"I hope you enjoy tonight. My clients don't always throw a party specifically to show off the work," she said as they entered the elevator.

"I'm sure you did a beautiful job." Shan pulled her close and wrapped an arm around her waist. They were alone and he dipped his head to kiss the spot left bare behind her ear with her hair up. "Just like you did with our home."

His lips were warm, his breath a whisper. His subtle praise of her work a sorely needed balm after last week's tirade. While his touch didn't make her shiver, it sent a gentle warmth along her limbs. Warm, not hot. Loaded with possibilities for someday down the road, but not for tonight. It was possible that with a touch of alcohol she might change her mind, but she was careful to not over indulge on nights like this. After all, she was technically working. To that end she had several business cards tucked into her small clutch purse.

"You smell delicious," Shan murmured against her ear. Another spiral of warmth slid down her spine, slow and comforting, much like a fire dancing in the grate on a cold night. "Let's not stay too long, hmm?"

"I need to stay a couple hours at least. And mingle. This is a networking event for me, Shan. You know that."

He sighed and kissed her nape. "I know. But I'm not feeling very businesslike tonight. Can I help it if I just want you to myself?"

"No, I suppose not. However, please remember the purpose here. You may make some contacts yourself, but I need to network tonight."

The reflection from the polished steel doors showed Shan's frown. "Have pity on me, woman. I've been thwarted almost at every turn since our engagement."

"I know, and I'm sorry. There will be times your business interrupts plans, so I ask for reciprocal patience."

"Of course." Although his words agreed, he still didn't smile. He just scowled less.

The door opened and it was easy to tell where the party was. Laughter and music came from a doorway down the long hall. The Shultz's had a corner condo with gorgeous views of the Golden Gate and Bay bridges.

At the door, Meilin paused, both hands holding her clutch low in front of her. When Herr Shultz, a robust man who worked at the German Consulate, saw her, she gave him her most modest smile. At his loud announcement that the star of the moment had arrived, she bowed her head. Exactly as her mother had taught her. Frau Shultz, a good twenty years younger than her husband, exclaimed and rushed to take Meilin by the arm and lead her to the center of the room. Chattering a mile a minute, she gushed over the reactions they'd had so far. Everyone loved Meilin's work. Especially how she'd managed to work an authentic Black Forest cuckoo clock into the design with other touches of home tucked in with furniture, fabrics, and rugs from other countries and continents. It took a minute, but the Shultz's noticed Shan and Meilin introduced him as her fiancé.

"Oh the poor men of San Francisco!" Herr Shultz exclaimed to a round of chuckles and twitters from the guests. "A great beauty has been removed from the marriage market."

"You must be so very proud of her," Frau Shultz said to Shan. "A beautiful woman with such great talent. I hope you don't stick her in the kitchen, constantly pregnant and changing diapers!" She laughed at her own witticism, and Meilin inwardly cringed even as she caught Shan's extra polite smile. One that made her cold. The kind of smile a polite person used with people he considered beneath him.

Yes, the German's were a tad crude, earthy perhaps in a way she wasn't used to, but they weren't bad people. And their money spent as well as anyone else's. For what they'd paid for the design, they deserved her best. And if that meant overlooking their unsolicited advice, then so be it.

"Of course I'm proud." Shan's arm tightened around her waist, making his possession clear to any who watched. "She has the choice to work or not. While we believe in the traditional family values, we're modern enough to believe in a partnership."

Meilin nearly choked on his declaration. After the captain of the ship speech, his suggestion last week that she close her business, and how inconsequential her work was in comparison to his, now he was telling strangers he believed marriage was a partnership? Staring at the floor was the only way she could hide her shock.

"Ach. 'Tis a lovely thing in theory," Herr Shultz boomed. "But in practice, life is so much better when the wife is at home." That earned him a playful slap on the arm from his twittering wife.

Although his face remained neutral, Shan's body stiffened and his arm tightened. Dear Lord. Shan didn't like these people. Not that she especially liked them, but this was business, not personal.

Fortunately the party guests started crowding in and Meilin became a tour guide, showing the various elements of the design. There were even before photos for comparison and the comments were favorable. She noted with relief that Shan found people to talk to while keeping an eye on her. Not once did she see him taking in her work. No approval, no disapproval. Either reaction would have been fine, but no reaction at all? Did he not want people to see his support of her work? Whether he took in her answers to questions, she had no idea.

After catching him either looking at his watch or glaring at the cuckoo clock for the fifth time, Meilin was ready to go two hours later. She only had a few business cards of her own left and a purse full of cards from potential clients.

With a sense of pride in a job well done, she was happy to have Shan loop her hand around his arm and escort her from the building into the soft night air. "Thank God that's over. How did you do the job without stabbing those people?" The valet arrived with his car and Shan opened the door for her.

"Shan! Really, do you honestly like every client? As long as the deal works, you don't have to be bosom buddies with them. They're clients. The job is done."

"Is it like this after every job?" he asked once they were tucked into his car and pulling away.

"No. This was an exception." Meilin sighed, truly relieved the night was over. "Most jobs are much smaller, one or two rooms instead of the entire condo or house. Usually a living room, bedroom, kitchen. Or converting a room into or from a nursery." Like his place, this had been the entire condo and had taken several weeks of planning and staged work. And had netted her a healthy profit. Enough to finally hire an additional designer full time.

"A nursery," Shan mused. "Now there's a worthy job." He gave her a smile and reached for her hand. "Come to my place tonight? We can start planning the nursery."

The comment should have thrilled her. Instead the little wine she'd drunk sloshed around her stomach along with the few bites of food she'd had. She still didn't feel a stirring of longing for a child. Was it something wrong with her, or was she not ready to make such a commitment to Shan?

"I'm tired, Shan." Not really a lie. "We have this weekend. Why don't we wait until then and make it really special?" Of course he wanted to consummate their physical relationship. She expected to do so soon, but tonight didn't feel right. Before the thought of sex without great passion hadn't really bothered her, but each time she met up with Drew, touched him, felt the bolt of physical attraction, she felt less inclined to follow through with Shan. The feelings inside her were getting more and more mixed up rather than settling down into an acceptance of how things were going to be once she married by contract.

Shan answered with a sigh, but he lifted her hand and kissed the back of it. "I'm looking forward to it. I've made a reservation at a small, very romantic hotel. I'm not letting you escape this weekend."

"And I'm looking forward to it," she rushed to reply. "I don't want to be pressured by having to get up and go to work in the morning, and Arnie wants my help with tutoring his students Friday night. I'll be ready Saturday morning to give you my full attention."

"I can live with that." He obviously wasn't happy with it, but he could deal with it. "Will I have to attend all of these open houses in the future? Those people were awful. I wanted to walk out the moment we walked in."

Meilin hoped he wouldn't attend, especially not if he was going to stand around making his impatience known. "No. You can pick and choose which ones might interest you. But I can't skip them when my clients want to show off."

"It's not that I don't support your work…"

"No, no. I understand how tedious these affairs can be. A lot of standing around, talking to strangers, listening to them try to impress us with their knowledge of art or whatever, when truly they have terrible taste and worse manners."

Shan's teeth gleamed in the ambient light from the streetlamps they passed. "You were very good with them. But even I can recognize a Ming vase and not mistake it for Tang Dynasty."

Meilin forced a laugh. "I hope so, considering your mother has one of each in her living room."

"Now you know how far my interest in decorating goes. Or doesn't. As long as there will never be a Black Forest cuckoo clock in our home, I feel safe in letting you do as you wish."

"No cuckoos, I promise." She actually agreed with him on that point, although some of those clocks were amazing works of art. Too bad the Shultz's hadn't been. But it had been a wedding gift, therefore it was important to them, which made it an important piece of the design.

"I might be convinced to put an elegant grandfather clock in the foyer, but no little birds popping out or miniature figures drinking beer spinning about."

"I swear to you, only the most tasteful items will be displayed."

Shan kissed her hand again. "Thank you."

Miraculously Shan found a parking spot in front of her building. He climbed from the car, opened her door, helped her out, and escorted her to the door tucked into an alcove off the street. "Invite me up for a night cap? I promise to stay no longer than an hour."

She really didn't want to, his manners hadn't been much better than her clients', but in the interest of payback for making him endure the evening, she handed him her set of keys. "One hour. I have a busy day tomorrow."

Shan easily opened the door and followed her in with a hand on her lower back. He didn't say anything, but she saw him holding back a sneer at the sight of the small lobby. A large mirror hung on the wall to the right and under it stood a large table where the mailman left the things that wouldn't fit in the small mail boxes—magazines, newspapers, and small parcels.

She took a moment to scan the pile and picked out a design magazine with her name on it. Then he followed as she mounted the stairs and began the climb to her third floor apartment.

Chapter 18

"Now I know why you have such great looking legs," Shan said. "And such a beautiful ass."

She stopped on the stairs and turned with a gasp. "Shan!"

He looked up from two steps down. "What? It's very beautiful, just like the rest of you."

A heat flush crawled up her body. "Do you kiss your mother with that mouth?"

He laughed. "I do. And I'll kiss you and your beautiful ass, all over, with this very same mouth."

Flustered, she turned and continued climbing, well aware of where his eyes rested. Her brother might have talked like that when they were teenagers, but generally the men around her held those comments to themselves. Even past lovers had kept that kind of language from crossing their lips around her.

No, she wasn't a stranger to cursing. Why did she feel like such a prude over his simple use of the word ass? Why did that word coming from his mouth feel like the worst obscenity? Trying to push the issue away, she continued up and around to the last flight to her floor. Used to the steps, she wasn't breathing hard, just a little heavier than usual. Shan wasn't winded in the least. At the top he caught up to her and placed a hand on her hip. The same large, warm hand slipped to rest on one butt cheek, startling her enough she nearly dropped her key ring as she unlocked the door.

Now that she had him here, at her apartment door, she didn't want to allow him in. But there was that damn engagement. How should an engaged woman act? No, she wasn't in love, not even in lust, but there were protocols. A prescribed way she should act. Despite the fact he'd agreed to wait until their weekend away, she wondered if he'd push the issue tonight. Any other normal couple would be forgetting about the promise of a drink and looking forward to embracing.

Kissing.

Undressing.

Making love.

Two bodies meeting, joining, seeking the ultimate release. That would be normal.

They stepped into the apartment, the foyer really little more than a rug with a small table against the wall to the left at the start of the short hallway to the bathroom, the living room directly in front. She set her clutch and magazine on the table. Shan stood close, his arm brushing her shoulder as he closed the door. Now his breathing sounded a little increased. The heat from his body covered her back. He stepped closer, both hands now on her hips.

Breathless from the sudden tension in the air, she peeked up at their reflection in the mirror over her table. Shan's dark eyes met hers and she saw them looking truly together for the first time. They looked good together, the perfect modern Chinese-American couple. Her ivory silk dress a perfect foil to his dark wool suit. They could have just come from City Hall on their wedding day, if one were being fanciful.

Their image might have looked newlywed, but she didn't feel it. Instead of anticipating their first night alone, she trembled for an entirely different reason. For the first time she questioned Shan's intentions as a gentleman. Especially since he pressed closer against her back, trapping her between him and the tiny table.

His stare never left her gaze in the mirror. Slowly, he pressed closer yet, his dark brown eyes dilating to nearly full black as his body, hard in every way, touched her from shoulders to thighs. He wanted her. Of course he did. He'd chosen her to be his wife. Now he was reinforcing the message. His hands slid from her hips around to meet over her stomach. The muscles of her abdomen fluttered under his hands. Shan's gaze intensified.

"I said I'd wait." He paused as a gasp escaped from her. "I'll wait. But you have to know, it's about killing me. It's no secret I want you." One hand pressed low on her stomach, letting her know he was aware of her reaction. "I won't press you tonight, not unless you say you want me to."

Meilin swallowed deeply again and opened her mouth to speak, only she didn't know what to say. "I'm..." Words failed her as her brain tried to find them.

Gaze not leaving hers, he dipped his head and touched his lips to the tiny spot behind her ear. "You bewitch me, Meilin. I don't mind the chase. I enjoy the tension, but like a spring wound too tight, at some point the tension will break. I'm not to the breaking point... yet." With a slow, subtle thrust of his hips he let her know how tightly he was wound at the moment. "But soon, Meilin. Soon. This tension needs some relief."

Again her mouth opened only to be empty of words. Shan's gaze narrowed, his chest expanded with the deep lungful of air he drew in. A decision was reached, she saw it in his eyes a heartbeat before he turned her in his arms, removing the reflection and replacing her view with the real thing, much closer.

His head lowered again, his stare held fast to hers. His warm breath fanned her face a whisper before his lips touched hers. "Soon."

The kiss hardly took her by surprise, but all the same she wasn't prepared for it. What had she been imagining? A buss on the cheek? A simple peck on the lips? It was ludicrous to think she could avoid the carnality of this kiss forever.

Warm and soft, his lips touched her. She had a breath to get used to it, and then he pressed closer. Urging her mouth to open, one large hand captured her by the nape, the other slid from her hip to her rear, cupping, pulling, encouraging her body to melt into line with his, settling her curves to his hard planes. Half her mind noted the physical sensations, the taste of his tongue as it touched hers, the firm yet gentle hold of his hands on her body, the scent of his cologne overlying the scent of his skin. None of it was unpleasant. None of it was intoxicating.

The half of her brain not involved in cataloging sensations jumped into an inner dialogue. *Yep, he wants you. Nice to know you're still attractive. Especially to a man like him.* She'd seen other women look him over, and send him coy smiles and come hither glances. Shan was a good looking guy. He exuded wealth and control. Refinement. The power that came with the best business contacts. All things attractive to the female of the species. The fact he'd chosen her should have impressed the hell out of her. Well, it did. In a way. Just not in the way he obviously expected. Yes, she was impressed as all get out. She just wasn't turned on at the high level setting. Not the way she should be. Instead of high heat like on her stove, she was more on medium heat. Maybe a smidge above.

Definitely not on deep fry, broil, or full rolling boil.

Oh, she supposed making love with Shan would be pleasant and, really, that should be enough to build a long marriage on. Everyone knew passion that flared too hot, too fast, burned out too soon. So yes, she could probably work up enough excitement to have a decent sex life with Shan.

Good Lord she was confused. Could she be anymore conflicted about this man? Or the one with eyes so blue she thought of swimming in a mountain pool? Where did her heart lie? It was a question she had to figure out soon. Very soon.

Shan lifted his mouth enough to change the angle a little. He murmured her name, his hands tightening, pulling her closer as he sealed his mouth to hers once more. Going deeper, his tongue swept the inside of her mouth, his breathing growing increasingly ragged. Her senses aligned with his and she did her best to respond, sliding her hands up his chest to his shoulders. Strong shoulders covered by fine wool. While her tongue dueled with his, she moved her hands up around his neck, spearing into the thick, short hair as soft as a shaved beaver pelt. He really did smell good. Much better than most of the men she'd dated in the past. His scent reminded her of home. Warm, slightly spicy, exotic in a blend of Chinese perfumes and clean male skin. His cologne or aftershave was very similar to one her brother used.

God. She was kissing her fiancé and thinking of her brother. Now that was messed up. Shan's hand moving from her butt up her side distracted her from that line of thought. Thank God. Other than her father or grandfather, the very last person she should be thinking of at a time like this was her brother. She should be thinking about sex. The way she'd been thinking about it when she'd kissed Drew. Now there was a man to turn a woman's mind to making love.

No! No, no, no. She wasn't going to think about the tall Englishman while kissing Shan. Groaning with disgust at herself, she broke from the kiss and let her head fall back. Not that Shan noticed anything was wrong. No, his lips glided across her cheek to her ear and the tender spot behind it. From there he kissed downward, the tip of his tongue leaving a trail of small, moistened dots down her throat. Of course he thought her groan was one of desire inspired by him, his kisses, his touch on her body. A touch that grew bolder with each passing second. The hand that had been holding her nape dropped to her shoulder blades while the other hand brushed at the outer curve of her breast, his thumb sweeping along the underside, learning her shape. She only had time for a gasp before that very thumb brushed over her peaking nipple. The shock of his touch shot through her body. It had been so long since anyone had touched her that way her body reacted on pure instinct without her permission.

She'd never thought of herself as that kind of woman. One who could make love with one while thinking of another. This was wrong. She forced her hands back down to his shoulders and pushed. It was like pushing against an immoveable wall.

"Shan," she said, not expecting her voice to betray her too. It had come out far too soft, too much like a whimper of need, not shame.

"I'm here, *ai ren*." His mouth closed on her skin, just above her collarbone, sucking, licking.

Great, now he was calling her beloved in Chinese. "Shan." Much stronger that time. "Don't."

"I won't stop, baby. I promise. I'm yours to have anytime you want." The heated words brushed over her skin as her head tilted sideways, sending entirely the wrong message.

She tried again. "No." Once more she pushed at his shoulders, their bodies too close for her to press against his chest. "Stop."

Shan grew still, his breath sawing in and out, sending warm breezes over the newly dampened skin, raising goose bumps. "What?"

"Stop. Please."

A new tension tightened his arm at her back and the hand now covering her breast. "Why? I thought…"

Desperately she searched for a reason that wouldn't piss him off. Something like *I don't really want you. I was thinking of someone taller and blond.* "Too fast." Did her voice have to sound so wispy? So breathy?

It took him some effort, obviously he didn't want to submit to her demand, but slowly the tension eased from his body. His hold gentled. A sigh ghosted over her face as he raised his head, eyes heavy with a desire so strong it nearly weakened her knees. The hand holding her breast slipped away with one last fleeting brush of his thumb over her traitorous nipple before slipping down her side to her waist.

Much safer. The breath she'd been holding escaped as a sigh. Instead of stepping back, Shan pulled her into a hug, his other hand rising to cup her head and hold it against his shoulder. Both of them fought to control their breathing.

"Right." The word disturbed the hair at her temple and the shudder that wracked his body took the last of the passionate tension from his body as a new tension replaced it. "Too fast. You're right. But you can hardly blame me. The way you responded, damn, Meilin. You're driving me wild. It's going to be so good between us."

Weak with relief—he could have so easily pressed the issue, ignored her words—she accepted his hug, resting her head against him. Without agreeing with him, she hummed a little. Just enough to let him know she'd heard him.

"I guess I'd better go. My self control isn't very strong." Shan kissed the top of her head. "Dinner tomorrow night." It wasn't a question. It was a confirmation of a commitment.

"Yes. I'll be ready by six thirty. Do you want me to meet you there?" His hand relaxed enough she could lift her head.

"I'll pick you up. I'll call when I'm outside if I can't get a miracle parking spot like tonight." He kissed her lightly, a mere pressing of his lips to hers. "I can hardly wait for this weekend."

"Mmmm." She let her hum give a noncommittal response. One he interpreted as agreement if the heat in his eyes was anything to go by.

"Wear something tasteful but sexy tomorrow. I want to show you off." He gave her another soft kiss, then stepped back, letting her go and opening the door. "I want the world to know you're mine now."

The smile she forced on her lips was weak. Only the role she'd chosen to play kept her at the door, watching him stride toward the stairs where he looked over his shoulder at her before heading down.

Too tired to slam the door, she closed it quietly to keep from disturbing her neighbors. Now Shan thought she was falling in love with him. However, it wasn't his dark eyes she saw as she leaned against the door. It was a sea of blue that filled her vision, and she had no idea what to do about it.

She was so in trouble.

Chapter 19

Drew stared at the door of the cafeteria. Over the past week the lessons had been a bit clearer, but no less difficult. It had been harder to concentrate not knowing for sure whether he'd see Meilin again anytime soon. Then this afternoon his teacher had mentioned she was coming tonight. The whole class had perked up at that. Not that they didn't like Professor Chung, but Meilin had provided a different touch. One they all responded to. And in the back of his mind he'd kept wondering if she'd get to see the homework she'd assigned. Five sentences.

Once they'd matched the characters to the words, the whole class had laughed. Love. Heart. Family. Cat. House. It had been hard forming short sentences that didn't give him away. Things along the lines of, *My heart wants to form a family with you in a house of love with a cat.* Although he'd prefer a dog. Then again, he didn't really care if it meant spending time with her. A pet wouldn't matter in the least.

All week the catering staff had spent one day on a menu pertaining to each culture in the school. Monday had been Chinese. Tonight was Italian. He'd liked German night, and Russian hadn't been bad. Indian night had been a little bland, the curry not up to the spiciness he was used to. So far Italian was pretty typical with spaghetti and garlic bread with a green salad. He was looking forward to the dessert table where it looked as if they'd tried to make tiramisu. Gelato would have been better, but the summer heat seemed to defy the attempts to serve such a large number. Rumor had it tomorrow was Japanese day.

He could only hope Meilin would show up in time for dessert.

"Hey, what's with you?" One of his classmates nudged his shoulder, bringing his attention back to the group. "You've been dancing in your chair like you've got ants in your pants."

Drew snorted and swirled his fork in the long strands of pasta smothered in red sauce. "Just been a long week," he told Bob, a thirty-something exec from New York who was headed to China to take over IT operations for his company.

"Only two down. Eight to go. No point in getting stressed out this early in the game."

"Just looking forward to a little time with the family." Dad and Mum were only in California for another week before heading back to London. He'd talked with them every few days, had taken a walk over to his apartment last night to hang out with Birdie for an hour, so he'd had some breaks. No way was he confessing his desire to see Meilin. Birdie had taken off this afternoon to go home for the weekend. That meant their apartment was empty. Was it possible to convince Meilin to go there with him tonight? He wanted as many stolen hours of privacy with her as he could get.

Yeah, and he was a bastard for wanting to distract her from her engagement. A right rotten sod. The irony didn't escape him that he'd be pissed as hell if he were engaged to her and another man was trying to make off with her. In this case, he was the outsider, the other man, the one trying to cuckold another. Wrong in every way except how much he wanted her.

Yeah, he was as dishonorable as a highwayman. He nearly laughed at the vision of himself dressed in boots, breeches, full sleeved shirt, long coat, mask, and tricorn hat, riding up on his black charger to rob the coach of the well-dressed lady inside. She'd be wearing voluminous skirts that would billow out as he plunked her down on his horse and rode off into the night with her captured in his arms. Guess he'd read *The Beggar's Opera* too many times. He was as bad as his sister, who loved the historical romances where some masked man swept the beautiful heiress off to a life of decadence and debauchery, only to find himself tamed by the lady and reformed to living a life of decency with wicked depravity confined to the four walls of their Mayfair bed chamber.

Oh he was a gentleman all right. A large drop of spaghetti sauce dripped from his pasta and made a splodge on his light blue polo shirt. Yeah. A right proper gent.

"Oh dear." A small hand reached over his shoulder to the center of the table and grabbed a wad of paper napkins.

Damn. Meilin. It just figured she'd show up the second he made a spectacle of himself.

He dropped his fork and accepted the napkins while she greeted each student. She took the open chair to his right, and he could feel her scent going directly to his brain.

"You have another spot," she said.

He shot her a sideways glance and caught her smile. At least she wasn't full out laughing. Trust him to lose his cool and make an idiot out of himself in front of her. Hadn't happened since he was six and got caught throwing cake at a neighbor's granddaughter during a tea party turned tiny food fight. The humiliation suffered that day had taught him to be very, very careful in social situations. He'd worked very hard to evolve into the suave and sophisticated man his mother had expected him to be. Although he hadn't liked her methods, more than once he'd reluctantly acknowledged the value of her lessons. California's relaxed ways must be rubbing off for him to let down his guard enough to make a splash of red sauce all over his shirt.

He dunked one of the napkins in his water glass and set about trying to sop up the stain. Stains. Hell, he'd be better off just buying a new shirt.

"Give it to me before I leave tonight. I'll get the stains out," she murmured, then turned her head away to answer a question from one of the female students a few seats around the table.

She'd clean his shirt? Still scrubbing, he gave her another glance and imagined towing her up to his room and stripping off the shirt there. Would she notice the thousands of crunches he'd done when he couldn't make it to the gym? The tan he'd cultivated since arriving in this warm climate? With a flash of heat, he remembered her half-lidded eyes as she took in his shirtless torso once he'd changed into swim togs at the party week before last. Shifting as something else started to take note of her presence and his fantasies, he tried to blot up the excess of water now soaking two parts of his shirt. Damn, that was cold against his skin.

Janice from across the table loaded her dishes onto a tray. "Anyone else ready for coffee and dessert?"

To Drew's left, Bob stood. "I'll help you. How many want dessert?"

Every hand rose. Even Cindy, their resident teenager at barely nineteen.

"Coffee?" Janice asked.

No one put their hands down. "Right. I'll bring back cream and sugar."

"Don't forget the forks and spoons," Dave called after them.

Cindy rolled her eyes. "Come on, big guy, the least we can do is clear the decks." She started stacking plates on her tray while Dave groaned. But he moved and started collecting trays and utensils. In a minute the table was clear, leaving Drew alone with Chung and Meilin.

"So," he ventured. "Did Teach over there pass on our homework to you?"

Meilin grinned. "He did. You all did a very good job. Did it take long?"

"Only two nights," Drew said with a groan. "We did learn how to use the Chinese to English dictionary going both directions."

Two seats to Drew's left the professor chuckled and drained his water glass. "I'm not sure I want to know what prompted those particular characters, but I must say you were all very creative. Especially you, Mr. Robinson. Makes one wonder at the type of upbringing you had over there in Merry Old England."

"Oh, it was very typical of an over-privileged Sussex youth. Loaded with tales of knights and their heroic acts, highway robbers and heiresses, lords and ladies of the court. My father once told me Winnie the Pooh had come through our woods hunting for honey. The search for the bear and the bee hive filled the better part of one summer." Until his mother had caught on and told him no such thing could ever happen. Odd, now that he thought about it, his father had been the one to read the better bedtime stories. The nannies had kept a wide selection on hand, and Dad had picked the most adventurous of the lot.

"I'm more curious about your upbringing." Drew split his glance between the two. "You both spent time in China. What was it like?"

"You'll find out when we get there in a few weeks." Professor Chung waved a hand. "As American born, we were never fully recognized for our Chinese heritage. We're still Americans to them, wouldn't you agree, Meilin?"

She nodded. "I do agree. Even being raised bilingual didn't help so much. I was better at listening, not so good at speaking. The Aunties and Uncles constantly reminded me, but at the end of two years they professed to be sad to see me go. They said I was almost like a Chinese." The two of them laughed.

"Pretty much the same for me, but I was much younger when I went to live with relatives. I hated that my parents sent me away, but living in a smaller town really perfected my language ability."

"Now people in Chinatown think he was Chinese born." Meilin teased him with a twinkle in her eyes. "How did the week go?" she asked Drew.

"Pretty well. I'm still not sure I'll ever really get the hang of it, but I'm recognizing a little more. Pronunciations are killing me."

Professor Chung laughed. "The English accent might be hindering you a bit, but as you speak with the accent of the upper social class, it's not as bad as if you'd been raised speaking Cockney or Welsh."

"Or Aussie," Meilin added.

"That darn Eton, paying off again," Drew joked.

"What's the joke?" Dave asked over their chuckles as he approached with a tray containing a few coffee mugs, sugar, and cream. Bob followed him with another loaded tray of mugs and a carafe. The ladies followed with trays holding plates of dessert.

"Oh," Meilin said. "It all looks delicious. Glad I didn't have dessert tonight."

"Did you get dinner?" Drew asked.

"Drive-through. Egg rolls, crab rangoon, fried shrimp, and barbeque pork with a steam bun."

"Didn't know you could get anything other than burgers or tacos from a drive-through," Chung said.

"New place. Not bad. A little dried out, but easier to eat than noodles while driving."

Next time he went out clubbing, Drew decided, he'd try it out.

"Field trip," Janice said.

Coffee and dessert were passed around, and the professor led them back into speaking simple Chinese.

Eventually they moved back to the classroom to escape the noise of many other languages being practiced. The tonal sounds of Chinese were best learned in a quiet room without the competition of all the others. Although Meilin spent her time also helping Bob and Janice, she sat close to Drew. Close enough he was tormented by her perfume and the soft quality of her voice slowly repeating the vocabulary words they'd been given that morning.

Drew almost cursed his parents for not putting him in a bilingual school from the time he was three. Almost. But who would have guessed then he'd need to learn Chinese? French, Spanish, and a little Italian had been a part of his school years, all of them close enough to make learning one more a little easier. But Chinese? What had ever gotten into his head?

Near ten o'clock a large yawn stole over him. Shaking his head to clear it, he looked up to see everyone else trying to hide their yawns.

"Enough," the professor declared. "It's late, you've all studied hard this week. We won't start until ten tomorrow. Get yourselves out for a walk, run, bike ride, or sleep in, but get some down time. We'll pick it up then and tomorrow afternoon I have some language videos. We'll get some culture in while letting you hear the words spoken slowly enough you may understand it."

"No closed caption subtitles, eh?" Cindy laughed.

"Only in Chinese," Chung quipped and was answered by good-natured groans.

Drew groaned because it meant saying good night to Meilin, again. With his eyes, he asked if he could walk her out. She nodded slightly and finished packing her briefcase before turning toward the door.

Excitement tore through him and suddenly he felt as if he could leap tall buildings. No, it wasn't pure imagination. This woman meant something special to him. He only had to find a way to make her accept and act on the attraction between them.

Piece of cake.

Chapter 20

With Drew a few steps behind her, Meilin exited the building. At her car, she unlocked the door, and Drew took her briefcase and tossed it inside.

"Come for a walk. It helps clear the mind after a long day."

She'd just opened her mouth to protest when her phone rang. "Excuse me." It was Shan's ringtone, and if she didn't answer, well, she wasn't sure she wanted to face an annoyed Shan in the morning.

"Hello?"

"Oh good, you're awake," he said. "After my fuss about you canceling on me last weekend, I really hate to do this…"

"You have to cancel this weekend?" She peeked up to see Drew grinning from ear to ear.

"Yes," Shan said heavily. "Believe me, I'm extremely unhappy about this, but…well. No point in whining about it. I need to fly out tonight. Don't suppose you could drive me to the airport?"

Meilin cringed and put an apology in her voice. "Arnie's study session just let out. I'm in Palo Alto. What time is your flight?" At the thought of driving home, only to turn around and make the drive to the airport and back home again… The fact remained she was already tired from the long week.

"A lot of driving so late on Friday night, and I need to leave now. I won't ask." His words were mild, but his tone held an edge.

"If you let me know when your return flight arrives, maybe I can pick you up."

"Since I don't know exactly when I'll be back, might be Monday, might be Wednesday, I'll have to get back to you on that."

"All right. Text me the details when you know. I'll do my best to be available."

Shan chuckled. "I like that last sentence. I was so looking forward to tomorrow. Tomorrow night. Sunday morning." He sighed. "The wait will make it so much sweeter. I'll change our reservations to next weekend. Will you miss me?"

"Of course. Be safe."

"For you? Always. Text me when you're home so I can leave with an easier mind."

Meilin murmured her agreement, then disconnected. Her shoulders sagged and she leaned into her car, forehead against the roof.

Large, warm hands settled on her shoulders, lightly massaging. "Bad news?"

Meilin raised her head. "Depends on how you look at it."

"Tell me."

She dropped her head back against his shoulder. "My plans for this weekend fell through. That means I can sleep in tomorrow and spend the day in my pajamas with a carton of cottage cheese, a bag of barbeque chips, and a good book."

"An odd combination. I have a better idea." He took her hand, pulled her away from the car, and shut the door. "Beep it locked, will you?"

She did as he asked, then followed as he pulled her along, taking a different path than before.

"What happened?" Drew asked, pulling her up beside him.

"Leaving town on business. Flying out tonight." A simple enough answer.

"So you're free the entire weekend?"

"Yes."

Drew grinned down at her in a way that lifted her heart and made her forget she was tired. "Have your day of indulgence, but not too indulgent. Let me take you out to dinner tomorrow night. Nothing stuffy, but something fun. When was the last time you played tourist down at Fisherman's Wharf?"

Meilin laughed. "It's been years."

"I'm dying for some fresh seafood. Also haven't had time to play down at Pier 39." Drew swung their hands between them. "What d'ya say? Sound like fun?"

"But what about class?"

"I'll take off just before dinner. That'll give us a few hours to eat and play tourist. Please? Pick you up about five-thirty? We can talk in Chinese, and that should count for study time."

She couldn't help it. Drew was too adorable, too playful. When was the last time she'd played? Too long, she decided, choosing to ignore her day of sailing with Shan. That hadn't been anything lighthearted as she felt with Drew. Still walking, she looked up at him from under her lashes. "Tell me what you're thinking."

"Maybe get a snack first from a street vendor, work our way up one side and down the other of Pier 39, then meander over to Alioto's for some crab and shrimp. We'll finish off the evening with a stroll along the waterfront. No set destination, no agenda, just wander where we want like real tourists. If we had all day, I'd love to take the Alcatraz tour, but…"

"If we went Sunday, we could have the whole day. If you can spare the time from your studies, that is."

"And you'd get your day of down time." Drew looked ahead, as if seeing something in his mind. "Okay, it's a deal. I pick you up at ten on Sunday. We'll do the whole day." He focused on her once again. "For now, I want to show you a spot I know."

It wasn't far. Around a bend, behind a building dark for the summer, they approached a small grove of trees and bushes. And in one dark corner, a bench so private it was easy to believe they were entirely alone.

"What do you want to talk about?" she asked.

"Nothing special." He put an arm around her shoulder and pulled her close to his side. It felt so perfect; she wondered if it was true two people could be specially made for each other. "Maybe I just want to be here with you. Did you ever think about that?"

She couldn't resist his grin or the sparkle in his eyes. "You're a bad influence."

"But in a good way, I hope."

Meilin chuckled and rested her head on his shoulder. "I shouldn't be here with you. Shouldn't be making plans."

"Stop the guilt train right there. We're just spending time together. Being friends."

"I don't usually cuddle on dark secluded benches with my friends."

"Neither do I, but we're a different kind of friend to each other. We can talk about dreams, plans, silly politicians, or last week's art show. You can tell me about your latest job, or the most exciting one waiting for you to get to it. Tell me your philosophy on life and the state of trade relations with China. I don't care. We can talk about anything or nothing."

"All right then, tell me about your favorite American thing."

"Oh, that's easy. Actually I have a short list."

"Let's hear it."

"Football, Thanksgiving dinner, sunny pools, girls in bikinis, almost anything cooked on the grill, and"—he pulled her close, staring down into her eyes—"beautiful women with jade green eyes and sweet dispositions. Now that I think about it, I have to say you're my favorite American thing."

The descent of his lips to hers was slow enough she could have pulled away. She should have pulled away. But the electromagnetic energy that had sparked between them from their first touch was in full force that night. A force that made it as natural as breathing to open her lips to his.

The kiss started slow. Lips brushing against lips. Air was exchanged, each one breathing in the other. One hand curled behind her neck, cradling the base of her skull. The other slid down between their bodies, the back of his fingers caressing her side to her hip, then thigh where he slipped his hand under and pulled her leg across his legs. With little urging, she scooted fully onto his lap, bringing her face even with his.

She brought her hands to his face, his golden stubble soft and prickly against her palms. His skin was warm to her touch, his jaw firm, his hair perfectly soft for tunneling her fingers into. The faded scent of his aftershave blended with his skin, making a perfume that was all Drew. He had the power to drug her senses and leave her feeling mellow and energized all at once.

Pulling her top loose from her skirt, his hands found the skin of her back, then front, one cupping her breast, the other loosening the hooks of her bra in back. "Drew," she said on a moan.

His hands stilled. Lips still touching hers, he quietly asked, "Stop? Or more?"

She should say stop, but instead demanded, "More."

A rush of air that sounded like a sigh of relief brushed over her lips. "As m'lady commands."

The hand cupping her breast slipped beneath the loosened bra, as his kisses moved across her cheek to her ear. She gasped when his tongue licked a secret spot just behind her ear. A rumble of approval accompanied the tilt of her head to one side giving him more access.

"You taste so good," Drew whispered.

"You feel so good," she answered, as her hands clasped his shoulders. In her sandals, her toes curled with each kiss, lick, and the gentle kneading of first one breast and then the other. Restlessly she moved against his hand, wanting more, needing something… His thumb and index finger lightly pinched one nipple, rolling and teasing as she arched her back to press closer.

His head still gripped in her hands, he dipped lower, trailing hot, wet kisses down her throat, to her shoulder. One strong hand braced her back while the other slipped the strap of her top and bra from her shoulder, tugging the cloth downward, exposing her to more attention from his hot mouth.

"There," she whispered when his lips closed around her nipple, suckling, biting, driving her crazy. Between her thighs, deep inside, heat rose so fast she squirmed a little, hoping to release the pressure, ease the ache.

Drew groaned. Oh Lord. That was him, the presence pressing up against her thigh. She'd never felt that sitting on a man's lap before.

"Easy, love. We're just doing a bit of snogging now. Not actually going to do the deed out here in the open."

"Then—oh!" The man had some moves with his tongue. "We should stop. Yes, we need to stop."

Drew lifted his head, buried his face in her shoulder, and wrapped his arms tight around her. She clung to his shoulders, wishing she'd dared to pull his shirt off.

"I know you said we need to stop, and you're right, this isn't the place, but my sister is across the bay tonight. With the parents. We could go to—"

Meilin placed a finger over his lips to stop that idea right there. "We can't. I can't."

Drew sighed and put his forehead against hers. "I know. But I can dream, can't I?"

"We can both dream, but it's not something to be acted on."

"At least you didn't say it could never happen."

Lord she wished she could. Her contract with Shan demanded she should walk away from Drew and never look back. Somehow doing so would feel like walking away from life. And that she just couldn't do. But neither could she take the path of temptation and follow him home.

It was a hell of a mess.

She'd been the good girl all her life, and what had it gotten her? Just this once she wanted to bend the rules, test her limits, live a little. And if that meant spending one day out of her planned life with a young, handsome, fun man while her fiancé was away, then that's what she'd do.

* * * *

Drew was so excited for Sunday he made Birdie come back early so he could take the car.

"You're going out with who?" Birdie asked the moment she walked through the door of their apartment.

Because he'd stayed up so late studying to make up for playing hooky today, Drew stood at the kitchen counter practically mainlining coffee.

"I'm playing tourist today in the city, and I want to pick her up like a proper gent."

"Meilin, right? Isn't she engaged?" Birdie stood at the door, hands on hips, a disapproving frown on her normally sunny face.

"She is, but he's out of town. I figure since she's a San Francisco native, she'd know the best places to see. We're playing tourist down on the waterfront. No room for getting naughty."

Birdie laughed and turned, shaking her head. "Right. Anywhere with you is a place to get naughty." Before she left the kitchen she stopped and looked over her shoulder. "Don't mess things up for her. You're leaving in a few weeks. It would be cruel to sidetrack her committed relationship, then walk away."

The reminder of how short time was twisted his gut. "Not my plan, Bird." Granted he didn't know what his plan was, entirely, but he had to go with his gut. Every instinct cried out Meilin was something extra special to him and only him.

"Yeah, well, you'd better get going. The car needs gas." She flipped her hair over her shoulder and headed down the hall to her bedroom.

With heavy sarcasm, he called after her, "Thanks, ducks!" Damn female.

Following Google and Meilin's directions, he arrived outside her building five minutes early. The only parking available within a block was right in front of the garage door that led to the lower level of the building next door, so he texted a message saying where he was illegally parked.

His phone dinged with a response: *Be right down.*

He couldn't think of a better start to a perfect day.

Meilin directed him to a parking spot a few blocks from the wharf, at a house belonging to a friend who said they could park there for the day.

The sun was bright, the breeze just enough to keep it from being too hot, the crowds thick all around. To him it felt like one big carnival with the street vendors hawking their wares, performance artists seemingly on every corner, and the general bustle around them. Alcatraz was creepy, but interesting, the boat ride there and back spectacular with the sail boats racing across the water. He loved it all and took every opportunity to take selfies of the two of them.

His favorite pictures were the ones of Meilin when she wasn't aware of him shooting them. Especially one with her face turned up to the sun, San Francisco rising behind her, the sun glinting off her glossy hair, a sublime smile on her face. He'd have that one blown up and printed for framing.

Better than the pictures were the times she snuggled against him, arm about his waist. She fit perfectly against him, and he didn't want her ever to be any place else.

They were strolling away from Pier 39 where he'd bought her a silk scarf painted in shades of red, black, and gold when she looked up at him. "You got quiet. What are you thinking?"

Hugging her closer to wind their way past a knot of people, he sniffed the air. "Thinking about dinner."

"What's for dinner?"

"Anything on the menu at Alioto's. We have about thirty minutes before our reservation."

"Mmm. Sounds wonderful. Can't remember the last time I ate there."

"Figured Sunday evening would be good as far as fewer tourists and maybe more locals."

"Possibly. Can't go wrong there."

Drew couldn't help but wonder if she was concerned about running into someone she knew there. Hadn't been the case during the day, but what about dinner out?

As they followed the maitre d', his hand lightly touching the small of her back, he wondered some more. Although she was subtle, she looked around, noting faces, but apparently not recognizing anyone. They were seated at a window looking over a marina full of small boats.

"Is this good?" he asked when they were left with menus.

She smiled. "It's perfect," she said, and waved toward the Golden Gate Bridge in the distance beyond the small forest of masts. "Sometime you'll have to have dinner at the Claremont in Berkeley. They also have a fabulous view of the bridge."

"Maybe we can do that next time."

When she smiled, his heart lifted. For someone who lived for the fun in life, he was finding there was nothing simple about this date. Whether she worried about being seen or not, he did.

"Would you rather not stay here for dinner?" he asked, wanting nothing more than to reach across the table and hold her hand.

"Only if you're uncomfortable?" The delicate brow she raised indicated she seemed to be reading his mind.

"I don't want to put you in a bad position if someone you know sees us together."

She sent him a sweet smile. "I'm not worried."

"All right then." He opened his menu, taking her at her word. If she wasn't worried, he'd not waste more time thinking about it. "What looks good to you?"

Orders placed, wine delivered, and a basket of fresh, warm sourdough bread between them, he began his gentle interrogation.

"Tell me about your family."

"What do you want to know?"

"The complete story. Mother, father, siblings, the family business, how many cousins do you really have...the usual."

"Not asking for much I see." She laughed. "Okay, the basics. Father and mother. Father, until recently, held the reins of the family business, which is a few restaurants and a restaurant supply. One brother who worked both sides of the business, is now taking over. My father has two brothers who now work for my brother. Their sons run the day to day restaurant business. More cousins work the various parts including cooking, serving, cleaning, deliveries, marketing, and purchasing. I can't give you a total count as the number grows with each marriage and birth. Many babies." She grinned. "Which is why I've never felt a need to add to the numbers. A few of us have escaped, such as Jack who is part of another branch from my father's grandfather's line. As you know, he chose law. Arnie, that would be An Cheng Chung to you, whose great grandfather was a brother to my great grandfather, chose to teach. There are a few academics down his branch. A few doctors and scientists as well."

"Sounds vast and complicated."

"Yes, very hard to track exactly how each one is related. My father can tell you, but I've chosen not to study the genealogy in depth."

"All pure Chinese descent?"

"No, not at all, although the direct line to me is. What about your family? All English gentry?"

Drew laughed. "They'd like to think so, but down the line we had a Viking who contributed the blond hair. I'm pretty sure we have a Highlander back a few centuries ago, and one great-grandmother was French. Basically Northern European to the bone."

"I think I can see the Viking raider." Meilin winked as she teased.

"If the stories are true, he was quite the character. He probably provided the travel gene that sent other ancestors across the sea to make their fortune. And spun off one rogue who came to a bad end as a highwayman."

Meilin chuckled. "I think I can see that too."

Throughout an excellent meal, they traded stories and rumors of less than arrow straight ancestors, each tale more outrageous than the last.

He'd even ventured into a few stories about working his way up inside the family business, especially a few of his bolder moves in the legal department that had set his course on law school. By the time coffee and dessert came around, his stomach ached from laughing. He couldn't remember a more fun dinner, or a more gorgeous sunset with an even prettier companion.

He saw the waiter coming and pulled out his credit card before handing it over without even looking at the bill. "Where would you like to go next?"

"I believe you mentioned something about a walk."

"Care to do it on the beach?"

Meilin laughed. "You're such a tourist. You have no idea that the beach is probably fog covered, or the wind is blowing like a gale and colder than winter."

"Maybe." Of course he hadn't had time to do much beach walking since he'd arrived in California the previous September. Hadn't even spent any of the longer breaks here but back home in Sussex. "Why don't you prove it to me?"

Chapter 21

Meilin nervously took one last look around her apartment. Shan already had her overnight bag over his shoulder as he waited for her to lock up. She finally pulled the door closed and used the key to set the deadbolt.

This weekend, twice postponed, was something of a chance to make up and get refocused, according to Shan. His business had kept him out of town a full week, and he'd spent most of it simmering because she hadn't called him back the night he flew out. Being with Drew had completely sidetracked her from her promise to let Shan know she'd made it home safe that night, and he'd had something to say about it. She just felt lucky he hadn't called while she'd been out on the town with Drew. And if anyone had seen her with him, no one had said a word to Shan. Another stroke of luck.

Shan took her hand and led her to the stairs. His excitement was palpable. Hers, not so much. Nervous energy apparently convinced Shan she was as excited as he.

"It's a perfect day for a drive. I have reservations at a place in Calistoga. There's a spa attached, so let me know if you want to indulge later this afternoon," he said.

"Oh, I don't want to interrupt your plans," she protested.

"Not an interruption." He winked at her as he pulled open the door to the sidewalk. "Indulging you, pampering you, is my focus this weekend."

Almost what she was afraid of.

Tonight was the big event.

It.

Doing it.

Shan had made it clear this weekend was about tonight and finally making love.

She wasn't ready. Especially after last night. After another tutoring session with Arnie's students, she and Drew had taken another walk.

Something that felt more and more comfortable each time they did so. It had been midnight before she made her way back home.

It had been three o'clock before she'd finally fallen asleep. Shan's call at eight had woken her from a dream of making love to Drew. It didn't take a shrink to tell her she had conflicted feelings.

Shan handed her into the car, then opened the trunk and set her bag inside before sliding behind the steering wheel. The excitement poured off him. "The weather is expected to be clear all weekend."

"Wonderful," she murmured.

Shan started the car, adjusted the volume on the radio to something low enough for conversation. He smiled at her. "This is going to be great. We're headed for Sonoma first. There's a winery I want to check out. But once we get over to Napa, just sing out if there's someplace in particular you want to visit. I'd like to stop at Mumm, but any place else is your call."

"Mumm is good." The smile she gave him in return felt weak.

Oh God. How was she going to get through this weekend? In fact, why was she even engaged to this man? She definitely wasn't ready for a weekend away, much less a lifetime, with this man. But could she really break it off? She'd been raised that once a promise had been given, it couldn't be broken. Just how heavy would the fallout be if she even brought up the subject?

Shan steered onto Park Presidio heading north toward the Golden Gate Bridge and Highway 101. Well, he was right about one thing—it was a pretty day with clear blue sky and ocean fresh air. Once on the bridge the view toward the bay was spectacular with a veritable forest of white sails on the water. A perfect day for sailing. Which brought back memories of their day on his boat. Memory of his one captain of the boat and family speech was enough to further dampen whatever enthusiasm she had for the day. At least one good thing had come of their adventure, the owner of the fishing float had contacted her and she had an appointment to meet with him and his wife later in the week.

They both opened their windows to let the fresh air blow through and Shan chatted as he drove, talking about his favorite wines, or some little shop he thought she might like. Meilin let him talk, occasionally offering a small comment. Enough to let him think she was listening.

All the while she worried.

Shan wasn't being unreasonable expecting her to have sex with him. They'd been engaged a month now. Nor was he unreasonable for expecting her to fully, and enthusiastically, participate. The trouble was, she wanted to, but not with him. Yeah, that was the kicker. She wanted

Drew to be in the driver's seat. She wouldn't have cared where they went as long as it was with him.

With Shan, she didn't care where they went, as long as she didn't have to have sex with him.

So, while they threaded their way north, she worried about what she was going to do. Did she go ahead and have sex with Shan? They were engaged after all. But then she'd feel like she was cheating on Drew, which was stupid, because even if she weren't engaged to Shan, a relationship with Drew presented enough problems on its own. And while she hadn't actually had sex with him, they'd come close enough she felt a little dirty, as if she'd cheated on Shan. Okay, so she had cheated in a way. But damn. It was hard to feel too terribly guilty about it.

Staring out the window of the car, she rested her elbow on the sill and twisted a lock of hair around her finger, a nervous habit she'd worked very hard to eliminate. One that had driven her mother crazy and had earned her hand slaps aplenty.

"Meilin? You still with me?" Shan's voice had a teasing quality to it, but when she turned to look at him, there was a hard glint in his eyes as he glanced at her.

"Oh, sorry. Was thinking about how to incorporate the beautiful trees around us into a design. You're right; today is the perfect day for a drive."

It was possible he believed her, but she guessed he didn't. He reached for her hand and she accepted his touch.

"Don't be nervous about tonight. We'll take it slow and easy. You're in charge as much as you want to be." Was he always so astute?

A slight chill that had nothing to do with the air conditioning slipped down her spine. "What if"—she swallowed deeply and asked the question that had been bugging her for weeks—"we aren't compatible physically?"

Shan glanced at her sharply. "Is that what's making you so nervous?"

So he had noticed. Not much of an actress, was she?

"Yes. I'm…concerned about not, well, being right for you." Mentally she rolled her eyes. Could she sound any more lame?

"I don't think that's an issue." The smile he sent her came close to a leer. "I've felt you respond to me when we kiss, Meilin. I think I've made it clear I'm hot for you, and I think it's just a matter of us being alone to show you just how responsive to me you are."

"But what if I can't, well, respond the way you want? What if it just doesn't work?"

With a slight frown on his face, Shan shrugged. "It's only one aspect of marriage. I don't see it being a problem, but if it is, we'll work through it and create our heirs. If it truly is an issue, something I honestly don't anticipate, then we'll deal with it the way our ancestors did—conduct discreet affairs as needed. Not my ideal marriage, but I don't see it as a deal breaker. We can still have a good relationship and raise children who have no idea what's going on behind the scenes."

The temperature of Shan's hand didn't change, but hers grew icy. "So, we'd keep love nests to hide our extra-marital activities. Condoned cheating." It was not the way she'd been raised. Although her parents disdained public shows of affection, the signs were there. She also knew her mother would have committed murder had she ever found herself the cheated upon wife. Her father, as well, in the reverse.

Was this evil Shan described a part of his life? Had his parents conducted themselves that way? She could recall nothing that indicated affairs of any kind.

"How did you ever come to think this way?" Surprised her voice came out calm and casual, she fisted her free hand in her lap.

"I've seen it in the so-called best families." He shrugged. "From China to the very upper crust of San Francisco society, and the like around the world, marriages are made to form family or business alliances. Sometimes those marriages are blessed by love and respect. Many times love is absent and respect is barely more than a shadow. But those families refuse to be brought down by scandal. As long as people are discreet and respect the alliance, the elders turn a blind eye to small affairs."

Shan glanced her way and squeezed her hand. "I don't anticipate us going in that direction. I want a true marriage. Respect for one another. Affection certainly. I pray for the growth of love as we get to know each other. We just need time together. Time such as this weekend. A chance to shake off the social dictates. Time to be physically close and let our touches speak instead of our words. Hands, lips, and eyes can say so much without a word being spoken. A touch, a sigh, a blending of two bodies in perfect rhythm." His finger stroked the top of her hand, but the expected intimacy did not appear. Instead she felt colder.

"What you say has merit. However, I'm still not sure I'm ready for that step." Might never be. No, knowing how she felt—responded—to Drew, she knew she wasn't frigid. She also knew Shan didn't draw passion out of her. Knowing that, the future looked far more grim than ever.

"We'll take it nice and easy today, Meilin." Shan sought to soothe with his voice. "Do not feel pressured. When we come together tonight, I expect it to be with mutual desire. I don't want you afraid of me. I want you hot for me. As I am hot for you."

They didn't speak for a long time. Soft, classical music filled the silence as they drove the highway leading north, twisting and winding up past Corte Madera, through San Rafael and onward.

"Don't worry, sweetheart," Shan said, his hand still holding hers, his thumb rubbing over the diamond of her ring. "We're going to relax, taste some wine, have a picnic, a nice dinner. Maybe an hour or two at the spa is a good idea."

"I'm not really worried," she lied. Of course she was worried to the point of making herself sick. She was also pissed at his cavalier attitude about a potential future of hidden affairs. But there was no sense in telling him so. He'd only work harder to convince her they'd be good together in bed, and be that much more anxious to get her there tonight.

And there was so much more to consider. Sex wasn't the only aspect of this marriage contract. Although she hadn't taken the time to read the fine print, she'd trusted that to her parents and their lawyer, there were other promises made. Promises that affected more people than just her. Her father had said more than once how happy he was about the union. But why? Not to be dismissed, there were five generations of pride at stake. And that was just the California ancestors. Never mind the Mainland Chinese ancestors. Those generations were uncountable. Briefly she wondered if her white or black friends ever felt this kind of pressure.

None of them had ever mentioned arranged marriages. Those who were married, happily and not so happily, had all chosen their mates based on the elusive idea of love, or in some cases, pure lust. A few had chosen society marriages, but even then emotion had ruled more than what was good for business, or so it had seemed to her.

"Let your worries take flight. We'll choose wine for our wedding. We can do whatever you want." He squeezed her hand, then pressed it down on his thigh.

She was both relieved and more agitated. At least with her hand on his leg he wouldn't notice the sweat on her palms. On the other hand, she was awfully close to his groin. Neither situation seemed ideal to her. Instead of fidgeting, she left her hand where he'd placed it, desperately praying he didn't move it higher.

"Do you like the idea of a spa visit?" he asked, giving her a moment of panic trying to remember what he'd been talking about. The spa. Right.

"Yes. Sounds good to me. And the picnic you mentioned could be nice if we find a place with tables under some shady trees."

"One thing about wine country, plenty of picnic places."

Another half an hour and Shan pulled off the highway, following a side road until it led to the parking lot of the first winery on their itinerary. She recognized the sign and relaxed a little. It was one she liked.

Shan apparently felt the need to impress her with his wine knowledge. They spent an hour in the tasting room choosing between Chardonnay and Riesling. In the end, Shan purchased a case of each. At least it was an hour out of the confines of the car.

After another stop, this time for reds, a case of a very nice Zinfandel and another of Cabernet Sauvignon joined the others in the trunk. Any more cases and they'd have to move their luggage to the back seat.

Making their way toward the Silverado Trail in Napa County, they found a small restaurant and pulled in for lunch, which suddenly sounded much better than an intimate picnic out of the public eye. Not normally a big drinker, the closer they came to their night at the hotel, the more Meilin sipped. Lunch helped buffer the buzz she had building. What would Shan say if she were too drunk to have sex? A small giggle threatened to escape, especially when Shan caught the twinkle in her eye.

Chapter 22

Guilt and a healthy dose of disgust stabbed her as Shan reached across the table and placed his hand over hers, a definite light in his gaze as it traveled from her face to her chest pressing against the thin material of her silk tee. His fingers stroked the finger wearing his ring; satisfaction and desire lit his face, making him more handsome. No denying it. He was a very good looking man. He just didn't warm her blood the way blond hair and blue eyes did.

"Thinking about a spa treatment?" he asked. Obviously he was thinking about how soft a mud bath and massage with oils would leave her skin, and how the treatment would relax her. There was no way he could know it would only enhance her guilt, her tension.

"No, not really. Maybe another stop. Don't you want to visit a couple champagne cellars? There's Domaine Chandon in addition to Mumm."

"How right you are. Have some dessert first?"

The waiter arrived and cleared the dishes of their entrees.

"Oh, no, I don't think so. Lunch definitely filled me up." She grinned up at the waiter. "My compliments to the chef."

"Thank you. I'll pass on your kind words." The man was a little older than the usual summer student working for tips to pay for college. He was thin with long brown hair sporting a healthy frosting of grey in his ponytail.

"Yes, excellent lunch." Shan had to get the last word in. The man of taste and distinction, at least in his own mind.

The waiter discreetly winked at Meilin and took the dishes away.

Shortly afterward they left the restaurant.

Shan handed her back into the car. "We'll go down Highway 29, then head back up the Silverado Trail, that way we'll get both sides of the valley. Pick out your two favorites and we'll finish with Mumm. Then tomorrow we can find a few more, if we're not too tired. Sound good?" The man actually winked at her.

By the time they reached the Mumm tasting room, Meilin had a buzz going once again. More than she usually allowed herself. It helped keep a lid on her nerves as she continued to wrestle with the issue of did she or didn't she. Sleep with Shan and lose some of her self respect, and possibly all of Drew's trust? Or find a way to put Shan off and endure his frustration and possible anger? Would he be angry? And how would he show it? Shan was martial arts trained, but was he the kind of man to keep his reactions physically leashed or would he strike out? The unknown of both sides of her internal argument terrified her. Both choices battled with her need to please everyone. There was no pleasing anyone. So how was she going to please herself, and what, exactly, did that entail?

Shan practically pulled her from the car after parking near the tasting room door. The parking lot was crowded, and she could hear people at the picnic tables under the trees. But that didn't really concern her. What caught her attention fully was Shan pressing her back against the car, inserting one thigh between her capri-covered legs, pressing high as he pinned her between the hot metal and his hot body.

She had no time to speak or protest as his lips covered hers, hard and insistent, his body equally hard and insistent as he pushed against her hip.

His bold move surprised her, causing her heart to leap in shock, her tongue doing its best to evade his without appearing to be avoiding him. She was able to make a protest in the form of a groan easily mistaken for a moan of passion. Exactly how Shan interpreted it, big surprise there, his hands sliding off the car to her shoulders, then down her body to her waist. Meilin's hands were trapped between them on his chest. Was she pushing or pulling? Not even she was fully sure as her head spun from the wine and the passion rolling off Shan in tsunami-sized waves.

"Meilin," he moaned between kisses when he took a break to change the angle of his attack.

"Shan...don't..." she gasped.

"Don't stop. I get it." Once more he took control of the kiss, grinding his erection against her belly. "We can skip this stop. I already know what I want to order," he murmured in her ear while nibbling her ear lobe. "We can head right for our room."

"No, Shan. Stop." The gasp wasn't nearly as authoritative as she wished. Panic began to crawl up her spine and a faint whistling crept past the blood pounding in her ears.

"Get a room, man!"

Meilin opened her eyes enough to see a group of giggling women staggering past them into the parking lot.

"There are kids here!" someone else called out.

"Shan," she gasped again. A little stronger this time.

"Anything you want, baby." The growled diminutive made her cringe.

"Not here."

"Right. Let's go to our room."

"No, let's cool it down a bit. I've been looking forward to this stop all day." Not particularly, but if she didn't stop him now, she was that much closer to having to make a decision that could very well compromise every ounce of her self-respect.

Shan dragged his lips away from her neck and placed his forehead against hers. Both of them breathed heavily. Her in relief, him in dissipating passion. "Give me a minute."

Okay, she got that. He was hard as a lead pipe, and it would probably take him several minutes to calm down enough to walk without sporting a tent in the front of his chinos. Shan's hands moved from her hips to fold her into a hug, holding her close against his chest, his hands slowly stroking up and down her back.

Relief made her sag against him and rest her head against his shoulder. When his body relaxed, she felt the kiss he placed on the top of her head.

"You're so much more levelheaded than I am when it comes to this attraction, Meilin. I wonder if you want me anywhere as much as I want you. Or even a little. I need something to build on."

"This is hard for me, Shan, but I'm trying. I've never slept with a man unless we'd been on several dates. Not just three or four dates in a few weeks, but three or four months. This is fast for me."

Shan hugged her closer. "Okay, okay. I get it. You're not cheap and easy. I respect that." A huge sigh lifted his chest and brushed her hair as he released it. "It's okay, baby. I'm trying not to push, but I'm just so excited we're finally spending time together. No pressure, no time schedules, no meetings. Just you and me. I promise to slow down until tonight. Okay?"

Mortified at what he obviously expected and with no good plan on how to put it off any longer, she could only nod against his shoulder, thankful her face was turned outward.

"It's getting hot out here," Shan said as he backed up one step, hands sliding around her body and down her arms to take her hands. "Let's go inside and pick out a bottle or two for tonight. Wouldn't you like some chilled champagne and strawberries tonight?"

"Yes. Yes, it sounds wonderful." She started to wonder if she could get him drunk enough to pass out before it came time to undress.

Inside they found one small table open. So small their knees touched under it. Meilin moved hers to the side. Shan rested his elbows on the table and leaned forward, taking her left hand in both of his. She wondered if he were more impressed with her ring than she was. Probably. Still reluctant to have such intimate contact with him, she felt marginally better about it with the table between them and the many tasters crowded around them.

It took awhile for their selections to be brought to them, and while she felt awkward about the silence between them, she had no more small talk at the moment. Sobriety was beginning to return, and she only wanted the oblivion of her buzz back. At least then she could smile at him with something resembling the adoration he expected. A silly, tipsy smile. God, she was starting to feel guilty for the subterfuge.

Not that Shan noticed. In fact, his state of sobriety, or lack thereof, was possibly becoming something of a concern. He'd been matching her drink for drink since lunch and now she could see the effect of the wine on both of them. Maybe a walk would sober him enough to drive safely.

Meilin felt relief that Shan knew what he wanted and was able to place his order for two cases. It would take a little time to get the order up and out to his car, so Meilin suggested a short stroll, an idea backed by the salesgirl. A tipsy, off-balance Shan was one thing, but a drunk one? No, she didn't want to go down that road. Not until they were in the room and he might pass out before putting any moves on her. But until they reached that point, she didn't want to worry about him driving. She certainly wasn't clear enough to drive them. If he'd even let her behind the wheel of his fancy car.

So she took him by the hand and led him to the trees lining the walkway to the parking lot. In the shade, the temperature of the late afternoon became tolerable. Shan pulled her to a stop, his phone in one hand.

"Let's get a selfie here."

A giggled worked its way up her throat. The wine had certainly loosened him up. Come to think of it, she'd loosened up as well. "You do selfies?"

"This will be my first. Let's see if I can figure it out."

By the time he figured out how to click the photo one handed, they leaned against one another in laughter.

"So very dignified, Mr. Lin."

Shan snorted in a manner she'd never expect from him. "Dignity can be over rated at times. Although I try not to mock it in public."

Meilin herself snorted. Seemed like every time she thumbed her nose at dignity it was unfortunately very much in public. Turning around to see if anyone had witnessed their silliness, she saw a young man wheeling

two cases of wine out to the parking lot. "Looks like us." She grabbed
Shan's arm. Why did they have to be so fast with the delivery? Every
moment out here was one further away from having to decide whether or
not to sleep with him. She waved to the man who was looking around for
them, letting him know they were on their way to the car. He waved back
and stopped, waiting for them to catch up.

Shan spun to look around and orient himself, saw the man with the
hand truck, and started forward. Only he skipped the path and tripped
over a rock used to mark the way and protect the landscaping.

Meilin felt her mouth form an astonished O as Shan fell face first into
a small garden of rocks and succulents. There was nothing she could to
do break his fall. Despite that, she rushed around the rock he'd tripped
over, hoping to do something. Anything. But the sound of his head hitting
a smaller pile of landscape rocks made her wince and cry out.

"Shan!" She knelt by his side and reached for his neck. Right. Like she
knew how to search for a pulse?

The winery employee ditched the wine and ran in their direction while
calling out over his shoulder for help.

In a daze, Meilin knelt at Shan's side until someone pulled her up and
out of the way of the people trying to help. They got him rolled over and
a compress on the large, bloody, swelling area on the right side of his
forehead. Smaller abrasions dotted his cheekbone, jaw line, and arms. In
fact, his right wrist didn't look quite right at that angle.

Paramedics arrived along with a police escort about the time Shan
started coming around. In a daze she let an officer lead her to a seat on a
rock and answered all his questions, making sure she let him know it was
Shan's own mistake that led to the accident. She wanted the winery to
know she held them blameless. And all the while, inside, deep within the
concern for his health, a very teeny bit of her sighed in relief.

Shan wouldn't be up to sex tonight.

Chapter 23

Drew had just popped open a fresh beer and settled into his favorite backyard lounge for an after dinner nap when his cell phone rang.

He'd escaped from the school for a night and just wanted to soak up an hour of setting sun before jumping into the spa on the far side of the pool to boil for an hour or two. Anything to relieve the stress knotting up his shoulders. He figured Meilin and her fiancé were probably getting dressed for dinner by now. All day he'd been following her Facebook updates with their locations. The last had been Mumm Napa, about five hours ago. Was she too distracted being wined and dined to update her status?

He answered his phone on the fourth ring.

"'Allo?"

"Oh, Drew, thank God."

Drew's brow's shot up, his heart kicked into high gear at the breathless sound of Meilin's voice. Was she crying? He sat up straight, all thought of relaxing vaporizing.

"What's wrong?"

"Oh my God, Drew, it's awful. I didn't want to sleep with him, but I never imagined Fate intervening on my behalf this way! I don't know what to do. Shan's making a fuss and being a bully."

"Slow down," he said cautiously. "What's going on?"

By the time she got the story out between sniffles and hiccups, his gut relaxed with relief. The man not only had a concussion, complete with black eye, badly bruised cheek, and a couple bruised—possibly cracked—ribs, but he'd broken his arm and ankle as well. And he wanted to sue everyone from the winery to the nurse taking his vitals. Since Meilin wasn't there to see him, Drew didn't hold back his grin. Served the arsewipe right. Still, this he could help with.

"You say he's threatening to sue everyone?"

"It's awful. He tripped over a rock, ignoring the path, so it's his own fault, but really. He was a little tipsy. Not enough for a DUI, the cops did a breathalyzer and the hospital did a blood alcohol test, so he's not being charged, but those people did everything they could to help him. And now he's demanding I find his lawyer. He shouldn't be trying to sue them. Good God, they acted in good faith! I can't talk him down from it, Drew. Do you think you can talk some sense into him? How fast can you make it up here?"

Drew was already on the move. "What hospital?"

"Queen of the Valley, in Napa."

"I'll find it." He strode into the house and to his room. "I'll try to make it in an hour. Keep your phone on so I can find you. Do you need help with his car? Should I bring Birdie to drive mine back?"

"No, no, I can drive him home. They want to keep him overnight. He really should stay longer, but, well… The way he's throwing around his lawyer's name, everyone will be happier if he's at home with personal care."

If the man was being that much of a pain, yeah, the hospital staff would love to see the last of Shan. "What about you? Did you, don't you, have reservations?" In his room he switched his phone to speaker and tugged off his swim trunks, changing into jeans and a T-shirt, then tucking his wallet into a pocket and slipping his feet into socks and cross-trainer shoes.

"We had, have, reservations in Calistoga. It's a little far from the hospital. So I probably should call and cancel. He'll probably expect me to stay overnight…"

"No, don't stay at the hospital. You'll need all the rest you can get if you're to drive him home tomorrow." Drew grabbed his keys from the dresser and threw open his bedroom door, surprising Birdie, who was leaving the steamy bathroom wrapped in a robe with a towel turban around her head. "I need the car," he said shortly.

"Wait a minute!" His sister protested. They'd already flipped a coin and she'd won the toss to take the car for the evening. Not that he'd cared much, he hadn't been in the mood to go out, but they'd had to play the game.

"Emergency trumps fun time. Ask Mum to borrow her car."

"You ask her." Birdie stomped behind him to the hall leading to the foyer.

"Meilin." Drew returned his phone to private. "I'll call when I get close. I've got GPS, so I'll find the hospital. Just hold his hand"—Drew winced at his own advice—"and try to keep him calm. You'll have to tell me how to find you when I get there."

Drew paused at the living room, looking toward the reading nook where the parents were cuddled on a love seat, each with a book in hand, but neither were reading. "Let me get on the road and I'll call you back."

"Okay," she whispered. "And...and thank you."

"No thanks necessary. I'm on my way as soon as I let the family know where I'm going. Hang in there, love."

No sooner had he disconnected than his family stood around him demanding answers.

"Meilin's fiancé, your friend Shan, had some sort of fall, knocked himself wonky, and broke a few bones."

Silence fell immediately, his father looking at him shrewdly. "And she called you because...?"

"We've become...friends. She was the substitute teacher a couple weekends ago. She's stopped by a few times to tutor and to help with homework. The professor is a cousin of hers. Anyhow, it's not important. I need to get going. They're at a hospital in Napa, and she wants my help talking him down from making litigation threats."

Dad's eyebrow rose a little more. Randi's soft hand landed on his arm. Birdie snorted and crossed her arms.

"We had a deal," his sister reminded him. "You usually get the car. This time it's my turn."

"You can take my car, Drew," Randi said and squeezed his arm. "We're staying in tonight and not going anywhere tomorrow. I assume at this hour they're keeping him overnight?" Everyone glanced at the clock on the mantel. Eight o'clock in the evening.

"Yeah, she said they wanted to keep him over," Drew confirmed.

His father dug out his wallet and separated several bills from it. "Here. You'll probably need to find a place to sleep or get some food at least. This should get you through the night."

"Right." Randi squeezed past him and headed for her purse on the kitchen counter.

"Thanks, Da." Drew shoved his keys and the money into the front pocket of his jeans. "I'll be going. I'll call once I find out something."

Randi met him in the foyer and passed over the keys to the new car, a gift from his father. One with real power, Mum's brand new Jag. Birdie hadn't been given the option of driving it yet, and he could see it roasting her arse that he got to drive it first. Too bad. He didn't have time to fight about it. "Ta, Mum." He bent to kiss her cheek, then headed out to the garage.

"Take care of my car," she called after him. "No tickets!"

He tossed a wave over his shoulder before letting the door bang shut. He'd do his best, but he wasn't making any promises.

* * * *

Meilin paced the floor outside Shan's room, impatient for Drew's call. Yes, she'd asked him for some legal advice, but if she were honest with herself, she just wanted him here. His level head, his calm presence. Everything that Shan had not demonstrated upon his injury. At least Shan was out of it. The doctor had ordered a sedative, and everyone had breathed a sigh of relief when Shan had slipped into sleep.

The fracture of his ankle, while bad enough to hurt, was a simple break easily straightened, then encased in plaster to keep it straight. Same with the broken arm. The worst part was both breaks were on his right side, a double inconvenience he'd already noted. Even without those breaks, the injuries to his head and ribs would have sidelined him from driving anyway. Either he'd have to let Meilin drive his car home, he'd observed sourly, or he'd have to hire a limo and a tow truck. She'd met this comment with a raised brow that had shut him up. For a bit. From there he'd complained of the pain in his head, knee, arms and any other place he could think of. Thankfully the pain pill had kicked in, further pulling him under so he'd mostly sleep through the hourly checks by the nurses.

The simple fact Shan hadn't yet grasped—but the doctor had been frankly clear about with her—was he would be out of commission for several weeks. He was going to either need to stay in the hospital a few days, or he'd require competent nursing care around the clock. Preferably in bed. And since he couldn't use crutches with the broken arm and the injured ribs, it would mean using a wheel chair during recovery. The doctor provided her with the name of an ambulance service who could get Shan home, and a nursing service who could care for him once he got there. Obviously the doctor wasn't going to insist Shan stay for a few days. She didn't blame him a bit.

What concerned Meilin most was how awful he'd acted to every single person trying to do their job, helping him. From the moment he'd awakened on the ground at the winery, to the moment he'd fallen asleep, he'd grumbled and loudly complained, even snapping at her, brushing her off when she tried to comfort him. Talk about a grouchy patient. Not that she had much experience with trauma that involved ambulances and emergency rooms, but she had a feeling the people staffing the rescue positions didn't deserve his ire. Not when he'd tripped all on his own.

And then he'd had the nerve to demand the nurses find a cot for her to sleep in his room. The last very thing she wanted to do. Had he been sweet, or at least calm and reasonable, she wouldn't have hesitated. To be ordered about... No, that she could not abide. If it weren't in poor taste, she'd set his ring on the table and walk out. But while she wouldn't stand for his verbal abuse, neither would she dump him while he was down. That wouldn't be any nicer than how he treated everyone working so hard to see to his comfort and healing.

One thing this day had made crystal clear—she had zero desire to marry the man. She couldn't see herself spending her life with him. No more waffling on that topic for her.

And if he thought she'd let him bully her about getting back to the city in the morning, he had another think coming. She'd happily stuff him into a limo, then drive his precious car home. By herself. She should have let Drew bring his sister along to drive their car back and he could ride with her for the two hour drive to the city. And that was only if traffic was light.

The more she thought about it, the happier she was she'd called Drew first. Of course she'd also called her parents. Shan's parents. His assistant and housekeeper, who were both focused on getting home care set up by noon tomorrow. She'd even called Jack because of his recent law degree. If anyone in the family counted as a personal injury lawyer, he sure did. He'd also approved of her calling Drew, as he couldn't reach the hospital in less than five hours. Another glance at her watch, the clock on the wall over the nurses' station, and her phone, revealed the same truth. Barely an hour had passed since she'd spoken with Drew. He could arrive at any moment now. Right?

At the end of the hall, she turned around and began pacing back the other direction, wanting nothing more than to fall into a comfortable bed and sleep. The wine buzz had worn off long ago. Right about the time the adrenalin had kicked in as Shan was still falling. A sight and sound she'd never forget. Although it had happened very fast, within a matter of a second or two, it kept playing over and over in her head in excruciating, slow motion.

Hearing the impact of Shan's head in her own made her wince yet again. The man was lucky to have most of his brains intact. Hopefully he'd see that soon. There was little the medical staff could do for him beyond pain relief. She'd already helped reposition his broken leg and arm a dozen times. Once more she mentally thanked the staff for sending him off to la-la-land.

The opening of the elevator door along with a little ding announcing its arrival had her turning in anticipation. At the sight of a tall man with blond hair, her heart skipped a beat, then jumped into double time.

Drew.

He was here.

One footstep led to another and soon she was close enough to run the last few steps and launch herself into his arms. His very strong arms that caught and held her.

He held her close as she clung to his neck, her face buried there, absorbing his comfort, his scent, the warmth of his body, the way his big hands cupped her bottom as she tightened her legs around his waist.

"I'm here, I'm here," he repeated over and over again.

"I'm so glad," she whispered on the edge of breaking down. "I'm so, so glad." Until this moment, she hadn't truly realized how tightly wound she was from the stress of the day. She wasn't one to freak out, but today had pushed so many unknown buttons. If the very strength of her reaction right now surprised Drew, she could only say she was more surprised. Didn't mean she'd let him go before she had to. He felt so good holding her.

From behind, a throat cleared. "Excuse me? Miss Wu?"

Meilin recognized the night nurse who'd taken the brunt of Shan's most recent verbal abuse. She unwrapped herself from Drew, and with his hands on her shoulders, turned to face the truly kind older woman. "Yes?"

"Mr. Lin is waking up and asking for you." Her curious gaze passed over Drew, silently questioning, but saying nothing more.

"Of course. We'll be there in a minute."

"Very well." Professional in the face of her curiosity, the woman held a blank face, although a hint of a twinkle had sparked in her eyes. Most impressive.

The nurse turned on her heel, and Meilin grabbed Drew's hand like a lifeline.

"I have to tell you," she whispered, "I can't marry him. But I can't tell him right now." A shudder shimmied down her spine from shoulders to hips. "Please, I may need your support on this. I'm not really sure how he's going to react to anything. He hasn't followed my predictions so far."

Drew squeezed her hand gently. "I'm not going anywhere until you tell me you want me to leave."

"He's already bitching about me driving his car home." She scoffed. "Like I'd ever wreck his precious Aston Martin."

Drew choked back a laugh, she was sure of it, but his expression was neutral and mild when she glanced at him. "Don't worry about the car. We'll figure it all out."

Meilin paused at the door to Shan's room, sucked in a deep breath, then marched across the threshold. Shan's eyes cracked open enough to see Drew beside her.

"Excuse me?" he said in a tone so frosty ice chased down her spine.

Opening her hand, she dropped Drew's and moved to the side of the bed, leaving Drew at the foot.

"I called Drew. He's here as a temporary legal counsel until we can find your lawyer. Apparently he's off climbing a mountain in the Sierras. I couldn't reach Jack, either." So she lied a little. "He's in Tahoe or Vegas, but that's neither here nor there. His phone is off or out of power. You said you wanted a lawyer, and I didn't know who else to call." She took Shan's hand, as much as she hated doing so, especially in front of Drew. But it seemed to calm Shan, and she sensed he'd been building up to another outburst, something not good for his head, blood pressure, or her peace of mind. "Please, accept Drew's advice for now. You're seriously injured and on some strong pain medicine. You shouldn't be upsetting yourself over liability issues as of yet." Or at all. He should be worried about his own close call with the law.

Shan's half-lidded gaze settled on hers. "Why him? Are you sleeping with him?" He ignored her gasp of outrage and focused his glare on Drew. "I told you to stay away from her."

"You're not in control of everything, Lin. Circumstances have thrown us into contact. And since you're drugged, I'll ignore the insult to her, for now. Make no mistake, the lady is not sleeping with me, or anyone else."

Meilin looked from one man to the other. Is that what had set both their backs up a few weeks ago?

"Right now, old man," Drew continued, "you'll have to make do with me. Meilin and I will get you home tomorrow, and then you can harangue your lawyer to your heart's content. But for now, this is the way things are."

Meilin held her breath until Shan blew out his pent up breath. "Fine. For tonight. Tomorrow, when I'm more awake, I'll better be able to locate the necessary people or their backups. I suppose there's really nothing to be done tonight."

"No," Drew said. "There isn't. You're injured and medicated and in no condition to make legally binding decisions. Let Meilin take care of you for now. There'll be time enough to threaten people with malpractice and safety issues later. Let the hangover wear off first."

Although Drew kept his tone light, Shan's face flushed red and his breath sounded as harsh as an angry bull. Something in what Drew said pissed Shan off more, if that were even possible. Not for the first time in the last three hours, she wondered if Shan's cracked veneer was showing his true character. Something he kept carefully hidden? How deep did this unreasonable anger go? Deep enough that one day he might crack completely, enough to physically beat her? The thought that chilled her was a reminder of his black belt.

"For tonight," Drew continued, "you're under excellent care. Meilin is exhausted and needs a good night's rest as much as you do. Possibly even more so, since she doesn't have the benefit of sedatives to help her sleep. We can do this two ways. I can make sure she gets settled in a hotel, or I can stay here and make sure you don't say something you'll regret later. Which would you prefer?"

"Either way she leaves, is that it?"

"Yes. If she has to get you back to the city and set up at home tomorrow, she must get some sleep."

"I've already canceled the hotel in Calistoga you booked," Meilin added. "I'll find a motel much closer."

Shan opened his mouth, she wasn't sure what he'd say, but then he closed it again and glared at Drew before drawing in a breath. "Take her to a hotel, then come back here. I want to talk to you."

Meilin glanced over her shoulder to see Drew nod. "Sure thing. Might take about an hour because I'm not sure she got dinner."

Shan heaved an impatient sigh. "Fine. Get her dinner, settle her in a hotel, then come back here."

The subtext was he didn't trust her with Drew. Or Drew with her. Whatever. Them together had Shan getting crankier.

"Come here," Shan ordered her. Although his hand was bandaged from being scraped, it was strong enough to pull her down. "Kiss me good night, baby."

The diminutive annoyed her, but she pressed her closed lips against his in a show of affection she should be feeling without reservation. He noticed the lack of passion because his hand tightened around her nape, holding her beyond her comfort zone. She squeaked a protest as simply uncomfortable began to hurt. She'd probably have bruises on the back of her neck in the morning.

Finally, he let her go. "See you in the morning. Be here by eight. And if you get one scratch on my car…"

Of course she wouldn't, but she hurried to reassure him she wouldn't leave so much as a fingerprint behind.

"In fact, leave my car here and let him drive you over. He'll get you in the morning, or I'll have a limo driver pick you up."

"Whatever you say, Shan."

The nurse quietly closed the computer she used for making notes on his file and turned to leave, but not without a wink in Meilin's direction. It was the best behaved he'd been yet.

Chapter 24

At dinner, Drew savored the sight, sound, and touch of Meilin. They'd found a small diner, far from the elegance of the more famous restaurants around. But it was between the hospital and the motel they'd located not far away.

Meilin played with her salad and nibbled on garlic bread. Drew did justice to a French dip sandwich and coffee.

"Didn't you say you'd already had dinner?" she asked.

"This is just a snack." He winked at her. "Mum says I'm still a growing boy."

"I can't imagine your food bill." Meilin smiled at him, teasing.

"I like to keep active and sitting all the time in class is killing me. I'll have to start getting up earlier and run a few miles in the morning or find a pickup rugby game on Sundays. Have to keep those muscles stretched and flexible." Drew winked. "Especially if you're going to start leaping into my arms." There, he'd made her blush.

"I… I don't know why I did that," she whispered and reached for her water glass, eyes lowered modestly.

"I'm glad you did. You can do that every day for the rest of our lives."

The blush deepened. "I don't know if that's possible. Even dumping Shan won't solve all the issues between us." She peeked up at him. It was one of the cutest things he'd ever seen her do.

"Dumping Shan is the first step, the biggest step, to us being together. After that we need to evaluate the future of our careers. Either I convince my father to open a satellite office here, or you come to China with me. I'm sure we can find a way to keep you busy. I'll need to travel so I'll need an interpreter I can trust, and someone with an educated eye for quality. You could fill both positions without blinking an eye. It would also mean you could send items back for your business. You'd just need to hire another designer or two to implement your visions, which can be worked out by e-mail. Or put your customers on hold pending the results of an extended buying trip."

Meilin's mouth dropped open. "Excuse me?"

Drew pushed his plate aside and leaned forward on his elbows. "I've been thinking about this a lot. You mentioned the obstacle of your already built career versus mine just starting. It doesn't need to be an obstacle. One slight change in direction for either of us, or both of us, and we can have the opportunity to understand what this is between us. Explore our impressions, define our feelings. See if there really is a relationship that can grow. I'm short on time here. I don't normally push so hard, but I need to know if there's hope." He'd never pushed so fast, ever. Nor had there ever been a hint of forever with the girls he'd dated. All his relationships had been casual. With him leaving in two weeks, he wanted a hint of possible commitment this time.

Meilin set down her water and leaned back in her seat, a small frown on her face. "You've been thinking about this. I need to think it over more."

"Of course you will, and now is not the time to make decisions of that scale." He picked up one of the few remaining fries on his plate and dipped it in the small puddle of remaining au jus. "The bigger issue right now is getting you some sleep, then tackling the issue of getting Lin home and set up with nursing care." He shoved the fry into his mouth.

Meilin dropped her head back with a sigh. "Yes. His assistant is looking into care professionals covered by their insurance. Not that he can't afford it," she muttered the last.

"So he'll have someone at his place by the time we get him home tomorrow. That means you'll be home tomorrow night."

"If they can't find someone on such short notice I might be forced to stay with him until Monday. The good news is he won't be pushing for sex."

Drew frowned and stopped in the act of lifting his coffee cup. "Did he force you...?"

"No!" Relief filled her face and his blood pressure dropped back into the normal range. "But he made it clear we'd share a bed tonight." A delicate shudder shook her shoulders. "If I'd thought of it myself, I would have pushed him over a rock much earlier."

Tortured green eyes gazed directly into his. "I wasn't looking forward to it. I never wanted to sleep with him, and I was nearly frantic trying to figure out how to put it off again. I think someone was on my side when he went over the rock the way he did." A tiny smile lifted one corner of her mouth.

He didn't even try to hold back the wide grin stretching his face as he lifted the coffee cup for a sip. Once he swallowed, he set the cup down. "I'll take credit for putting some voodoo down on him to cause his accident if you like."

Meilin laughed as he hoped she would. "I like to think one of my ancestors interceded on my behalf. Good timing either way."

Drew set down his coffee cup and reached across the table. "Yes. Perfect timing. So, what are we going to do about it?"

Meilin put her small hand in his much bigger one. "First I need to extract myself from the contract. That will be tricky. Until that's taken care of, I don't feel right about exploring whatever it is we have here." With her free hand she waved at the space between them. "I won't be the one to break the contract by infidelity."

Although they'd already come damn close. But, he reminded himself, the choice to take the next step had to be hers. Didn't mean he couldn't nudge her a little toward his way of thinking. "You're not married yet. In your mind the relationship is over but for returning the ring." All's fair in love and war, so the sages said.

Intently, she stared back at him. "There's more to it than simply returning the ring, and until the families are clear that the engagement is broken, I can't move forward with anything else. I must make the break clean."

Frustration built inside Drew. Of course she had to be honorable. Didn't mean he didn't want her. Fiercely. But at least she was willing to talk about a potential future with him. It was something.

"Okay. I can deal with that." He lifted her hand and kissed the fingertips. The jolt of sizzling energy that burst through him was visible in her reaction. She sucked in a breath, her eyes dilating, a flush washing her skin. Her hand trembled a little, and it thrilled him right down his soul, and the part of him hardening to the point of pain. God, he wanted her with every atom in his body. So much his own hand shook. "You have to know how much I want you. I can be patient. You need that from me, but it isn't easy keeping my hands off you. I might slip up a little. Just remind me I'm a patient man. Deal?"

Her eyes closed, then opened only a little, as if her lids were heavy with overwhelming passion. "Yes. Deal. And thank you. I won't take advantage of your patience. Not if I can help it at all."

They both jumped when the waitress set their ticket on the table. "Want me to clear away anything here?"

Reluctantly, they separated their hands. "I think we're done."

Meilin nodded. Tiredness radiated from her slender frame. Drew glanced at the bill while the waitress stacked dishes, then dropped a few bills on the table. "No change. Thanks."

With barely a blink, the waitress stuffed the money into her pocket and lifted the stacked plates away. "You all have a good evening, now, folks."

Walking Meilin through the check-in process and making sure she was safe in her room was one of the harder things he'd ever done. Knowing he was leaving her there for the night made him uneasy. Although the room was scrupulously clean, the chain well-known, it was a motel on a main thoroughfare with a door opening to the street. If Shan got extremely obnoxious, Drew vowed to come back here and crash on the second full sized bed in the room. Unless she invited him into her bed. He'd be a bloody fool to turn down such an offer.

"If I come back, I don't want you opening the door until you look out the peep hole," he told her. "I'll make sure you can see my face, okay? Don't let anyone else in. And do up all the locks."

She gave him a long look of exasperation. "I know how to be safe in a hotel room."

"All the same. You're a woman alone. A small woman. Alone." He pulled her close and lifted her by the waist until their lips met. The kiss was soft at first, then deeper, harder, hungry. Over the pounding of his heart in his ears he barely noticed the ring of a cell phone. A tone he didn't recognize, didn't want to acknowledge.

Meilin pulled away with small nibbling kisses. "We can't do this. Not now. Not yet." The breathless whisper thrilled him to his core. She was affected as him.

"Can't help it. You feel good. Smell good. Taste even better." He kissed her again, and once more her phone began to ring.

"Ugh!" She pulled away and wiggled to be set down. "That's Shan."

"Guess that means I'd better go." He missed her warmth immediately. She was the perfect arm-full, and he wanted nothing more than to wrap her around him again. Instead he let her go to answer the phone.

"Yes, Shan. I just got to my room. We found something a little nicer than a drive-through for dinner." She paused and glanced at Drew. "I'm at the motel just down the road from the hospital. Near the highway junction. It's safe and clean. No, not fancy, but I'm only here overnight, and hope to sleep most of my time here." She propped her free hand on her hip, a frown twisting her face. "Drew is on his way back. Not sure what you're worried about. I'm an engaged woman, remember?" Meilin threw her hand in the air and her head back to stare at the ceiling. "Sure,

sure. Glad to know you trust me. Right. Fine. I'll see you in the morning.
I asked a guard at the hospital to keep an eye on your car overnight. It's
parked next to a Lamborghini and a Ferrari. It will be safe. Yes, I'm sure.
Okay. Good night."

She stabbed the screen to drop the call. "Bastard. Glad I've
decided to call it off. Every time he opens his mouth now I get more
and more annoyed."

"It will all be over soon, and we'll start something new." Drew cupped
her chin and lifted her face. Her beautiful face. He dipped his head and
kissed her lightly. "I'll call when I'm on my way back. The sooner we get
him checked out of there, the better."

"I agree." She kissed him back. "Now go. I hope you get some sleep
tonight. I'd ask you to blow him off, but right now I don't want to tweak
his temper. God only knows what he'll say or do then."

Chapter 25

The night at the hospital was long and uncomfortable. Drew was grateful that at least the room had a reclining chair and the nurse gave him a pillow and blanket. God only knew why he stayed to play babysitter. Other than a few moans of pain, followed by opening his eyes to confirm Drew's presence, Shan Lin slept most of the night. Probably due to the compassion of the nurses, who certainly didn't want to deal with him any more than necessary. From his phone, Drew pulled up a site for a local florist and ordered a fruit and flower basket for the nurses' station, sent a text to his father, then did his best to fall asleep, mentally cursing the older man in the hospital bed.

In the morning it was even more of a cluster fuck. Shan finally calmed down when it was determined Drew would drive his precious car with Shan in the passenger seat—at least as a Brit he understood, and respected, the Aston Martin—while Meilin followed in Randi's car. Which made no sense until they were on the highway and Shan started grilling him about his association with Meilin.

"We're relatively new friends," Drew said for the third time as they drove through Marin County headed for the Golden Gate Bridge.

"I've already told you I don't want her to have friends like you," Shan stated baldly as he shifted, trying to find a more comfortable position. They'd picked up a pile of pillows from Target to help make him more at ease in the passenger seat. An idea that worked marginally well.

"Not up to you, old man. America is a free country and, like you, Meilin has a right to make friends with whomever she likes."

"Stay away from her. We're getting married in a couple months, and nothing will stop it. Not you. Not her family, no one. She's signed the commitment contract."

"You make it sound like she's entering a mental institution. Hate to tell you this, but a broken engagement isn't worth pursuing in court. Your contract doesn't mean much in this country."

"It's a contract. She signed it, witnessed by a ballroom full of people we all know. Family, friends, my lawyer. It's legal and if she tries to break it because of you, you won't like the consequences. After all, you're not American."

Drew merely gave him a sidelong glance. "Why don't you try napping again? I'm sure it's the pain making you a grumpy Gus." It had taken all his stiff upper lip training to say that with a straight face. A phrase he'd learned from his sister.

"Asshole," Shan muttered.

Drew laughed. "Glad you figured that one out, but probably because you are one yourself. What's the saying? Takes one to know one."

"If I didn't respect your father, I'd have your ass deported in a heartbeat. Don't think I might not."

"My visa is tight. And now with my stepmother and sister being citizens, I've got a little more clout in that area. You can kiss my arse." He said it with a smile when he felt more like punching the man in the face. Then again, Lin already had enough injuries. "And you might as well forget about suing the winery. The borders of the walkway are clearly marked. The hospital and the police have your blood alcohol on record."

"I was under the limit."

"Just. You barely avoided at citation at best, a DUI at worst. My advice is to send the winery a thank-you note for their fast action in getting you medical care. Wouldn't hurt to also commend the hospital staff for putting up with your belligerence."

"They were fumbling, incompetent fools. Once I see my own doctor that will be confirmed."

"Your choice." Drew shrugged.

* * * *

Meilin was thrilled to see Shan's assistant and housekeeper at his condo with a personal care nurse in place, a big Samoan man who looked like he'd take no trouble from Shan. They'd also had a hospital bed installed and other items needed for an incapacitated man. Although Shan protested her leaving, Meilin was happy to escape when Drew insisted. Later she'd pay for Shan being thwarted, but just then it felt good to dodge the guilt.

With Shan's car safely secured in its underground parking spot, she settled into the passenger seat of Drew's vehicle with a sigh. When he reached for her hand, she grasped his. Strong and warm, his hand wrapped around hers and lightly squeezed. The shock and simmer between them made it impossible to let go.

"You okay?" Drew's deep voice with the sexy accent calmed what little upset remained.

"Yes. Now I'm okay." Rolling her head on the back of the head rest, she looked at him. "With you it seems I'm always okay."

"I know I'm happier with you." He smiled back at her with another squeeze of her hand. "I mean it. I just know we're meant to be together. I don't care what we do, just as long as you're with me."

"I'm beginning, possibly, to think you're right," she said slowly, her heart beating so fast she felt lightheaded.

"Then don't worry about the future. It will take care of itself. The only question is, what's the next step?"

The next step? The next step. "I break the engagement contract. It won't be easy."

"Sure it will. In this day and age engagements are broken all the time."

"But this contract was written between our families using lawyers. It's a big deal."

"Well those lawyers can just undo the contract. Who do you need to call first?"

"My parents, I suppose." And wouldn't that just be the most fun. In fact, while making the call sooner rather than later would be better, she didn't relish the thought at all. In fact, it terrified her because she'd have to do it in person. Face to face.

All too soon Drew came upon her building, pulled a U-turn in the street, then slid into a parking spot just vacated by another resident.

"Pretty slick parking job," she teased.

"Try parking in London sometime."

"Thanks, but I'll pass. Which makes it more impressive you did it on the correct side this time."

After a teasing glare over his shoulder, Drew checked for traffic, then stepped from the car and walked around the hood to open her door. "I'll get your bag."

Meilin sucked in a deep breath as she watched his movements, beautiful with athletic grace. The art critic in her appreciated the lines of his body, the economy of movement, the sheer beauty of him from the way he smiled to the way he slung the strap of her bag over his shoulder. Sunlight touched on his golden hair, disheveled from sleeping at the hospital, and she had the feeling of looking upon one of the gods, a being so beautiful mere mortal man couldn't look upon him without being incinerated for daring to do so.

The air stilled in her lungs, and she had to remind herself to breathe. As dizzy as she was, she was grateful when Drew snaked his arm around her waist and pulled her up against his side. Heat flooded her system, gathering low where her body clenched around a sudden wash of moisture. The gaze they shared was so intimate she could almost feel him sliding inside her body.

His voice, low and husky, thrilled her further when he asked, "Do I get a tour of your apartment?"

Too excited by his presence to answer, she nodded and dug into her purse for her keys.

Chapter 26

When Meilin dropped her keys, Drew bent down and picked them up from the sidewalk. She trembled as he once more slid his arm around her waist. There was no place he'd rather be, no place he'd rather she be, but in his arms. Unless it was in his arms in a bed. His bed, her bed, he didn't care. Her bed was certainly closer. Now that she'd made the decision to dump old Lin, Drew wanted to convince her they were perfect together in all ways. With only two weeks left until he left for China, he had to work fast.

In silence they made their way into the older building. He followed her to the stairs and up to the third floor. Mostly he noticed her. The fit of her slacks and how they hugged her ass as she climbed. The gentle sway of her hips, the slender line of her back, and the way her hair swung just above her shoulders. She was erotic poetry in motion. Each step tightened his need to touch, kiss, and make love to her.

At the top of the stairs, she turned right down a hall painted a faded butter yellow, the hardwood lined with a worn runner of beige carpet. At the last door on the right she stopped.

"Which key is it?" he asked and held out her dangling keys. The blush that bloomed on her cheek was charming as she pointed to the right one. The one pinched between his fingers.

"Good guess."

Wanting her more than he wanted anything else in his life, including the superman costume for his sixth birthday, he concentrated on not fumbling the key. In short order the door was opened, they stepped through, and Drew used his shoulder to ease it shut.

Meilin reached for her bag. "You can drop the keys on the table."

He dropped the keys in a small bowl to his left, but held on to the overnight bag. "Where's this go?"

Meilin's hand landed softly on his arm. "In my room."

"Lead the way."

The pupils in her eyes dilated, and not just from the dim room. By the catch of air at the back of her throat, she felt the weight of attraction between them. She wanted him as much as he wanted her. Thank God.

Meilin's hand slid down his arm to where her fingers meshed with his, their palms pressed together, the conduit for the electricity cycling between them. Walking backward, her gaze locked on his, she slowly led him through a small sitting room and into a bedroom. The apartment smelled like her. Rich with cinnabar, exotic florals, and another spice he couldn't name. It all whispered her name to him. The high bed was set on an old-fashioned brass frame and covered with a deep comforter of black with swirls of bright colors that gave the impression of flowers and birds. The bed was very much her. Rich, sensuous, inviting.

He dropped the bag at the foot of the bed and reached for her. This was the moment. This was the place. It had all come together to make this moment perfect.

Meilin came into his arms, her head tilted back, lips raised for his kiss. Only his kiss. The only kiss that would ever matter to her, he'd make sure of it.

What he didn't want to see was the hesitation in her eyes as she looked up at him. "I... I wasn't going to do this just yet. Remember? Just last night I said I wouldn't."

Framing her face with his hands, he told her, "You can say stop at any time, I promise, but know that I might suffer bodily harm if you do." At least one of them laughed. He wasn't entirely joking about the bodily harm, but he'd never push her. Tease, entice, and seduce, but never push or force. The choice was hers.

"I don't want to hurt..." She lifted her face to him.

All teasing left him. He shook with desire and dipped his head. "I need you," he said against her lips.

"I need you more," she said, rising up on tiptoes to meet him, her arms moving around his waist.

From their previous kisses he thought he knew what to expect. But the electric storm between them took him by surprise. Like a tsunami, the kiss ripped away all their previous experiences and nearly took him to his knees. Needing support, he released her face, lifted her onto the bed, and followed her down. There. Perfect for the seduction he'd dreamed of. The seduction he'd follow through on now.

Staring into the multilayered jade depths of her eyes, Drew speared his fingers into Meilin's soft, smooth hair. Like threads of heavy silk, the strands flowed over his hand, the pins holding it up loosening and falling away.

Mesmerized, he watched the glossy lengths fall to the bed under them. The pins fell soundlessly on the thick pile carpet at the sweep of his hand. Meilin's head slowly tilted back, her eyes closed, lips parted, her sweet breath touching his face in soft puffs.

Her smooth as pearls skin glowed with a faint flush. Black lashes lay like delicate fans on translucent skin beneath her eyes. Red lips parted, tempting him closer, promising him kisses sweeter than ruby red cherries. "You're so beautiful," he murmured.

Meilin's eyes opened enough to look at him through her long lashes. "You're the beautiful one."

The thumping of his heart increased, the blood rushing to his groin pulling elegant words from his brain. Little ability to speak remained, leaving him only with the roughly spoken words, "I want you."

A slow smile lifted one side of her lips. "Then make me yours."

Heart too full to speak, he dipped his head and tasted sweet nectar from her sweetly swollen lips. The short nails of her fingers gripped his shoulder and forearm, holding him to her, driving up his need. Her lips opened to him and he pulled her breath into his body. He wanted to dive in and plunder, but the drugging influence of her scent slowed him down, urged him to draw out the moment, savor each nuance. Savor her.

The fingers digging into him sank a little deeper, meeting resistance in the hard muscles of his arms.

"Drew…"

He cut off her moan and nipped at her full lower lip. "Easy now. I want to record this moment forever in my mind." Teasing, torturing, his lips whispered over hers. "I want to live right here, right now, for all time."

His lady's humor came to the surface. Her soft laugh was more a moan that tugged at his inner most soul. Her hands loosened their grip and glided over his arms, up over the cotton of his shirt, to his shoulders where they tightened again. Pulling him closer until he felt the softening of her breasts against his chest, the softness of her stomach against the rock hardness of his groin. She pressed her lower body closer, shifted and moved, testing him. Her hands then traveled down his back, to his ass where they gripped hard again, forcing him closer yet.

"Don't take too long," she ordered in a voice barely stronger than a breeze rustling the leaves outside the window. "I'm hungry. I want to devour you."

Lord, she tested his resolve to make this special. Granted, the fact they were together now was special. A prayer answered. A miracle of bloody freaking biblical proportions. He'd be sure to offer a true prayer of thanks later. For now he had to worship at the altar that was Meilin.

Needing to get closer, he sealed his mouth to hers. Willingly she molded to him, extending her small sweet tongue to meet his in the middle. There they touched, like two dancers allowed only to touch fingertip to fingertip. How his ancestors had to have been frustrated by the little-to-no-contact rules at the formal balls they attended. How they must have reveled in the scandal of the waltz that allowed them so much closer to the untouchable ladies of society. The very wickedness recognized by other cultures who insisted the sexes dance segregated.

Breaths mingled and Drew's desire burst into an explosive flare of heat. Teasing done, he plunged his tongue into her mouth. Meilin rose up to meet him, passion for passion, the kiss now deep, their mouths fused. Their breathing harsh, yet perfectly in tune.

Meilin's hands came around to the front of his body, squeezing between them, following the line of his belt.

It became a race then. He searched out the zipper of her pants. She loosened his belt buckle. Arms tangled as he pulled her shirt up, her hands fumbled for the button on his trousers. With a little laughter, their outer clothing fell away as Drew toed off his shoes. Somehow he found a move that allowed him to sweep their clothing from the bed. Impressed with himself, he managed all that without breaking the kiss.

At last he stretched out on the bed beside her, the silk of the coverlet nearly as smooth as the skin rubbing against him. Only her lacy bra, panties, and his briefs remained between them. A situation that needed to change.

Reluctantly he left her lips and kissed his way to her jaw, down her throat, stopping to lick the hollow at the base of her throat. The beating of her pulse teased him and he stayed to taste her skin until she moved restlessly against him. As much as he wanted to touch and taste, he wanted to see. Torn by the need to rush forward and conquer, he resisted and pulled back to let his eyes catch up. Meilin offered a protest as he distanced himself a few inches.

"Hush, love. I just want to see." Propped up on one elbow, he looked. Against the dark silk of her bed spread, her skin glowed like a sacred statue of twenty-four karat gold.

If he wanted to look, she did as well, her gaze stroking his body every bit as much as his study took in hers. When he touched her with a single finger, she mirrored his movement, gilding him with her light touch drawing across the upper bulge of his pecs as he traced the swells of her breasts.

Not overly large, not small, the perfectly sized and shaped breast cupped in his hand was in a state that begged attention. Attention he was more than happy to provide.

He was also thrilled to see the front closure on her bra. A truly wonderful invention. But he didn't stop to wonder other than to flick it open. Her breasts were large enough to hold on to the cups, as if reluctant to bare herself to him completely. One gentle brush of his hand unseated them and at last his eyes feasted on the dark rose of her peaked nipples. They rose and fell with each deep breath she took. Just air being exchanged in her lungs, but the effect was like the gentle rise and fall of the ocean.

Meilin rolled to face him, her hand stretching down, reaching for him. "If you get to stare, I get to touch, learn by feel." She found him, wrapped him in the warmth of her hand. He sucked in air, lost for a second in the feeling, so much so his head spun.

"Careful, I'm too close. Don't want to finish too fast."

"Then don't stop."

Gaining control again, he tugged the strap of her bra down, interrupting her torture. Once her arm was free, he rolled on top of her, settling between her legs only to endure a new torture. Her body held his just right, the warmth of her embrace a perfect cradle for him. This was home as he'd never known it before.

"I won't stop. Not now, not ever. Not unless you want me to." He sealed his promise by capturing her lips again and rolling a little farther to fully free her from the upper garment.

Once the wisp of cloth vanished, he pinned her hands to the bed on either side of her head. "Don't move," he warned her.

Eyes darkened and cheeks flushed, she sassed him back. "Not fair."

"No one ever claimed life was fair. Now behave while I finish unwrapping my present." The warm, exotic scent of her was driving him wild, and he wanted to taste and thrill her before he let go.

Content when she huffed out a small protest and surrender, he pushed up to gaze upon her. The look of passion on her face almost drove him to the main event, but he fought against the pull of desire. They weren't going to rush this. She was too precious for that.

Weight on his elbows, he cupped her breasts, plumping them, raising the nipples to his lips. Slowly, he took the first one in his mouth and teased her, first with his tongue, then by suckling. The other breast he gently squeezed, then rolled the nipple between his fingers. To his satisfaction she pressed her head into the pillow, raising to meet him, writhing against him. Alive in his arms, warm and enticing, she drove him onward to please her more. At the small wail that rose from deep in her throat, he switched breasts, teasing the other with his mouth, pinching and rolling the wet nipple he'd just left.

Against his stomach the lace of her panties was no barrier to the wet heat coming from deep inside her. He rubbed against her, pressing himself into the bed below, the silk beneath them a caress nearly as exciting as her hand.

Meilin shuddered beneath him, whispered words of need a sweet song to his ear.

In that moment, in a flash of understanding, finally grasping what had eluded him weeks before, he knew why poets lived to breathe life into their words. He pushed up, rising above her to feast his eyes on her beauty. He also knew, truly and deeply, why painters and photographers were driven to capture their visions for all the world to see. He understood the lyrics to every love song ever written. Not very lawyerly or logical, but all was suddenly clear as crystal to him. This was why men conquered and pillaged. They did it all to feel this bliss. To seek more. Cavemen had used clubs to drag their lady loves back to their caves. Modern men became artists, or climbed to the pinnacle of business, or became warriors of a different sort. To claim the mate of their dreams. To feel this one connection, soul to soul. It made gods of men and goddesses of women. The very hubris that earned them the jealousy of petty deities.

Were the Chinese deities as jealous as the Greek and Roman pantheons? Were they courting disaster?

Determined to drive her mad, and revel in his new insight, he lowered himself until he could kiss each rosy nipple, then continued the kisses down her body, over her quivering stomach to her cute navel. A small giggle escaped her as he dipped his tongue into the divot.

"Keep going," she ordered.

"Ticklish?" he asked.

"Not a bit," she lied. It was bold attempt, but he knew. Later he'd explore each spot. Just something more to look forward to. There was so much he wanted to do with, and to her, he suspected it would take a lifetime. Something not yet guaranteed at this point, but he'd do his damndest to make it happen.

Moving down, he kissed her lower abdomen, enjoying the growing scent coming from her center. So delicious he couldn't hold back much longer. Soon his fingers found the waistband of her panties and he tugged, pulling them down until she was exposed, her thighs trapped. The longer he played, kissing the sparse soft black hair on her mound, the more she writhed to sweet sounds escaping her throat.

At the feel of her fingers along his scalp, he nipped at her skin.

Meilin arched up against him, urging him to take what he wanted. Give what she wanted. It all blended into one. Pressing his lips to her mons, he settled between her thighs still restricted by her wispy panties.

"Andrew," she complained. The moan pleased him. He might even forgive the use of his full name. But later. He needed to taste her now.

* * * *

Meilin groaned. Drew was taking his time, teasing her with only his breath against her most private parts. She didn't care what he did, as long as he did it. Soon. Kiss her there, touch her with his fingers, or best of all, crawl up the length of her body and fill her. This torture was almost too much and when his lips touched her, she let out a little cry of joy. "Yes!" she encouraged him. She'd say anything to get him moving a little faster.

She wanted him so much she didn't flinch when he tore her panties away. The only thought that crossed her mind was she could finally open her legs and let him in. He left her no time to think further as his lips briefly closed about her. One tiny swipe of his tongue, that's all he gave her before pushing her thighs wider. She melted at the touch of his mouth, and quivered as he stroked, licked, and sucked. Although she was far from cold, she imagined herself an ice cream cone he devoured. When he used his thumbs to open her inner lips, she accommodated him by lifting her legs from behind the knee and pulling them up.

Drew growled and she glanced down to see his gaze fixed on her face. The pure hunger shining from his beautiful eyes made her hotter still. As if she could be any more turned on. With that look, and a deliberate touch of his tongue, he closed his lips around her clitoris and sent her straight to the stars. He held her there, a finger sliding into her body and stroking, as his lips suckled, he kept her coming until she couldn't sustain it, couldn't breathe anymore, and collapsed as a balloon deflating. Dampness coated her skin, and her chest rose and fell as fast as her heartbeat, sucking in as much air as she could. Surely she'd held her breath for a full minute as she rode the crest of her climax.

A smug grin on his face, Drew slowly worked his way up her body, his touches, kisses, and small bites lighting tiny fires along her nerves. By the time he reached her nipples, desire once more thrummed in her veins. How did he revive her so fast? As he suckled and pinched, she writhed against him, post orgasmic lethargy forgotten.

"Now, Drew. Now."

"In a minute."

The sweet agony he put her through... There'd be payback when she got her chance.

He lingered so long over her breasts she nearly came the instant his sheathed tip touched her. When had he managed that trick? They both gasped with pure pleasure as he slowly entered her, first an inch, then he drew back, only to enter a little deeper. His patience had her close to growling for him to speed up when he pushed up over her, his arms straight, and finally, finally entered her fully.

Then he stopped.

Dumb with disbelief she stared up into his blue, blue eyes which even now twinkled with passion and mischief. "Andrewww..."

He grinned, then pushed deeper still. "You feel amazing."

"I... I wasn't sure you'd...fit." On a moan, she arched upward as he pulled back.

"Oh, we...fit." Staring into her eyes, he slowly thrust into her again. "Perfectly."

"Yes, oh yes. Do that again."

As securely as he filled her, his gaze held her rapt. So much emotion filled his eyes, she felt it as a physical caress. No one had ever shown her so much of themselves. His intensity humbled her, filled her heart with emotion so strong she feared it would burst. He warmed her from the inside out to every extremity, and she wanted to give it all back to him. Such a sharing soul, surely he gave her the power to fly as one with him. Only him.

"Drew..." She couldn't find the words. Instead she cupped his face with its sexy golden stubble, and held him, doing her best to convey her heart with only her gaze.

"I know," he said roughly. "I know."

From there words were useless. They spoke with their eyes, their hands, lips on skin, the melding of their bodies. He lowered himself to rest on his elbows as he continued to stroke her deep, deep inside, his hands curling over her shoulders from beneath her, holding her secure against their movements. She lifted her legs to wrap them around his hips, never breaking eye contact. It was the most erotic thing she'd ever experienced.

His chest, lightly furred with golden down, teased her nipples, keeping them at attention, begging for more.

A part of her wanted to close her eyes, let her body feel every sensation, every slide of flesh against flesh. His eyes held her. Now dark blue, the pupil dilated to full, for the first time she could appreciate the phrase about the eyes being the window into a person's soul. Did he see in her eyes what she saw in his?

Forever.

She saw forever in his eyes. Them holding hands long into their twilight years, grandchildren tumbling at their feet. Grown children, puppies, and kittens. Travels to far off places. The vision was so profound her heart stuttered.

Drew's eyes focused more intently, his lips curved in a smile, then touched hers. Her heart raced to catch up as the most exquisite bliss stole over her like a category five hurricane. Hungry for it all, every last ounce of pleasure, she rose enough to seal her mouth to his, at last closing her eyes and letting the bliss take full control.

As the pleasure peaked, Drew's arms tightened, holding her as if he'd never let go, his body stiffening as he joined her in falling through the heavens.

They held each other tight, his weight on her slowly increasing as the vibrations they shared slowly decreased, then faded away, leaving them both breathless and covered in a fine layer of moisture.

She still held his face between her palms. Their kisses eased to nibbles until his head dropped to her shoulder and she slid her arms around his neck, holding him to her, kissing wherever her lips landed. Slow kisses, barely more than pressing her lips to his temple, hair, ear. Worshipping the man who'd just transformed her into a new woman. One with a future worth fighting for. With him.

Before either of them had fully caught their breaths, Drew lifted his head and stared into her eyes once more. Without a word, he slowly flexed his hips and still hard, still touching every inch of her inside, he smiled.

"Ready for round two?"

Chapter 27

The ringing of a cell phone woke Drew from a light doze. It came from somewhere on the floor and he recognized his sister's ringtone. Shit. The real world was calling.

He was able to make out the bedside clock. Five in the evening. And his parents probably wanted to know if he'd be returning their car any time soon.

"What's that?" Meilin asked, her voice muffled against his chest. Right where he liked her.

He cupped his hand around her head where it lay and lightly combed his fingers through the hair at her temple. "My sister. I hate to say it, but I think our time-out is over."

Meilin's sigh brushed over his skin. "I suppose it has to be."

"I better get it." He didn't want to leave her, leave the bed, or God forbid, leave the apartment.

Meilin kissed the hollow at the base of his throat just as his stomach rumbled. "And we'd better find you some food."

"Let's kill two birds with one stone. Have dinner with me. We'll meet up with my parents and sister, and she can drive me back to school."

Meilin rolled to her back, freeing him to get his phone from the floor, if only he wanted to roll out of bed to do it. The ringing stopped, then started up again.

In short order Drew and Meilin agreed to meet his family at a restaurant not far from Meilin's apartment in an hour. That left time for a leisurely shower, and Drew made the most of it, stroking every inch of her skin under the pretense of washing her.

Despite being only a few blocks away, they arrived just as Drew's father opened the door for the two women with him. Fortunately his dad and Randi both kept their thoughts to themselves, and if they found it odd he and Meilin sat close, trading glances and small, secret smiles, they never mentioned it. Birdie wasn't quite so polite, but held herself to questioning looks.

The hour they spent in the restaurant was a special kind of hell. Knowing his last few moments with Meilin were shared, knowing he wouldn't see her again soon, possibly for days, he wanted to turn back the clock and do the day again. Without the part that included driving Shan Lin home.

Thankfully his parents kept the topics neutral. Weather. Sports, although with football season not starting for weeks, there wasn't much Drew wanted to discuss there. Meilin told Randi about an art show at the DeYoung and that took up all of fifteen minutes between Meilin's lessons in Chinese food, particularly dim sum. Mostly for his benefit he guessed.

Once the bill was paid, his dad sat back and patted his stomach. "That was delicious. Never enjoyed a Chinese meal more. Hate to say good night, but we old folks need our sleep."

Birdie rolled her eyes when Court winked at her mother. "Daaa-ad," she complained.

Meilin laughed, albeit a little embarrassed. "Yes, tomorrow starts another busy week. I have some delicate business to conduct and will need all my rest for it."

"Anything I can help with?" Randi asked.

"No, but thank you. It's a family matter and could be quite dicey."

As Drew well knew, it involved talking to her parents about breaking the engagement.

"Hey, Bird, Meilin's apartment is about three blocks from here. How about we give her a lift?" Drew pushed back his chair and stood, holding out a hand to assist Meilin.

"Not a problem," his sister said.

"Or we could give her a lift?" Randi offered. "We were thinking of trying to catch the sunset while crossing the Golden Gate."

"Oh, no," Meilin protested. "I don't want to put anyone out. I walk the three blocks all the time."

"Nonsense," Drew said. "I want to see you home safe and sound."

"Well that's settled." Court stood and held out his hand for Randi. Despite their age, the two looked darn right together, his father tall and fair, his stepmother small and fairer still with her red hair and milk pale skin. Put them in medieval costumes and they'd be perfect for the roles of Lord and Lady.

Now he and Meilin were lovers, he wanted a photo of them side by side. Did they have the same glow as his parents? "Hey, Mum." He held out his phone to Randi. "Take a pic of us, will you?"

"What a wonderful idea!" Of course Randi loved it. From the look in her eyes, she knew. Trust the newlyweds to notice something like this growing between two people. Although her gaze still held questions. Questions he hoped to answer soon with his own announcement.

But first things first. Meilin had to lose the jerk.

Chapter 28

It took three days, but finally Meilin worked up the courage to talk to her parents. She'd called Shan each day and listened to his petulant complaints about trying to do work while laid up at home and increasing his demands for her attention. Each call reinforced her vow to bring it all to an end. On Wednesday evening, she arrived at her parents' house in the Sunset District with her father's favorite dessert in hand. Chocolate cherry cheesecake from his favorite bakery. Didn't win her points with her mother.

Dinner was endured, the proprieties observed. Not that she could eat much. Mother had noticed, but not Papa. At last, dessert done, the teapot emptied into the last cup, she broached the subject.

"Mother, Papa, I have something to discuss with you."

"Of course," her father said. "We're all ears." Sadly, his contentment would shatter in a moment. He was, after all, greatly in favor of a marriage to Shan.

She drew in a deep breath, folded her hands on the tablecloth and bowed her head respectfully. "I have decided I do not wish to marry Shan Lin."

The world grew still, her mother's hand stopping mid-air in raising a teacup to her lips.

"What did you say?" Mother asked quietly. "I hope it's not what I think I heard."

"You heard correctly," she said softly, her stomach in knots. "I no longer wish to marry Shan Lin."

Papa finally found his voice. "No, you're mistaken. You're annoyed about something, which is normal, but you must marry him. You're practically married, all but for California law." The lowered brows and the crease between his eyes was an exclamation point to his fierce expression and reddened complexion. No, she hadn't expected him to be pleased.

Papa's hand hit the table, making her jump and leaving her heart pounding. "I forbid you to speak of this again. The wedding will go on and you will learn to be happy with Shan Lin."

Okay, she hadn't quite expected that. Still, she had to speak up for herself. This wasn't China where she was expected to do as her father said. This was America; she was a grown woman with her own income. She ran her own business and made decisions on a daily basis. This was no different, other than being more personal. Longer term. "I respectfully disagree, Papa. I will not marry Shan Lin. I don't love him and will not ever love him. I have lost respect for him, and his character is not that of one I'd choose to be my husband. He's…said things. Things I cannot agree with."

"This is no impediment to marriage, Meilin," her mother said. "Husbands and wives have had differences of opinion for centuries and still found ways to live together. You must simply adapt."

Fingers knotted in her lap, she answered. "It's not that simple, Mom. I can't adapt to what he sees in our future. I apologize for any embarrassment this may cause you, but I simply cannot marry the man."

"What is so objectionable about a wealthy man with a good heart?" Papa demanded.

"For starters, he does not respect my career."

"That is of no consequence. Once you have children they will be your career." Mother waved away her first objection.

"I cannot marry a man who does not respect my desire to work. To not respect my wishes is to not respect me."

"Nonsense!" Papa shouted.

"It is not nonsense," she said. "Also, he has said that once we have two children, if we find we're not compatible intimately, he would free me to have an…an affair, which means he'd be free to do the same. I can't forsake marriage vows in that manner."

"Again," Papa shouted. "That is no reason to call off a wedding. There are bigger issues at stake than intimacy between partners. Besides, once you have your children it is only natural for the passion to fade. You'll be too tired, too busy with the children. He'll need to find comfort elsewhere."

Meilin's mouth dropped open and she stole a horrified glance at her mother. "I can't believe you'd say something like that, Papa."

He at least had the grace to look abashed. "Some men have told me that's how they felt when their children were born. Not that I'd know anything about it."

She couldn't believe he'd try to backpedal in such a manner. Mother sat still, a fierce look growing fiercer with each second as she stared at Papa. "I also cannot believe you'd justify such an abhorrent view. Makes me wonder where you really were when you claimed to be working late while I was home with two toddlers who drained every last ounce of my energy." Angry spots of red colored her cheeks, and Meilin sensed a shift in the room. The anger moved off her as Mother aimed a terrible scowl at Papa. "How dare you suggest our daughter put up with a husband who would condone cheating under any circumstances!"

Mother threw down her napkin and stood, knocking her chair backward. "Meilin, on that alone I will support you in breaking the engagement. There are other reasons for the marriage to take place, but I can't see selling you into a loveless relationship. Shan promised us he'd win you over, make you love him, but..." Voice clogged with deep emotion, possibly tears, much to Meilin's astonishment, Mother abruptly turned away.

It was Papa's turn to gape like a fish, his mouth moving with no sound for several seconds. By the time he found his voice, Mother had stomped from the room, down the hall, and into their bedroom where she slammed the door.

Papa spluttered while Meilin stood to collect the remaining dishes, feigning a calm she did not feel.

"That woman!" he finally shouted, then turned his anger on Meilin. "It's still not enough to break a marriage contract such as you have with Shan Lin. You will marry him!" His face was fully infused a deep red, his expression angry and...pained.

Plates and cups in her hands, she stood tall. This was no time to crumble. Her entire future counted on her holding firm. "I will not. Now, do you call the lawyer or do I?"

"I forbid you to take this path!" Papa lurched to his feet.

His anger was a terrible thing to see and Meilin trembled at it. But in her mind, she saw Drew, standing tall and confident. She borrowed from her vision. "I will not marry Shan Lin. I'll call the lawyer tomorrow." With as much dignity as she could muster, she turned on her heel and carried the dishes into the kitchen. Unable to stop the trembling setting in, she set the rattling stack in the sink, washed her hands, and left the house with Papa shouting after her.

Once in her car, she gripped the steering wheel, her knuckles white, and made herself breathe. Deep breath in to the count of three, long breath out to the count of five. It took ten minutes, but finally she was calm enough to drive home. At home, she kicked off her shoes, removed her clothes, and crawled into bed. Curled in a fetal position, she closed her eyes and held back the tears.

Finally she'd spoken up for herself. It felt awful to face such anger. Never had she made her parents so angry. Usually Papa fawned over her, praising her beauty and her intelligence. Oh how differently tonight had ended! He'd shown a side she'd never seen before and she didn't like it. Not one bit.

But what had she expected? That they would coo and soothe? Try to talk her into rethinking her decision? Instead, it seemed she'd tossed a bomb between her parents, dividing them as she'd never seen before. Sure, Mother had yelled at Papa in frustration before, but Meilin had never seen her retreat with slammed doors.

It was all too much to deal with while her mind was numb with hurt and shock. She needed to end the engagement, but she hadn't expected to cause problems between her parents. If their reaction were anything to go by, then how would Shan's parents take the news? How would he? Could marriage contracts be defended in court? Engagements were broken all the time, but then again, few were ever accompanied by legal contracts other than pre-nuptial agreements, which kicked in when divorce was on the table.

What else was in the contract she'd skimmed?

Wasn't their contract essentially a pre-nuptial? She tried to recall the details, but much beyond the fact she had to be married to him ten years before expecting any sort of compensation in a divorce, she hadn't taken much note. To her it had been a matter of marry once and for all time. She hadn't gone into the marriage expecting much more than financial stability. She hadn't once given thought to California property laws or how she might benefit in a divorce. Marriage was a forever deal in her mind. She'd been prepared to meet her end of the deal—provide a serene home, give birth to a minimum of two children, be a hostess and help to her husband in his business and social obligations. The unwritten agreement was that eventually they would fall in love with each other and love would add strength to their union.

The flaw in her thinking was now crystal clear. Find love first. Without love, marriage would be a cold and lonely prospect. Especially if she knew her husband felt free to find a mistress to see to his physical and emotional needs, and expected her to find a lover to do the same for her, as long as no one knew.

No. She could not tolerate that kind of life. Better to remain single than to go knowingly into a marriage that had little hope of being anything more than lukewarm with respect and little affection. If she found herself alone in her old age, she wanted memories of love and laughter to comfort her, even if the love and laughter came from her nieces, nephews, and friends.

Love and laughter such as one young Englishman could give her. One with golden hair and twinkling blue eyes filled with affection and teasing. A shiver of longing to be in his arms again eased the tension in her muscles. Memories of making love, of losing and finding herself right here in this bed, soothed the last of her tremors. A whisper of his scent clinging to her pillow melted the icy angst from around her heart. If his memory could affect her this way, what would seeing him, loving him, snuggling with him every day do for her well-being?

Did this mean she loved him? Was in love with him? She tried to look into the future and imagine her life without him. But his laughing eyes kept intruding, warming her, making her smile.

Maybe she was in love. Truly, deeply, in love. For the first time. A weight lifted from her heart and she wanted to jump up and sing. A thought that made her smile to herself.

Well. Seemed her decision was made.

Meilin sat up and pulled her knees to her chest. If making the decision was half the battle, then why did she still have one tremor of fear?

Pictures of Shan's angry face flashed before her. She sighed and closed her eyes, rocking back and forth. Confrontation wasn't something she'd been raised to handle. Tonight had been the first time she'd seen anything resembling true trouble between her parents. If they'd had strong disagreements, they'd carefully kept the children shielded from the discord. Father's word, mostly, was law, her mother often demurring with down cast eyes before witnesses.

Was that what she wanted for herself? To be second to a man? Funny how she'd never really taken the time to think about what she wanted out of a relationship. Or even if she really wanted one in the first place.

Although conflict rarely entered her world, she usually didn't run from her problems. With that in mind, she faced the future now. First, she considered her life as it was. Alone, solely dependent on her talents and brains. Making her way in the world without relying on anyone more than she had to. Employees she paid. For fun she had friends. Friends who one by one were taking up the shroud of married life, tying themselves to a man, and happily taking on the burden of children. Their lives now left little time for her or other friends not involved with the schools their children attended or the social clubs their husbands belonged to. A life very much like the one she'd take on by marrying Shan.

It sounded like a busy way to live, but it could be as lonely as her current single life. Without the satisfaction of knowing she could take care of herself, or knowing her partner had her back as well as her heart, just as she'd have his. Is that what made all the difference?

Had her friends really traded independence for a life of security? Dependent on a man who might one day decide he wanted someone younger? A man who might die in an accident or have a heart attack? What would become of her friends then if their husbands didn't leave behind enough life insurance or savings? It didn't sound very secure to her, but did love make the risk acceptable?

But she had options. Drew had said she wouldn't have to give up her career to be with him. Just redirect it a little. He was young enough and focused enough on his career that children probably hadn't crossed his mind. And as the sole male heir to his father's business, someday children would become a priority. Would she be ready for children then? Would she be too old? Would it even matter now his sister was in the picture? If she married and had children, it was possible Drew would be relieved of providing the next generation.

And yet, for the first time in her life, she felt empty at the thought of never holding her own child. Drew's child. What a time for her biological clock to kick in!

Overwhelmed by the questions, she dropped her face into her hands. The future was so uncertain. To marry or not?

Marriage to Shan was out. Definitely.

Marriage to Drew… Well, that thought wasn't even on the table, couldn't be. Not until she'd dealt with calling off her engagement to Shan and all that entailed.

Although it was after nine, she reached for her phone to call the lawyer her father had used for the marriage contract. Another distant cousin and one who wouldn't mind the late call. No time like the present to set things in motion.

Chapter 29

After a very long, very hellish day, Meilin dragged herself up the stairs to her apartment. Never had those three flights felt so endless. Never had she climbed them with her heart so heavy.

A cloth bag containing a few groceries bumped against her leg with each step. Just a little salad and some basics to see her through dinner tonight and breakfast for a couple days.

She reached the top of the steps and leaned against the wall for a minute. Enough to give her the strength to walk into her apartment before she collapsed completely. Physically, mentally, and emotionally. All levels had been hit hard today. Hell, every day for the week plus a few days. And she was no closer to finding a good to solution to even one of her problems, numerous as they were.

On a deep breath, she straightened. Standing out here wasn't going to fix a single one of them, either.

At her door, the bag slipped off her arm and hit the floor with a loud, cringe-worthy thunk. It was after nine and Edna would be asleep. Making noise in the hallway was rude enough, but something so loud?

She managed to get her key slipped into the first lock when her neighbor's door opened behind her.

"Meilin, honey. Everything okay?"

Great, now she'd disturbed the older woman who needed her sleep. The door was solid against her forehead when she let her head drop against it.

"Meilin?"

"No," she whispered. "Everything's not all right. Nothing's even remotely okay."

Two gnarled hands grabbed her shoulders from behind, urged her to turn around, and she found herself hugged to the thin, but far from weak, person of Edna.

The kindness of the gesture was too much. Meilin burst into tears. Being rocked by a woman more than twice her age and several inches shorter was immensely comforting, almost the same as when she'd been a small child and her great grandmother had cuddled her after kissing away whatever small trauma had happened just then.

"Come on, honey. This needs some tea."

Meilin let Edna tug her toward her apartment's open door, then sat when she pushed Meilin over to a sofa. A tissue box landed in Meilin's lap next. She grabbed several and bent to bury her face in them. Edna's slight form sat next to her. It didn't take much encouragement for Meilin to lean on the smaller woman and let her bony arms surround her. Dear, dear Edna. The thought of leaving her behind someday made Meilin cry harder.

At last, long minutes later, the tears slowly dried. When she could breathe without gasping and hiccupping, she sat up slowly. Edna kept a hand on her arm, gently patting.

"There now. You collect yourself and I'll make some tea." The elder woman rose, then made her way into the kitchen. "There are clean washcloths in the bathroom if you want some cold water on those eyes."

By the time Meilin came out, Edna had a tray on the coffee table with her prized vintage Chinese yixing teapot and a pair of chipped white ceramic mugs.

"You didn't have to do that," Meilin said.

"Nonsense. My pleasure." Edna settled on the sofa and pointed to the spot next to her. "But I will let you pour."

The teapot, one Meilin had found for Edna in an antiques market, was hot to the touch and fragrant from years of brewing a fine oolong that they both preferred. It made her smile to see it being enjoyed.

Once they both had cups and sat sipping, Edna said, "Want to talk about it?"

"Oh you don't want to hear my problems. It's bad enough I'm here past your bedtime." By nine every night Edna folded up like a morning glory waiting for the next day's sun.

"I was awake. Not even in my nightgown yet."

True, Edna still wore one of the cashmere sweater and wool skirt sets she preferred.

"Sure you want to hear all this? It's very dramatic. Melodramatic, even."

"Make my night." Edna grinned and raised her cup for a sip.

Meilin took her own sip, then sighed. "You know I became engaged."

"Yes. Handsome man, but too old for you. I'm surprised you accepted him, but assumed you knew what you were doing."

Meilin laughed. Her first in many days. "No, I didn't know what I was getting into." As briefly as she could, she brought Edna up to date as far as Shan's accident.

"I'd decided I didn't want to marry him," she explained.

"And that's where the blond hunk comes in?" There was hope in Edna's question and face.

"No. Yes. Maybe. He's not really a part of the central drama. That all revolves around Shan and my parents."

Edna nodded. A signal to continue.

"Well, I finally told my parents who were not pleased. Especially my father. Mother walked out leaving us to finish the…discussion."

Edna snorted. "I imagine it was more of a fight then."

"Mostly it was Papa yelling at me. He forbade me to break off the engagement."

"Then what happened?"

"After I got home, I was reaching for the phone to call my lawyer when my brother called. Not long after I left their house, Papa had an… episode. That's what they're calling it. A small-ish heart attack." God, would the feelings of guilt never go away? She'd brought the attack on. Although Mother never said the words, the truth was there between them. It hovered in the hospital room each time she went to visit her father. A huge, flaming, hot pink elephant sitting right there.

"Silly man for not staying on top of his health. He brought it on himself," Edna declared firmly.

"Yeah, well, I was the detonator."

"Not your fault, honey. But keep going. That's bad enough in itself, but there's more going on."

"Yes." She sipped some more tea and let it warm her inside. "Turns out there was more to the engagement agreement than they'd told me. Once I marry Shan, he'll assume all the expenses for my father's care and retirement. That way he can leave all the assets for my brother to take over the family businesses. They do well, but not well enough to fund my parents' retirement, especially with my father's health. This heart attack will put a huge burden on the group insurance." Closing her eyes, she slumped against the nubby fabric of the mid-century sofa.

"So, the wedding is still on?" Edna's voice rose. "What about you? You'll sacrifice a relationship with a hot young Brit for your father?"

"There's no other way, Edna. I can't afford to take on their medical bills, neither can my brother. Mom can't get a job to make enough. Her job is now to nurse our father. She needs to be at his side to take care of him. While this episode wasn't huge, it did enough damage that Papa will need constant care and watching over. No more chocolate cherry cheesecakes for him."

"But you don't love Shan. In fact, I sense you don't even like him. Possibly might even despise him. If not now, in a few years for sure. Surely they don't think it's right to marry him under those circumstances?"

"They do."

"But...why?"

The distress on Edna's face was the motivator to set down their cups so Meilin could hold her hands. "Because in China, when you injure another person, it becomes your responsibility to care for that person for the rest of their life. Although my parents were born American, they were raised to be as Chinese as possible. They follow the old traditions as much as modern life allows and raised me to do the same. Because my father's episode was brought on by my wish to dissolve the engagement, it is therefore my fault he's in the hospital, and the easiest path is to marry Shan and let him pay for everything. The hospital, the nursing home or home health assistant, therapy, and medications."

"That's nonsense." Edna snorted. The noise was so cute Meilin nearly smiled.

Edna's outrage also made Meilin feel a little better. She wasn't alone in feeling the unfairness of the situation. They hadn't told her this was part of the contract. Had she known, she might have refused to sign. She sighed. Or not. Knowing what all was on the line, she might have shrugged and signed anyway. Before meeting Drew.

After meeting Drew... Well that was the critical turning point. A test of her loyalties to her family. A test she was failing, miserably, to the great disappointment of her mother. Her brother had a little more sympathy, but didn't hesitate to point out how marrying Shan was best for everyone. Best for him, Mother and Father, however no one mentioned how it would be best for her. They didn't care if she was happy about it or not. She'd signed, accepted the proposal, and now she was committed. The end.

In their opinions.

"And how does the beautiful blond man with the English accent feel about all this?"

Meilin looked into Edna's watery emerald eyes. Hair that had once been red was now thin and white. Skin once smooth as alabaster was wrinkled and translucent, showing signs of aging that would never be reversed. The thin shoulders inside cashmere were slightly hunched. Blue veins stood out on the hands knotting with arthritis. Hands that could still knit a sweater, afghan, or baby bootie. In her gaze, there was little sign of age, unless it was decades of life responsible for the wisdom there. The kindness was innate.

"He doesn't know about the latest. I mean, he knows I was engaged and determined to get free of it. He knows I don't want to marry Shan. He knows I love him, although I've never said the words. He also knows Shan is not the only obstacle in our way. Were Shan not around, we'd still be facing the issues of age. He's ten years younger than I am. Just out of college, for Christ's sake!"

Edna snorted. "Age is merely a number. Besides, a younger man will keep you young longer. What does your heart tell you?"

Meilin stared at their hands. Hers smooth and strong. Edna's gnarled and stronger yet. "My heart says he's the one. Nevertheless, we still have other problems to consider." In a few sentences she outlined Drew's new career and how it didn't match with hers. She also told Edna what Drew had said about that.

"Listen to your heart, my dear. He's wise, your young man. Talk to him. I bet he has solutions you haven't even dreamed of. I bet he has ideas so outrageous they have to work. I have the feeling he'll do anything to keep you from marrying where your heart doesn't wish to go."

"What if his solution is the same as Shan's? Marry me and take on the burden of my parents?"

"What if it is? Didn't he mention you could work for his father's company? I bet they have some sort of insurance program that would cover your parents. My son put me on his so that when I need a nursing home, the insurance will help with most of the costs. Not that I intend to go quietly when he decides I'm too senile to take care of myself." A wicked twinkle entered her eyes. "Beside, when I go into a home, I want to be spry enough to pinch the butts of the orderlies."

Meilin laughed. "I'd pay money to see that."

"Just come see me when the time comes, and I'll consider it payment enough. You can sneak me in some cigarettes and booze. By then I'll want the end to come quickly, so don't try to tell me how those things will kill me."

Laughter rose again. "I promise. Might even hire a male stripper to make the deliveries from time to time."

"Only if you're off gallivanting around China or England. Lovely as a stripper would be, I'd rather see you."

Meilin sobered again. "I've already told my family I'll go ahead with the marriage. I never got the chance to tell Shan. In fact, he is insisting

I move into his condo this weekend. He wants me to care for him rather than the home health aide and his housekeeper. And he wants to prove to me how well we'll get along married." Only three days away. Tears swam in her eyes again at the thought. "For so many reasons, I don't want to. I have commitments I just can't drop and keep my business reputation, and yet he's demanding I do so."

"Then don't." Edna shook their still clasped hands. "Talk to Drew. Don't give up and roll over. You're made of stronger stuff than that."

Sniffling back her tears, Meilin nodded. "You're right. I'm a modern woman who started her own business from scratch. I need to find my own solution here that doesn't involve a man bailing me out."

"Well, let Drew bail you out a little. Hire on with his company and take the insurance option. That will mean making your contribution, not throwing yourself solely at his mercy. It will make you more equal, which is the way marriage works best. Partners who bring their own talents to the relationship. Whether that means you keep the house so he can concentrate on making a good living, or both of you working and sharing household duties, or him staying home while you work, it's all up to the two of you to find the balance. Not what your parents and millennia of ancestors determine. You determine how your marriage should work. That's what should be traditional these days."

Leaning forward, Meilin carefully took the fragile woman in her arms. "The world needs more of your wisdom. I'll do it. I'll talk to Drew."

Chapter 30

At the end of two very long weeks, Drew was hard pressed to paste a smile on his face. Hell, he was hard pressed to remember to shave or do laundry. More than once he'd sat brooding over his choices from choosing law school to ultimately moving to China. Was it really what he wanted from life? Was he crazy for ever starting down this path? Had it been his idea to begin with, or a careful manipulation by his father or grandmother? And with the move from Stanford to Peking University imminent, he had no time to work things out.

The Mandarin lessons certainly seemed to be a huge miscalculation on his part. Almost everyone in the class had voiced the same doubts at least once, so possibly he wasn't wholly off track. Although, the lessons seemed to be progressing. However, for him, not quickly, not easily, and he still questioned his intelligence for thinking he could learn Mandarin. For one, he was lacking the musical ear that could help him hear the subtle tones. He had a greater appreciation for foreigners learning the crazy way English had words with similar spellings, but far different pronunciations.

Learning Mandarin and getting ready to move to China were big items, but neither truly quite topped his list of things that seemed bollixed up. Meilin took the top spot. She hadn't answered a single text in over a week. Not knowing how she was doing, or what she was doing to break herself away from Lin, was driving him up a tree. All he knew was her father was in the hospital with some severe health issues. A tidbit he'd learned from Arnie after nearly a week of silence from Meilin. Something Arnie had learned only by calling to beg Meilin to come help with the evening tutoring.

All Drew had to comfort him were the pictures on his phone and a framed copy of the one of him dipping Meilin at the wedding. Him with the damned garter on his arm, her holding the flower, the two of them looking into each other's eyes. It was the most painfully romantic photo he'd ever seen.

He wanted to call, but held himself to one text a day. A simple message of, *I Miss You.* For three days she'd answered with, *Miss You Too.* Then nothing for eight excruciating days.

Here it was, Friday night and no word if she'd show for tutoring. Or to see him. Or anything. Didn't stop him from keeping an eye out for her.

Dinner was nearly done when she appeared in the doorway. He was so glad to see her he nearly jumped from his seat and captured her in his arms. A very public display they'd agreed couldn't happen. He was past caring. The need to hold her, to kiss her silly, was almost too strong to rein in.

The hesitant look on her face stopped him from following his impulse. Barely.

Instead of running to catch her up in a hug, he stood and held out a chair for her. The small, tentative steps she took toward him were worrisome. The tired expression on her face also had him concerned. Her eyes looked pained, her lips pinched, and weariness seemed to bow her shoulders. She'd lost both weight and the lustrous shine from her skin.

One glance confirmed the absence of the ring on her finger. The desire to catch her up in his arms intensified. Questions poured into his brain. Did it mean what he hoped? Then why did she appear so stressed? Was her father's health so precarious? Had a business deal gone bad? Was Lin harassing her for wanting to break the engagement?

But when her gaze met his, she gave him a brief, tiny, tremulous smile.

It lifted his heart so high he could barely breathe. Just seeing her eyes light up dissipated his cloud of worry and brightened his world. Once more he believed he could conquer anything, even learning Mandarin. All he needed was her by his side.

As she approached the table, she quietly greeted each of the students by name, asked simple questions in Mandarin and smiled at their responses. No, no one had the accents close to perfect, but even he could tell the difference just five weeks into the program. Maybe there was hope for them all.

Meilin swept her skirt under her bottom and gracefully settled into the chair he pushed in for her, never giving away her feelings, until he sat, and then she slid her foot up against his.

With a small sigh, her shoulders relaxed and her posture straightened.

She needed contact with him as much as he needed the contact with her.

The last of his doubts lifted away like a puff of smoke.

He didn't care what it took, this woman was his. The other half of his soul. With her at his side, he'd conquer new worlds, travel many mountains, explore valleys deep and mysterious, and cross all the oceans of the planet. One day they might add a child or two to their adventures, but for now, just the two of them would be perfect. And the minute he got her alone, he'd tell her so.

Holding back and following the motions of studying, working through pronunciations, he stumbled through the evening hours until Professor Chung called a stop at half past nine.

"It's Friday," the teacher said. "Tomorrow we'll start at ten. More fun vocabulary followed by a few videos in the afternoon. Tomorrow night you get a break. Those who want to go into the city for some authentic Chinese food, in a restaurant where the menus are in Chinese, let me know in the morning. We'll make a night of it. Perhaps even hit a night club to blow off some steam. We're at the halfway point and you're all making great progress. We're ready for the next step, five weeks in China. Longer for some of you."

Everyone smiled except Cindy who frowned unhappily. "I can go for dinner, but night clubbing…" She shrugged.

"Right," Drew said. "I don't think we have time to get you a fake ID."

Cindy's eyes flew open in shock while everyone but Chung snorted with laughter.

"Invite your parents," Chung offered.

She nodded with resignation. "I suppose. Or I can go over my final packing."

Meilin shot her a sympathetic smile.

"Count me in," Drew said as he stretched. "Who's driving? I think my sister will claim the car again." Damned nuisance now that they had different schedules.

"I can take three in my car," Bob volunteered.

"I call shot gun," Drew jumped at the offer.

"Professor, let me know the final plans, and I might be able to meet up with you," Meilin said, gathering her purse and briefcase. "I have a client meeting in the afternoon, but don't have solid plans later."

Drew stole a glance at her and bit his tongue to keep from cheering.

"Let me walk you out," he said, standing and taking the briefcase from her hand. So what if he'd just announced their connection to the small class? He didn't care. He wanted the world to know. And he wanted the details on the missing ring.

As soon as they stepped from the building into the warm night filled with the song of frogs and cicadas, he swept her up into his arms and hugged her tight. The kiss followed naturally and he thrilled to her immediate response.

"Meilin, Meilin, how I've missed you. Worried about you. I've been slowly going mad day by day."

She clung to him, arms tight about his neck and buried her face in his shoulder. "I've missed you so much."

The words sounded on the edge of a sob.

"Hey, we're here now. Together. Let's take a little walk and talk."

Her quiet agreement nearly broke his heart it was so faint.

They dropped her briefcase and purse in her car, locked it up, then hand in hand strolled down a path to a private bench. Their private bench. The dark summer air enveloped them, protected them from prying eyes, the way lit by lamps bright enough to illuminate the path, but not so bright as to simulate the harsh sun.

Once they reached their spot, under the sheltering branches of a tree that provided more shadow, and settled close beside one another, the question burst from him.

"Is it over?"

Meilin folded her hands in her lap and dropped her head. "No."

"What? You're not wearing his ring." He grabbed her hand and turned to face her. "Tell me."

Meilin took a deep breath before raising her face to him. "The first move has been made. I told my parents. It didn't go well. My father grew very angry with me, and my mother became very angry with him. I was about to follow up that meeting up with a call to the family lawyer. Instead, my brother called. Told me that Papa had collapsed soon after I left their house. A heart attack."

Drew squeezed her hand.

"I went to the hospital where my mother all but accused me of causing the heart attack by being selfish." Tears welled in her eyes, but she drew in a deep breath and blinked them back. "These last eight or nine days, I've lost track, have been horrible." It took some time, but eventually the whole story came out. Halting nearly every sentence, she told him every bit.

It took all he had to let her get to the end without interrupting other than to squeeze her hand or gently prompt her to continue.

When she stopped completely, Drew spoke. "So, it is, or was, your plan to go through with the marriage to care for your parents, even though your family knows you don't want to marry him. And that doesn't matter one bit to them? That you don't love him? You have no hope of ever loving him?"

Eyes downcast, Meilin nodded. "He's caught whispers of my plan to end the engagement but is still convinced he can woo me into loving him. By taking care of my parents, I'm supposed to see how kind he is. He doesn't know Edna told me differently."

"How is Edna?" Drew smiled. He hadn't yet met Meilin's neighbor, but she'd told him stories. He had a feeling he'd love the lady on sight.

"Still feisty. Mom's right about one thing; I love Edna as much as my own grandmother. She comforted me last night when I was barely clinging to the last knot on my rope. It's because of her support I'm here tonight. She insisted I needed to tell you what's been happening."

"I want to buy her some flowers. Wise woman."

Meilin nodded. "She is."

"What did Edna tell you about Lin?"

Meilin's mouth flatlined. "One evening when he came to pick me up, he passed her on the stairs. Didn't acknowledge her or offer to help carry her groceries. Nothing. Passed her like she was a bag lady on the street." Temper sparked in her eyes. "He's kind and concerned only when there's an audience."

"Selfish bloody wankstain."

Meilin gasped. "What?"

"Wankstain. A waste of..." Damn he was blushing now, Meilin never swore, and he'd made a point to be polite around her. "...well, just a waste," he muttered. "Someone should have cockblocked his father way back when."

Meilin covered her mouth and...giggled. Not a sound he'd ever heard from her.

"Sorry. I don't usually resort to crude language, I notice you don't either, but, well, sometimes there are no other words." He rubbed the back of his neck, hoping to dissipate the heat gathering there.

Meilin laughed outright. "You're right. I don't care much for crude language, but as you said, sometimes it's the only option. Especially with a British accent."

A sigh of relief escaped. "So. What other wise words did Edna share with you?"

Meilin bit her lower lip and looked away. "Um, she mentioned an option that might work out better than selling myself to Shan Lin."

"Yes? If she said you should marry me, then I'll send her flowers every day for the rest of her life. And then weekly to her grave site."

Meilin shook her head, then looked down at the ground. "Remember you once said I could easily fill a position at Lynford? Art and furnishing acquisitions and interpreter for you? What would the compensation package be like for such a position?"

Drew stilled, a small part of him shocked. She wanted a job? Well, yes, it would be a tailor-made fit, and yes, he'd suggested it. It would also allow them the time to get to know each other better. Give her a chance to be sure of his love for her and to know in her heart she loved him too. They wouldn't need to marry immediately, possibly putting her under undue pressure, but rather, allow her to grow into the idea. Okay then.

"What sort of compensation package would you like? I'm pretty sure we could come up with something to fit you like a glove." Reaching into his pocket, he was prepared to call his dad and get the process started. Meilin's hand on his stopped him from dialing.

"I'm aware there are some companies with insurance benefits that cover nursing home care for parents of employees. Does Lynford believe in such programs?"

"If it isn't one of our benefits, it should be. I could see it being a huge perk. Let me call my dad and find out."

Meilin's hand still prevented him from making the call. "And if it isn't a current benefit, I'm guessing, hoping, salaries are generous enough it won't matter." Her eyes were wide as they searched his.

"I'm positive we can find a way to make it work out. And if you choose you want to marry me, I'll make sure your parents are cared for. I'll even put it in a pre-nup, if you want one written."

Meilin's eyes widened more as she shook her head. "I don't expect you to take on my problems by way of marriage."

"I care about you and your worries. By loving you, and hopefully marrying you, helping you becomes my privilege. Not an obligation, not a contractual line item, but merely by extension of what you love, I love. If your parents need help, we help them. Likewise, should my parents ever need help, we help them. It's what love does."

At that Meilin's face crumpled and she threw her arms around his neck, pulling him close. "Oh, Drew. You said it perfectly. You wouldn't hold my parents' needs over my head to force me to marry you. That's love."

Hot tears watered his neck, but he didn't care. He pulled her closer until she cuddled on his lap. "It will all work out. We'll make sure of it. You and me. On our schedule. No one else's. I love you and want to be with you, however you'll let me be with you. The minute you say you're ready to marry me I'll have you before an Elvis impersonator in Vegas just to seal the deal. Then we'll follow up with church ceremonies here and England. Just to make sure everyone knows we mean it."

Meilin's laugh was watery against his neck. "Oh, Drew. I do love you. So, so, much."

After long minutes of kissing, touching, stroking, Drew pulled away to catch his breath. "I'm calling my sister and telling her to find another place to sleep. She can take my room at the dorm. Tonight, the apartment is ours."

Chapter 31

Unaccountably nervous, Meilin smoothed the red silk dress embroidered with a gold dragon from shoulder to knee over her thighs. After spending the night in Palo Alto, she and Drew had driven into the City together for dinner with the class.

She badly needed this night out. While Drew had been in lessons, she'd called Jack's Uncle Za for his advice. Turned out he hadn't much liked Shan Lin before she told him about the engagement agreement. Afterward, he wanted to tear Shan apart in court. Publically. He wasn't exactly thrilled with her parents, either, but for her he'd treat them with respect when quizzing them in further detail about the written, and unwritten, items in the contract. Since she had brought her copy in her briefcase, Za sent a courier to pick it up that afternoon and promised to get a hold of her early the following week. It was a relief to have something moving forward the way she wanted.

Dinner had been fun and full of laughter as the students learned the characters for delicacies such as squid and octopus, then ate the results of their orders. Most had been surprised to find they liked the unusual dishes. Unsurprisingly, Drew had dived in with great enjoyment and no sign of trepidation like a few of the others. He even handled his chopsticks like a pro.

Now they stood at the entrance of the night club where she'd first met him so many weeks ago, nervously wondering who she knew who might be at the club that night. More importantly, who there might know Shan Lin and report to him she was with Drew.

"There's a table opening," Drew nearly shouted in her ear to be heard over the music.

It was a miracle they found enough seats for everyone, and Junlei was there to take their orders. Meilin sent her a grateful smile, which was returned with a wink.

"As soon as you get the first round, set up the second," Meilin told her. "First one is on me."

"Sure thing!"

Fortunately it was busy enough, and loud enough, Junlei didn't have time to verbalize the questions in her eyes. Obviously she recognized Drew, and the absence of an engagement ring on Meilin's finger. No, Meilin didn't want to go into it tonight. Instead she shrugged and turned her attention to the dance floor. Hopefully no one she knew would be here. Wasn't Jack still out of town?

Arnie, still oblivious to the attraction between her and Drew, held out his hand. "I get first dance," he yelled.

Happy for the distraction, she accepted. It felt good to shimmy and sway to the hip-hop beat. Like a physical touch, Drew's gaze followed her from where he sat guarding the drinks and purses left behind, a secret smile on his face. Every dance move she made was for him, and his eyes ate her up. The slim silk dress fit her like a second skin and she let her hands trail down her sides, watching his eyes follow them before his gaze captured hers again. It was a tease and a torment for them both. A building of anticipation.

For a full hour she danced. Switching partners with each song. Arnie didn't last long and traded places with Drew. While presumably their group danced together, she and Drew knew they danced with each other. They found plenty of opportunities for small touches, each one adding to the heat in Drew's eyes. Adding to the heat that pooled low in her belly. Finally, a slow song entered the mix and Drew reached for her. In his arms, she flew back to the night they'd met, only now the electricity between them flared twice as strong.

He bent, placing his mouth close to her ear. "I want to kiss you."

A gasp of desire escaped and she pushed him back an inch. "Not here. Not now. There's only so far I can go."

"I know," he said as he spun her, drawing her closer for a moment. "I know what's at stake. I won't compromise you that much in front of the class, but it's killing me." He smiled and spun her out, then pulled her back.

She laughed with pure joy. No one danced like Drew. No one made her laugh, or float on candy clouds, like he did.

The music faded out for a second, and Drew took her hand and tugged her back to the table. "Don't know about you, but I need something to drink."

"Me too." Meilin fanned her face.

Junlei had just reached their table with a tray of fresh drinks as Meilin dropped into her chair, reaching for a napkin to blot her damp face.

"Perfect timing," she shouted at the waitress.

"I live to serve." Junlei laughed. "You look thirsty."

"I so am." She used the napkin like a fan.

"Meilin! There you are."

Both women startled as a man shouted from behind them. Junlei dropped Drew's beer on the table, and it would have spilled but for his quick reflexes.

Ice formed and dribbled down Meilin's spine. A tremor of fright coursed through her even as she turned to see Shan behind her in a wheelchair pushed by his health aide. "Shan? What are you doing here?" Who had called him? How had he known? As far as she knew, he never came to places like this.

Anger turned his handsome face into something ugly and frightening. "Looking for my fiancée who hasn't been answering my calls for the last two days."

Junlei gasped, her dark eyes round in surprise. "This is your fiancé, Meilin?"

Confused, Meilin looked at her friend. "Well…" Lord, what did she say?

"You didn't tell me this low-down, cheating, conniving, double-crosser was your fiancé," Junlei shouted, pointing a finger at Shan.

"What?" Meilin was even more confused and noted the conversations around them dropped off and everyone was turning to watch. "You didn't ask, and I didn't think you knew him. How do you know him?" She looked at Shan and saw his face slide into an expression of granite. "Do you know Junlei?"

"I don't know her. I'm here for you. But I find you with"—Shan lifted his casted hand and pointed at Drew—"this upstart, this *boy*! I knew there was something going on between you two!"

With a scream, Junlei grabbed Meilin's drink and flung it in Shan's face. The red wine ran down his face and stained his white shirt almost like blood. "You lying, two-timing, son of a bitch! You know me, asshole. I've been trying to find you ever since I discovered you got me pregnant!" She lifted her tray over her head and would have whacked Shan on the head had Drew not caught her arms.

"He got you pregnant?" Meilin's hand flew to her throat. "When?"

Using a white linen handkerchief to wipe the liquid away from his face, Shan stared past Junlei as if she didn't exist while she struggled to break free of Drew's hold. "The dirty rotten creep came here one night, maybe five, six weeks ago, because he was feeling 'itchy,' seduced me with his smooth talk and slick flattery, then tossed a handful of bills on my pillow and told me not to look him up because he was engaged to a *lady*," she snarled. Giving up on getting her tray back, she spit on Shan's face. "You're the father of my baby, you dirty, stinking, rotten user! I'm a lady! How dare you treat me like trash!" She spit again and Drew pulled her farther back as a pair of bouncers arrived.

With a look of disgust on his face, Shan used the sopping, stained handkerchief to wipe the spittle from his face. "She's delusional."

"What's going on here?" one bouncer demanded.

Meilin was in too much shock to answer. Shan was too stiff with indignation or anger, she couldn't tell which, to say a word. It was Drew who stepped in, Junlei's tray safely in one hand, the other around her arm, holding her back from assaulting Shan further.

"We have a case of a two-timing Lothario here. It seems both ladies object to his presence," Drew told the two security guys.

The bigger bouncer scowled at Shan Lin and flexed his enormous fists. "You messed with Junlei? Man, that was a bad, bad move. It's time you leave." By the awful grin on his face, Meilin was pretty sure the bouncer wanted to get a few punches thrown in before letting Shan go. Maybe push his wheelchair off the curb…pointing downhill.

The smaller, but not by much, bouncer took Junlei from Drew's hold. "Babe. You got him good. Let us get him out of here, and then you can tell us all about it, okay? Anything you need? Like his name or phone number?"

"I have those," Meilin quickly said. "I know exactly where to find him." For good measure she scowled at Shan. "Do you remember the day, Junlei?"

Junlei fumed, but she nodded and quieted down, folding her arms across her body. "It was about a week after you were here last. Middle of the week. Wednesday night, I think. He came in about nine or nine-thirty."

Mentally scanning her calendar, Meilin thought hard. "A Wednesday night?"

"Yes."

"Then," Meilin turned a fiercer scowl on Shan who was still held by the bouncer, "that would have been the night of the Schultz's party." The night they'd made out by the door of her apartment. "You left me and came here." Not a question, but a statement. He'd been aroused and talking of going to bed. Had almost pressed himself on her.

Shan's face tightened before growing blank. It had taken him an effort to tamp down his emotions, which made her confident in her guess.

"You lying piece of garbage! You try to get me into bed, but when I turned you down, you came here and hooked up with my friend!" Her arm lifted, almost as if it had a mind of its own and started to swing. Drew caught her arm.

"Don't do it, love. You've got your easy out from the contract."

Knowing he was right, Meilin reached out a hand to her friend. "I want to know. I need to know. I'm breaking things off with him, but I need your account. Please."

Junlei didn't look too happy with her, but she nodded again. "Oh don't worry, I'll tell you all about it. You're better off without him. He's no good."

"I agree," Meilin soothed, running a hand down Junlei's arm. "I didn't know he'd been with you. If I had known he'd go find someone else the first time I turned him down, I never would have agreed to marry him. I'm just glad to find out now, before the wedding."

Junlei nodded again, then burst into tears and threw herself into Meilin's arms.

"I'm so sorry," she cried.

"What have you got to be sorry for? It's all on him." Meilin hugged the younger woman tight. "It will all work out, don't you worry. We can get a DNA test to prove he's the father. I believe you, but a test will guarantee he has to take care of you. I won't let him hurt you anymore. I promise."

Shan tried to shake off the bouncer's hand on his shoulder, but when he couldn't, he crossed his arms over his chest with a wince. "This does not break the agreement. You know how much your family will suffer if you don't follow through. Your father never planned for catastrophic illness. His insurance won't cover it, and he doesn't have the savings."

"I'll take care of my father," Meilin pronounced over Junlei's sobs against her shoulder. "It's my responsibility. I didn't ask you, and my father had no right to make such a deal. It was a low, underhanded move on your part to make it part of the contract."

"It's a business deal," Shan sneered. "Not only did I agree to take care of your parents, but I promised to inject some funds into the restaurants to help your brother get a stronger foothold. If you back out, then I can sue for breach of contract and your family will suffer. You'll be in no position to help them once I ruin your business. Your name won't get you a cup of coffee in the entire Bay Area once I'm done with you. You'll work the rest of your life to pay off your debt to me. If you can find a job outside your family's restaurants."

Junlei straightened and accepted a handkerchief from Arnie. "You'll do no such thing to Meilin! She can sue you for breach of contract because you fathered a bastard on me not two weeks after your engagement to her. I'll make sure everyone in Chinatown knows you go screwing around and then refuse to accept the consequences of your actions. That will sure put a dent in your reputation for being kind and generous."

Shan blanched but he didn't otherwise acknowledge Junlei's words. "Meilin." He spoke low, as if it would make him sound dangerous or something. "Come with me now and I won't take legal action. Hold up your end of the agreement and make everything right. I promise you it will be a good marriage. You won't want for anything."

"Other than honesty? You'll give me everything else but the truth? Will you get a head start on your other life? Have you already picked out your mistress?"

Shan glared. "I don't know what you're talking about. I only want you."

"And yet, once you didn't get me into bed the night of the Schultz's party, you found another, got her pregnant and refuse to acknowledge it, and you expect me to marry you even now? Your lack of integrity bothers me. A lot. If you were the last man on earth, I wouldn't marry you." So angry she shook, she started to move forward to slap him, but again Drew held her back.

"Easy, love. We've got him. And you've got witnesses. Besides, he's injured enough."

Meilin looked up at him, then around the nightclub to find a dozen or more phones aimed their way. Easily half a dozen were close enough to have picked up the conversation. It was then she noticed they weren't shouting to be heard over the music, which had quieted to background level.

From the crowd someone shouted, "We've got your back, Meilin! Everyone who works in a low level position in Chinatown knows what a prick Shan Lin is."

A round of cheers went up in agreement.

Which made her wonder, if these people hated him, then who had told him she was here?

"Shan, how did you know where to find me?"

His face remained stoic. "I just knew. Now, Meilin, this is quite enough. It's time to leave and it's time to take your proper place. With me. Not him." Shan nodded toward Drew at her back.

"That's where you're wrong, Lin old man," Drew said, his accent crisp and clear, sounding more royal with every word. "Her place is wherever she wants to be. Her job is to do whatever she wants. If that means she chooses to be by my side, then that's her proper place. Not at any man's beck and call. But rather there as a partner. Something you never offered her. Now, I suggest you prepare to meet her lawyer. He'll be in touch very soon."

The DJ jumped into the action then. "And that concludes tonight's floor show. Leroy, Alex, show the man out. The rest of you, save those videos, I'm sure they'll be appreciated in court. Now, let's dance!"

The music kicked up to full volume and Meilin had to laugh. Drew grinned wide as he dragged her out to the dance floor to Aretha Franklin belting out R-E-S-P-E-C-T from the sound system.

Chapter 32

Meilin gripped Drew's hand as they deplaned in London's Heathrow airport.

The last several weeks had been such a rush, she hardly knew where she was anymore, but what counted most was she was with Drew.

Drew had been able to put off flying to Beijing with his class for a few days while they'd met with his parents, her parents, and Shan's lawyers getting everything straightened out. Thank God for Shan's cheating ways or they'd be in court about now wrangling about the voiding of the contract.

Drew's father, in particular, had been a huge help in smoothing things over. Not only had he presented her with the perfect job offer, he'd advanced enough money to help her wrap up things in the city. She'd been able to concentrate on getting her visa, hiring and training a designer to oversee her business, and she'd paid six month's rent in advance on her apartment. Randi had advised her to keep the place because Meilin and Drew would want their own home when they made trips back to San Francisco. It was a solid idea and one Drew approved of.

It hadn't been easy, but she'd pulled everything together to arrive in China for Drew's final week in the program. She'd traveled with his parents, who'd put her up in the company apartment not far from the China head office. It was big enough for two families, and there were tentative plans made for a family gathering there sometime in the future. Eventually she and Drew would find a small house of their own.

But for now, after nearly twelve hours in the air, she and Drew were visiting London for a short break before they both started work in earnest. She'd never logged so many air miles in so short a time. By the time they returned to Beijing, by way of a fast trip through San Francisco, it would be her first complete trip around the world.

"All right, love?" Drew tugged on her hand. "You're looking a little shell-shocked."

Loving indulgence softened her heart as she gazed at her tall Viking warrior with the golden hair. "I am a little, but it's all good."

He leaned over and kissed her. "Wait until you see the house. We're headed straight for Sussex for a few days. After that, we'll have a day or two to hang out in London and get indoctrinated with the company line, but I want you to see the house first."

Both Drew and Randi had talked about it, of course. She knew it was big, built in the Tudor era, very formal, but family friendly as well. Drew had described summers running through the parklands surrounding the house with trees, ponds, and the adventures to be had. She wanted to see it all, but mostly she wanted some time to just hold Drew's hand and walk in the forest.

The usual hassle with Immigration and Customs seemed to go a little smoother, and in what seemed like no time at all, they were pulling their suitcases toward the sidewalk of Arrivals.

"Look, there's Martin," Drew said and tugged her to the right where several cars down a black Land Rover waited. The butler she recognized from the party stood beside it talking with an airport cop. Martin was impeccably dressed in a dark suit with white shirt and blue tie. Just the color that matched the Robinson eyes.

As they approached, they overheard Martin saying, "Look mate, there they are. I'll be out of this queue in less than three minutes. I appreciate your need to keep traffic moving, and I'm moving." Putting action to words, Martin moved to the back of the vehicle and opened the rear. "Right here, Mr. Drew. Pleased to see you again, Miss Wu." He took their bags and hefted them into the vehicle. "Just climb right in, now, and we'll be on our way so the good man here can go assist someone else who needs him more."

The officer tipped his hat and wandered to the next car at the curb.

Drew held the door for Meilin, then climbed into the back, taking the seat near her.

"Bloody, officious, meddling, traffic cops," Martin was muttering as he climbed behind the driver's wheel. "Everyone buckled in? Right, let's be off."

Drew laughed. "Still giving the authorities a bad time, Martin?"

"Not me, Mr. Drew. It's them giving me a hard time. I'm just a good law-abiding citizen trying to mind my own business. Have a good flight?"

"Flight was fine."

With Drew's arm around her, Meilin listened to the two men bantering, and stared out the window watching the city turn to country as they traversed the highway. On the wrong side of the road. Of course they'd had the discussion about right versus left hand driving, but since Beijing went with most of the world, despite Hong Kong adhering to the British system, neither one had actually climbed behind the wheel of a car over there. Going along with Court's recommendations, because traffic was so horrendous, the laws so mysteriously confusing, they either rode the public transportation or hired a car and driver. Or would, when they were there longer. She'd barely had time to unpack the few boxes she'd checked on the plane before Drew had completed his course and spent a week at the office before they were on a plane again.

With her head still spinning, she found it easier to just relax against Drew, still taking in the direction of her new life with him, and just absorb the world as it rushed past her beyond the vehicle.

"Not far now," Drew murmured in her ear. "You can see the chimneys." He pointed to where red brick rose above the trees in the distance.

"Big house."

"Just a house. Not a castle or anything so grand."

"Is it more like Pemberley or Longbourn?" She strained to see more as the road curved and once more it hid behind a grove of trees.

"Let me guess, a Jane Austen reference?" The teasing laughter in Drew's voice caught her attention. "What is it with you ladies? Randi said almost the same thing, word for word."

"You haven't read it or seen the movies?" Honestly, it was the best way for Americans to make the comparison. Presumably the Brits had their own way, which she'd probably figure out in a decade or two.

Drew theatrically shuddered. "I suppose my mum made me watch it once. It's only since Randi and Birdie have come into our lives that I've heard it discussed. And then it's more along the lines of who made the best Darcy."

"Colin Firth, hands down." She smirked at him.

"I believe Randi is of the same opinion. As for the size of our house, I believe she determined it's something in between."

Martin slowed the car, then turned between a pair of large brick gate posts. If there had once been gates across the drive, they were missing now. The lane narrowed and was almost a living tunnel beneath the trees forming a canopy from where they lined the sun dappled gravel trail. What seemed like miles later, the trees opened up and the lane resolved into a large oval before a very tall, three story house of red brick. Tall windows reflected the sunlight and all manner of plant life surrounding the grand house.

"Now that's not just a house, Drew. That's a country manor. And it doesn't look Tudor. Where are the beams and whitewashed stucco?" In fact, it wouldn't look out of place in Pacific Heights back home.

"The house is clad in tile. Another renovation over the years, and it's a house. Just a little bigger than what you're used to. It has bedrooms, bathrooms, a library, dining room, even a kitchen."

"And many other rooms, I'd imagine."

Martin pulled the car to a stop before a set of steps leading to a grand double door, probably carved from good solid English oak.

Gazing at the house, she asked, "What year was it built?"

"The Lynfords built it about 1550. More or less. It's been through several renovations and additions, depending on family fortunes at any given time."

Meilin accepted Drew's hand and stepped from the vehicle.

"I'll see to the bags, Mr. Drew," Martin said. "Mrs. Robinson said to put you both up in your room…?"

"That's fine, Martin. Thank you. Anyone at home?"

"Your father said they were going to be out for the afternoon, but everyone will gather in the drawing room at six-thirty before dinner. If you need anything pressed or steamed before then, please let me know."

"I think we're good." Drew turned to Meilin. "We have time for a lie down if you want a nap. I know you didn't rest well on the plane."

No, she hadn't. Too excited. Not that she thought she'd be able to nap now, but if she didn't, she'd probably fall asleep face first in the Yorkshire pudding, or whatever was on the menu for dinner. "A nap sounds great. A shower even better."

"Come. We'll ring Cook for a tray of tea to tide us over."

Martin slammed the back of the vehicle shut. "I'll just take these directly up, and then I'll ask Cook for some refreshment. I wouldn't be surprised if she has a tray set up already."

"We'll take a quick tour of the ground floor, then head up."

"Very good, sir."

Martin headed up the wide stone stairs, his arms loaded with suitcases. Meilin felt guilty for packing two, but not knowing what she'd need… oh well. Drew had stuck to one, but as he'd said, he had a closet full of clothes not only here, but also at the house in California. She didn't have any such luxury.

"Come on." Drew took her hand and led her into a grand foyer paneled with what looked like hand carved oak.

"Is this all original?" She spun in place, taking in the hall that looked like a set from Henry VIII.

"Every bit," Drew confirmed.

The wood glowed from centuries of polishing. A few treasures hung from the walls; old swords, a shield, paintings of people in period dress ranging from stiff ruffed collars to Victorian bustles.

"There are more modern paintings around the house. Up the stairs, along the halls, a few in the library." When she'd made a full circle, Drew grabbed her hand and towed her toward the first of many closed doors. "The front drawing room."

Meilin was speechless with wonder. A state she retained while Drew led her from room to room. The library was the coziest. The long dining hall the most impressive with its darkened solid oak beams overhead and a table large enough to sit forty.

"We can squeeze fifty in here for Christmas."

"Fifty people at one table?" Meilin strolled the length of the room. "It's amazing. I can almost hear the musicians playing while the guests eat, drink, and be merry."

"It's a pretty big deal." Drew stood watching her, hands stuck in his pockets.

There were two doors at the back flanking a fireplace large enough to stand in.

Drew nodded at them. "Those doors lead to a very modern kitchen. Bea's mark on the house. It was originally a butler's pantry, but she wanted the kitchens moved up from the cellar, so she added on and rearranged things a bit."

"It's amazing, Drew. This is like walking into history." The panels on the walls were smooth under her fingers. Probably due to very liberal doses of oil over the years. The light came through glass panes wavy with age.

"The bedrooms upstairs are more modern. Well, if you consider the Victorian period modern."

Meilin laughed. "Compared to the Tudor years, it sure is."

"We had a morning room down here until last year, but when Grandmother broke her hip, Dad had it converted to a bedroom with handicapped accessible en suite and sitting area. It's where Grandmother hangs out when she's here. The old bird is done with stairs, and Dad's not likely to install an elevator any time soon."

One of the doors from beside the fireplace swung open, and a cart loaded with plates and silverware was pushed through by a tall, thin woman with a shock of red curly hair barely contained in a ponytail.

"Mr. Drew!" she exclaimed in a bright Irish accent. Meilin figured she was in her mid thirties, not much older than she.

"Cook!" Drew replied, taking long steps until he reached her and gave her a big hug. "We're home for a bit."

"Go on with you now." Blushing like a teenager, she pushed him away with a laugh. "A tray's just gone up to your chambers for you and your lady."

"Cook, I want you to meet Miss Meilin Wu. She's one of Lynford's newest employees." He turned and stretched out his hand for Meilin. "Meilin, this is Sally O'Brien, also known as Cook around here. No finer chef in this part of England, I dare say, possibly all of England. She keeps us well-fed. Has been with the family since she was barely out of chef school when I was a tot."

"No better family to do for." Sally gathered her apron and gave a short curtsy. "Now don't let your tea grow cold and let me get about setting up for dinner."

Meilin eyed the cart. Seemed to her like there were enough plates for at least a dozen people, maybe more. Big dinner tonight?

"All right, ye bossy one," Drew drawled. "We'll get out of your hair. Want to wash the plane smell off and get a couple winks of shut eye."

"Pleased to meet you, Sally," Meilin said. "Looking forward to dinner tonight."

"Nothing but the best." The woman grinned, then made shooing motions to get them on their way.

"She seems very nice. Also looks like a large dinner party tonight," Meilin said as Drew led her up a wide staircase with the promised ancestors hanging on the wall.

"I suppose Dad and Mum invited a few folks to meet you. Mostly relatives tucked up in nursing homes. Any excuse to break them out for an evening here and there."

His casual tone was hiding something, but she was too tired, too fascinated with the house to call him on it. At the top they turned right and continued walking until the last door on the left.

"This is us. I just hope Mum hasn't done too much redecorating." Drew turned the knob and pushed the door open.

Another room that took Meilin's breath away. The first thing she saw was an enormous bed on the left wall, two heavily draped windows on the far side. A fireplace was centered on the right wall lined with more oak panels. In front of the fireplace two wing chairs upholstered in navy sat at an angle, a tea table holding a loaded tray between them.

"This is a Victorian fantasy," she said. The hand carved bed was the most solid one she'd ever seen. The tall posts held up a carved canopy and heavy navy blue velvet drapes hung at each corner. The massive headboard had to weigh four hundred pounds on its own. At the footboard sat a large, solid wooden chest.

"Just a room," Drew said.

Meilin glanced at him and caught his grin.

"Figured you'd like it," he added, then pointed at two doors flanking the fireplace. "One on the left is the bathroom, the one on the right the closet, which is probably where Martin put the suitcases. Both are a little cramped as they were once one large dressing room."

"It's a wonderful room." She ran a hand down the bed curtains, enjoying the soft velvet. "Immaculately kept."

"I'm pretty sure the room's had a pretty good airing out recently." He came up behind her and wrapped his arms around her waist, setting his chin on her shoulder. "A spot of tea first, or would you rather take a long soak in the tub?"

"Tub?"

Drew chuckled. "A very fine extra large claw footed tub. Much like the one in your apartment, only big enough for two. I had an ancestor who loved their baths and he installed the finest available back in the day. Of course we've updated the plumbing, but where possible, retained the finer fixtures, or had them restored, and when they were too damaged, had as true to the period replicates installed. Fortunately, my rooms are fairly authentic, as are Dad and Mum's. A few bedrooms were lost when converted to en suites. Everyone wants their own bathroom these days."

Under Drew's hands, her stomach rumbled.

"Guess that answers that question. Kick off your shoes, m'lady and let's dig in while the tea is hot and the scones are fresh."

Meilin reluctantly let him pull away. "Yes, I'm a little hungry, feeling a tad grimy, and would dearly love a nap."

Drew glanced at a clock on the mantel—also hand-carved oak—and said, "We have about three hours until it's time to gather for before dinner drinks. Let's take full advantage."

He led her to a chair in front of the fireplace. "Not yet cool enough for a fire, but maybe later tonight."

"This looks fine." Cook had outdone herself, and Meilin didn't know whether to start with the scones drenched in clotted cream and strawberry jam, the variety of finger sandwiches, or the fresh looking raspberry tarts.

She curled up in one chair and watched as Drew poured tea from a fine china pot into delicate porcelain cups.

"Probably the oolong," he said.

She let him add cream and one sugar. If she was going to die and go to heaven here, might as well go down with as many sweet calories as possible. When he held a tart in front of her lips, she opened up and bit down on the best treat she'd ever tasted. "Oh. My. God," she mumbled around the mouthful.

"Never going to find a better tart anywhere in England, I might even dare to say the world."

He sat in the opposite chair and fed her bites of delectable treats between sips of tea until she couldn't take another bite.

"Mum says she's afraid to spend too much time here. Seems to think we'll have to use a piano case to bury her if she eats like this every day."

"I can appreciate her worry." Meilin wiped her fingers on a linen napkin. "That was so good. I hope your father pays Cook very well."

"She's been here twenty years, so I'd say she's happy with her lot in life."

"She made it through chef's school as a teenager?"

Drew's laugh filled the room. "She was twenty-five when she started here." He stood and reached for Meilin's hand. "Time for a soak? Or would you rather nap first?"

"I'm too grimy to climb into those fresh sheets. Bath first."

The glow in Drew's eyes inspired her cheeks to heat. "Excellent. I'll play lady's maid and help you prepare."

"I'll help you prepare." She reached for the buttons on his shirt. "You need a bath too."

Didn't have to ask him twice. Meilin found herself stripped and in a tub filling with hot water, Drew at her back, in a matter of a minute. She was even more surprised when he reached for a jar of peach colored bath salts and dumped a large handful in.

"Mmm, smells good."

"Not as good as you." He nuzzled her nape where a few strands escaped her hastily twisted knot of hair.

As the water rose, she leaned back in his arms, not one bit surprised when his hands found and cupped her breasts. Judging by the column of hard flesh against her backside, the bathroom would probably end up better soaked than they would.

"Turn off the water with your toe, would you?" His lips moved against her neck.

Not easy to do, especially with him tormenting her neck and nipples, she somehow managed the job by the time the water was two inches from the rim of the tub.

Since they'd already established equal opportunity teasing was fair, and expected, she reached behind her back with one hand until she found him just the way she liked him, hard and ready to please her.

As her hand tightened around him, his fingers tightened ever so slightly on her nipples, pinching and rolling them until she squirmed.

"I seem to have caught a mermaid. I surely can't resist the siren's song," he spoke through increasing harsher breaths.

"Oh, I'm better than a mermaid."

"How's that?"

"Did you never wonder how a human male could make love to a mermaid? For that matter, how does a merman make love to a mermaid?"

"Unless it's all by mouth, hmm, I suppose you have a good point there." He groaned as her hand traveled up his length and her hand cupped the tip. "I seem to have miscalculated the order of events here."

"Oh?"

"We should have gone to bed first and saved the bath for after."

Meilin laughed low and throaty. "No, the order of events is fine. I feel much fresher already. After more than fifteen hours since my last bath, there is no way I'd taste, or smell, very good. I love you, darling, but I prefer clean flesh when making love."

"You always smell, and taste, scrumdiddlyumptious to me." Drew flexed his hips enough he slid through her hand. "You feel even better."

"Scrumdiddlyumptious?" The delicious streams of arousal twisting from her nipples to between her thighs made it hard to follow any type of conversation, especially one with such a silly word that made her think of chocolate.

"I grew up with Roald Dahl. Dad read me *Charlie And The Chocolate Factory* quite early on. First chapter book I read by myself."

"I love the movie. The first one."

"I bet you taste great with chocolate smeared all over you."

Just the thought of him licking chocolate off her... They'd have to try that. Whipped cream too.

Without warning, his hands left her breasts and moved to her shoulders. Before she could figure out his move, he had her flipped over and facing him. His ran his hands down her back until he cupped her bottom and lifted her against him. "Straddle me, woman."

There was just enough room for her knees to squeeze his hips in the tub. She rubbed up and down his erection, bringing forth a groan of pleasure from him.

"That's right, drive me mad." His fingers delved between her cheeks, touching the edges of her labia enough to heighten her lust. He lifted her, helping, driving her against him while she clutched his shoulders.

Because they'd had the tests, and she was on birth control, she readily slid over him without a condom, taking him in an inch before sliding up, then down again, taking a little more of him inside. Water didn't make a great lubricant, but he had her hot enough it didn't worry her too much. Slowly, inch by inch, she worked him into her. His face found a home between her breasts until he turned his head and took one into his mouth. The sucking motion of his mouth was timed perfectly with their efforts to fully join below. It didn't take long for her to finally seat herself against his body, him deeply embedded in her.

"Yeah, that feels so good. I love being in you," he said with a growl around a mouthful of her breast.

The feeling of pleasure was so great she couldn't speak, only feel. Him hard inside her, her soft inside his mouth except for the nipple he pushed up as he suckled. Heart pounding, breath sawing in and out of her lungs, she moved with him. His hands pulled her open, allowing him to drive deeper. Eyelids too heavy to open, through her lashes she watched him watch her with equally heavy eyes.

"Yeah," he said. "Just like that."

Flexing her hips, she rotated a little and stared back as his eyes darkened.

"You vixen." His fingers gripped her rear, stroking the valley between, moving lower with each rise and fall of her lower body, until the tip of one finger rested where she'd never been touched before by a lover.

"Drew?" She stiffened.

"Relax. It's okay." The finger retreated. "We'll talk about it another time."

He latched on to her neglected breast and his other hand came around to the front of her body, sliding between them, finding her sensitive nub, stealing away all thoughts as he stroked her into resuming her movements.

She rushed toward completion so fast that later she wondered if just that hint of something dark and dirty had been more of a turn on than she'd ever expected.

Chapter 33

At the sound of a gong from the lower floor, Drew and Meilin were already on their way downstairs. He'd worn the blue tie she said matched his eyes. She wore a matching silk dress embroidered with birds and flowers made in the Mandarin style with a high neck that fastened across her shoulder with silken frogs. The side slits in her long dress were high enough to show off her gorgeous legs. Her shiny hair was twisted up in a French knot to show off a pair of dangly gold earrings with blue topaz beads.

He'd never felt more proud of any woman on his arm.

She'd taken up his challenge to try a new life, and so far everything was going their way. He'd never been more sure of anything in his life.

Now, to find out if she liked surprises.

Voices came from the drawing room and he steered her that way.

"Sounds like more than just a few people," she said.

"No idea how many the folks have invited." But if he had to guess, there were close to twenty people gathered for dinner tonight.

Just outside the drawing room door, Drew stopped and turned to face Meilin. "In case I haven't said so lately"—he picked up her hand and brought it to his lips—"you grow more beautiful every day. Tonight you positively glow."

The soft smile she gifted him turned his heart to mush. "And you grow more handsome. I never knew I could love anyone as much as I love you."

When she said it like that, there was no way he could turn away without kissing her. It was just getting good when a loud voice interrupted from the open doorway.

"Hey now, kids. Save that for later. There are people here waiting to see you two."

Meilin dropped her forehead to Drew's chest. "What's Jack doing here?"

"That's the problem with kids these days," Jack continued in a loud voice and threw open the other half of the double doors. "You introduce them, make sure they meet up a few times, and then they go off together and you never see them. They don't call. They don't write. And if you ever want to see them again, you have to invite yourself to their parties." He made a show of tsking and shaking his head. "I tell you. The kids of today, there's just no—"

"Jack!" A man's voice came from inside the room and Meilin's head rose, a look of shock on her face. "Let them come in."

Meilin turned and gasped. "Papa? Mother?"

Drew couldn't keep the grin from his face any longer. "Surprise." He slipped his arm around her shoulders and guided her into the room.

Randi came forward and took Meilin's hands. "Since we didn't get to meet your parents while we were in California, we thought it might be nice for them to come and visit. See that Drew comes from a good family. I know they were feeling less than confident about your choice to take a position with Lynford in China, so this seemed like a good time to gather the family and make introductions all around."

"But—" Meilin started to protest but Jack interrupted again.

"Since they only had me for a character reference"—Jack slapped Drew on the shoulder—"I came along to assure them they were traveling safely to England. Also to help care for my uncle who is showing great progress in his recovery."

"This house is a great place to recover in peace," Randi jumped in again. "We thought they'd enjoy the scenery, and we'd get to know each other at the same time. We gave them the room on this floor so it's easier on your father."

Meilin's mouth moved like a fish out of water and Drew rubbed her back. "They've been here a week and they're having a great time from what I've heard." Her father looked less pale and more relaxed than the one time Drew had met her parents in San Francisco. Her mother looked happier too with a pale pink blush on her cheeks. Both were responding well to the English countryside.

"Come, let's make introductions." Drew guided her from one person to the next. "My grandmother Robinson, who I believe has taken over the cottage in the garden this week. You may have met her at the graduation party."

"Of course I remember you, young lady," his grandmother said. "You made a wise choice joining this den of thieves."

Drew laughed and Meilin smiled.

"Next we have my aunt and uncle and their sons…" Drew continued around the room, pleased and somewhat surprised Bea's parents were there, and ended with the vicar who set aside his sherry long enough to shake Meilin's hand. Each one had something nice to say. Even Larry, while Oswald kept watch from one side of the room and Birdie hovered near their grandmother. Both Birdie and Oswald carefully ignored each other. No change there.

Drew managed to keep Meilin busy enough mingling that she had no chance to ask him why her parents and Jack were there. She wasn't buying the meet and greet story Randi had dished out. But she was noticing her parents getting along quite well with his father and grandmother. Randi flitted about keeping everyone's drinks fresh.

Still, his woman had questions in her eyes every time she glanced at him. He merely smiled. There were traditions to uphold. Protocols to follow. He had a plan and he wasn't going to deviate from it. Martin saved the day by announcing dinner just as Meilin had him cornered. Would have to send the man something special from China for that.

In the dining room they found Randi and his grandmother having a quiet discussion. When his grandmother told everyone to look for their place cards, Drew caught the exasperation on Randi's face and the resignation on his father's as he escorted his wife to her seat at the foot of the table. Far, far away from her usual seat next to him.

Drew seated Meilin on his father's left, then drifted down the table to find his seat. Of course, on Randi's left, while she directed Meilin's father to her right. He held back his chuckle as he seated his grandmother on his left, then took his own chair.

"Giving up the hostess spot," he said to his grandmother.

She answered with a harrumph and a nod of satisfaction, and turned her attention to his Catchpole grandparents.

Despite the new seating arrangement, Randi handled dinner well and the courses flowed as smoothly as ever. Conversations were bright and he exchanged many glances with Meilin who seemed quite bemused. Just a little longer and then he'd answer her biggest question—exactly why this dinner was being held.

Once dessert was served, Drew looked across the table at Meilin's father. The solemn man gave him a nod. Okay then. Show time.

Pushing back his chair, Drew picked up his champagne glass and a fork. Carefully tapping it against the crystal—his grandmother's eyes narrowed on him to make sure he didn't break it—he called the dining room to order as the last server slipped back into the kitchen. Only Martin remained beside a table with bottles of wine and pitchers of water at hand.

"I suppose you're all wondering why we're gathered here tonight." Chuckles met his statement. "All right, most of you know, but Meilin does not." He set down the fork and started toward the head of the table.

"It's been a wild ride since the night I met Meilin. I knew immediately there was something special between us, but it took a lot of fast talking and fancy dancing to reach this point. The fact is, I've never been happier." He rounded the table behind his father's chair, his gaze locked securely on his target. "There's a new road ahead of me and while the people in this room will be a part of it, there's only one person I want by my side."

Meilin's eyes widened as he reached her seat and set his champagne on the table.

"Tonight I carry on a long standing family tradition. There's always been one place where the Robinsons make these grand gestures. The grander the better. And while it's tough to beat my father and his grand gesture last Christmas Eve, made in this very room"—the family thumped their fists on the table with mutters of "hear, hear"—"I have my own grand gesture to make."

Meilin raised her napkin to her mouth and moisture twinkled in her eyes.

"I want the world to know how very much I love you, Meilin. I want them all to be a part of this, but the honor is reserved for this small crowd."

He put a hand back and his father slapped a velvet box into Drew's palm. He dropped to one knee and held the box out to Meilin.

"I know it's been fast, but I've never been more sure of anything in my life. I don't want to go a step further without knowing you'll be my love, my partner, my wife. Please, accept this token of my intention to make you the happiest woman on earth, as you've made me the happiest of men."

Meilin dropped the napkin in her lap and covered her mouth with both hands. The tears shimmered in her eyes and he could see her trembling.

Nerves hit him then, and praying with all his might she wouldn't turn him down, he opened the box and thrust it at her. "Please say you'll marry me."

Her gaze never left his as she reached out. She bypassed the jeweler's box and touched his cheek. "Yes," she whispered. "Yes," she said louder. "I love you so much, Drew." She threw her arms around his neck and hugged him close.

His arms wrapped around her waist and he clung to her, his heart so light he feared he'd drift into the rafters with the ghosts if she didn't hold on.

"So let's see the ring," Grandmother Robinson called out. "How'd you do? Does it fit?"

Meilin lifted her head laughing and wiping at the tears spilling down her cheeks. "Yeah, Drew, how'd you do?"

Once more he held out the ring with a three carat diamond surrounded by the finest rubies to be had in Beijing. More were set into the carved gold band. "I learned red is the color of good luck in China."

Meilin lifted the ring from the box and slipped it on her finger. "Indeed it is. I love it. I love you."

Exaggerating his sigh of relief, Drew stood and pulled her into his arms. "I'm the lucky one here." He tilted her backward in his arms, just as he had for the photos in June. This time he kissed her with everything in his heart and soul. Meilin kissed him back without reserve.

Behind him his father stood. "Lift up your glasses, ladies and gents. The lady said yes!"

By the time they came up for air, they were surrounded, but it didn't matter. Meilin was the only one he saw, the only one he could hear as she whispered, "The day I met you was the luckiest one of my life."

"To date," he said and kissed her again.

The End

Keep reading for an excerpt from the first novel in the series

HER FOREIGN AFFAIR

Twenty-two years ago, she ran out on the love of her life—
and took a secret with her.

When Randi Jean Ferguson fell for Courtland Robinson while studying
abroad in London, she was ready for a life of tea and crumpets. But when
she discovered Court was being forced into a shotgun wedding, there was
no way she could stay—or tell him she was also pregnant with his child.
Now widowed, Randi is just starting to consider finding Court—when he
shows up at her door. With his son. Randi's not ready to reveal everything
to Court, but if she doesn't, will both their children end up scarred?

The best thing to come out of Court's unhappy marriage was his son. But
he's spent the last twenty-two years thinking about Randi, his California
girl, his first—and only—love. Now a widower, he takes a chance he's
only fantasized about and seeks her out. At last he'll solve his heart's
greatest mystery—but that won't be the only surprise in store for him.

A Lyrical e-book on sale now.

Learn more about Shea at
http://www.kensingtonbooks.com/author.aspx/29498

Prologue

A soft spring breeze tugged a long curl from Randi Jean Dailey's carefully styled up-do. She paid the cabbie his quid, stepped from the car with the help of the hotel doorman, and gave him a smile. The cabbie let out a satisfactory wolf-whistle before zipping back into London traffic.

Jean's heart pounded with excitement. Instead of climbing on the plane to go home after her semester abroad, she'd primped and polished and put on her perfect little black dress accented with proper pearls and sexy stilettos. The ones Court had bought for her two weeks prior. The ones that made her short legs look a mile long, he said. The black shoes she'd worn to seduce him last night. The ones that had driven him so mad with lust he'd made love to her all night long.

With a long bittersweet kiss, they'd parted at noon. His promise to follow her to California as soon as he possibly could were the last words spoken between them.

She adjusted the lace shawl around her shoulders and headed into the hotel where the Lynford International Importers new hire reception was being held. As an only-just-hired summer intern, she'd received her job acceptance and invitation to the reception shortly after Court had left her studio flat. The afternoon had been spent madly running around making arrangements to stay in England another three months. To start.

But that wasn't all the good news she had for Court. Instead of only the summer, she'd be extending her stay indefinitely. Forever. The thought made her dizzy with delight.

Upon reaching the doors to the reception hall, Jean stopped and rested a hand over her abdomen. She had one more surprise for Court. One she prayed would thrill him to his bones. One that would give him the leverage to work around his father's manipulations. Like the song from a few years before, their future was so bright, they'd both have to wear shades. A silly grin crossed her face as she started through the wide open doors.

Soft string ensemble music drifted across the room. The event was exactly as Court had predicted. Proper Englishmen and their ladies talking quietly, mingling, as much to see as to be seen. For a week, he'd bemoaned the fact that instead of seeing her off at the airport, he had to attend this stuffy reception put on by his father's company. Not interested in the décor, she searched the sea of bodies in semi-formal wear, looking for one particular blond head. The men wore sharp suits of worsted wool with silk ties, the women cocktail gowns in various levels of fashion and expense. The student interns and freshly graduated new hires were easy to pick out, by not only their youth, but by the less expensive clothing and the nervous smiles on their faces. Because Court's family owned the company, she looked beyond the students and concentrated on the older attendees. The people Court had known since the day he'd been born.

One bright head stood out. Danielle Richards, the hiring contact. If not for Danielle's call hours before, Jean would have been boarding a plane just then. Jean headed for Danielle, who certainly knew Court and could help Jean find him. She merely had to work her way through to the other side of the large ballroom.

Descending the steps into the crowd, she plowed ahead, exchanging nervous smiles with the three or four people she recognized from classes.

Among the glittering bodies, various scents perfumed the air and queasiness assaulted Jean for a moment. Something that had never bothered her before the past week. She and Court figured she had a mild touch of flu, or possibly food poisoning like she'd had right after arriving in January. The call from the student clinic this afternoon had negated that theory.

A glint of Danielle's bright copper hair through the crowd assured Jean she was still on the right path. A few more steps and her gaze briefly met Danielle's. Someone stepped in and cut off the line of sight before Jean could take a second look at what appeared to be mild alarm on the other woman's face. Jean glanced behind her to see what might be happening that would cause the hiring director's reaction. No, nothing unusual there. Jean pressed forward once again.

Like the sun prying back a thick layer of dark clouds, she saw his golden blond hair through a parting of bodies. His back to her, he stood near Danielle, part of a circle of immaculately groomed men and women, a mix of older and younger.

Finally, she eased past a knot of distinguished men and stood directly behind Court. On a deep breath, she assessed the situation. The group he stood with contained two older couples, important looking men and their society wives, all perfectly dressed and bejeweled. A younger woman with a sleek blond bob stood at Court's left. Too close, but he came from people who knew people and had friends he'd been raised with. This could be one such. Across the small circle, Danielle was the only other person Jean recognized. A person who'd been friendly. Although the expression on Danielle's face wasn't exactly comforting.

Court began to speak, and Jean was able to hear him clearly, see clearly as his left arm came up to encircle the waist of the blond woman at his side, the action surprising her. If his shoulders looked a bit stiff, the movement a tad forced, she seemed to be the only one who noticed.

"Danielle, I'd like you to be among the first to know, Bea and I will be married next weekend. There isn't time for formal invitations,"—his chuckle was forced—"we're expecting, however, we'd love you to attend."

The timbre was Court's, but the tone and the words couldn't be his. Dizziness surged in Jean's head. She took a step back and clamped both hands over her now roiling stomach. The air had evaporated from the room and darkness framed the edges of her vision.

"Court..." Danielle said, doing her best to keep her face clear of emotion. Jean could see it, could hear the strain, as the other woman's electric blue gaze locked on her.

Jean swallowed against rising nausea and took another step back, bumping into someone's chilled glass of something. The shock of cold liquid dribbling down her back froze her in place.

In an almost dreamlike parody of slow motion, Court's arm dropped from the woman, and he slowly turned. Jean's gaze flew to his face as it came into view. His skin took on an ashen cast, as his eyes widened above his slackening jaw. For a long moment, it was all she could see.

"Courtland?" The sharply spoken word from the blond woman broke the spell. "What is it, darling?"

Jean's breath rushed back into her starved lungs, and her heart jolted into triple time, rushing adrenalin into her system. It was the spark she needed to turn on her heel and push through the crowd.

"Jean!"

She heard him call after her. Heard Danielle call after her, but didn't stop. Escape was the one thought in her head. Later she'd think about Court's announcement. But now there was room for only one instinct pounding through her veins. Run.

Snippets of his history came to her as she forced her way past people now expressing their shock at her rudeness. The girl he'd practically been engaged to since they'd been in nappies. The horrible break up days before Jean had tripped him in the library. The stories of his family and how he was expected to take over the business one day, like generations of Lynfords and Robinsons before.

Above all, the vision she couldn't reconcile with the words he'd just said, Court's face smiling down at her. His voice saying, "I love you. I'll come for you. We'll have a wonderful life."

As she broke through the edge of the crowd and rushed into the lobby, she thought she heard Court call out her name one more time, but from a distance. She didn't look back. Couldn't look back. Adrenalin pounding through her veins powered her forward. A doorman opened the heavy outer door.

"Miss?"

His enquiry went unacknowledged as she rushed by, headed for the cab parked at the curb.

"Taxi!" she called out.

Surprised, the doorman who'd recently helped her from a cab, leaped to open the door for her.

"Miss? Everything all right?"

She shook her head and climbed into the cab.

"Where to, miss?"

"Home." It was all she could think of. She could be at Heathrow in a few hours where she'd wait until a seat opened on a plane headed for New York. From New York she'd get a plane to San Francisco. There, she'd figure it all out.

"Where's home, miss?"

"Away from here." Tears blurring her vision, she met the cabbie's gaze in the rearview mirror. "Just drive." No one had followed her out the door. Especially not Court. His words echoing in her head tore her heart to shreds. The cabbie turned around and slowly eased into traffic.

Unable to stand it, she gave into temptation and looked back through the tears welling in her eyes and spilling down her cheeks. The sidewalk remained empty of anyone she recognized. Only the doorman looked after her.

The image of Court's face rose in her mind. Merry blue eyes, laughing at her driven need to experience everything Anglo, jokes about her attempts to learn the Brit accent, the little presents of Earl Grey tea, crumpets and flowers he brought her. The rose petals he'd scattered on her bed last night where they made love pretending to be in an English garden. The flower pressed between the pages of her favorite novel, a sweetly scented bookmark and reminder of his promise they'd be together.

From the dark and dreary February day when she'd accidentally tripped him in the library, her world had been filled with sunshine and laughter. He took her places, both physical and emotional, she'd never have discovered without him. Small shops, hidden parks, intimate pubs, classic tea houses, historical sites, and the places known only to locals. To heaven, where he wrapped her in soft clouds of love, like the weekend in the country where they hiked green fields and pretended to be Robin Hood and Maid Marian. A better friend, guide, and lover she couldn't have asked for.

"I need an address, miss. Or an intersection at the very least."

Of course the man needed a direction. Jean wiped tears from her cheeks and wrapped her arms around her middle. "Houghton Street," she said. She needed a direction, too, knew where she was headed in the next twenty-four hours, but had to take baby steps to get there. "Houghton Street and then Heathrow." One step at a time.

Chapter 1

Twenty-two years later
East Bay Area, Northern California

Bent over the open oven, Randi figured only serendipity could have timed her daughter's arrival for Thanksgiving dinner quite so well.

Already up for six hours, most of that time spent in the kitchen, Randi was ready for her first glass of wine. A real glass, not a sip from the bottle she'd poured over the bird. So much for her resolve to become a new woman in her fabulous forties. A couple years in and she still harbored doubts about how fabulous the forties were. However, a person should always seek to improve herself, right? All well and good, nevertheless, this new woman clung to a few old habits she didn't want to give up, such as nipping from the bottle of wine intended for basting the turkey.

"Mom!" Birdie's voice rang through the house like a bell.

"In the kitchen," she called back. Steam from the oven frizzed her hair and bathed her face as she basted the bird. There went the efforts of an hour spent plucking eyebrows and applying her makeup just so. Well, instead of a fashion plate, the picture of a sophisticated California hostess, she'd be Wyatt's picture of the perfect woman—glowing from the heat of the kitchen and probably smelling of turkey as well. Too bad he wasn't here to celebrate. Death had a way of ruining family gatherings.

Instead, Randi expected her father and Birdie, both bringing visitors from out of town with no place else to go. Strays had always been Randi's specialty, especially for holiday dinners.

"Smells great, we're starving!" Birdie moved into Randi's peripheral vision. As bright as a sunny day with her long, honey blond hair, Birdie lit up any room, especially with her smile, cheerful disposition, and her clothing. Occasionally, Randi considered her child's bubbly nature positively nauseating. But not today. The semester had dragged on and contact with her daughter remained too infrequent. Stanford may have been a mere hour across the Bay, but it might as well have been across the country for all the time Birdie had to spare.

Randi shoved the heavy bird back into the lower of the stacked double ovens and straightened with a hand on the small of her back as she lifted the door shut. Yeah, cool sophisticate she so was not. Had she wanted to present such an image, she would have ordered the complete meal, cooked and ready to serve, delivered from the upscale grocery store down the hill. "Bird should be done on schedule this year. This time I bought a fresh one, not frozen."

"Your dinners are always perfect, and thirty minutes late doesn't count. Mom, come meet our guests."

Ah yes. The mysterious Drew, a grad student from overseas Birdie had met the previous week after tripping over his big feet in a coffee shop. Not only Drew, but his father, as well, visiting the states on business, timed for Drew's first big American holiday. The widowed father. A match to her widowed mother status.

Great. It was bad enough her father also asked to bring a guest, a single man of a certain age. In other words, old enough for Randi. But now her daughter had joined the game? Lately, it seemed as if an invisible milestone had passed, one declaring her mourning period complete, and, apparently, someone had declared open season on finding dates for her. Funny, her heart hadn't reached the same conclusion yet.

Well, let these possible future dates get a good look at the new woman. The one thinking about thinking of dating again.

Since Birdie generally preferred jeans, Randi raised an eyebrow at the dress her daughter wore. Navy flats were more in keeping with her personality, though Birdie showed off a pair of still nicely tanned legs. Randi was about to comment, but Birdie beat her to it.

"Wow." Birdie stopped and stared for moment. "Great look," she whispered, then took Randi's arm and dragged her into the foyer where two tall men stood. So the extra hour of shaving, shining, plucking, and painting had been worth it? Despite the steamy glow she certainly sported at the moment, and no time to powder it away.

Not wanting to acknowledge the matchmaking attempt of her daughter—the man was a foreigner for crying out loud and wouldn't be around long enough to get to know—she wiped her hands on her apron, then extended one to the younger of the two. Dark blond, he had deep blue eyes and a smile every bit as cheery as Birdie's. As Randi gripped his hand, hers warmed with dreaded perspiration. She made her shake firm and brief, dropping his hand almost immediately.

"Mom, this is Drew. Drew, my mother Rand—"

"Jean?"

"—ee Ferguson," Birdie stumbled to a stop.

Drew hadn't interrupted. No, it was the man behind him. The boy's father. The one Randi didn't want to look at. The resonance of his voice, the rich British accent that made the plain name she'd used for one semester sound exotic, it was an illusion, an echo from the past, a hallucination induced from too little sleep.

Reluctantly, Randi let her gaze slide past Drew's startled eyes and collide with those of the older man one step back, looking more stunned than startled. More amazed than surprised.

"Not Jean Dailey?" he asked, head tilted a fraction as his gaze bore into her.

There was only one thought in her mind as her heart thudded to a momentary stop, and her blood froze into crystals. *It can't be.*

This must be a delusion leftover from last night's dreams. The ones brought on by the romance novel she'd found in a box last week. The one sitting on her bedside table still exuding the soft scent of the rose pressed between the pages of the love scene. He'd been invading her thoughts too much lately. He couldn't really be here, in her foyer. This scene was purely a figment of a mind set to wandering by plain old loneliness.

Randi grasped Birdie's arm, holding her as much to stay standing as to keep Birdie from moving to the side of the younger man. There was no way God would play this cruel a joke on her after so many years. Yet, as she stared into those blue, blue eyes, the years peeled away.

"Jean is my mother's middle name," Birdie supplied helpfully, despite her apparent confusion, breaking the silence that had held for nearly a full minute. Words abandoned Randi, leaving her throat too tight, too dry for speech. "Her full name is Randi Jean Dailey Ferguson."

Hell, no point in trying to hide her true identity now, as if that had ever been a remote possibility. Not only did Birdie give it all away, she babbled to fill in the extremely awkward silence.

The gaze of the apparition who resembled, well, *him*, sharpened, and his lips quirked in satisfaction. The heat of his regard wouldn't allow Randi to deny the exceedingly male presence in her house. All the air evaporated from the foyer, and her heart kick started so hard it threatened to leap from her chest. Her mind might be screaming denials, but her body knew. And despite the first sluicing of ice through her veins, heat rushed in behind.

Those damn blue eyes stared into hers, and a spark of something ancient and irrepressible settled in her heart, causing it to beat triple time.

Yup. God was that cruel.

From her past, the one man she never once imagined she'd ever see again stood in her foyer. Impossible that he should have found her. Dad would have never given her away had anyone knocked on his door looking for her. Google searches on the various combinations of her name turned up little other than notices in school newsletters. All those years ago she'd married, changed her name, given birth, and moved from the parental home to start a new life as a new woman. The girl he'd known as Jean Dailey became Randi Ferguson. All the heartache of betrayal had been left far behind in Merry Old England more than twenty-two years ago. The only reminder? The nearly twenty-two-year-old beauty standing at her side. The child who towered over her, so like her father, if the truth be known.

All those years ago, God had held her feet to the fire to face her future, but this time she faced the past. And why did that past still have to be so damn handsome?

No, not a hallucination. He was real. So very, very real.

It was him, looking barely five years older than he had so long ago. His thick hair still gleamed gold under the soft glow from the skylight, though there were hints of silver at his temples, and his forehead seemed a tad higher. Great, gray looked good on him. He was still lean, his eyes remained as piercingly blue. Light blue that looked right into her soul. His face had filled out a little, developed a few lines at the eyes, and the cheekbones were no longer quite so prominent, the jaw a slightly smoothed granite instead of freshly chiseled stone, but essentially the same.

Yes, he still looked the same while she'd grown rounder and squatter. Thank heavens for the impulse that sent her to the salon a week ago. At least she wasn't gray. At the moment. And of course, makeup, underwires, and Lycra hid a multitude of other imperfections.

Whereas he… Well, he looked damn fine in his light blue tailored shirt, gold cufflinks, perfect navy slacks, and expensive leather shoes.

Just like his son.

She wanted to push them out of her house right then, send them both back to England, far, far away from Birdie.

Oh, no, no, no. This did not fit with Randi's plans. She needed to regain control of the situation. Time. She needed time. Yes, she'd planned to tell Birdie all about this part of her past, but after Christmas. Before the New Year. After getting some more information from an investigative resource. Not like this, not now. Lord, not now! When Birdie was already looking at her as if she'd lost her mind.

Control. Right. Shut the rest away and pretend there was nothing going on. Randi eased up on her daughter's arm when she murmured a protest.

Oh God. Birdie's attracted to… She couldn't complete the thought too horrible to think.

A first date she'd said, right? Did that mean they hadn't progressed beyond coffee? No hand holding? No kissing? God forbid… How would she break this up without Birdie knowing she'd brought home not only her brother—half brother—but father, for dinner? Her very gorgeous, missing from her entire life, father.

As she watched his face, drinking in every detail, his eyes warmed, then hardened. He didn't seem nearly as surprised as she felt. Had he been looking for her? Had he used his son to find her through her daughter?

Birdie pinched her arm, bringing Randi back to the moment with a small jolt. Oh Lord, she was standing there like an idiot, everyone looking at her with expressions of curiosity and puzzlement. Hoping to find her cool hostess voice and not a strangled, choked voice, she gulped.

"Hello, Court."

Meet the Author

Shea McMaster lives for traditional romance. Born in New Orleans, raised in California, Shea got moved to Alaska in 1977, where she attended high school before running back to California to get her English degree from Mills College. Alas, once back home she met and fell in love with her own forever true hero, a born and raised Alaska man. Since then she's had a love-hate relationship with America's largest state.

With her one and only son through college, and out of the house, Shea is fortunate to spend her days with her fur baby, engaged in daydreaming and turning those dreams into romantic novels and novellas featuring damsels in distress rescued by their own brains and hunky heroes. She also writes steamy romances under the name Morgan O'Reilly.

Discover more about Shea at sheamcmaster.com, and on Facebook: http://www.facebook.com/pages/Shea-McMaster/240251469328338

www.ingramcontent.com/pod-product-compliance
Lightning Source LLC
Chambersburg PA
CBHW020752250626
47155CB00003B/1034